Lady Mary's life was bound by the men who ruled it. . . .

King Charles II—Her charming uncle. His affection for Lady Mary did not hinder him from sacrificing her happiness for his own ends.

The Duke of York—Her loving father, later King James II, whose ardent Catholicism brought only grief to his Protestant daughter.

Prince William of Orange—Her husband, unloving and unloved. He scorned his beautiful young wife and used her as a stepping-stone to power.

The Duke of Monmouth—King Charles's dashing illegitimate son, Mary's cousin. He turned to her for help and then went on the attack.

Gilbert Burnet—Later Bishop of Salisbury. A committed anti-Catholic and Mary's trusted advisor, who helped to strengthen her for the tribulations to come.

WILLIAM'S WIFE

Jean Plaidy

FAWCETT CREST • NEW YORK

A Fawcett Crest Book
Published by Ballantine Books
Copyright © 1993 by Jean Plaidy

All rights reserved under International and Pan-American Copyright Conventions. Published in the United States by Ballantine Books, a division of Random House, Inc., New York.

This book, or parts thereof, may not be reproduced in any form without permission.

Library of Congress Catalog Card Number: 92-32588

ISBN 0-449-22284-5

This edition published by arrangement with G. P. Putnam's Sons

Manufactured in the United States of America

First Ballantine Books Edition: May 1995

10 9 8 7 6 5 4 3 2 1

Contents

The Lady Mary

Early Days

There have been two people in my life whom I have loved beyond all others, and it has always weighed heavily upon me that I was called upon to decide between them and, in choosing one, I betrayed the other. I did what my heart, my faith, my sense of duty dictated and ever since I have suffered from the torment of knowing of the pain I inflicted and from which I myself will suffer to the end of my days.

I want to go right back to the beginning, to project myself into the past, to see it more clearly than I could when it was happening. I want to ask myself: what should I have done?

I was born in St. James's Palace at a time when my birth was of little interest to any except my parents, for a most significant event was taking place. My uncle, King Charles, recently restored to his throne after more than ten years' exile, was about to marry the Infanta of Portugal—an event which generated great excitement and expectation throughout the country. In any case, I was only a girl, and fifteen months after my birth, a boy was born to my parents, a fact which robbed my birth of any importance it might have had.

In the beginning the world was a wonderful place; the days were full of sunshine; I was surrounded by people who loved me and, being cherished by all, I was led to believe that the world had been created for my pleasure.

The best times of all were when my parents visited us. Everyone was so respectful to them that I quickly realized how important they were. My mother would take me up into her arms. She was like a big soft cushion into which I could sink with a feeling of cosy security. She would caress me, murmur words of love to me, and pop a sweetmeat into my mouth and show me in a hundred ways how much she loved me. But the most important of all was my father. When he came into the nursery crying, "Where is my little daughter? Where is the Lady Mary?" I would stagger or toddle and later run to him, and he would pick me up and set me on his shoulder so that I could look down on everything from my lofty perch. I loved all those around me but no one so much as I loved my father.

Once I heard someone say, "The Duke loves the little Mary beyond all others."

I never forgot that and I used to say it to myself when I was in my bed alone. I would listen for his coming; and often in later years, when I was haunted by memories of the fate which had overtaken him, I would recall those days and, sickened with doubts and self-reproaches, I would contemplate the part I had played in his tragedy.

How often then did I sigh for those days of my youthful innocence, when I thought the world a beautiful place in which I should be happy for ever.

When he visited us he would not let me out of his sight. I remember an occasion when he even received some of his officers to discuss some naval matter and he kept me there with him. He was Lord High Admiral of England then and I remember his seating me on the table while he talked to them; and, to please him, I know now, the men commented on the extraordinary intelligence, vitality, and charm of his daughter—and how delighted he was.

Sometimes it is difficult to know whether I really remember certain incidents from those days or whether they were talked of so frequently that I convince myself I do.

There is a miniature of me painted by Nechscher, a Flemish artist of whom my father thought highly. I am holding a black rabbit. They told me how my father used to join us at the sittings and watch me fondly while the artist was working. In my mind's eye I can see him clearly, but was I really aware of him at the time?

There are some days which I do remember and I can be certain of this. I was nearly three years old. It was cold, for it was the month of February. I knew something important was taking place. Snatches of overheard conversations came to me.

"I hope the Duke and Duchess will get what they want this time."

"Well, I don't know. The boys are sickly and I reckon he wouldn't change the Lady Mary for all the boys in Christendom."

When my father came to see me, after the usual rapturous greeting, he said, "You will be happy to hear, my daughter, that you have a little sister."

I remember my bewilderment. A little sister? I already had a little brother. There were always nurses around him and he did not mean a great deal to me.

"She will join you here," my father went on, "and you will love her dearly."

"You love her?" I asked.

I must have shown my father that I feared she might supplant me in his affections, for he gave me a smile of immediate understanding.

"I love her," he said. "But whoever came, it would always be the Lady Mary who had first place in my heart."

Excitement followed. Young as I was, I was to stand as sponsor for my sister; and Anne Scot, the Duchess of Buccleugh, was to be the other. Later I learned that this honour had been bestowed on her because she had recently married my cousin Jemmy, who had become the Duke of Monmouth.

I certainly remember that occasion well. It was presided over by Gilbert Sheldon, who was the Archbishop of Canterbury at the time, a very stern and formidable man of whom I should have been very much in awe but for the presence of my powerful father who would never be stern with me, nor allow anyone else to be.

The new baby was christened Anne, after our mother, and in due course she joined the nursery at Twickenham.

The house in Twickenham belonged to my grandfather—my mother's father, the Earl of Clarendon. He was a very important man, I realized, though I saw him rarely. There was another grandfather, whose name was always spoken in hushed whispers, because he was dead, and when I was very young indeed, I knew there had been something very shocking about his death.

Some people called him The Martyr. Later I learned that he had been king and that wicked men had cut off his head. I shivered every time I rode past that spot in Whitehall where they had performed this dreadful deed.

I was growing very fond of the new baby. My sister Anne was a placid child. She rarely cried and smiled readily. She was always eager for her food and everyone was delighted because of this. I was with her a great deal, and thought of her as my baby. She seemed to like me to sit near her cradle. She gripped my finger in her dimpled hand so tightly when I held it out to her and I found that endearing.

And then suddenly the peace of Twickenham was shattered. There was commotion everywhere; people were running back and forth, all talking at once. I had to find out what was wrong.

Then I heard that one of the maids had been found dead in her bed. There was no mystery as to how this had happened. It seemed they had thought we were safe at Twickenham, but the dreaded plague which had been sweeping through London had reached us here.

"The Plague!" Those words were on everybody's lips.

My parents arrived. I was caught up in my father's arms. Anne and my brother were examined by our mother. My father did the same to me.

"Praise be to God!" he cried. "Mary is well. And Anne and the boy?"

"All is well," said my mother.

"There is no time to be lost. We must leave at once."

The next thing I remember is riding away from Twickenham and on to York.

I was happy in York. The time sped by. We saw our parents more often there, although my father was absent now and then for long spells which seemed intolerable. The Fleet was at that time stationed on the East Coast and he was often with it.

There was war as well as plague. We knew little of that in York until we heard of the glorious victories not only off the coast of Lowestoft but also at Solebay.

These names sent a glow of pride in me for years after because my father was always mentioned in connection with them. He had been in charge of the Fleet which had beaten our wicked enemies, the Dutch. I loved to hear of his successes. I only regretted that he had to go so far away from us to do these wonderful deeds.

I heard one of the attendants say, "These victories will bring a little comfort, and the Lord knows, we need it in these terrible times."

I had heard only a little of the scourge which was sweeping through the country and devastating the capital. All it meant to me was that we had had to leave in a hurry for York, where I saw more of my parents than I had in Twickenham. It was only after that I heard accounts of the red crosses on the doors with the words "God have Mercy on us," which meant that there was plague in the house. I did not hear until much later of the macabre death carts which roamed the streets, and the dismal cry of "Bring out your dead," and how the bodies which were piled into those carts were taken to pits outside the city walls where they were hastily buried.

It was much later when I heard of the terrible tragedy which had followed the plague year, when London faced another monumental catastrophe and was almost completely destroyed by fire.

And when I did hear in lurid detail of the horrors of

those burning buildings, of weeping, homeless people, of the crafts on the river into which they crowded with as many of their belongings as they could hope to save, my thoughts were dominated by two men, the brothers who had gone out unceremoniously into the streets, wigless, short sleeves rolled up, sweat streaming from their faces while they gave instructions and supervised the blowing up of buildings to make gaps and so stop the fire spreading further. For those two men were the King and my father, his brother, the Duke of York.

He was a hero, my clever, wonderful father. He had saved the country from the Dutch at Lowestoft and Solebay as he had helped to save London from that all-consuming fire.

Of course, I learned all this later. In the meantime I was kept in my cocoon of safety.

The memories of York were of days of great happiness, broken only by occasional clouds when my father disappeared for a while. Then I heard that his absences would be even longer, because the King had summoned him to attend Parliament, which was now held in Oxford, because of the state of the capital.

Then my dismay was great, but he consoled me by saying he would come to see me whenever he could.

"When you are older, I will tell you all about it," he said. "Now all you have to do is wait and as soon as I am free I shall be here to see my little Lady Mary."

"I will come with you to Oxford," I said hopefully.

"Ah! What a pleasure that would be!" he replied, smiling. "But, alas, there is no place for little girls in the King's Parliament. But one day . . . soon . . . we shall all be together . . . your little brother, your little sister, your mother . . . the whole family of York."

It was a long time before we were.

And so I was growing up. There were times when I was vaguely aware of trouble. My grandfather Clarendon suddenly disappeared from the scene. We had never seen a great deal of him, but it seemed strange when his name ceased to be mentioned. I knew he had been very important and Lord Chancellor and a friend of the King and my father, having been with them when they were in exile. He was my mother's father, so it seemed strange that we should stop speaking of him.

I did hear someone say that he was lucky to have escaped to exile before he lost his head. There was enough against him to bring about his downfall, and his continual carping at the King's way of life meant that even that long-suffering monarch was eager to be rid of him.

I was bemused by these scraps of gossip which I tried hard to understand. I had one grandfather who had lost his head; and here was another who, it appeared, had escaped in time before being deprived of his.

I knew my mother was deeply affected by his departure and I believed my father was, too.

But when they were with us, they were always their affectionate selves. I think my sister Anne was my mother's favourite, though Anne did not resemble her at all except in looks. I had heard it said: "The Lady Mary is Stuart from head to toe. The Lady Anne is a Hyde." I was tall and at that age slender, dark-haired with rather long almond-shaped eyes. Anne was always plump; her hair was light brown with a reddish tinge in it. I was pale; she was rosy. She would have been very pretty but for a slight deformity of the eyes. Her lids were contracted a little which gave her a rather vague look. It had affected her sight in some way.

Anne was very good-natured, rarely cross, and fundamentally lazy. She did not like trouble of any sort and, in her sunny, good-natured way, she made a very good job of avoiding it. When she was tired of doing something, and as we grew older that particularly meant lessons, she made the excuse that her eyes hurt.

We were very happy together in those days. She laughed at me for wanting to learn about everything.

"You do it, sister," she would say, "and then you can tell me all about it."

I quickly realized that my mother was reckoned to be

clever. It was true that she often decided what was to be done. My father used to say, "You are right, of course, my dear." She was very friendly with a great number of the serious people at court. I had heard the King refer to her as "my serious-minded, clever sister-in-law." I was rather surprised that she should have doted so fondly on Anne, who had little to say and refused to learn. Their only common interest seemed to be their love of sweet foods. Many times I had seen them sitting close, a dish of sweetmeats between them, and they would be eating all the time.

There was an occasion when the physicians pointed out that my sister was growing unhealthily fat and could damage her health if she did not give up the habit of consuming sweetmeats at every opportunity.

My mother was frightened. Perhaps she blamed herself for allowing her daughter to share her own weakness. In any case, Anne was sent away for a while with one of my mother's ladies. She was to be watchful of what Anne ate and my mother could trust her friends to keep a sharper eye on my sister in a different house than in her own, for there she suspected that her friends would give way to her pleadings for more of the sweetmeats she loved so much.

I was very sad to lose my sister. Life was not the same without her good-natured smiles. I pictured her on a strict diet, deprived of her sweetmeats. Perhaps she was taking it all in her good-tempered manner.

It was a happy day when she returned, good-natured as ever and, if not exactly thin, less rotund than she had been.

Everyone declared that the cure had been a miraculous one, but it soon became clear that the temptation presented by a dish of sweetmeats was still irresistible. However, we were all so delighted to have her back that we could only smile at her indulgences.

During Anne's absence I missed her so much that my parents decided I must have a companion to compensate me for the loss of my sister and, to my great joy, Anne Trelawny joined the household. She was a few years older than I and we were firm friends from the beginning. It was wonderful to have someone to confide in; and Anne was sympathetic, understanding, and all that I could ask for in a friend.

My sister Anne must always have what I had and when she came home and saw that I had a friend, she must have one too.

She made this desire known to our mother who immediately set about looking for someone suitable.

My mother had been particularly interested in one of the maids of honour, a certain Frances Jennings who came from a family of somewhat obscure origins. It was something of a mystery that she should be received at court, but Frances herself was very engaging—not exactly beautiful, but attractive and quick-witted. My mother, herself of a lively mind, liked to have people of her own sort about her, and she was more attracted to intelligence than ancient lineage. Hence she took a special interest in Frances and when a connection of the noble house of Hamilton was attracted by her, my mother helped to advance the match.

Frances had a younger sister, Sarah, whom she was anxious to bring to court and when the young girl was introduced to my mother, she found her very bright indeed. She was about five years older than my sister Anne, which seemed no drawback, and she would, my mother was sure, be a lively, entertaining companion for our somewhat lethargic Anne.

A position in our household was naturally accepted with alacrity by the ambitious Frances for her sister, and I am sure now that from the moment Sarah entered our household, she was fully aware of the advantages which had opened up for her.

She knew exactly how to behave with Anne and, almost from the day of her arrival, they were the closest friends. We were a happy quartet: Anne Trelawny and myself, my sister Anne and Sarah Jennings.

Then a certain anxiety crept into my mind. I felt something was not quite right. My mother had changed. She seemed a little absent-minded at times. She would smile and nod but her thoughts seemed elsewhere. In spite of her plumpness, there was a drawn look about her face. I noticed that its colour had changed. Her skin had a strange yellowish tinge and now and then she would put her hand to her breast and wince.

I thought at first that she was anxious because her father had gone away, and when I thought of what I should feel if I lost mine, I could understand her sorrow. But there was only one Duke of York and Lady Mary; and no father and daughter loved each other as we did. My mother had lost her father, who had run away to save his head. But there was something else. Once I saw her walking in the gardens with Father Hunt, a Franciscan; and they were talking earnestly together.

I knew that Father Hunt was a Catholic and I was sure that Gilbert Sheldon, Archbishop of Canterbury, would not be very pleased to see my mother in close conversation with him. Then I saw my father join them and the three of them walked off talking closely together.

I did not think very much about that at the time, until I heard that the people did not like my uncle's marriage to Catherine of Braganza, because she was a Catholic, and the English did not like Catholics.

This and the change in my mother's looks were like vague shadows, but so slight that they did not linger long in the warm sunshine of those happy days.

My mother was going to have a baby. That was the reason for her being ill, I supposed. She was so plump and her figure so round that her pregnancy was scarcely noticeable.

Anne and I eagerly waited to hear whether we should have a little brother or sister. We hoped for a sister. Brothers were a disappointment. They were always ill.

To our delight it was a little girl. They named her Catherine, in honour of the Queen.

We talked a great deal about her—or rather, I talked and Anne listened. Anne preferred to listen. Sometimes I thought she was getting more and more lazy.

My father came to see us. It was a cold day in March and the year was 1671. I was at that time nearly nine years old and Anne already six. I was greatly alarmed because I saw the pain and suffering in my father's face.

He sat down and, putting an arm round each of us, drew us to him and held us closely. Sobs shook his body. I was filled with horror as well as sadness to see my invincible hero so broken with grief.

"My dearest daughters," he said. "The most terrible of calamities has befallen us. How can I tell you? Your mother . . . your mother . . . "

I kissed him tenderly, which only made him weep the more.

He said, "Children, you have no mother now."

"Where has she gone?" asked Anne.

"To heaven, my child."

"Dead . . . ?" I whispered.

He nodded.

"But she was here . . ."

"She was so brave. She knew it could not be long. She was very ill indeed. There was nothing that could be done to save her. My children, you have only your father now."

I clung to him; so did Anne.

He told us that he had been with her at the end. She had died in his arms. She had died happy . . . in the way she wished. We must try not to grieve. We must think of her happy with the angels in the true faith of the Lord.

We were bewildered. We could not believe that we should never see our mother again. Neither of us could visualize what our lives would be like without her. There would be changes.

We were soon to discover that.

We had lost her, yes. But there was something more than that. What we did not know then was that, on her deathbed, she had received the *viaticum* of the Church of Rome and that my father was also wavering towards the Catholic faith.

Unfortunately, my father was not keeping this a secret.

He was too honest. He believed he would be false to his faith if he tried to disguise it. I was to learn that he was a man of very little judgement. Already he had taken the first step which was to lead to disaster. And we children, because he was after all his brother's heir, were not without importance to the State.

So there were changes. In view of his religious leanings, which were becoming public knowledge, the Duke of York could no longer be allowed to supervise his children's upbringing, and because of their position in the country, it was necessary for the King to take the matter in hand.

Richmond Palace

It was decided that the old palace of Richmond should be our new home. Lady Frances Villiers was to be our governess and in charge of our household; and our tutors would be appointed by the King.

The Palace of Richmond had originally been called Sheen, but when the Earl of Richmond, who became Henry VII, took the crown after defeating Richard III on Bosworth Field, he called the palace after himself and it became Richmond.

When much has happened in a place, some of the past seems to linger there and people like myself become fanciful. My sister did not feel this at all; but Anne Trelawny understood immediately and I talked of it to her.

I remember approaching the palace with our party and thinking: this is to be our new home. There were several buildings, but they did not seem to match each other, though they all had circular towers and turrets. I noticed the chimneys. There were several of them and they reminded me of inverted pears.

My grandfather had lived here once—that grandfather whom we mourned every January. He must have stood in this very spot, where I was at that moment, looking at those upside-down pears. It was a dwelling of ghosts and shadows. I hoped my father would come often.

It was rather intimidating, on our arrival, to be greeted by Lady Frances Villiers. She was smiling, but I sensed she could be formidable. She curtsied, but I fancied she meant to imply that this gesture was a formality, necessary be-

cause of our rank, and that we should have to submit to her
will.

I was surprised to see that there were six girls with her—
some obviously older than I was.

I glanced at my sister. She was not very concerned.

"Welcome to Richmond Palace," said Lady Frances. "We
are so happy to be here, are we not?" She turned to the
girls, who stood a pace or two behind her.

The tallest of them answered, "We are very happy to
serve the Lady Mary and the Lady Anne, my lady."

"We shall be a most contented household," Lady Frances
went on. "It gives us great pleasure to be here. I and my
daughters have come to serve you and I know we shall all
be good friends. Have I your permission to introduce my
daughters to you, Lady Mary, my Lady Anne?"

I nodded my head in as dignified a manner as I could
muster, and Anne smiled broadly.

"My eldest daughter, Elizabeth . . ."

I often wondered long afterwards why some fate does
not warn us when a meeting which is going to have a great
impact on us takes place. I feel there should have been
some premonition to tell me of the effect this girl was going to have on my life. So often I have said to myself, from
the first moment I met her I knew I had to be wary of her,
that she was sly, clever—far cleverer than I could ever be—
and that she disliked me because she, who considered herself my superior, should have to pay homage to me simply
because I had been born royal.

But no, I thought that afterwards, when I knew. It took
me a long time to discover how devious she was. But I was
young and innocent; she had the advantage. I could easily
have had her dismissed. I only had to say to my father, "I
do not like Elizabeth Villiers," and, although he was no
longer in control of the household, my wishes would have
been respected. But she was subtle. She did not betray herself. That was where she was clever. She knew how to deliver a barb where it hurt most, but it would be couched in
soft words so that only those who understood could be

aware of the venom. She was too clever, too subtle for me. That was why she was always the victor, I the victim.

But I deceive myself. None of this was at all clear to me at that first meeting.

She was by no means handsome, but there was something unusual about her looks. Perhaps this was because there was a slight cast in her eyes. It was hardly perceptible. I caught it at times. Her hair was of an orange tinge. "Ginger," Anne Trelawny called it, and Anne, my dear friend, liked her no more than I did.

The other daughters were being presented.

"My ladies, my daughters, Katharine, Barbara, Anne, Henrietta, and Maria."

They curtsied. Anne Villiers reminded me of her sister Elizabeth; she had shrewd eyes and a penetrating look. But she was less impressive—perhaps because she was younger.

And so we were installed in the Palace of Richmond.

Life in London had settled down to normality. The city had been almost rebuilt and was a much more beautiful and cleaner place than it had been with its reeking gutters and narrow streets.

My father, with the King, had taken a great interest in the rebuilding. They were often in conference with the architect, Sir Christopher Wren, while the work was in progress.

My father at this time was not a happy man. I guessed he was grieving about my mother's death, and the failing health of my little brother, Edgar, gave him great cause for concern.

He talked to me at this time and I learned more from him than I ever had because I believed he was so distressed that he did not always consider his words, and sometimes it was as though he were talking to himself.

I was glad in a way, though sad because he was, but I did begin to learn a little of what was happening about me.

He was angry on one occasion.

"Bishop Compton will be coming here," he said.

"To us?" I asked. "But why?"

"The King has appointed him. He is to instruct you and your sister in religion."

"That does not please you?"

"No. It does not please me."

"Well, why do you let him come?"

He took my face in his hands and gave me one of his melancholy smiles.

"My dearest child, I have to submit to the King's wishes in this matter." He was angry suddenly. "It is that or ..."

He released me and turned away, staring ahead of him. I waited.

"I could not face that," he murmured. "I could not lose you."

"Lose us!" I cried in alarm.

"Well, they would take you from me. Or ... they would restrict our meetings. My own children ... taken from me ... I am unfit to take charge of their education, they say. And all because I have seen the truth."

This was beyond my understanding. I could only think of being taken from him and I could visualize no greater calamity. He was aware of my concern and was my loving father immediately.

"There. I have frightened you. There is nothing to fear. Anything but that. I shall see you ... as always. I would agree to anything rather than that they should take you from me."

"Who would take me from you? The King, my uncle?"

"He says it would be for the sake of the country ... for the sake of peace. He says, why do I not keep these matters private? Why do I flaunt them? But you must not bother your little head ..."

I said firmly, "My head is not little and I want to bother it."

He laughed and seemed suddenly to change his tone.

"It is nothing ... nothing at all. Bishop Compton will be here to instruct you in the faith you must follow, according to the laws of the country and the command of the King. You must listen to the Bishop and be a good little member of the Church of England. Compton and I have never been great friends, but that is of no moment. He is a hardworking fellow and has the King's favour. He will do his duty."

"If he is not your friend . . ."

"Oh, it was a long-ago quarrel. He had the temerity to dismiss a man who acted as secretary to your mother."

"Did my mother not wish him to be dismissed?"

He nodded.

"Then why? Could you not . . . ?"

"This was the Bishop of London and the secretary was a Catholic. It is over. Your mother was not pleased. Nor was I. But . . . the people here . . . they are so much of one mind and they will listen to no other. Now, my dearest, let us have done with such talk. The fault was mine. Bishop Compton will come to you and he will make good little girls of you both. It is the King's wish that he should come, and we must needs make the best of it."

"But you are unhappy."

"Oh, no . . . no."

"You said that we could be taken from you."

"Did I? Let me tell you this . . . nothing, nothing on earth will ever take my children from me."

"But . . ."

"I spoke rashly. I did not want this Compton fellow to be here, but I see now that he is a good man, a religious man. He will obey the King's commands and make good Protestant young ladies of you. That is what the King wants and you know we must all obey the King. He says it is what the country wants and the country must see it being done. That is important. He is right. Charles is always right."

"Then you are not unhappy?"

"At this moment, with my dearest child, how could I be unhappy? You are to have a French tutor. You will like that. I believe you are interested in learning."

"I like to know."

"That is good. And Anne?"

I was silent and my father laughed.

I went on, "She does not care for books because they hurt her eyes."

He frowned. "She certainly has an affliction. Poor child. But she has a happy nature and we must keep it so."

When he left me he had banished my fears.

I was learning more of what was happening around us. There was always gossip among the attendants; the girls naturally heard it, and the elder ones, like Elizabeth Villiers and Sarah Jennings, understood what it was all about.

These two had taken a dislike to each other. Sarah, by this time, had complete domination over Anne, and my sister was hardly ever seen without her friend. It was not that Sarah was sycophantic. Far from it. There were times when one would have thought she was the mistress, and Anne the attendant.

I think Elizabeth Villiers resented her. She had not succeeded in forming that sort of alliance with me; and she probably recognized in Sarah one of her own kind. They were both ambitious and knew that to have one foot in a royal household was one step up the ladder to power.

They realized far more than we did then what our position could be and that there was a chance—though remote—of our reaching the throne if certain eventualities were to come to pass. They recognized in each other a rival for power, and that made them natural enemies. In their way they were both formidable, though their methods were different. Sarah spoke her mind without fear; Elizabeth was soft-spoken and sly. I think, on the whole, I preferred Sarah.

We were all sitting sewing one day. I quite enjoyed needlework. Anne would sit idly with the work before her, not attempting to use her needle. It hurt her eyes, she usually said. Sarah would laugh and do hers for her. I liked to do something with my hands while I listened to the music one of the girls would play; and sometimes there was reading.

On this occasion, Elizabeth Villiers said, "The Bishop

will soon be here. He will make sure that the Lady Mary
and the Lady Anne keep to the true faith."

"He is a very clever man," said Sarah.

"And of the right persuasion," Elizabeth went on, "which
is very necessary."

"Do you think the Duke is happy with the appointment?"
asked Anne Villiers.

Elizabeth smiled a little superciliously. "The Duke will
realize it is the best possible conclusion."

Sarah commented that the Duke would know it was what
the people wanted and it was always wise to listen to them
and let them think they were getting their way.

"They are certainly getting their way on this," said Anne
Villiers. "I am not surprised the Duke does not like the
Bishop."

I must have shown that I was listening intently, for I saw
Elizabeth's eyes on me as she said, "We all know that the
Bishop had Edward Coleman dismissed from the Duchess's
household while she was alive and all because he was a
Catholic, which the Bishop thought was a bad influence.
The Duke held nothing against Edward Coleman for that
but, of course, he could not save him."

I was thinking of what my father had told me and I remembered seeing him with my mother in the company of
Father Hunt, the Franciscan. The trouble was all about religion and that was why Bishop Compton was coming here
to teach us.

Elizabeth had turned the conversation round to great
families. She had succeeded in bringing to my notice that
my wonderful father had to bow to the will of the King, not
realizing that he himself had already told me that. Now she
wanted to attack Sarah in the same oblique way.

She was growing more and more annoyed by the influence Sarah exerted over Anne, and I dare say she thought
that if she were not careful Sarah would have more power
in the household than she did. She was hinting now that
Sarah was of low birth, and she would stress the fact by

saying that she was very sorry for those who lacked the advantage of birth and breeding.

"I have the utmost admiration for those who rise above it," she said, smiling benignly on Sarah. "Of course, we Villiers are of an ancient family. The name is enough to tell you that. We have been known at court through the centuries. Our kinsman George Villiers, the present Duke of Buckingham, is one of the King's greatest friends. Oh yes, it is certainly good to be of noble lineage. Do you not agree, Sarah?"

Sarah was ready. "That would depend," she retorted. "It can be of an advantage, of course, but it can also be a disadvantage. When there is a disaster in a family, a little anonymity can be very desirable."

"Nothing can alter the glory of an illustrious name."

"Ah, but the higher the family, the greater the fall. One does not have to look very far for an example. A great family such as yours must find the exploits of The Lady very distressing."

I saw the colour rush into Anne Villiers' cheeks. Elizabeth looked coldly at Sarah and the cast in her eyes had become almost a squint.

"I don't understand you, Sarah," she said.

"Oh, didn't I make myself clear? I am sorry. You were speaking of your illustrious family name and I was saying what a pity it was that one member of it should make it . . . notorious."

"What . . . do you mean?" stammered Anne Villiers.

"I refer to Barbara Villiers, of course. Your cousin, is she not? My Lady Castlemaine, no less. I believe they sing lampoons about her in the streets."

"She mixes in the highest circles," said Anne Villiers.

"Indeed, yes." Sarah obviously could not resist going on. "That is why she has become so well known not only at court, not only in London, but throughout the country."

"There are many who would be greatly honoured by the King's friendship."

"Honour?" Sarah went on. "There are times when it is

difficult to differentiate. What is honour? What is dishonour? It is for all to make up their minds." Sarah was smiling triumphantly, because she knew Elizabeth Villiers had been trounced.

I was rather bewildered by this conversation and took the first opportunity of consulting Anne Trelawny.

"It seemed to me that they were talking in riddles," I said.

"Not they. Elizabeth Villiers does not like Sarah Jennings, so she wants to remind her all the time of her obscure origins, and that it is only by sheer good luck that she has a place here. But Sarah is not going to take that lightly. She retaliates that people in great families can act scandalously, and, of course, Barbara Villiers is the notorious Lady Castlemaine, and is the cousin of these Villiers girls."

"Anne," I said, "people seem to want to keep things from me. Don't you, please. I am not a child any more."

"I dare say you will be going to court one day and you will know about these matters. You would soon discover that Lady Castlemaine is the King's mistress, for they make no secret of this. He spends much time with her. She is most indiscreet. And everyone knows what happens between them."

"But the King is married!"

That made Anne smile. "It makes no difference. It happens with people in high places."

"It does not happen with my father," I said fiercely.

Anne was silent. Then she said, "The King is so often with Lady Castlemaine."

"But what of the Queen? Does she know this?"

"The Queen most assuredly knows."

"The poor lady."

"Yes, that is what many say. But life is like that."

"I like my uncle so much. He is so merry . . . and kind."

"He is much liked."

"I cannot believe he would act so."

"People have many sides to their natures. This is one of the King's. Lady Castlemaine is not the first by any means.

You know of your cousin, the Duke of Monmouth. You know he is not heir to the throne, but he is the King's son."

"I do not understand."

"He was born when the King was in exile. He is without doubt the King's son. The King accepts him as such. But he is not the King's legitimate son and therefore cannot inherit the throne. As you grow up you learn to accept that such things happen."

"I am glad my father is not like that."

She looked at me a little sadly but with great affection.

"I think the Queen must be very unhappy," I said. "I am sorry. She is such a kindly lady. I shall never like the King so much again."

The Bishop had arrived. He was a man in his early forties, I imagined, which seemed ancient to us. He was not unkind, nor very severe, but he was determined that he was going to teach us to become good Protestants.

I understood later that he was not very learned academically and that side of our education was neglected to some extent. What he was determined to do was set our feet on the right path and, in view of our parents' religious inclinations, it was very important that we should not be contaminated by them.

That was exactly what he had been ordered to do and I realized later that it was a perfectly reasonable arrangement. My father was, at that time, heir to the throne, for it seemed that Queen Catherine was barren; my mother had died in the Catholic faith and my father leaned strongly towards it; and the English were determined never to accept a Catholic king.

I learned too how the King was exasperated by my father's attitude towards religion. But my father was a good man, an honest man; he could not deny his faith; he was like one of the martyrs who suffered so much during their lifetimes and were so revered after their deaths. He would have died for his faith—or lose a crown for it. People might say he was a fool. That may have been from their point of view, but he was a good fool.

He had been told that if he tried to bring his children up in the Catholic faith, they would be taken from him; and that was why Bishop Compton had been sent to teach us.

I was quite pleased that a more serious attitude was being taken about our education. It was true enough that we were never overworked, and if we did not wish to attend lessons there was no compulsion to do so. Anne hardly ever sat for them; that was why in later years she had to exert herself just to write a letter. I was different. I liked to learn, and I was happy to work with my French tutor who was delighted with my response.

Both Anne and I learned to paint and our drawing master caused a certain amount of amusement when he arrived, for he was a dwarf, only three feet ten inches high, and he had a wife who was more or less the same size as he was. He was an excellent miniature painter, very dignified and always behaved with very special decorum.

I liked Richard Gibson and enjoyed the lessons with him. He was well known throughout the court and he and Mrs. Gibson were a most unusual pair. They were by no means young, having lived through the reign of my murdered grandfather and the days of Oliver Cromwell to the restoration of my uncle Charles. They were great favourites at court.

They had had a wedding in my grandfather's court, which had been celebrated in verse by the poet Waller. There had been a banquet in honour of them which the King and my grandmother Queen Henrietta Maria had attended. People marvelled at them, for they must have been nearly sixty years old at this time and they had had nine children, all of whom were of normal size.

Even Anne enjoyed drawing under Richard Gibson's tuition.

And eventually my father became reconciled to the fact that the King had undertaken the education of his daughters.

* * *

The year after my mother's death, baby Catherine and my little brother Edgar, who had been ailing all his brief life, both died. My father was very sad. He had suffered so many misfortunes.

He took a special delight in being with Anne and me, and our continued good health was a great comfort to him.

Edgar's death had made a difference and, growing up as I was, I sensed it. Something had changed. Anne and I were more important, especially myself. It was clear why.

Queen Catherine, poor lady, continued to be barren. My father, next in line, had lost his wife and there were no remaining sons of the marriage; and after him came his daughters.

There was a certain amount of whispering about my father's preoccupation with the Catholic faith, which grew stronger rather than diminished.

I once heard someone say: "If he must be so, why let the whole world know it?"

Because he was an honest man, was the answer. There was no deceit in him.

The people were uneasy and that made them forget his glorious naval victories which at the time had made him so popular. They wanted my father to understand that they would never accept a Catholic king on the throne of England.

It was for this reason that Anne and I must not only observe all the ceremonies of the Church of England, but we must be seen taking part in them.

Oh yes, the death of my mother, followed by that of little Edgar, had given Anne and me a new importance.

And particularly myself.

I was eleven years old now and learning more every day. I was not excluded from the gossip as I had been; and there was a good deal of it among the girls of the household. Sarah Jennings was very interested in what was happening— and so was Elizabeth Villiers. I think they were both rather excited to be in such a household as ours which was really right in the centre of affairs, although it might not seem so to us who were living in it.

Of course, a certain amount of attention would always be given to the heir of the throne, but for a long time it had been thought that the King would certainly have a son. He had enough illegitimate ones—lusty at that—to prove that the inability to get an heir was not due to him. It was ironical that he could beget them on so many of his fair subjects and fail with his queen. It seemed to be one of the perversities of life. Poor Queen Catherine! I can sympathize with her now.

Intrigue was rife. The Queen could not produce the heir: the Duke of York was suspected of being a Catholic. There was, of course, the Duke of Monmouth. Illegitimate, yes, but a Protestant and young and handsome, a favourite with the people. Surely he could produce healthy sons. An illegitimate Protestant would be preferred to the true heir who was a Catholic.

That was the opinion at the time and I was not unaware of it.

It changed the attitude of the girls. They were more free with their gossip. Elizabeth Villiers was particularly watchful of Anne and me. Anne was completely obsessed by Sarah Jennings. It was always "Sarah says . . ." or "Sarah doesn't do it that way," "I must ask Sarah." Sarah had Anne's heart and mind, it seemed. And there was I, with my dear friend Anne Trelawny. Nor had I made a confidante of any of the Villiers girls, although there were six of them.

I did not realize until later that Elizabeth would have liked to have the same dominance over me that Sarah had over Anne, for it was just possible that I might become a very important person indeed.

She was jealous of me. I understand a great deal now which I did not at that time. She would have loved to be in my position! I think Elizabeth Villiers wanted power beyond anything else. I know now what lay behind that intent gaze which I had often found fixed upon me. She was thinking: this girl, this stupid creature, if events shape as they may well do, could be Queen of England one day. And I, brilliant, clever, capable Elizabeth Villiers, will be nothing . . . or someone of comparatively little importance—perhaps—if I am lucky—in *her* household.

That would have been galling to someone of Elizabeth Villiers' nature. There were times when she tried to win my favour, but there were others when her envy got the better of her good sense and she sought to wound me.

She knew of the love between myself and my father and she tried to undermine it. She was well aware that to me my father was the hero of many naval victories, the man who had fought the flames during the Great Fire of London, the loving father adored by his children; and she wanted to show me that my idol was not all I thought him; and in her way, which was subtle enough for a young and innocent girl of my age, she set about doing it.

It was when we were all together at one of our sewing sessions that she began to talk about someone named Arabella Churchill. It was the first time I had heard the woman's name mentioned.

"It really is most scandalous," said Elizabeth. "How can she be so brazen? This is the third, and all born out of wedlock. A boy this time, they say, and healthy. These children always are. Is not fate unkind? Sons of a marriage die one after another while the little bastards live on."

"And they say she is by no means beautiful," said Anne Villiers.

Elizabeth laughed. "Well, some like them that way. She has other attractions doubtless."

Henrietta Villiers asked, "Is it true that her legs were the great attraction?"

"Yes indeed," replied Elizabeth. "She had an accident in the riding field and her legs were very much in evidence. They happened to be seen by a certain person . . . and he fell in love with them."

"With a pair of legs!" giggled Henrietta.

I was only half listening. I supposed this was another of the King's amours. They included court ladies, actresses from the theatres, women of all sorts and classes. This Arabella Churchill would be one of a crowd. I always felt uneasy when they discussed the King's morals. After all, he was my uncle. He knew that there was gossip about him but he was just amused. He was very good-tempered.

I heard Anne Villiers saying, "She is very tall and nothing but skin and bone—not good-looking at all."

"Only a magnificent pair of legs," said Elizabeth, raising her eyes to the ceiling in an expression of wonder. "Yet she inspired a personage."

Sarah said that there was so much beauty at court that perhaps it was refreshing to find a lack of it.

"The gentleman concerned," went on Elizabeth, glancing at her sisters, several of whom could not restrain their giggles, "is said to have an odd taste in women."

I was getting more perceptive. The pauses and the exchanged glances startled me. I thought suddenly, I believe they are talking about my father. I could not believe this though. This Arabella Churchill had had three children. When the first would have been born, my mother was alive. It was nonsense. But the suspicion remained.

I said to Anne Trelawny when we were alone, "Arabella Churchill's lover? Who is he?"

I saw the flush in her face and she did not answer.

I said, "Was it my father?"

"In a court like ours these things happen," she said uneasily.

I could not forget that while my mother was dying, he had been in love with Arabella Churchill's legs. I discovered that her first child had been born in 1671—the year my mother had died—and now there was this one.

I remembered my father's sorrow over my mother's death. How he had wept and seemed to care so much, and all the time he was making love with Arabella Churchill. And I had believed he was heartbroken by my mother's death. How could he have been?

Life was full of hypocrisy. People lied. They deceived. Even my noble father.

Elizabeth Villiers had succeeded in what she had intended to do. Nor did she leave it there.

She had a clever way of steering the conversation round to the way she wanted it to go. In the days of my innocence I believed that it happened naturally, but now I was beginning to see it differently. She was clever; she was subtle; she was five years older than I and when one is eleven that is a great deal.

At this time her aim was to poison the relationship between my father and me. It may have been because she thought he might yet turn me into a Catholic and so jeopardize my way to the throne and, as my attendant, she would be without the benefits accompanying such a position. Or it might have been that, disliking me as she did, she could not bear that I should know such happiness from a love the like of which I imagine could never have been hers.

When one of the courtiers began acting strangely and it was said that he was suffering from a bout of madness, Elizabeth remarked that he reminded her of Sir John Denham.

One of the younger girls asked who Sir John Denham was.

It was obviously what Elizabeth had expected, and she said quickly, "It was something which happened some time ago. It was very unsavoury and perhaps best forgotten, though there will always be people to remember it."

"Oh yes," said Anne Villiers. "Whenever Sir John's name is mentioned, people will remember."

"Do tell us what happened," begged Henrietta.

And then I heard the story of Sir John Denham.

It had started in the year 1666, just after the Great Fire. Sir John Denham had gone mad suddenly and thought he was the Holy Ghost. He even went to the King to tell him so.

Henrietta and Maria Villiers giggled at the thought and my sister joined in.

Elizabeth reproved them rather primly.

"It is not a joke," she said. "It was very serious and you should not laugh at the misfortunes of others."

"It was due to his wife, was it not?" said Anne Villiers. "He had married her when she was eighteen and he was a very old man. You can guess what happened. She had a lover."

Elizabeth was giving me a covert glance, so I guessed what was coming.

"Sir John was so upset," she went on, "that he went mad. And then she died. It was said she was poisoned. The people blamed Sir John at first. They gathered outside his house and called on him to come out that they might show him what they did to murderers. The people are fickle. When he gave his wife a fine funeral and wine was served liberally to all the people who had come to see her buried, instead of attacking him, they said he was a good fellow and it must have been someone else who murdered his wife."

"Who?" asked Henrietta.

"I really do not think we should talk of this," put in Elizabeth. "It is not really a very pleasant subject."

"But I want to know," said Henrietta.

"You are not to . . ." Elizabeth made a great show of embarrassment, as though forcing herself to be silent.

Sarah looked at her cynically. Sarah was more shrewd than the rest of us. That was why she and Elizabeth were so wary of each other. I wondered whether she would discuss the case of Sir John Denham with my sister when they were alone together. Anne might be too indolent to ask, but she seemed to be listening with interest; I supposed it would depend on whether Sarah wanted Anne to know.

I did bring the matter up with Anne Trelawny. I trusted her completely and it was always a joy to talk over things with her, because she never tried to impose her will on mine.

"Do you remember all that talk about Sir John Denham who thought he was the Holy Ghost?"

"Oh yes," said Anne reluctantly. "It happened a long time ago."

"Round about the time of the Great Fire."

"I thought they said she died the year after the Fire."

"She had a lover."

"They said so."

"Who was it?"

"Oh, people will talk!"

"Was it my father?"

Anne blushed and I went on, "I guessed it was by the way Elizabeth Villiers talked."

"She's a sly creature, that one. I had even rather have Sarah Jennings, though I must say *she* can be a trial, and I could well do without her."

"What happened? Was there a big scandal?"

"I suppose you could call it that."

"And my father?"

She shrugged her shoulders.

I said, "I now know about Arabella Churchill. She is still with him, is she not?"

"Both the King and the Duke can remain faithful to those who really mean something to them. The King had been very friendly with Lady Castlemaine for some years and there is this play actress, Nell Gwynne."

"Pray do not change the subject, Anne. I said I want to know. One of the Villiers girls said that when Sir John provided the wine, someone else was accused of the murder."

"They had to blame someone."

"My father?"

"No . . . not your father."

"Then whom did they blame?"

"Well . . . they said . . . your mother . . ."

"My mother! She would never have done such a thing!"

"Of course not. As a matter of fact, the postmortem proved that Lady Denham had not been poisoned at all. So it was a lot of lies."

"Not all," I said. "I suppose Sir John did go mad and his wife did take a lover, and that lover was . . ."

"Dear Lady Mary," said my friend Anne. "You must see the world as it really is. You cannot shut your eyes to the truth. Your father is not unlike the King in this. They were both born to love women. It is part of their natures. I sometimes think that the King is so greatly loved because of this weakness. He is the people's charming, wayward King. He has so much that is good in him and must be forgiven this foible. And as for your father, he loves you dearly, as you love him. This love between you is a precious thing, the best you will ever know until you have a husband who will love you, too. Accept what is good in life. Do not allow others to influence your feelings towards those you love."

"I wanted him to be perfect, Anne."

"No one is that. Life is very rarely perfect and never for long. If you are going to savour the best of it, accept what cannot be changed and enjoy it while you are able. When you have learned to do that you have mastered as valued a lesson as ever Bishop Compton can teach you."

The Stepmother

My father came to see me. He wanted to be alone with me and I knew he had something of great importance to tell me.

"My dearest daughter," he said. "I want to talk to you very seriously. I know you are young, but I want you to try to understand the position in which I find myself."

I nestled closer to him. No matter what evil stories I heard about his relationships with women, I still loved him the same. To me he was always the tender, loving father, and whatever he felt for those women did not touch us.

"You must know that the King cannot get children," he began.

I wrinkled my brows. I had often heard that this woman or that was going to have the King's child.

He noticed this and went on, "No child who could inherit the throne. The Queen, it seems, cannot produce one. Now this is of some significance to us. I am the King's brother and, if he were to die . . . oh, do not look alarmed . . . he is not going to die for a long time. He is hale and hearty. But there are those who say, yes, but suppose there was a riding accident . . . some mishap. Who knows in this life? And if your uncle died tomorrow . . . well, we must be prepared. I should be king then."

"I know that," I said.

"Well, I have two beautiful daughters and God knows I love them well, but the country looks for sons. People have this obsession for the masculine sex. That is a custom. They will take a woman, yes, but they would rather a man and they maintain that it is the duty of the heir to the throne to get sons if he possibly can."

"My mother is dead now," I said.

He looked mournful. "Alas," he murmured. "But that is why they expect me . . ." He paused and, gripping my hand firmly, he went on, "to marry again."

"To marry? Whom would you marry?"

"Ah! That is the question. The matter is being raised. Believe me, my love, there are many who would like to give birth to the heir of England. So I must needs put the past behind me. I must take a wife. I must show them that I will do my best to give them an heir."

I could not help thinking: you will do that with ease. If Arabella Churchill, with the enticing legs, were your wife you could have several already. I did not say that. I would have wounded him deeply. He would not want me to know of such matters. But I kept thinking of my mother, with the pain in her face just before she died, and at that time he was Arabella Churchill's lover.

These thoughts persisted, and I remembered what I had heard about the days when they were young and in exile at the court of the Princess of Orange, and how my father had fallen in love with my mother and proposed marriage to her. Then there came the Restoration and the Duke of York was no longer a wandering exile, and the marriage, which might have been acceptable when he had been, was no longer suitable for the brother of the King. There had been opposition, but my father had remained true to his word. I had liked that story. It fitted in with the image of him which I had created for myself.

And now he was going to marry again, so that he could get an heir to the throne because, although he already had my sister and me, boys were preferable.

"So you see, my dearest," he was saying, "your father must do his duty. I hope you will like your new mother."

"I could not have another mother," I said. "I had one and I have lost her."

He nodded and looked mournful again. Perhaps I was

growing cynical, but I fancied he was not displeased at the prospect of having a new wife.

It might be that she would be young and beautiful, so that he would not have need of those others.

Everyone was talking about the proposed marriage of the Duke of York. It was freely discussed by the girls. There seemed to be no reason to be discreet about it, even though he was the father of Anne and me, since it was being spoken of throughout the court.

The Duchess of Guise was highly suitable. Would it be the Duchess? Then there was the Princess of Wirtemburg. There was also Mademoiselle de Rais.

"I wonder which one it will be," said Elizabeth Villiers. I imagined she did not want it to be any of them. Or if there had to be a marriage that the bride would be ugly and barren. I imagined she was hoping that one day—some time ahead maybe—I was going to be Queen of England.

To me it seemed preposterous and I could not conceive its ever coming to pass. The idea filled me with dismay. But if my father married and there was a son, the household at Richmond would sink into insignificance.

Poor Elizabeth! How sad that would be for her!

Then there suddenly appeared another candidate for marriage into the House of York. This was Princess Mary Beatrice of Modena.

My father had sent the Earl of Peterborough to the Continent. It was said he was to spy on these ladies and to report secretly on them in such a way that none should know the true verdict but the Duke of York himself. But by some means we heard of the reports.

The Duchess of Guise was very short and not elegantly shaped: nor did she appear over-strong and it seemed unlikely that she would produce the much-desired heir. Mademoiselle de Rais? The Princess of Wirtemburg? Fair enough, but in the meantime my father had seen a portrait of the young Mary Beatrice of Modena.

I like to remember that when he made his choice he came first to me.

"She will be your companion," he said. "Peterborough sent home such a report to me. She is of middle height, which is good, for although I would not choose one who was low in stature, I would not care to have a wife look down on me. Her eyes are grey and she moves with grace. She has a sweet innocence, for she is but a child yet. She is strong and very young. She would bear sons, this little lady. Peterborough reports that, although she is gentle and of great modesty, yet she discourses with spirit. Methinks you will like my little bride from Modena."

"It is not for me but for you to like her," I said.

"You are right, but I should like to have my dearest daughter's approval. She will give it, I know, when she knows that is what I wish. My dearest child, I am going to bring you a little playfellow."

She was young and very frightened. I liked her from the moment we met. My father was proud of her and must have thought himself very lucky to have such a beautiful bride.

There was, of course, a faction who were against the match. They called it the Papist Marriage and tried to prevent its taking place; and when they heard it had actually been celebrated they suggested that my father should retire and lead the life of a country gentleman somewhere away from the court. This the King refused to take seriously.

I did not know at that time how intense the feeling against my father was becoming. If only he had not been so frank, so honest. If he had only been like the King, who leaned towards the Catholic faith but was wise enough not to let his subjects know this, how different everything might have been! But my father was no dissembler. To deny his faith would be a mortal sin to him.

At this time I could only be glad that he had acquired such a charming bride. I understood absolutely how he had been prevailed upon to marry; and although I could never forget my mother, I ceased to mourn for her so acutely and began to like my stepmother.

My father had said he was providing us with a playmate and this was true in a way. She was about the same age as Elizabeth Villiers and Sarah Jennings, but she seemed younger and, in spite of the fact that she was the daughter of a great house, she lacked the air of superiority which characterized those two. Fifteen was young to be married, particularly when the union brought with it two stepdaughters only four and six years younger than herself.

I sensed that she was very unhappy to have been taken away from her home and sent to a strange country and to a husband who must seem very old to her. My father was, in fact, twenty-five years her senior, but, I told myself, she would soon discover what a wonderful man he was—the best in the world—and when she did, she would cease to regret her marriage and would stop mourning because she had not become a nun, which was the life she would have chosen for herself.

Because of my understanding and the closeness of our ages, she began to confide in me.

"The thought of marriage was very unpleasant to me," she told me in her musical voice with the quaint accent. "I had set my heart on going into a convent."

I felt very sorry for her, putting myself in her place and imagining being forced to leave my father and go off to some foreign land.

When I learned a little more about her life, I thought it was not such a tragedy for her that she had come to us. Her childhood had not been as happy as mine had.

Poor Mary Beatrice, born to the illustrious House of Este, noted for its chivalry, its bravery, its encouragement of literature and all forms of art and civilization in general!

Unfortunately, her father Alfonso was a victim of crippling gout and depended on his forceful wife, the Duchess Laura, who ruled not only her household but the country. Mary Beatrice could scarcely remember her father, for he had died when she was very young. There were two children, Mary Beatrice and her brother Francisco, two years her junior.

Her father's brother, Rinaldo d'Este, was appointed guardian of the children on Alfonso's death, but it was Duchess Laura who assumed command.

"My mother is a very good woman," Mary Beatrice told me. "We did not always understand that when we were children. We thought she seemed very harsh, but it was because she was always concerned with what was best for us. You see, she thought we must never show weakness so that we might grow up strong."

"So she was very severe with you."

"For our own good," insisted Mary Beatrice. "I hated soup. It made me sick once and ever after I did not want to take it. My mother said that was weakness. Soup was good and nourishing. I must overcome my petulance and folly. I must learn to *like* soup because it was good for me. So every day I must sit at table and take soup. There was always to be soup for me."

I shivered and had a quick picture of my mother sitting on a chair with my sister Anne beside her, a bowl of sweetmeats beside them. I could hear my mother's voice, laughing as she said, "You eat too many sweetmeats, child. I fear you are as partial to them as your mother is. So no more, eh? Let us be strong or the palace will not be big enough to hold us. Look at this plump little hand . . ." taking Anne's hand and kissing it. And a few minutes later that plump little hand would be reaching for a sweetmeat and my mother, watching, would laugh and jokingly scold as she took one herself.

How different from ours Mary Beatrice's mother must have been!

"I was not allowed to leave the table," she went on, "until every drop of the soup had gone. But I did teach myself not to be sick. My mother is a very strong, good woman."

"I should have hated to be forced to take what I did not want," I said.

"The soup was usually well watered with my tears. She

was right, of course. One has to learn to do things one does not like. It makes it easier to face the world."

I wondered whether drinking soup she had hated had made it easier for her to come to England. I did not believe it had for a moment and I felt very critical of Duchess Laura and a fresh flood of sadness for the loss of our kind and clever mother.

"Our lessons were not easy either," said Mary Beatrice. "Many times I was beaten because I could not remember a verse in one of the psalms. You see, my mother wanted the best for us. She wanted us to be clever, so that we were prepared for anything that might happen to us. It was all for our benefit. The doctors once said that my little brother was not strong enough to sit so long over his lessons. He should be more in the fresh air. But my mother replied that she would rather have no son at all than a dullard. So poor little Francisco had to persevere with his lessons."

How different it had been with us! I remembered Anne, lolling indolently in her chair. "I shall not do lessons today. My eyes will hurt if I try to." And everybody said she must not hurt her eyes. Lessons were there if we wanted them, but no one in the household should think of forcing the Lady Anne to learn if she did not want to.

Poor, poor Mary Beatrice—although it must be rather pleasant to have learned as much as she appeared to have done.

"You will find my father very kind," I assured her. But I could see that she was unsure and uneasy, although she had already been charmed by the King.

I was a little piqued to realize that she wished my uncle had been her bridegroom instead of my father—and not because of his superior rank. I had heard it said so often that the charm of the King was unsurpassable. Kindliness was at the very essense of that charm and, because of her youth, and perhaps her beauty, he had made a very special point of showing affection and kindness to his new sister-in-law.

He appeared often at St. James's Palace, which was my father's official residence and, of course, with him would come the courtiers so there were some very lively gatherings.

My uncle obviously liked Mary Beatrice. He was always attracted by beauty such as hers, and I realize now that he made such a show of favouring her because of the unpopularity of the marriage. He wanted to soothe the people's fears regarding it. But at the same time, he deplored my father's preference for the Catholic faith—or rather his refusal to keep it a secret.

This show of favour had its effect on Mary Beatrice and she was no longer the melancholy girl she had been on her arrival.

The shock of meeting her husband who was so much older than she was had subsided a little. My father was making her see that he was not an ogre. In fact, I thought she was beginning to like him, but her uneasiness had not entirely disappeared.

Elizabeth Villiers talked of the great excitement there had been on Guy Fawkes Night, the fifth of November, just a short time before Mary Beatrice arrived in the country.

"The fires were bigger than ever this year," said Elizabeth. "There were grotesque images of Guy Fawkes. Hideous, they were. Well, he did try to blow up the Houses of Parliament, so it is understandable that people remember. It was all due to the Papist Plot. It will never be forgotten while there are Catholics in the country."

She began to chant,

"Remember, remember the fifth of November
The gunpowder treason and plot
I see no reason,
The gunpowder treason
Should ever be forgot!

"That is what they sing!" Her eyes were wide with innocence. "Why did they make such a special occasion of it this year?" she asked.

This was Elizabeth stressing the unpopularity of my father's marriage.

I was pleased when it became clear that Mary Beatrice was not afraid of my father as she had been at first. When I grew older I realized that, with his great experience of women, and his considerable charm—although some degrees less than that of the King—he had begun to win her affection. I noticed the smiles they exchanged and that the melancholy which she had not succeeded in hiding on her arrival was no longer there. There was an acceptance of her new life which grew firmer every day.

Card-playing was one of the most popular pastimes at court and Mary Beatrice was expected to join in. She told me that she disliked it and that she found no excitement when she won and she hated to lose.

"Then if you do not want to play, why did you do so?" I asked.

"I am told it is expected of me and some of the company look very displeased when I show no enthusiasm for the game."

"But it is amusing!" I cried. "I play now and then. Even my sister does. We like it very much."

Mary Beatrice shook her head. But that was just a minor irritation.

During the months that followed and as my father was revealed to Mary Beatrice as the considerate and kindly man he was, she grew to love him. The lazy manner of our court must have seemed a great contrast to that of her mother's. She remained enchanted by the courteous attention paid to her by the King. And she was becoming a light-hearted girl of sixteen.

Of the four ladies she had brought with her from Modena two were young. One of these was Anna, the daughter of Madame Montecuculi, the lady who was in charge of them all; and the other was Madame Molza, who was only a little older than Mary Beatrice herself. The other lady was

Madame Turenie, who had been with Mary Beatrice since she was a baby.

Through the veiled remarks of Elizabeth Villiers and the sophisticated comments of Sarah Jennings and some of the older girls, I was getting a deeper understanding of my father's position.

There had been a time when he had enjoyed a popularity almost to rival that of the King. His dalliance with Arabella Churchill and involvement in the Sir John Denham affair were dismissed as romantic waywardness, to be expected in a man of the world; but what remained unforgiven was his adherence to the Catholic faith and now his marriage to a Catholic. The King and heir to the throne might be as lecherous as they pleased. Their religion was another matter. England had experienced Catholic Queen Mary, the bigoted daughter of King Henry VIII, and they were determined never to have another Catholic monarch on the throne if they could help it.

And as time was passing, it seemed more and more likely that my father would inherit the throne. Forgotten were the victorious naval battles which had made a hero of him. Now could be heard the first rumblings of the storm and I was to learn how significant that would prove to be.

There came a day when Mary Beatrice had some exciting news.

"I am going to have a baby," she said, her beautiful eyes alight with happiness.

We were all very excited, particularly my father. He embraced me with the fervour he always showed at our meetings.

"I am so happy that you and your stepmother are such good friends," he said. "Nothing could delight me more. And soon you will have a little brother ... or sister. That will be wonderful, will it not?"

I said it would, but I could not help thinking of those other little brothers who had lived a while in our nursery and caused great concern until they passed on.

I hoped this one would not be like them.

The Chaste Nymph

Our household was no longer at Richmond. It had been moved to St. James's, that ancient palace which had once been a hospital for women suffering from leprosy. That was years ago, before the Norman Conquest, of course. It was dedicated to St. James and the name remained when it became a palace. Like Richmond, it was a place full of memories, and because of my growing awareness of all the murmurings about my father's leanings towards Catholicism, I thought of my namesake, Mary, who had lived here when her husband, Philip II of Spain, had gone away. He had not been a very kind husband; he was obsessed by his religion and such people are often too busy doing their duty towards God to be over-concerned with people. Perhaps they felt people were not very important. However, in spite of the fact that nowadays I often thought of sad, cruel Queen Mary who had ordered people to be burned at the stake because they would not become Catholics, I was happy to be near my father and Mary Beatrice.

It was at this time that I first met Frances Apsley. Frances's father was a friend of my father, and because of this she had been given a place at court.

From the moment I met her I was entranced. When she was presented to me I felt that I should have been the one to kiss her hand and do homage to her because of her excellence which I could never match.

She was a few years older than I was and when she talked to me I was too bemused to take in what she had said. I did gather that her father was Sir Allen Apsley.

My father had been good to hers, she told me.

When she was about to leave, I said that we must meet again.

"I have my duties," Frances told me.

"I shall write to you," I said, and Frances replied that that would give her great pleasure.

I was so filled with admiration that I must have shown it, and when I met Mary Beatrice I spoke of Frances Apsley to her.

"Ah yes," said my stepmother. "A very pleasant girl, and a beautiful one. Your father is friendly with her father. They were together during the long exile. Sir Allen was always loyal and worked hard to bring about the Restoration."

It was the beginning of that passionate friendship which I shall remember all my life. I was very fond of Anne Trelawny; she was my confidante and had been from childhood—but this was different. Anne was to me just another girl, older than I, wiser in many ways, my very good friend. But Frances was like a goddess.

I thought of her a good deal and I decided I would write to tell her of my feelings. This I did and her response was immediate. She told me that she cared for me in the same way as I did for her and that we must meet whenever it could be contrived and when we could not we would write to each other.

So began our romantic correspondence. We would ask people to take our letters to each other. I prevailed on my drawing master, little Richard Gibson, to do it and he was eager to oblige. I noticed that people were very ready to please me nowadays. True, my stepmother was pregnant, and if she had a son my position would change immediately, but the son had not yet put in an appearance and royal babies had a habit of either being girls or not surviving.

Sarah Jennings was a good courier although I did not altogether trust her. I preferred to use my little dwarf.

Frances had given a new zest to the days. Each morning when I awoke, my first thoughts were of her. Should I see her that day? Would there be a letter from her? Life was wonderful. I loved and was loved.

I wrote to her and told her that I felt towards her as though she were my husband. My love for her was greater than I had ever felt for anyone before—even my father. I loved him dearly but he was just a father. This was different.

I was very young and totally innocent. I knew that this was how lovers talked to each other—in plays for instance. Unlike my sister Anne, I liked to read of romance and passion in those pieces where the lovers were a young man and woman: but I saw no reason why the lovers should not be of the same sex.

I gave Frances a new name. It was Aurelia, a character in one of Mr. Dryden's comedies. In this, Aurelia was a delightful creature whom everyone loved. As for myself—I must have a special name, too. It was difficult to find anything that fitted myself. Beaumont and Fletcher had written of a young shepherdess named Clorine, who was faithful through all sorts of trials.

So we became Aurelia and Clorine. It gave a romantic secrecy to our correspondence.

One day my father came to see me.

He said, "You are growing up, daughter. Twelve years old, no less, and Anne coming on a little way behind. The King thinks it is time you made an appearance at court now and then. After all, you are my daughters."

"What shall we have to do?"

"Well, he has an idea. He thought it would be rather interesting if you gave a performance. Some play . . . something in which you could sing and dance to show the court you have not been idling all this time."

"A performance! Do you mean act?"

"Why not? It will be amusing. You will enjoy it."

"Like actors on a stage?"

"And why not? But your stage would be Whitehall. I have a plan. I am sending for the Bettertons . . . the great actors. They will come to court and teach you how to say your lines. We shall make sure that you have some beautiful dresses. It will be a great introduction to court. I shall be so proud of you."

"Anne and I to act! Do you really think we can?"

He touched my forehead lightly. "Do not frown, dearest daughter," he said. "When Mrs. Betterton has coached you, you will act perfectly. You will enjoy it. Some of the girls can join in. Jemmy will help. He will want to be in it. He will be coming over to see you."

I was a little taken aback and I wondered whether Frances would be present to see me act. I should have to do my very best.

It was interesting to meet Mrs. Betterton. She was a very handsome woman and most deferential. She told us to read for her. I wondered what she thought of Anne, who could scarcely read at all. She said she was quite pleased with me.

She instructed us to say words after her. I enjoyed it, particularly when Jemmy arrived.

He was very handsome and tended to give himself airs. I did not mind that. I liked Jemmy. He was always very friendly towards me. I had heard Sarah Jennings say that he acted as though he were heir to the throne and seemed to forget he was born on the wrong side of the blanket.

I had long ago discovered what that meant and because of it Jemmy could not have what he had set his heart on. Jemmy was a very ostentatious Protestant, though I did not believe he was very religious in truth. He just liked to be present at all the ceremonies of the Church so that he could remind people of this. He was very popular, though there was a great deal of scandal concerning him at this time. It had something to do with a Mrs. Eleanor Needham, daughter of Sir Robert Needham.

When Jemmy arrived he was as blithe as ever. He snapped his fingers at scandal. I supposed he was too accustomed to it to take much notice.

He was a very good dancer and was going to perform

with us, but that would not be until the play was over, for that was for ladies only.

It was all very exciting. Even Anne was aroused to enthusiasm and made an effort to learn her lines; she really worked hard under Mrs. Betterton's tuition. Anne was to take the part of Nymphe in the play—a chaste nymph like myself.

The story of Calisto, the Chaste Nymph, was taken from Ovid's *Metamorphoses* and John Crone had been commissioned to write a play from it.

Jemmy was overcome with mirth about something and when I asked him what it was, he said he dare not tell me, but I could see that with a little prompting he would. In the story, Jupiter pursues the Chaste Nymph with the object that she shall be chaste no longer.

At last I prevailed on Jemmy to tell me what amused him.

"The noble Duke will not allow his daughter to be sullied, even by the greatest of the gods," said Jemmy. "Poor John Crone! He has to make a different ending. Depend upon it, dear cousin, my chaste nymph, you are in danger of losing your virginity, but you will be rescued in time. This is one occasion when wily old Jupiter will not have his way, for Calisto is in truth the Lady Mary . . . and the daughter of my Lord Duke must be rescued in time."

This seemed very funny and everyone laughed mightily.

It was a most enjoyable time and we were all very excited about the play. Sarah Jennings, of course, had a part, and Jemmy told us that Lady Henrietta Wentworth was going to play the part of Jupiter, which gave him great pleasure.

Frances would be present. I should act for her and I must be good.

Sarah Jennings, who was going to play the part of Mercury, had no qualms. She was sure she would give a superb performance. I heard her telling Margaret Blague, who was dressed in a magnificent gown embroidered with brilliants, not to be so nervous. *She* was not in the least.

Margaret was protesting, "I did not want to do this. I do not want to act. But they told me I must. Oh dear, I am sure I am going to spoil everything."

Mrs. Betterton said, "This is an attack of nerves which comes to most good actresses. Some say that if one is not a little nervous one will not give a good performance."

I could not help glancing at Sarah. She never felt nervous, I was sure. Sarah interpreted my glance and merely tossed her head. Rules which might affect others did not touch her; in her opinion she knew better than everyone else about any subject and that included acting; and even in the presence of a highly acclaimed lady of the theatre, Sarah would rely on her own judgement.

Henrietta Wentworth and Margaret Blague were talking together. How different they were! They were two of the most beautiful girls at court however. Henrietta Wentworth was rather boldy handsome; she would make an excellent Jupiter. Margaret Blague was shy and retiring; and she was sure she was going to make an inadequate Diana. Moreover, she was very religious and felt there was something not very moral about acting.

Henrietta Wentworth was admiring the beautiful diamond Margaret was wearing.

"It was lent to me by Lady Frances," Margaret explained. "I do not want to wear it. I hate borrowing things. I am always afraid I will lose them. But Lady Frances was insistent. She said it suited the part and my costume."

"Why should you lose it?" cried Henrietta. "I love jewellery and that is a very handsome piece."

The stage was set. Mrs. Betterton hovered about us, giving last-minute instructions.

"Do not forget, Lady Anne, plenty of feeling in your words. And you, Lady Henrietta, remember, Jupiter is a great god, the head of them all. He has come to woo Calisto. And Lady Mary, you must show your determination to resist his advances . . . just as I showed you."

"Yes, Mrs. Betterton. Yes, Mrs. Betterton," we all assured her we would remember what she had taught us.

The music had started and we were there. It was wonderful. There were one or two little mishaps. Anne forgot her lines on one occasion, but Mrs. Betterton's voice, hushed though clear, came from behind the scenes. Diana was not where she should have been at a certain point, but that also was put right. The ballet went well. I saw Jemmy dancing with Henrietta Wentworth and the audience seemed to like it, for they applauded with enthusiasm.

The King himself congratulated us all; then he kissed both Anne and me and said he had not known there was such thespian talent in the family, which made everyone laugh and applaud again.

We were all very happy, except poor Margaret Blague, who was in a state of dire dismay, for her fears had been realized and she had indeed lost the diamond which she had been lent by Lady Frances Villiers.

Poor Margaret! She had not wanted to be in the play in the first place. She had had to be persuaded that it was her duty, and now, to have lost a diamond which did not belong to her plunged her into the deepest gloom.

Anne said, in her light-hearted way, "You must not worry, Margaret. It is certain that it will be found. It must have dropped onto the floor. Let there be a search."

I could see that there would be no comfort for Margaret until the diamond was found and returned to Lady Frances.

Margaret was appalled to discover it was worth eighty pounds.

I felt very sorry for her. Margaret was different from the others. She was more serious; at one time she had been in my mother's household and my mother had thought very highly of her.

She had said once, "Margaret Blague is a really virtuous girl. She is deeply religious and lives according to her beliefs. One cannot say that of many. Oh yes, they will attend the church services; they assume piety, but when it comes to the virtuous way of life they betray that they are merely making a show. With Margaret her religion goes deep."

I knew she thought play-acting was sinful and I could

not agree with her in that. Poor girl. She had been more or
less forced into doing what she had not wanted to, and
against her judgement to borrow the diamond. It was ironic
that this should have happened to her.

A search was made but the diamond was not to be
found. It would be easy for someone to pick it up and
pocket it. Who would be the wiser?

"Eighty pounds," mourned Margaret. "I am not rich
enough to pay Lady Frances such a sum."

"She will not ask for it," I comforted her.

"But I must pay it nonetheless. Otherwise how will she
know that *I* have not stolen it?"

"No one could possibly suspect *you* of that."

"There will be some," insisted Margaret. "And how can
I be happy again knowing that I have lost this valuable
jewel?"

It was true. If the diamond were not found, Margaret
would remember it all her life.

I could not stop thinking of her. The incident had put a
blight on what should have been a happy evening.

My father noticed my preoccupation. He had come to us
full of enthusiasm.

"Calisto! Nymphe! My clever little girls," he cried. "You
were enchanting. I was so proud of you both. We shall have
Davenant wanting you to join his players."

"It was Mrs. Betterton who helped us," said Anne.

"Ah, she is a great actress and a charming lady, too."

"She made us say our lines again and again, didn't she,
Mary?"

"Yes, she did."

"What ails you, daughter?" asked my father. "Is something wrong? You cannot hide your feelings from me, you
know. Come. Tell me."

"It is poor Margaret Blague."

"What of her?"

"She has lost Lady Frances's diamond and is very frightened. She did not want to act in the first place, nor did she
want to borrow the diamond."

My father grimaced. "A little puritan, eh?"

"She is really very good and now so unhappy because she thinks losing the diamond is some judgement on her for playing when she knew she should not do so."

"These puritans can be something of a trial ... as we found to our cost. Tell her not to worry. Doubtless the jewel will be found. If it is not ... then it is lost."

"She says she must pay for it and she cannot because she is not rich."

"And that worries my tender-hearted little daughter?"

"I like her. She is very pretty and she looks unhappy now."

"And you cannot be happy and enjoy your triumph while poor Margaret grieves."

He understood, as he always had.

"Well," he said, "I refuse to have my daughter sad on such an occasion. I tell you what shall be done. I shall provide the eighty pounds, so that Margaret Blague can take it along to Lady Frances and so forget about the matter. How is that?"

I looked at him with adoration. He was indeed the best and kindest man in the world.

"So you are happy now you have this matter settled?" he asked.

"I am happy," I said, "to have the most wonderful father in the world."

Anne had been so excited by the performance that she wanted to do more. She had liked Mrs. Betterton so much that she had wanted to keep her at court. Of course, she was indulged in this matter and there was to be another play with a bigger part for Anne. We were all so pleased to see her enthusiasm. Good-tempered, good-natured as she always was, she was rarely excited about anything, so it was unusual to see her working on her lines with energy and real enjoyment. This was for the play *Mithridate*, and Anne was to have the part of Semandra.

Mr. Betterton was also at court and he was coaching the young men in their parts.

Anne had discovered my passion for Frances Apsley. She knew about the letters we exchanged and that Frances was Aurelia and I, Clorine. She did what was typical of her; she decided she must have a passionate friendship. I had Frances and, as there was no one to compare with my choice in Anne's opinion, she must have Frances too.

After all, sentimental friendships were the fashion. So many young women indulged in them and they were generally conducted by letters.

This had nothing to do with her allegiance to Sarah Jennings, any more than mine had towards Anne Trelawny. They were our true friends, our everyday friends. This was different. The object of our devotion in this case was an ideal being, a goddess to be worshipped.

I had found the goddess and she must be Anne's too.

I often wonder now what Frances thought of our outpourings. When I remember some of the impassioned words I wrote I can smile at my innocence. It did not occur to me at the time that others might think it was not exactly a healthy state of affairs.

However, Anne was soon corresponding with Frances in the same manner. Frances humoured her, as I expect she did me. We were the daughters of the Duke of York, heir to the throne, and if there was no son, I was second in line to the throne, Anne third. That had to be a consideration.

Not only was Anne writing to Frances—an example of her devotion and her determination to imitate me, for writing was an occupation she had hitherto avoided and I could imagine what those letters were like—but they must have their private names, as Frances and I had. So Frances was Semandra—from the play, of course—and Anne was Ziphares, another character from it.

It may have been this unusual activity on Anne's part that attracted Lady Frances's attention, and she may have felt that she should know what was going on. We were, after all, in her charge. She was especially watchful.

It happened that Richard Gibson, the dwarf, whom we often used as a courier, was away. Sarah Jennings, who was fully aware of the passion Anne and I shared for Frances Apsley, and no doubt laughed at it and clearly considered it no impediment to her domination over Anne, agreed to take the letters while Richard Gibson was absent. Thus, I supposed, she could keep a close check on Anne and share her confidences about what she would consider to be a silly and by no means a permanent arrangement.

One day, when I was having my dancing lesson with Mr. Gorey, our dancing master, Anne was in her closet, writing to Frances—never an easy task for Anne—and before she had time to finish her letter she was called to have her dancing lesson.

She did not want to leave the letter unsealed, so she took it with her to the class and, as my lesson had just finished, she gave it to me, whispering that I might be good enough to seal hers with mine and that Sarah had promised to take them both to Frances.

I went back to my closet and there wrote my letter to Frances, but just as I was finishing, Sarah Jennings came in.

"I shall have to go now," she said. "So I will take the letters."

"My sister's is not yet sealed. Will you please seal it for her while I do mine?"

As I gave her the letter, Lady Frances came in and I had a notion that she might have heard some of the conversation.

I felt my face grow scarlet. Suppose she asked to see the letter? I could not bear to think of those cool eyes reading the impassioned words. She would not understand at all and they would seem quite foolish to such a practical person. I had called Frances my husband and I was her adoring wife.

Sarah was calm enough. In any case, she had nothing to fear. She was just standing there with Anne's letter in her hand.

As Lady Frances came into the closet, I was so embarrassed. I stammered something about my new gown and asked how she liked it. I turned to the cupboard and opened it so that my back was towards her and she could not see my flushed face.

Lady Frances said, "My Lady Mary, what were you doing in your closet before I came in?"

Sarah stood there with an air of nonchalance, Anne's letter still in her hand.

"I . . . had called in Mistress Jennings to show me a new way of sealing a letter," I said.

Lady Frances looked at the letter in Sarah's hand and there was a slight pause before she said, "Mistress Jennings is very ingenious with such things."

There was an awkward silence and then she left us.

Sarah shrugged her shoulders. "Let us seal the letters," she said, "and I will take them to Mistress Apsley without delay."

After that I fancied Lady Frances was very watchful and when next I wrote and Richard Gibson was still away and Sarah was unable to deliver the letter, I summoned one of the footmen and asked him to take it, in spite of the fact that Frances had warned me not to send letters unless it was by someone whom I could trust.

I was sure then that Lady Frances was watching us closely, for that letter fell into her hands.

I was horrified when she came to my closet and said that she wanted to talk to me. She was very respectful, as always, but her mouth was set in stern lines and I saw that she was determined to do what she considered her duty.

She said, "You have been corresponding with Mistress Apsley." She held up the letter which I had given to the footman. She must have ordered him to give it to her.

"You . . . have read it?" I gasped.

"Lady Mary, your father has put me in charge of this

household. It is therefore my duty to know what goes on in it."

I was trying to think what I had written in that letter. I was always in a state of high emotion while I wrote them, words flowed out and I was never sure half an hour afterwards what I had said except that all the letters contained pledges of my constant love.

Then I remembered that I had mentioned something about the scandal concerning the Duke of Monmouth and Eleanor Needham and that the Duchess of Monmouth had taken the matter mightily to heart.

That had been indiscreet, of course, and I should not have referred to it. Nor would I, if I had thought anyone was going to read it other than Frances. I was rather proud of my eloquence and I remembered the end. "I love you with a love that never was known by man. I have for you more excess of friendship than any woman can for woman and more love than even the most constant husband had for his wife, more than can be expressed by your ever obedient wife and humble servant who wishes to kiss the ground where you walk, to be your dog on a string, your fish in a net, your bird in a cage, your humble trout. Mary Clorine."

I had been so proud of those words when I wrote them: now I blushed to remember them.

Lady Frances was looking at me very strangely. I noticed an uncertainty in her eyes. I had realized that she was not sure how to act.

She began, "His Grace, your father . . ." Then she shook her head; her lips moved as though she were talking to herself.

"It is a very excessive friendship," she said at length. "I think it would be better if we did not speak of it. And the Lady Anne . . . ?"

"My sister writes to Mistress Apsley because I do," I said.

"I must ponder this matter," she said, as though to herself.

"I do not understand. Is it not good to have friends . . . to love?"

"Perhaps it would be well if you did not meet for a while."

"Not meet?"

"And not . . . write such letters."

"I do not understand . . ."

"No," said Lady Frances briskly. "I am sure you do not."

"Not to see her . . ." I murmured blankly.

"I think you might meet, say on Sundays. You will be in the company of others then. And perhaps on Holy Days."

I stared at her in dismay. I had been in the habit of taking any opportunity I could to be with Frances.

I said, "Lady Frances, you have my letter."

She looked at me with caution in her eyes. I knew that she was eager not to displease me. It was a fact that my stepmother was pregnant, but who could be sure what the result of the pregnancy would be? And if the situation did not change, Lady Frances might be at this moment earning the deep resentment of the future Queen of England.

"We will forget this matter," she said slowly. "I think, my Lady Mary, it would be well if we were a little discreet."

She was smiling at me. Gravely I took the letter from her and she left me.

It was a bleak January day in the year of 1675. I would soon be thirteen years old. My father had been very disappointed because, instead of the hoped-for boy, Mary Beatrice had produced a girl. He tried not to show it and declared that he was very happy with our little sister.

I found Mary Beatrice in excellent spirits. She confided to me that she wanted the child to be baptized in the Catholic faith and she was afraid there would be some opposition to that.

"Your father desires it, too," she said. "And I am going

to be very bold. I shall command Father Gallis to baptize the baby before anyone else can do anything about it."

In view of the conflict which was growing over this matter of the Catholic faith, I thought this was a very daring thing to do. I knew that my father was very sad because Anne and I were being brought up as Protestants, and he only accepted this because if he had attempted to stop it we should have been taken away from him altogether and he would probably have been sent away from court.

I was amazed that the usually meek Mary Beatrice could be so bold; but I was learning that people will do a great deal for their faith.

It was no use trying to dissuade her, and Father Gallis baptized little Catherine Laura. The name Catherine was given to the baby in honour of the Queen and she was Laura after Mary Beatrice's mother.

Mary Beatrice had no qualms about what she had done. I supposed this was due to the fact that, whatever misdemeanour she committed at court was of no importance because she had done right in the sight of Heaven.

However, she did seem a little subdued when she told me, a few days later, that the King had announced his intention of coming to St. James's to discuss the baptism with her.

I was horrified.

"The King will be angry," I said. "You have been very bold. It is not that he will care very much. He is careless about such matters. But you have to remember that the people are not very pleased."

She held her head high, but I could see that she was apprehensive. I begged her to tell me quickly what the King said when he came. I felt she had gone too far, even for his good humour.

She kept her word and I hastened to her. I found her a little baffled.

She said, "I told the King what I had done but it was not as I expected. He did not show anger at all. He just smiled in a rather absent way and talked of other things. I was overjoyed. My baby is a Catholic, even though she was born in this heretic land."

"Do not be too sure of that," I said. "There are people around us who could create mischief."

The next day I was told that the baby was to be baptized in the Chapel Royal, according to the rites of the Church of England, of course, and one of the bishops would perform the ceremony.

I was astounded. Mary Beatrice had said the King had not seemed to hear what she had said.

"He did hear," I assured her. "He is sweeping it aside, as he does anything that is unpleasant. He understands what you did. Most people would have been furious . . . banished you to the Tower. But the King does not act like that, so he brushes it aside as though it has not happened. But he will have his way all the same and Catherine Laura will be baptized in the Church of England."

"But she is a Catholic!" Mary Beatrice was almost in tears. She was bewildered. She did not understand the ways of our court. The King, so charming . . . smiling, showing no signs of anger, had just swept aside her childish action. As far as he was concerned, it had never happened.

Soon after I heard that my sister Anne and I were to stand as sponsors and the Duke of Monmouth was to join us.

When it was over my father came to see me.

"The Duchess told you that there was a previous baptism," he said.

"Yes," I replied. "She did."

He was frowning and staring before him. "The King has spoken to me very seriously," he went on.

"The King behaved to the Duchess as though it were of no importance."

"He understood her motive. 'She is young,' he said, 'and quite ignorant of the significance of her action. She is not to be blamed, but watched that she commits no more such follies.' If this were known, Gallis would be hanged and quartered. As for myself and the Duchess, he warned me that at least we should be sent away from court. No one must know that this ceremony took place. Please, never speak of it."

I did understand. I was growing up fast. I saw that my father could be in danger.

I threw myself into his arms and clung to him.

"I promise, I promise," I cried.

The Orange Marriage

Life had changed since we had been launched on the court. We were often in the company of the King. Both Anne and I looked forward to those occasions, for he treated us with great affection and lack of ceremony, as always the kindly uncle. How differently I see such relationships when I look back now!

In those days I thought all the affectionate words and actions meant he really cared for us. He did, of course, in his light-hearted way, but I know now what his main aim was. We were in his care. We were good little Protestants. We were in line to the throne and my uncle wanted the people to know that, although he himself could not provide them with a Protestant heir, he would make sure that, in spite of his brother's love affair with the Catholic Church, those who followed him to the throne should be of the approved religion.

Although I know now how this matter was always there in our lives, I did not understand then how very important it was and how it would shape my life.

So we were now at court, and I must say we were finding the experience delightful. We were treated with the utmost respect wherever we went. Lady Frances was almost deferential at times. Elizabeth Villiers was wary, and so was Sarah Jennings. She and Anne were inseparable, in spite of Anne's passion for Frances Apsley. It was Sarah who was Anne's alter ego.

I continued to write to Frances and to see her when I could on Sundays and Holy Days; and both Anne and I discovered a pastime which we found fascinating. This was cards. How we enjoyed them! The excitement of picking up the cards to see what had been dealt to us, eagerly scanning them, deciding how we should play them—it absorbed us.

In fact, we became so addicted to the cards that there was criticism of us.

Margaret Blague thought it was sinful and, like all good people, did not stop herself from letting us know it.

"What harm does it do anyone?" I asked.

"It could harm the players," she insisted. "It is gambling and that should not be indulged in—especially on Sundays."

Margaret was very puritanical. She would have been happier under Oliver Cromwell, I thought. Hadn't she believed that play-acting was sinful?

My tutor, Dr. Lake, brought up the subject one day.

He said, "It has been noticed that you and the Lady Anne are at the card table almost every evening."

"It is a pastime we enjoy," I replied. "What harm is there in it? Do you consider it to be a sin?"

"It is not exactly a sin, but I think Your Highness gives offence by indulging in it on the Sabbath. The people would not like it if they heard of it."

I knew that we had to be constantly careful not to offend "the people," and I could understand that there might be some of them who would not like us to play cards on Sundays.

"I will speak to my sister," I said, "and we shall not play cards on Sundays."

Dr. Lake looked a little placated and I was so relieved that he did not attempt to curtail card-playing during the week, for that was something neither of us could have agreed to.

Something very unfortunate happened at this time and, although it was proved to be just the mischief-making of a man of evil reputation, it was very disturbing while it lasted.

A Frenchman named Luzancy announced that the Duchess of York's confessor had visited him in his lodgings. This Luzancy had been born a Catholic and was a convert to Protestantism. The Roman Catholic priest, he alleged, had held a knife to his throat and threatened to kill him if he did not return to the Catholic faith.

There was nothing more likely to arouse the concern of the people. They would never forget the fires of Smithfield during the reign of that queen whom they called Bloody Mary. Then Protestant men and women had been burned to death for their religious opinions. They had heard gruesome stories of what had happened under the Spanish Inquisition. Never would they have that sort of thing in England.

We were back on the old theme which seemed to be running through my life, and which was soon to be brought home to me in the most significant manner possible. But I suppose this was the case with many people at that time. It certainly affected my father's life more than any.

The matter of Luzancy was taken so seriously that it was brought before the House of Commons and Lord William Russell, the ardent Protestant, who hated the French and deplored the licentiousness of the court, took the opportunity to bring in new laws against Catholics, and as a result no English subject might officiate as a papist priest in any chapel whatsoever.

This was a criticism not only of Mary Beatrice but the Queen herself, who had been subjected to suspicion since she came to the country.

Even when witnesses to Luzancy's criminal career in his native France were produced and he was completely discredited, this law persisted.

I believe that Mary Beatrice did not realize the extent of her unpopularity. She was very young and was beginning to grow fond of her husband, whom she found to be so gentle and kindly; she was very fond of her royal brother-in-law; and she had her baby.

What a tragedy it was that little Catherine Laura should only live ten months!

I talked to Anne Trelawny about it. I said, "It is so

strange. The King has several children by women other than his wife, but the Queen cannot have one. And my father . . . well, he has only Anne and me, although he has had others . . ."

"And strong ones too," Anne reminded me.

"Why is it, Anne? Do you think it is a judgement on them?"

I could see that Anne thought this might be so but was afraid to say so.

"Because," I went on, "they are not faithful to their wives."

I thought how sad it was, how difficult to understand. The King loved the Queen, but he loved others, too. And I was forced to admit that my father was like his brother in this respect.

I did not want to think of Arabella Churchill and people like that. But they existed and there were several of them.

We tried to comfort poor Mary Beatrice over the loss of little Catherine Laura. It was not easy. I heard it whispered that the little girl's death was an indication. It was going to be the King's story all over again. Illegitimate children were easy to come by for the royal brothers. It was only legitimate ones who were denied them.

It was very strange indeed and I was convinced that it was indeed a judgement on their immorality. I wondered why two of the most charming people I had ever met should be afflicted in this way.

There was no long period of mourning for Catherine Laura and it seemed to me that her death was quickly forgotten at court.

Perhaps because my uncle now shared the view that it was very possible that my father like himself, would never get a legitimate son, he decided that Anne and I should be brought into prominence. We had achieved a little attention with our play and ballet and we went to the Lord Mayor's banquet and sat with the King and Queen that all might see us.

I was confirmed by Henry Compton, Bishop of London,

to make it clear to all that I was not following my father's religion, and I believe this event was viewed with great satisfaction by the people. They cheered us enthusiastically. They always cheered the King. I had heard it said that, in spite of the immoral life he led, the people loved him more than any king since Edward IV, who was a little like him. Licentious indeed, tall as Charles, and very handsome. My uncle could not be called that, but he had that overwhelming charm to make up for it.

I enjoyed being cheered and knowing that the people approved of me.

"There is nothing the people like more than a beautiful young girl," said my uncle.

And that was very comforting.

So . . . life was changing. I loved Frances as dearly as ever. True, we only met on Sundays and Holy Days, and then in the company of others, but my great joy was writing to her and knowing that she was there. I wished sometimes that we could go off together and live quietly in a country cottage, surrounded by a garden full of beautiful flowers. I should want Anne Trelawny, of course, and my sister Anne—and she would not come without Sarah Jennings. And my father and Mary Beatrice must be there . . . and one or two more.

I laughed at myself. I was just living in an impossible dream.

Mary Beatrice was considerably comforted because she was pregnant again and in the August of the following year, only ten months after the death of little Catherine Laura, she gave birth to another daughter.

There was the usual disappointment over the sex of the child, but at least she seemed strong and Anne and I were delighted to have a stepsister. She was called Isabella after Mary Beatrice's great-grandmother.

Life seemed very good at that time and then came the bitter blow.

I was fifteen years of age in April of that year. I was so

innocent in many ways. Life was good; I was surrounded by affection and I believed it would go on like that for ever.

I knew there were trials, but I did not take them seriously. There was the continual harping on the religious theme. It kept cropping up, but I did not think it was any great concern of mine.

How wrong I was!

I knew there was trouble on the Continent. There was constant talk of wars and treaties. That had nothing to do with me, so I thought. The Dutch were our enemies, then the French were; then we were friends with this one or that. What had that to do with life at St. James's and Whitehall? A great deal, I was to discover.

And then one day we heard that the Prince of Orange was to pay a visit to the court.

I had heard the name of this Prince mentioned now and then—and more frequently of late. He was some kinsman of ours. His mother had been the eldest daughter of my grandfather, Charles the Martyr, so he was the nephew of the King and my father—and my cousin.

He had a Dutch father and I had been brought up to hate the Dutch, though I learned later that the people liked them better than they did the French. My father and the King had always preferred the French, but then they were half French themselves.

We had been at war with the Dutch, so therefore the Prince of Orange would have been our enemy—but enemies of yesterday were today's friends and it appeared that we were making treaties with the Dutch, and it was for this reason that Prince William of Orange was coming to England.

There was a certain amount of gossip about him among the girls of the household. He had visited Whitehall seven years or so before. I had hardly been aware of it, but the older girls like Elizabeth Villiers and Sarah Jennings remembered it very well.

"He caused some interest when he was here last," commented Elizabeth.

"Notoriety," added Sarah Jennings. "Such a virtuous young man he was. He was very serious."

"And very religious," added Elizabeth.

"Of course," Sarah went on, "it was his aim to maintain the Protestant faith throughout Europe. He hated the French King because his aim was exactly the opposite. *He* wanted to crush the Protestants and make the whole continent Catholic. So you see how it was between them."

"Some would have thought," put in Anne Trelawny, "that, with all his might, Louis would have triumphed and soon silenced the Dutch."

"Oh, but the Prince would not give in," said Sarah. "He was determined and has the reputation of being a clever commander. His small country stood out against the French . . . and now here he is talking peace with England."

"Which the French won't like," said Anne Villiers.

"But the people here will," added Elizabeth. "They like the Prince . . . not for his charm . . . he is a little lacking in that . . . but because he is such a good religious man with ideas that appeal to the English. But in spite of his solemn ways, he caused a good deal of amusement on his last visit."

"What did he do?" I asked.

Sarah and Elizabeth exchanged glances and laughed.

"It was really funny," said Sarah, "and they shouldn't have done it. But he was such a virtuous young man that the temptation was too strong. He must have been about twenty then. He did not drink . . . only schnapps, a sort of Holland gin; he liked to retire at ten o'clock, so that he could be at work early in the morning. You can imagine what the King and the courtiers thought of that! Virtue is a challenge to them—a fortress to be stormed and overcome. So they decided to have some fun with him."

"They might have tried to be a little more like him," I said.

"Oh, Lady Mary!" cried Anne Villiers. "You could surely not expect that!"

"I will tell you what they did," added Sarah. "They took him to supper at the Duke of Buckingham's apartments, for they had this plan. They were going to make him very drunk and see what he would do."

"Surely he would not allow that," I suggested. "I thought he only drank that mild stuff they have in Holland and very little of that."

"Ah, but he was not in Holland, was he, Lady Mary?" Sarah went on. "They filled up his glass with something very strong—he did not realize how strong—and even when they refilled his glass he did not realize what they were doing to him until it was too late."

"And perhaps he enjoyed it when he tried it," said Elizabeth Villiers. "You have not said that they talked about the charms of the Queen's maids of honour and how they liked and expected attention from the courtiers and were very free with their favours. The Prince listened. He could never have heard anything like it before and it must have seemed to him that customs were very different in England from those in Holland."

"So they made him drunk!" I said. "I do not think that was a very kind or clever thing to do."

"You haven't heard what happened," said Sarah. "When he went back to Whitehall, he was so inflamed with the drink and the stories he had heard of willing maids of honour that he tried to get into their apartments. He was so angry when he found them locked against him and was told by the older ladies to go away that he broke a window and tried to climb in. So, there was your virtuous young man. Virtue had been defeated by strong drink and the hope of the pleasure he would get from the ladies."

"I think it was a very unkind trick to play on a visitor," I said.

"So did he," said Elizabeth. "Next morning he was very ashamed and contrite, but at least it shows that underneath this cloak of virtue he is just like most other men."

"That is not quite true," protested Anne Trelawny, "because he was sorry for what happened, and it was not his fault really."

"But," insisted Elizabeth, "he had always been so disapproving of other people's weaknesses and it was revealed that when intoxicated he was just like the rest."

"But he did not ask for the drink in the first place," said Anne.

Elizabeth shrugged her shoulders. "You are determined to defend him. The King was very much amused and liked him better for 'his normality' as they called it."

"That was a long time ago," said Anne Trelawny. "He will be on his guard, I dare say."

"Oh yes," agreed Sarah. "He will be watchful of what he drinks. I look forward to seeing him."

"I doubt not you will ere long," said Elizabeth.

I was surprised when my father told me that I was to be presented to the Prince of Orange. I had supposed that I would meet him sometime but it appeared from my father's manner that there was something special about this meeting. He seemed a little apprehensive.

He said, "It is the King's wish that you and your cousin should meet and be friends."

"I hear he is very serious."

"He is greatly respected throughout Europe," replied my father.

He himself came to escort me to the Prince. The King was with him and, when my father led me to them, my uncle came forward and, taking both my hands, kissed my cheek.

"This is my dear niece," he said to the Prince. "Mary, here is my nephew William, the Prince of Orange, a very welcome visitor to our court."

William of Orange bowed rather stiffly, and I curtsied.

"Now," said the King, "you have met. I do not think you had the pleasure of meeting my niece when you were last at Whitehall, nephew." He looked faintly mischievous and

I knew he was thinking of the solemn young man trying to break into the quarters of the maids of honour. William's face was impassive. I guessed that he dismissed that incident as unimportant.

He had penetrating grey eyes which I was sure missed little, thick brown hair, an aquiline nose, and thin lips. There was something rather formidable about him, although he was of small stature, very thin, and stooped slightly. His skin was mildly pockmarked, but he had such dignity that, in spite of his physical disabilities, one knew at once that he was a man to be reckoned with.

The thought occurred to me as he stood by the King that there could not be two men more unlike each other.

There were very few people present, which surprised me, and I only realized why this was so much later.

The King said, "My dear Mary, why do you not sit down and talk to your cousin? Tell him about our court and I am sure he will tell you about his."

My father was watching me, half-uneasily, half-proudly. I thought I detected a certain anger in his look, but not against me, nor against the Prince of Orange. He looked frightened, unhappy, and frustrated.

It was a strange experience, sitting there with this young man beside me while my father and the King stayed some way apart, talking quietly, so that I could not hear what they said. I wished the Prince would not look at me so intently. He did not seem to take his eyes from me.

I am not sure what we talked of. In fact, all the time I was wondering how long this interview was going to last and when I should be able to escape. He asked me about the household, how I spent my time, about the customs here. I wanted to ask him about his but that seemed out of the question. I was not sure why. I was, after all, an inexperienced girl of fifteen; he was a man of twenty-seven and a ruler of a country, an important ruler, or he would not have been received at Whitehall with such respect.

I was glad when the session was over and I could leave them.

My father took me to the door and kissed me gravely. He still seemed upset.

On the afternoon of the following day my father came to me. He looked very serious and took me into my closet so that we could be entirely alone. I knew now that he was very unhappy.

We sat side by side and he put his arm about me and held me tightly against him before he spoke.

Then he said, "Mary, my dearest daughter, there is something I have to tell you." He hesitated, as though it hurt him to go on. I was getting alarmed. Something rather terrible must have happened.

"Yes, dearest father," I said faintly.

"You are growing up, Mary. You are no longer a child and people in our position ... well, sometimes it is necessary for them to do something which might seem rather unpleasant at first ... until ... "

"Please tell me, father, what this is all about."

"Well, sometimes we have to do something which we would rather not do. It is our duty, you see. Everybody has to do something ... uncongenial ... at times, and for people in our position ..."

"Please tell me quickly what I have to do."

"You will like it ... when you get used to it. It is just that, at first ... well, I would have wished it could have been a little later. You are young yet ... but not too young. My child, you are going to be married."

"Married!" I cried in horror.

"You are fifteen years old. People such as we are ... well, it has happened to many. Your stepmother ..."

I felt blank, unable to grasp this stupefying fact. Then I burst out, "Who is it? Whom shall I marry?"

"Oh, it has not been arranged yet," said my father. "These things ... you know ... certain preparations. Documents have to be drawn up."

"Please tell me who it is."

"It is a kinsman of ours. You have already met him and

I see that you like each other. It is William, the Prince of Orange."

The Prince of Orange! That cold little man with the penetrating, critical eyes, who had asked all those questions. Marry *him*! He was too old. He was quite different from my father and the King and the men that I had seen about my uncle's court. All the time he had been talking to me he had not smiled once. He came from a far-off country. Holland! The thought struck me with sudden force. I should have to go away with him, that strange cold man, to a strange cold country, far away from my sister, my father, from Frances and Anne Trelawny. I thought of poor Mary Beatrice's arrival in this country, come to marry an older man. But he had been my kind, good father and I was for William of Orange.

This was too much to be borne. To be married to that strange man—to leave my home! I put out my hands as though to ward off this cruel fate.

"No, no, no!" I cried.

My father put his arms round me and rocked me to and fro as though I were a baby.

"Don't let them send me away," I begged.

"I shall be as unhappy as you, my dearest."

"Then you must stop it!"

He said slowly, "My poor Mary, my poor child. You must understand. You were born into royalty, and we all must needs do what is asked of us. That is our destiny and duty. We have to face it. The people will like this marriage."

"It is not they who will have to endure it."

He sighed. "You see, it is your position, my child."

"You mean the throne . . ."

"Oh, I know your stepmother and I have hopes of a boy, but there have been so many disappointments, and in view of your position, my dearest, the people want a Protestant marriage for you and there could not be a more ardent Protestant than Prince William. He has upheld that faith on the Continent of Europe and he is a very clever man. He is youngish yet, but he will make his mark on the world, never doubt it. He is a great man and you will be proud to be his wife."

"Father . . . dearest Father, I do not like him."

"Liking comes with marriage."

"So you want me to do this."

He shook his head sadly. "I want you to stay with me all my life, but I know that cannot be. Alas, we have our duty. It is the King's wish."

"I have always found my uncle very kind. Perhaps . . ."

He shook his head. "Your uncle would be kind, but even he could not release you from this. He wants this marriage. He is anxious to strengthen our alliance with the Dutch and this marriage is one of the terms. It is a great opportunity for William. You will learn to understand these things. If you spoke to your uncle he would show great kindness and commiseration, but that is his way. Beneath the kindness he is a wily ruler and this marriage is necessary to the country. William wants it and we want friendship with William. Therefore the King insists. Let me tell you, I have tried to dissuade him, but it is of no avail."

"Then there is no way out."

"I think you will find William a good man. He is dedicated to his country's welfare and that is a noble thing to be. And, of course, he has a claim to the throne of England—distant it may be, but there. An alliance with you will make that claim stronger. But this is not the time to talk of these things."

"I want to know everything. I did not think the Prince would want to marry me unless there were . . . advantages to him."

"You must not judge him too harshly for that. It is diplomacy. But he wanted to meet you, to see you for himself before he would enter into the arrangement. He has seen you and likes you well. So that is a good start."

"I hate it all. How can I leave you?"

"It will be a little time yet, but I wanted you to know. It will give you time to get accustomed to the idea. You will find it is not all bad, and I swear that in time you will look back on your fear and realize how unjustified it was. The Prince is a good man and your uncle thinks it will be a successful marriage."

"But you do not like it, I see you do not!"

"I wanted you for the Dauphin of France," he admitted.

"I should have had to go away from home then."

"I had rather it had been an alliance with France. But this is what the people want."

"But I am the one who has to marry him! I hate it!"

Then the tears came and I could not stop them. I wanted to plead with him, to beg him to stop this monstrous thing happening to me. But I could not speak. My sobs prevented me.

My sister Anne wanted to know what ailed me.

"I am going to be married," I said.

She stared at me in dismay.

"I shall have to go away," I went on piteously.

"You can't go away! I want you here. You've always been here. We belong together. You could not go away from *me*."

She was deeply upset, poor Anne. She had drifted so happily through life—as we both had, until now. When she had not wanted to do her lessons, she had merely said they hurt her eyes and no one forced her to. Of course, she could not read very well, but that did not bother her. She must not eat so many sweetmeats, they said, but they just smiled and shook their heads when she slipped the delicious morsels into her mouth.

Now she was genuinely distressed. I *must* not go. She could not visualize our household without her elder sister whom she rather slavishly copied and who had been there all her life.

She was twelve years old now and she knew this was a serious matter, for suddenly she started to cry and, throwing her arms about me, clung to me as though to defy all those who would attempt to separate us. We wept together; in fact I had scarcely stopped weeping since my father told me the news.

I wrote a letter to Frances, passionately telling her what they were planning for me. All the girls seemed enveloped in gloom. Lady Frances looked anxious. What would happen to the household? There was still Anne, of course. But it would not be the same. It would be of less importance. I was nearer to the throne than Anne. What would happen to them all?

They whispered together. There was pity for me on account of the bridegroom who had been chosen for me.

"The Prince of Orange!" I heard someone murmur. "And the Lady Mary!"

I knew what they meant. They did not admire him. He was quite different from the men whom they considered to be attractive. He lacked graceful manners; he was brusque, he dressed simply; he had none of that charm which the King possessed in abundance and which most of the men about him sought to emulate.

My misery increased as the days passed and preparations marched inexorably onwards. In the streets there were bonfires and signs of rejoicing at the prospect of a Protestant marriage—an indication that there could be a Protestant heir. Charles himself remained acceptable, in spite of suspicions that he had a leaning towards the Catholic faith. He was merry, charming, with a cheerful word for everyone. He had come back to them after his exile, the Merry Monarch. They were as anxious that he should not go wandering again as he was himself. They were happy enough in the present. It was the future which troubled them. Therefore my marriage to a staunch Protestant pleased them. It was only those immediately concerned, like my father and myself, who were uneasy.

I went to see Mary Beatrice. She was due to give birth shortly and if she had a son this marriage would be less desirable to many people. My hopes soared at the thought. What if William decided that he did not want to marry me after all!

That was nonsense. It was necessary for the treaty.

Mary Beatrice wept with me.

"My poor, poor Mary. He seems such an ogre, but he might be a good husband. At least he will not have a string of mistresses. There is a great deal to be said for fidelity," she added wistfully.

"I shall be sent away," I wailed.

"As I was."

"I know. You suffered, too, but you came to England, to my father, who is good and kind."

"William is a good man, they say."

"And you were beaten when you did not know the verses of the psalm, whereas I have never known anything but love."

"Oh yes, you have a most affectionate father. He would not let anyone punish either you or Anne, and you were always his favourite. Mary, this hurts him as much as it does you."

"Oh dearest, dearest stepmother, I have to leave you, too, and Anne."

She tried to comfort me, but in vain.

"They are saying that if you have a son, the Prince of Orange will not be so eager to marry me," I said, looking at her pleadingly, as though it were in her power to save me.

"I think he would want to marry you whatever should be. Your father tells me that he liked very much what he found when he met you."

"I did not realize then that I was being shown for that purpose."

"He would not have wanted to marry you if he did not like you."

I was not sure of that and, in any case, I did not like him.

"Think!" I moaned. "I shall have to leave you all."

"Holland is not far. We shall visit you and you will come to us."

I flung myself at her and clung. "I don't want to go. Pray something will happen to stop it."

There was nothing she could say to comfort me.

* * *

Elizabeth Villiers was excited.

She said, "I am so pleased because I shall be accompanying you to Holland."

"You!" I cried.

"Well, you will have your attendants and I shall be one of them. You will have familiar faces around you. My mother is to be in charge of the attendants and my sister Anne will be with us, too. Is that not good news?"

There was only one piece of news which would be good to me at this time—that there would be no marriage. I was not particularly pleased that Elizabeth Villiers was to come with me. I was fond of Lady Frances in a way. She was often stern, but then she had to be responsible for us and I understand now that she was watchful for the advancement of her daughters, which was what one must expect from a mother. I was glad she was coming.

Anne Trelawny came in then and I could see that she had had news which pleased her.

"Your father has said that you and I are such friends that I should be one of those who are to go to Holland with you," she cried.

We embraced warmly.

"I thought that would cheer you a little," she said emotionally.

"I am so glad you are coming," I told her. "It makes me slightly less miserable to think of that. There is only one thing that could make me really happy now."

"I know," said Anne, "but I shall do what I can to help and we shall be together."

So I was cheered a little.

My sister Anne was very mournful indeed. She looked pale and quite unlike herself. Her cheeks had lost that rosy glow which had made her pretty.

"I do not like this, Mary," she said. "It makes me feel quite ill. I begged our father to stop it."

"It is not in his hands."

"To separate us! We have never been separated. And

now there is this man, John Churchill. He wants to take Sarah away. I won't have it."

"John Churchill," I repeated, and I immediately thought of Arabella Churchill, with the wonderful legs, and what I had heard of her friendship with our father.

"He is very good-looking, I grant that," Anne went on. "Sarah is taken with him, though she won't admit it. He is always hanging around. Arabella Churchill is his sister. John Churchill was a page in our father's household. You must have seen him. People say that Arabella helped him on. Then he became an ensign in the Foot Guards. He has been abroad already in France and Flanders, even Tangiers. I must say, he is very attractive. Sarah says that if he comes courting her he will have to give up his philandering ways. Did you know, they say our uncle sent him to Tangiers because Barbara Castlemaine liked him too much. And now he is chasing Sarah."

I had rarely known Anne to speak so much. She was not usually given to conversation and liked to sit contentedly listening while others conversed, avoiding all unnecessary effort.

But now she was really moved. I warmed towards her and the tragedy of having to say goodbye seemed greater than ever. How I should miss my dear sister. How could they take me away from everything that had made up my happy life? What a silly question! They could and would do it—by marrying me to the Prince of Orange.

Anne went on, "Of course, John Churchill's family doesn't think Sarah is good enough to marry him."

I could not help saying, "I am sure Sarah doesn't agree with that."

"No. She is furious about it. That is why she keeps him uncertain, and he grows more and more eager to marry her every day. But she likes him, I know. That is what worries me. She must not marry him, for if she does she will go away. Suppose they want to send him abroad. I will not lose you *and* Sarah. Mary, you must not leave me."

There was nothing we could do but mourn together and my hope of release grew fainter every day.

The marriage now seemed a certainty. There was an occasion when the Council came to congratulate me. My eyes were red with weeping and I must have looked really miserable.

After that there followed more ceremonies . . . the Lord Mayor gave a banquet to celebrate the betrothal to which the whole court was invited. The people lined the river bank as our barges sailed along to Westminster Hall and the Prince and I were in the King's barge with my father. The King had his hand on my shoulder and the Prince was on the other side of me. I did my best not to show the misery I felt.

I was moving fast towards my marriage. I had to accept the fact that nothing could avert it now. I should have to marry this strange, silent man who seemed much older than I. Twelve years is a great deal when one is fifteen. It was only two weeks since I had heard the news which had robbed me of my content. It seemed like two years.

The ceremony was to take place in my bedchamber. An altar had been set up there for the service which would be performed by Bishop Compton, who had taken charge of my education, the Archbishop of Canterbury having been taken ill suddenly.

Early that morning Elizabeth Villiers came to me in some dismay and told me that her mother, Lady Frances, was ill—very ill indeed, and would not be present at the ceremony.

She added, "The Lady Anne is also indisposed."

As soon as Elizabeth left, I went to Anne's apartments. I remembered with concern how pale she had been looking of late.

I was horrified, for when I opened her door and was about to enter, Dr. Lake suddenly appeared.

"My lady," he said, "you cannot enter the Lady Anne's apartments. Your father has strictly forbidden it."

"What do you mean, Dr. Lake? Am I not to see my sister?"

"She is ill . . . and needs rest."

I was astounded but Dr. Lake would say no more. So I was to be denied my sister's company.

I went back to my room, bewildered. I had never been so unhappy in my life.

It was nine o'clock in the evening, and the ceremony was about to begin.

The Prince, the King and Queen, my father and his heavily pregnant Duchess were there with the Bishop of London and those officials whose presence was considered necessary. Not a great number for such an occasion, but enough to fill the room.

They had bathed my eyes and done their best to disguise their redness—the outward signs of my grief; they had dressed me as a bride. I was sure there had never been a more unhappy one.

My father took me to the alter which had been set up, and as he did so I turned an imploring look on him. Was it too late?

Of course it was. I saw the despair in his eyes and I knew that if it had been at all possible to save me from this marriage he would have done so.

The King was jovial and smiling. If he knew of my reluctance and terror, he gave no sign. My stepmother's eyes were full of compassion. I wondered that she was present, for she was very near to the birth of her child.

The King smiled at me affectionately and whispered that I was a beautiful bride and he was envious of the bridegroom, who was looking far from exhilarated by the proceedings. Perhaps he found it disconcerting to be confronted by an obviously reluctant bride.

"Where is Compton?" cried the King. "Hurry, man, lest the Duchess bring us a boy and then the marriage will be disappointed."

The Prince winced a little at this and there was a faint titter from some members of the company.

My uncle continued to regard his nephew with a touch of cynical amusement, which I had noticed on more than one occasion.

The service had begun. It was the culmination of a nightmare. I was in truth being married to a man I did not know and who, on a very brief acquaintance, frightened me and filled me with dislike.

The Prince was saying that he would endow me with his worldly goods and, symbolically, laid some gold and silver coins on the book as he pronounced those words.

Then the King, still jocular, cried, "Take them, my dear niece. Take them quickly and put them in your pocket without delay, for it is all clear gain."

I saw the Prince's lips twitch with annoyance and the service continued.

Then it was over and I was the Princess of Orange.

How did I live through the rest of that night? I do not know. For a long time I tried to shut it out of my mind.

I was only half aware of what was to come. I had heard only whispered comments and had hazarded deductions. I knew such things existed but I had never given a great deal of thought to the subject until the last few days when I knew the ordeal lay just ahead.

I felt more frightened than I ever had in my life.

There was a great deal of chatter and laughter. People came and talked to me, congratulating me. I drank some wine.

"Not too much, my dear," said the Queen. She pressed my hand.

She had come to England to marry a man she had never seen, but she had been older, much older—twenty-two, I had heard it said. Mary Beatrice had been only my age. But the Queen had come to marry the King and Mary Beatrice my father. They had come to our court. I had to go to this strange place with a cold, dour husband.

They prepared me for bed. I wished they would dispense with the old custom. I wished I could run away.

The Queen and Mary Beatrice were there. It was part of the hateful ritual. They undressed me gently.

Mary Beatrice looked so tired. I was sure the child's birth was imminent. Oh, why had it not come before? Why had it not been a healthy boy? And why had the Prince of Orange not said, as it was a boy, he no longer wanted this marriage! But the child was not born and I was already married to him.

I was told to get into the bed. I lay there, trembling. Then the Prince was beside me.

The King was laughing. He pulled the bedcurtains, shutting us in, and as he did so, he shouted, "Go to work, nephew, and St. George for England!"

I heard the laughter. I was aware of the darkness, and I tried to steel myself for the ordeal to come.

All through my life I have endeavoured to forget those events which disturb me. I have not always succeeded. The night following my wedding was one of those.

I awoke in a daze, hating the daylight, putting my head beneath the bedclothes to shut it out. With immense relief, I found that I was alone in the bed.

It was over—the night of pain, horror, humiliation, and horrific awakening. If I had been wiser, as so many of the girls were, it would have been easier. But I had been thrust from innocence into brutal knowledge and my initiator had been a cold, calculating man, impatient with my reluctance, my cries of protest, and my endless tears.

I sensed his irritation and that what had to be done was no more agreeable to him than it was to me. What he did was a necessary duty. He despised me and I was in great fear of him.

I kept asking myself, is this how it will be every night? Then I prayed in my foolish childish way that night would never come.

I lay still for a while, bruised, hurting, and feeling unclean.

My attendants came in. Elizabeth Villiers and her sister Anne and my dear Anne Trelawny, who looked at me anxiously and compassionately. She put her arms round me and kissed me tenderly.

"I shall be with you in Holland," she reminded me.

That was like a faint glimmer of pleasure in a dark, dark world.

"You have been crying again, my lady princess," said Anne Villiers.

Elizabeth looked amused, and I hated her. I wondered if I should ask my father to stop her coming with me. It seemed a trivial matter in the midst of all my misery.

"I will bathe Your Highness's eyes," said Elizabeth, practically. "They are rather swollen."

I was dressed. I did not know whether the Prince would come again. I prayed not. I did not want to see him.

A visitor did arrive. It was William Bentinck, and the sight of the man set me shivering, for I knew he was the most favoured of my husband's attendants and that there was a very close friendship between them. I gathered that there must be something very unusual about this man, for the Prince was not one to show affection for the people around him—and he undoubtedly did show some regard for this man.

Bentinck said, "I come from His Highness the Prince of Orange. He has asked me to bring this to you."

With that he bowed and put a casket into my hands and, with the air of a man who has completed a mission, he begged leave to retire, bowed deeply, and was gone.

I was left holding the casket. Elizabeth was staring at it with curiosity.

"Is Your Highness going to see what it contains?" she asked.

The two Annes showed a curiosity to match Elizabeth's, yet I stared at the casket with repulsion, as though I expected venomous snakes to emerge, because it came from him, that man who struck fear into me such as I had never known before, who in a few weeks had ruined my happy and peaceful existence.

Trembling, I opened the casket. Therein lay several jewels, among them a pendant of rubies and diamonds on a golden chain.

Elizabeth held her breath in admiration.

"They are beautiful!" cried her sister.

"You must try on the pendant," said Anne Trelawny.

"It is the custom to send jewels on the morning after the wedding," said Elizabeth.

I felt the cold jewel on my neck as Anne fastened the chain. I was thinking, I shall never be able to forget. And this is only the beginning.

"Is it not beautiful?" cried Elizabeth. "Think what it costs!" Her eyes squinted. I thought, she is envying me. Oh, if only she were in my place and I in hers!

I said, "Take it off and put it back in the casket."

They looked surprised, all of them. Even Anne Trelawny did not understand. They were all overwhelmed by the beauty and costliness of the jewels.

I saw him briefly the next day. He hardly looked at me. I think that night of horror had not pleased him either. My hopes rose at the thought that perhaps it would not be repeated.

The day was taken up with receiving deputations and congratulations. It seemed that everyone was pleased about the wedding except my father and stepmother and, of course, the married pair.

That night I lay in my marriage bed and waited. For a long time I lay there, listening for his footsteps. Once I dozed and awoke with a start. It was well into the night before I could believe, with an overwhelming joy, that he was not coming to me.

I was at St. James's, our dear home. It was some days since I had seen my sister Anne. She had been too ill to be visited, they said. She must rest. I wanted to talk to her and I was sure, however ill she was, she would want to see me.

My ladies were all talking about the Prince of Orange. I knew they thought he was very strange. They were saying that there was nothing of the ardent lover about him. He did not spend any time alone with me and when it was necessary for us to be together, he hardly looked at me; he never seemed to show the least sign of affection for me.

He was eager for all the ceremonies to be over. I expected he was as bored with the continual congratulations as I was, but I felt that if he kept away from me it was the best thing that could be hoped for in a situation which would have been more intolerable if it were the reverse.

Two days after the wedding Mary Beatrice's baby was born.

My father came to see me and I could see at once that he was very pleased, though he embraced me with an expression of mingled anxiety, commiseration, understanding and self-reproach for what had been done to me, and tenderness. I wanted to tell him of my miseries and let him know that I was aware that what had come about was due to no fault of his.

"My dear," he said, "I have come to tell you that I have a son."

My first thought was: how cruel that it should be now instead of a week before when he might not have married me.

"A son," he repeated. "Yes, a son."

"And the Duchess?"

"She is well and overjoyed, of course."

"And the child?"

"He will survive."

"Dear Father . . ."

"Dearest daughter, if only . . ."

It was no use talking of it, but it was comforting to know that he understood.

"The Prince, your husband, will not be pleased," he said.

I shook my head. "He should have been born before . . ."

I did not finish, and my father took me into his arms and held me against him.

I said I wanted to see the Duchess and he told me she was very tired just now, but soon she would be receiving visitors and I should be the first.

When he had left me, I felt a certain pleasure because my husband would be cheated of his hopes. He had married me because there was a fair chance that one day I should inherit the throne. In spite of his love of his country, which was the most stable Protestant state in Europe, he longed for the crown of England, and to obtain it he was ready to marry the girl whom he despised and now he was saddled with her and his hopes of the crown were fading fast. It was his just desert.

I wanted to see my sister, but they continued to say she must not be disturbed. I could not bear to be parted from her any longer. I decided I would insist on seeing her.

When I went to her apartments, Dr. Lake appeared, as he had before.

I said firmly, "I have come to see my sister."

"Pardon me, Your Highness, but you cannot do that. The Lady Anne is very ill and it is the Duke's order that you shall not visit her."

"Are you saying that my father has given orders that *I* shall not see her?"

"That is indeed so. Your Highness, I have to tell you that the Lady Anne is suffering from smallpox and your father is anxious that you shall run no risk of being infected."

"Oh no . . . no," I cried. "And . . . er . . . Lady Frances?"

"Lady Frances is also suffering from the same, Your Highness."

I was horrified, but I said, "I want to see my sister."

"That is not possible," replied Dr. Lake. "The Duke's orders were very firm on that point."

I knew that this was another example of my father's love and care for me.

He had his son now, his little heir to the throne, but I believed he loved his daughters as he could never love any other of his children. And one was stricken with the dreaded disease which was very often fatal and he was going to lose the other to a man for whom he could not care.

My misery on account of my own desperate situation was overshadowed by my fear for my sister. I shuddered to think of her suffering from that affliction from which few survived, and if they did escape there was often a lifelong reminder in those ugly pockmarks which marred the complexion. The Prince of Orange had such marks on his face.

I had seen very little of him since the wedding night. I fancied he must have felt as ashamed as I did. He was only doing his duty, of course. That was how he would see it. How different he was from the King and his courtiers, who sinned so joyously! There was no joy in my husband.

He came to St. James's and I was in a panic when Elizabeth Villiers told me he was on his way to see me. She hovered very respectfully in the background. When he entered, she curtsied and lowered her eyes. His gaze lingered on her for a few seconds before he turned to me.

There was no love in his eyes; there was nothing but that coldness. I believed he was already deeply regretting the marriage, the importance of which had been so greatly lessened.

He said, "Prepare to leave for Whitehall at once."

Leave my sister! I would not do it. I felt stubborn and angry. I loved my sister deeply. I knew I should have to go very soon, leaving all that I loved and cared for, but until that moment I would not leave the place where she was. Suppose she called for me? I had to be there.

I heard myself say, "No!" in a voice which surprised me by its firmness.

He stared at me incredulously. He had told me what I should do and I had refused without preamble. I could see that he was convincing himself that he had not heard aright.

He said, "You will leave at once."

"No," I repeated. "I shall not leave my sister."

He looked amazed. I was aware of Elizabeth Villiers, watching me closely. There was silence.

Then Elizabeth said, "Your Highness, I will prepare for our departure."

I stood very still. I did not care what happened to me. I was not going to leave St. James's one moment before I had to.

"Do you know that there is smallpox in this place?" he asked.

"Yes," I answered.

"Your sister and others have fallen victim to this plague. It is folly to stay here one moment longer than need be. So prepare to leave at once."

I cried passionately, "I do not care about the smallpox."

I saw a faint colour appear under his pale skin. It made the ravages of the disease more noticeable. I did not care what he said. I was still under my father's care and he would understand. But this man did not know anything about love, of caring for people so much that one must be near them, however great the danger. I could not leave Anne now.

"This is folly," he said quietly. "You do not know what you say."

I was determined now to stand out against him. I wondered why he did not tell Elizabeth Villiers to go.

He turned suddenly and strode out of the room. I looked at Elizabeth. I fancied there was a certain amusement in her sly eyes.

She said, "Should Your Highness have been so vehement? After all, there is pox in the place. He is your husband. You have defied him. He will not like that . . . and after his disappointment about the newly born baby!"

My father came to see me that day.

"So," he said, "you have refused to leave your sister."

I nodded.

"The Prince is not pleased. In fact, he is determined to leave for Holland at the earliest possible moment."

I went to him and buried my face against him.

"He is not a happy man at this moment," I said. "He was hoping the child would be a girl or stillborn. He married me only for the reason that one day I might have inherited the crown. I am glad he has been cheated of that."

"The treaty was important to him, but he would not sign it until he had seen you and after the marriage. Also, my dear daughter, he liked what he saw or there would have been no marriage."

"No. He hates me, as I do him."

"This is just the beginning. He is a fine man. Your uncle has a great respect for him."

"My uncle always seems to me to be laughing at him."

"He is amused by his rather abstemious conduct and his stern religious views. But as a man . . . as a statesman . . . he is reckoned to be one of the best in Europe. You will be proud of him, Mary, one day."

"I wish he had never come here. I wish we did not have to be friends with the Dutch."

"But you will like the Dutch. They are good, law-abiding people. They are devoted to their Prince and they will be to their Princess. And you will like them when you see how much they will like you."

"You have come to comfort me. I suppose it is to prepare me for my departure."

He was silent, and I knew that I was right.

"There is to be a special ball in two days' time," he said. "For the Queen's birthday. The King thinks the following day would be a good time for you to leave."

I caught my breath. "So soon?"

"It may be that the weather will prevent it."

"But it has to come," I said sadly.

He was silent for a while, then he said, "Lady Frances, I fear, will not be with you."

"She is very ill, I know."

"And makes no improvement."

"I am so anxious about Anne."

"Anne is young. We can hope. I cannot believe that God will be so cruel as to take both my daughters from me."

We clung together in silence.

At length he said, "Lady Inchiquin will take the place of Lady Frances. She is a mature, married lady."

"Another of the Villiers family!"

"They have found favour with the King. He wants you to have people about you who will help you through the first difficult days which always follow starting a new life in a strange country. The two Villiers girls who have been with you here, Elizabeth and Anne, will be there, and also Anne Trelawny. I know she is a favourite of yours. Then there will be Henry Wroth's girl, Jane, and Lady Betty Selbourne. They are both pleasant creatures. So you will have familiar faces about you."

"This has all happened so quickly," I said piteously.

"Sometimes it is better that way. Oh, my dearest, how I shall miss you!"

There was nothing we could do but mingle our tears.

I hated every moment of that ball. It was a glittering occasion to celebrate not only the Queen's birthday but our marriage.

What mockery! I knew the Queen was not completely happy. She loved the King devotedly and it was not possible to hide from her his many infidelities. So how could she be happy? And as for celebrating our marriage— William was far from pleased with it and, as for myself, it had ruined my life. What an occasion for a ball!

Not once did William speak to me during the evening. He was not the man to grace a ball. Brusque, plainly dressed, what a contrast he made to the King and my father! I thought how well he would have suited Oliver Cromwell; he had no place in our glamorous court where good manners, appearances, wit, and grace were so important. He stood out among the rest, dour, ungainly, disapproving, and displaying such an assurance of his wisdom and worthiness that I began to wonder whether there might be some truth in it.

Everyone had noticed his neglect of me. I think the King was amused by it. I could imagine his comment, "My poor nephew. To be disappointed at the post! This little fellow whom the Duchess had produced has a good chance of survival. What a way to treat a God-fearing man! Is there no reward for virtue? What are they doing up there, neglecting their own, for the sake of the sinners?"

Anne Trelawny was very angry. She was worried at the time because of the illness of her father who was at St. James's. It was not a healthy place to be in and I supposed William was right when he had suggested my leaving. My refusal to do so was another piece of folly in his eyes.

Anne said, "It was cruel the way in which he behaved at the ball. He is nothing but a monster. I am sorry but I cannot help saying it."

Jane Wroth, whom I liked because she was warm-hearted and natural and spoke before she thought of what effect her words might have, said, "That is true. He is nothing but a Dutch monster."

Sarah Jennings, to whom I should soon say goodbye, because naturally she would be staying with my sister, commented, "He reminds me of Caliban. He looks as though he is plotting something."

She felt free to speak of him thus, I supposed, because I should soon be gone, and he with me.

I heard them talking about him later. They called him the Dutch monster, Caliban.

And this was my husband.

The time had come. There could be no further delay. My father had given orders at St. James's. Anne, who was now dangerously ill, was not to be told that I was leaving, for he feared the effect it might have on her in her weak state. As for myself, I was expressly forbidden to go near my sister, for fear of catching the infection, so I must leave without saying goodbye. I wondered what further blows fate could deal me.

I was realizing that I was really fond of Lady Frances and was deeply sorry that she was not accompanying me, that I was a little afraid of Elizabeth Villiers, and did not really care for her sister Anne. I did have Anne Trelawny though, and frivolous little Jane Wroth and lively Betty Selbourne were very pleasant to be with.

I spent the night before I was due to sail writing two letters to my sister Anne. I sent for the Duchess of Monmouth and asked her to give them to my sister as soon as she was well enough to receive them. I wanted her to know that I was thinking of her and how it grieved me to leave her.

William had not approached me since our wedding night, and it was becoming more and more clear to me that the experience had been as unpleasant to him as it had been degrading to me.

I think I began to like him a little better then, although I had not been in the least displeased to hear those whispered comments in which he had been referred to as the Dutch monster and Caliban.

He found me a disappointing wife now that I was further removed from the throne, but I saw that he did not hurt me out of malice. He just acted naturally and we shared our regret for a marriage which need never have taken place.

On that dreaded day I left St. James's and went to Whitehall to say goodbye to the Queen.

Queen Catherine was a gentle, kindly lady. She had trouble of her own, but still had sympathy to spare for me. She understood my feelings and reminded me of how she had come to England to marry a man she had never seen.

I burst out, "But, Madame, you were coming to England and I am going from it. You came to the King . . . and I . . ."

I said no more. She understood. She had come to the most kindly and charming of men and I was going to one completely lacking in these qualities. She had come to what would have been great happiness if it had not been tainted by perpetual jealousy. Poor Queen Catherine. It seemed there could be no perfect happiness.

I left her tearfully, feeling I should never see her again.

At Whitehall Stairs the King was with my father and there were crowds on the river bank. William was there with Bentinck beside him, and others of his suite. They were saying that the wind was fair for Holland, and my heart sank, for now there would be no postponement. It could only be a matter of hours.

We sailed down the river to Erith. There we dined and after that there was the last farewell.

The King kissed me tenderly. He said I must come back to Whitehall whenever I wished. There would always be a hearty welcome for me while he was in his court.

I clung to my father. There was no ceremony now. He could not restrain his tears. I believe he had loved me more than any other and this marriage was as much a tragedy for him as it was for me.

And then we sailed down the river towards Sheerness where the Dutch fleet was waiting to take us to Holland. There, what I had prayed for in my childish way happened. The wind had changed and it was decided that we could not sail until it took a more favourable turn.

William looked angry. He was impatient to be gone and this delay was frustrating him.

A message came from Whitehall. It was from the King. Why did we not return to the court? He could promise that we should pass the time pleasantly enough while waiting for the tiresome wind.

William had no desire to return to the frivolous court. He preferred to remain at Sheerness and we spent a night there and were entertained by Colonel Dorrel, the Governor. William continued to remain aloof from me, a fact which comforted me considerably and made me dislike him a little less, though I was still filled with misery and resentment.

William, I know now, was one of the most astute of men. He firmly believed that one day he would take the crown of England. There had been a prophecy at the time of his birth, of which I will write later. He was a man who would always grasp an opportunity when he saw one, and often turned adversity into advantage. He was frustrated by the delay but decided to make use of it. He was fully aware that he lacked the charm of the King and my father but he had one great asset; his religion, and he knew that the marriage had been popular. If the time should come when I inherited the throne, he wanted the people to respect him.

I think that was why he decided that the Dutch fleet should move from Sheerness to Margate and that we should sail from there. The fleet could move at its convenience according to the wind, while our party could travel by road to Margate by way of Canterbury. Thus we should show ourselves to the people and if the great day came when William should return to the country as its king, he would not be a complete stranger to them.

It was devious thinking, but I was to become used to that, for he was indeed a great ruler and there was room in his life for little else.

So we travelled to Canterbury, and it was clear that the people on the route were pleased to see us. We had the approbation of the all-important people.

Most of the party had stayed with the fleet at Sheerness, and there were only a few of us: Lady Inchiquin, a maid to attend on me, William Bentinck, and another Dutchman named Odyke.

What followed was really rather extraordinary and I did not realize at that time that it was part of a plan.

We arrived at an inn where William declared himself to be short of money. This seemed incredible to me, for I knew he had received a part of my dowry which was forty thousand pounds. However, what he did was send Bentinck to the City Corporation to beg a loan, explaining that the Prince found himself without means.

This was, I understood later, meant to arouse the indignation of the people against my father, whom William despised and was beginning to regard as his greatest enemy. My father had tried to stop the marriage; he had not hesitated to show his dislike of it. William wished to be seen as the great Protestant leader who would save England from the Catholic yoke as represented by the Duke of York, the present heir to the throne.

I think this did have the effect William intended, as so many of his actions did.

Throughout the city there was great sympathy for the Prince who had married the Duke's daughter and been so meanly treated as to be left without money. Doctor Tillotson, the Dean of Canterbury, called on William and begged an audience.

This was immediately granted.

"Your Highness," said Doctor Tillotson, "this is a state of affairs which is greatly deplored by all the good people of Canterbury. I beg of you to honour the deanery with your presence. It is a scandal that you should be here without means, and I must tell you that it is the custom of people of your rank to stay at the deanery when visiting our city."

William thanked Doctor Tillotson for his offer of hospitality, but he said he was content to stay at the inn. However, he accepted the offer of a loan and said he would not forget Doctor Tillotson's goodwill.

There was a great deal of sympathy for William and criticism of my father who was blamed for William's poverty. This was, of course, what William had hoped for, and he looked more pleased than he had since our marriage.

More messages came from Whitehall inviting us to return and wait there for a suitable time, but William refused, rather ungraciously, and renewed his friendship with Doctor Tillotson who, I learned, had in the past preached vehemently against Catholicism.

During our stay we saw much of him. He was a man of much charm and gentleness. William did not visit me at night; I was still in England and I was faintly comforted.

It was a strange interlude and I had never before stayed in an inn, so it was a great novelty. It was here that I received the distressing news that Lady Frances Villiers had died of the smallpox. I thought then of my arrival at Richmond so long ago; and then of the discovery of Frances's letters. One remembers such things when one knows one will never see a person again.

I wondered about the Villiers sisters who would receive the news at Margate, where they were waiting with the Dutch fleet.

My fears for my sister Anne increased and I waited for news of her with great trepidation.

Then the wind changed and William wanted no more time to be lost.

I was relieved to be with Anne Trelawny again. The Villiers girls were grief-stricken by the news of their mother's death. I shared their sorrow but my thoughts were dominated by Anne.

November is not the best of times to make that treacherous crossing and, no sooner had we left Margate, than the wind arose. How it buffeted our poor ship! How cruelly it tore at the sails! I thought that my last moment had come. All the women, except myself, were sick. Perhaps I was too unhappy to let the storm touch me. I just sat in my cabin, not caring much what happened to me. If I were going to die, I should not have to go to Holland to be the wife of William of Orange. There seemed some comfort in that.

The wind had subsided a little as we approached the coast.

We had arrived, battered by the tempestuous journey. We landed at a place called Ter-Heyde and were immediately taken to the Hounslaerdyke Palace. I was glad because I was too exhausted to think of anything beyond rest; and on the first night in my new country, I slept long and deep.

The Princess of
Orange

A "Very Incognito" Visit

I suppose one cannot remain in deepest depression for weeks on end—especially when one is young. I was only fifteen, and young for my years, and the young, I believe, are resilient.

It was a relief to be on dry land after experiencing that turbulent sea and wondering if I would survive, and I had realized that, after all, I wanted to live.

I could not help being impressed by The Hague Palace to which we came after leaving Hounslaerdyke. It was a magnificent spot, grand indeed, with its Gothic halls and the lake, which they called the Vyver, washing the wall on one side.

It was the official residence of the Stadholder, which would account for its formidable formality, and much as I admired it, I was relieved to discover that I was not expected to live there.

There were two residences which were really part of the palace. One of these was the Old Court, which was a Dower Palace, and very pleasant, but the place which I really liked was the House in the Woods, and I was delighted to discover that this would really be my home.

True to its name, it was in a wood, but the house itself was surrounded by beautiful gardens. Two new wings had been built onto the house to accommodate my household.

It was about a mile from The Hague Palace and in front

of it was a long avenue, at the end of which was an impressive statue of the Stadholder William Henry, my husband's grandfather.

I think I felt a little more hopeful when I entered the House in the Woods for, in spite of its splendour, there was a homeliness about it. The walls of the domed ballroom were covered by paintings and among them was a portrait of my grandfather, the never-forgotten Charles the Martyr; and I was shown another picture of a member of my family. This was my Aunt Mary, who had married into Holland and become my husband's mother.

As the weeks passed, I entered into a state of resignation. I soon realized that I should not see a great deal of William. We did not meet even for meals because he usually dined at The Hague Palace with his ministers when my presence would have been undesirable.

There were occasions when he came to supper at the House in the Woods, and those were the times I dreaded, for I knew they meant we were to spend the night together.

I tried to understand his point of view. These occasions were as distasteful to him as they were to me, for I was perpetually on the edge of tears which frequently overflowed; and the manner in which I clenched my teeth in preparation for the ordeal was not conducive to lovemaking.

He was not the sort of man to hide his feelings or to make things easier for me.

"Stop crying," he would say. "Do you not understand that this is our duty?"

Oh yes, such an attitude must curb the most intense passion, except that of a sadist, of course, and William was certainly not that. He wanted to get the unpleasant business over as speedily as he could and he made no secret of it.

Perhaps I should have been glad of this, but there must have been something perverse in my nature. I did not want him, but with a certain feminine logic, I wanted him to want me.

I knew that I was by no means repulsive. I was rather

too plump, but I had been called beautiful. I was young and virginal—indeed too much so, it seemed. I believe my youth irritated him and my dread certainly would.

It was strange that I should feel this faint resentment because the "duty" was as repulsive to him as it was to me. I thought of Mary Beatrice and my father. In fact my father was constantly in my thoughts, and I longed for his presence. Mary Beatrice had been as young as I was and as frightened. It must have happened to her just as it had to me. And then, suddenly, she had ceased to be frightened and instead became jealous of Arabella Churchill and the rest. But she had come to love my father. Should I ever grow to love William? They were as different as two men could be. My father and the King had what was called the Stuart charm. That had completely passed over William without touching him. I must remember that people who paid compliments as charmingly as the King did did not always mean them. William would never say what he did not mean. William would never pretend.

And so the weeks passed. I learned to steel myself for those evenings when William came to supper and I found they were less unpleasant than they had been in the beginning. I knew what to expect and that is better than being taken by surprise. I very much liked the House in the Woods. I could wander out with my attendants and stroll in the woods whenever I had the desire to do so. We danced in the evenings, or played cards, and, apart from the suppers and their aftermath with William, I could be tolerably happy.

Then there was wonderful news from home. Anne had completely recovered and I was so relieved and delighted that nothing could make me miserable then.

I was still writing to my dear Frances Apsley, and still called her "my husband." I wondered what William would think of those letters. He must never be allowed to see them. But would he be interested? I was beginning to learn that little interested him except the government of the country.

I remember one day when we were sitting with our nee-dlework I heard the story of that strange happening at the time of William's birth. It must have affected him deeply, and made him sure of the destiny which awaited him.

I had noticed that Elizabeth Villiers liked to talk about William. Sometimes I would find her looking at me slyly, as though she were considering something. I did not under-stand her and I wished I had asked my father not to let her accompany me. I could tolerate her sister Anne, but there was something about Elizabeth which disturbed me. It al-ways had, but I had been so miserable at the time of the marriage that I had not been able to think of anything else. I should have been wiser. My father would have said im-mediately that if I did not want her she should not go, for indeed the purpose of these girls, more than anything else, was to be a comfort to me in a strange land. But it was too late to think about that now.

On this occasion, she said, "I heard a strange story the other day. It was about the Prince's birth. It is really very extraordinary."

We were all alert, listening.

"It was someone who knew the midwife, a Mrs. Tanner, who told me. Perhaps the Prince has told Your Highness of this?"

She was looking at me with that sly look. She knew that there was very little conversation between the Prince and myself and was hinting that it was very unlikely that he would have told me anything except not to cry, that I must not be foolish, a silly child crying for her father.

"What was it?" I asked.

"Well," said Elizabeth. "If you have not heard and do not mind my telling . . ."

"Do tell us," cried Anne Villiers. "I cannot wait to hear."

"It was a very sad time," Elizabeth went on. "The Prince's father had died only eight days before the Prince was born. The court was deep in mourning and the Princess hung her bedchamber with black cloth."

"Surely she changed it for the birth of her son?" said Anne Trelawny.

"No," replied Elizabeth. "Not according to Mrs. Tanner, the midwife. Even the cradle was hung with black."

"What a sad way to bring a child into the world!" commented Jane Wroth.

"What would he know about it?" demanded Elizabeth. "But that is not the point. When he was emerging into the world . . . at the very moment . . . all the candles went out."

"Who blew them out?" asked Anne Trelawny. "Or was it just the wind?"

"No one. They went out of their own accord."

"How difficult for them," put in Jane Wroth. "A baby about to be born in the dark."

"But that was so that the circles of light could be seen." Elizabeth spoke with great intensity and, watching her, I saw the squint was very pronounced. It made her look calculating, wise, witchlike.

She went on in very solemn tones: "And about the baby's head were three circles of light. Mrs. Tanner saw them clearly."

"What were they?" I asked.

"Your Highness, they were signs. Mrs. Tanner said they were like three crowns just above the baby's head."

"What did it mean?" asked Anne Trelawny.

"They said it meant that the Prince was born to greatness. His father was dead. There was no Stadholder. The fortunes of the country were low. And he had just come into the world. It was a sign, they said, that he would inherit three crowns."

"What crowns?" I asked.

Elizabeth looked at me steadily and said, "They speak of the three crowns of Britain: the crowns of England, Ireland, and France."

Elizabeth lowered those strange eyes. There was an air about her which I did not understand, a pride, a triumph.

She had always baffled me.

* * *

It was not long after my arrival in Holland when I received a request to go to The Hague Palace where my uncle Laurence Hyde, Earl of Clarendon, who was the English ambassador, had something of importance to impart to William and me.

I had long realized that my husband did not regard me as of any importance in state matters, but this was different. He needed my uncle's ambassador to remind the people here that I was his niece and Princess of Orange.

Wondering what this could mean, I went to the Presence Chamber in the palace where William, with Clarendon, was impatiently awaiting me.

My uncle greeted me with the deference due to my rank as the Prince's wife, and, having made his point, said that the news was for both of us.

"There is great sadness at Whitehall, Your Highnesses. Charles, Duke of Cambridge, has died."

Poor Mary Beatrice. Her little son, who had been born two days after my marriage, had been christened Charles and created Duke of Cambridge.

There was silence. My thoughts were with my step-mother. I remembered her joy when she had at last given birth to the longed-for son, and her hopes because it had seemed possible that he would live.

And how short had been his life! This was the child who had soured our marriage and filled William with such bitter disappointment.

I said, "The poor Duchess. How is she?"

My uncle replied, "Very sad, Your Highness, and the Duke with her."

I looked at William. I guessed what he was feeling and I marvelled at his ability to hide it. I saw him take a deep breath and then he said, "We must send our condolences to the Duke and Duchess."

"I will write to them at once," I said.

"It will comfort their Graces to hear from you," said my uncle.

"What was the cause of death?" asked William.

Laurence Hyde was uncertain. "There have been the usual rumours, of course."

"Rumours?" asked William with more animation than he had shown on hearing the news.

"It is gossip, Your Highness. There was smallpox in Whitehall. The Lady Anne herself . . . Praise God she has now recovered . . . but there were several deaths. The Lady Frances Villiers . . ."

"Ah yes," murmured William. "And now the little Duke. But these rumours . . ."

"The nurses, Mrs. Chambers and Mrs. Manning, were blamed by some for not applying a cole leaf to draw out the infection. They protested that they had done their best for him. I am sure they did, poor women. But there will always be rumours."

"And how is my father?" I asked.

"He is deep in mourning, Your Highness."

I wished that I were there to comfort him.

When my uncle left and I was alone with William, he said, "That message must be sent to the English court without delay."

A certain reserve dropped from him. He might have felt it was not necessary to hide his true feelings from me. I saw the slow smile spread across his face—a smile of satisfaction.

I was shocked. I could not stop thinking of the grief my father and stepmother would be suffering at this moment.

Perhaps he noticed this, for he laid a hand on my shoulder.

"You must not grieve," he said in a more gentle tone than he had ever used to me before. "It may be that they will have more sons."

But the smile lingered about his lips and I was sure he was convinced they never would. The way was clear. My father would have the throne, but for how long? The English would never accept a Catholic monarch. No wonder he felt benevolent towards me.

That night he came to supper. There was a change in him. He was less impatient, less critical.

He was implying that the marriage had been worthwhile after all.

I thought a good deal about William. In fact, he was not often out of my thoughts. He was a strange man, so aloof that I felt I should never know him. He had betrayed his feelings a little over the death of my little half-brother, but that had not surprised me. Quite clearly he had no affection for me, though he had a deep regard for my position. He thought I was a silly young girl. He had made that perfectly clear, and never more so than during those periods of "duty."

I sometimes had a conventional idea that, since he was my husband, I should try to love him. I began to make excuses for him. I pictured what his childhood must have been like, and I compared it with my happy one. Sometimes I felt that if I had not had such devoted parents, and particularly a doting father, I might have been able to understand him more readily.

He had been born fatherless and his mother had died when he was young. All through his childhood he had been taught that it was his duty to serve his country and that he must regain the title of Stadholder.

I had learned something of his country's turbulent history, of the Spanish oppression, of his great ancestor, William the Silent, who had stood out against the evils of the Spanish Inquisition. William the Silent must have been rather like William himself. They were great men; they were serious men—unlike my uncle Charles and the men of Whitehall and St. James's, whose main interest was the pursuit of pleasure.

I learned about the de Witts who had governed the country until some six years before, when the French King had invaded the country and William had declared he would fight to the last ditch and never give in.

He was a great soldier and a great statesman, and the

people of Holland recognized in him another William the Silent. I heard how they had rallied to him, the Stadholder, and had demonstrated against John and Cornelius de Witt, storming their house, dragging them out, and subjecting them to violent deaths by tearing them to pieces in the street.

It was horrible, but so much that was horrible happened to people. William had saved his country and was now recognized throughout Europe as one of the most able statesmen—important enough to marry the daughter of James, Duke of York, heiress to England—himself in line to the throne.

The three crowns! I thought: did he believe in the sign at his birth? I imagined he was no visionary, but it is easy to believe in prophecies which promise us great things, and his whole life had been moulded to one aim. Ambition. And the crown of England had been promised him at his birth. For that, it was worth marrying a foolish girl for whom he could feel only contempt.

I was beginning to understand William and it helped to change my feelings towards him in some measure. I still dreaded his coming, but I understood. He could not feel warmth for anyone. He had not been brought up to love.

And then I had a surprise.

I had always known that William Bentinck was a greatly respected associate of his, but I had not realized how close.

One day from my window I saw William riding away from the House in the Woods after one of our nights together, which always left me a little shaken, although I had come to accept their inevitability. William Bentinck came riding towards the palace. He had, I guessed, some message for William. He had almost reached him when the horse shied and Bentinck was thrown from the saddle.

I caught my breath in horror, but the horse had stood quite still and Bentinck hastily picked himself up. It was clear that he was unhurt. It was just a slight mishap. The horse must have slipped over a stone and Bentinck had slid quite gently out of the saddle.

It was what happened afterwards that amazed me. William had leaped from his horse and ran towards Bentinck. They were smiling at each other and then suddenly, to my astonishment, William took Bentinck into his arms and held him against him for a moment. Then he released him and they laughed together. I could not hear what was said, but I knew that William must be telling him how relieved he was that he was unhurt. I could not believe it. William looked like a different man. He was smiling as I would not have believed he could smile.

Who would have thought he could feel so warmly towards any man?

After that I became very interested in William Bentinck and wondered what it was about him which could attract William in such a way.

Bentinck was a year or so older than William—a nobleman who had been a page in William's household, a position which had brought them into close contact and, as they were more or less of an age, I supposed they would have interests in common, and so this friendship had begun.

He had accompanied William on that visit to England when the latter had distinguished himself by breaking the windows of the maids of honour's apartments; but, I learned, it was some years later when the friendship became significant.

I was a little hurt when I heard the story from others. William himself talked so rarely to me and never of his past.

It had happened five years after his return from England. The war in France was in progress and William was at The Hague Palace for a short respite, when he caught the smallpox. There was great consternation. This disease had killed both his father and his mother and people wondered if it was going to take him too. And at such a time when Holland needed his undoubtedly clever leadership!

His life was despaired of, for the usual eruptions did not appear and in such cases death seemed certain.

The doctors had a theory that if a young and healthy person who had not had the sickness would sleep in the bed of the sufferer and hold him in his arms throughout the night, these eruptions would be brought and possibly save the life. Was there a young and healthy man who would risk his own life to save the Prince's, for it was almost certain that the volunteer would catch the pox?

I could imagine the consternation among those young men about the Prince. It was William Bentinck who offered to make the sacrifice for the sake of his master and Holland.

For sixteen days and nights he shared William's bed and waited on him by day. The effect was as the doctors had said it would be. The eruptions were drawn forth and William's life had been saved. Alas, poor Bentinck had caught the disease very badly and come near to death. However, he recovered and ever since there had been a special friendship between him and William.

I liked the story. It proved that William had some warmth in his heart. He was capable of gratitude and Bentinck had risen high since that episode; he was always at William's side. William consulted him and shared confidences.

As William was capable then of firm friendship, I began to make excuses for him. His mother had died when he was nine years old and he had been devoted to her since his birth; perhaps it was through her that he had conceived that ambition to possess the English crown. She had been English, my father's sister—and she had put William in the charge of Lady Catherine Stanhope, who had gone to Holland with her on her marriage, having previously been her governess. Then, of course, there was Mrs. Tanner's vision of the three crowns.

I had begun to feel a little happier after that; and then, a wonderful thing happened. I was going to have a child. There was a long time to wait yet, but it had at last come to pass.

I was so proud. I even felt that all I had suffered would

be worthwhile. What would it be like to have a child of one's own? It would be wonderful. Everyone would be pleased, particularly if it were a boy. If it were a girl, that would be a disappointment, but only a minor one, for I was young. I could have sons, for I would have shown that I was not barren.

William was delighted. It was impossible for him to hide his joy. He smiled at me for the first time.

"That is good," he said. "We will pray for a boy."

He patted my shoulder. I smiled at him a little shyly and he continued to regard me with approval.

All my ladies were delighted, except Elizabeth Villiers. She congratulated me with the others, of course, but I caught an odd look in her eyes which I did not understand. Anne Trelawny clucked over me as though I were a little chick and she a mother hen.

It was early days yet, for there was a long time to go. I congratulated myself because I should enjoy the waiting period. No more suppers and after. What need of them now? Their express purpose had been achieved.

It was decided that while I was in the early stage of pregnancy it would be a good idea for me to show myself to the people of Holland, and in order to do this I and my ladies should take a journey through the country. The best way of undertaking this was by means of the canals. There I could sail through the land in the utmost comfort.

I looked forward to it with enthusiasm and felt almost happy.

I wrote to my sister Anne, to Mary Beatrice, and to Frances Apsley to tell them my news. I had not let Frances know how unhappy I had been; I never allowed myself to criticize William in any way. Now I did not have to pretend so much, for I was no longer miserable.

We had a great deal of fun preparing for our journey. Elizabeth Villiers acted a little strangely. She said she wanted to see me. It was very shortly before we were due to leave.

"I want to ask Your Highness's permission to remain behind," she said. "I have a certain weakness of the throat which I know would be aggravated by the damp air and I am afraid I should be ill if I spent much time on the waterways. I have been advised in this."

I was surprised. I had always thought she was particularly healthy, but I did not protest. I was never fond of her company and felt no great need for it—only a mild pleasure that I should be deprived of it.

That was a very pleasant journey. I was greeted everywhere I went by those kind and homely people. I was impressed by the cleanliness of their dwellings, the manner in which they conveyed their pleasure in seeing me, which seemed very sincere, so that I felt they really were glad to welcome me, for they would not have pretended to be glad if they were not.

There was less ceremony than at home in England. People would come and take my hand; they would bring forward their children for me to admire. I was really happy during those days. There was something peaceful about the flat green land, and when the children brought me flowers which they had picked from the fields, I was reminded that soon I should have a child of my own. Yes, for the first time since coming to Holland, I was truly happy.

The night air was indeed damp and one day, to my dismay, I awoke shivering intermittently. I tried to shake this off, but it persisted. In a day or so I had a fever.

Doctors were called. They said I was suffering from the ague. It was a change of climate, though the air around The Hague Palace was noted for its dampness.

Thus my progress through the country did not end as happily as it had begun. I was taken back to the House in the Woods.

Elizabeth Villiers was there. She looked taken aback when she saw me and, I fancied, disappointed.

"Your Highness is ill?" she said with a pretence of concern.

"It is the dampness of the air, they say," said Anne Trelawny. "Her Highness is to go immediately to bed."

Elizabeth continued to look displeased. I did not trust her. She made me feel slightly uneasy.

I began to feel very ill and then ... it started.

The pains were violent. I did not know what was happening to me. I lost consciousness for a while and when I regained it I found several doctors at my bedside.

It was morning—that very sad morning—when they came to tell me I had lost my child.

I had never been so miserable in my life.

William came. He looked very angry. The child of our hopes was not to be.

"What did you do?" he demanded.

"Nothing ... nothing ... it just happened," I stammered.

He looked at me with scorn. He was so disappointed and angry. Then he left me. It was almost as though he could not trust himself not to do me some harm if he stayed.

I felt a resentment then. I had wanted the child as much as he had. Why did I not tell him that? Why did I allow myself to be treated so? He frightened me. When he was not there I planned what I would say to him, but when he came my courage failed me.

I thought of Mary Beatrice who had only little Isabella left of all her children, and how she had lost the little Prince whose coming had so disappointed William and who, had he lived, would have ruined William's hopes of the throne, and I thought: am I to be cursed in the same way?

Anne Trelawny tried to persuade me not to despair because it was only the first. That did not help me. I had lost my child. I turned my face to the pillow and wept.

William, inspired by new hopes that there was no impediment to my inheritance, was determined to get his heir, and as soon as my health began to improve his visits continued, and it was not long before I was pregnant again.

One day there was a letter from England. It was addressed to William and it evidently annoyed him to such an extent that he could not help showing the bitterness of his feelings.

It was from my father. The relationship between them had never been cordial. They could not help seeing each other first as Catholic and Protestant. I could sympathize with William in this when I heard how his country had suffered under the Spanish yoke and how the terrible Inquisition had inflicted such extreme torture on the people of Holland. I had heard that some thirty thousand of them had been buried up to their necks and left to die unless they accepted the Catholic faith as the true one. William saw my father as a man who would spread this kind of terror throughout the world.

As for my father, he recalled Cromwell and his Puritans who had murdered his father.

They were born to be enemies. They were so different in every way—my father warm and loving, William cold and austere. How strange that the two most important men in my life should be so different and how sad that they should have been such enemies.

And now here was another cause for enmity.

William said to me coldly, "I have had an accusation from your father that I do not take good care of you."

"Oh no," I said.

"But yes. He thinks that it was strange that you should suffer from the ague which you never did under his care. He informs me that the Duchess, his wife, and your sister, the Lady Anne, wish to visit you."

I could feel nothing but joy. I clasped my hands and could not help exclaiming, "Oh, how happy that will make me."

"They propose to come, as your father says, incognito. 'Very incognito' are his words. They have already sent a certain Robert White on ahead to procure a lodging for them near the palace so that there will be nothing official about the visit."

"Why do they want to come in this way?"

He looked at me oddly. "They seem to think you are not

being well treated here. Perhaps you have given some intimation of this?"

"Why? What do you mean?"

He lifted his shoulders. "The good ladies are to assure themselves—and your father—that you are being treated according to your rank. It would seem they have been led to believe this is not so."

He was spoiling my pleasure in the anticipation of their arrival.

I said quickly, "You would not . . ."

"Refuse to allow them to come? I could scarcely do that. Rest assured, the lady spies will be well received when they arrive, though they will be 'very incognito.' "

Nothing could really spoil my delight and I joyously awaited their arrival.

And what a joy it was to see them. There was my dear, dear sister, who had been so ill when I left, now in radiant health.

It was wonderful to see me, she told me.

"When you went away, I wept for days. Sarah thought I should do myself some harm with my sorrow. Dear, dear Mary, and how do you like it here?"

She looked around the chamber. It was attractive, she said, but not like dear St. James's and Richmond.

She was talking a great deal—for Anne—but this reunion was a very special occasion and even she was moved out of her usual placidity.

Then there was my stepmother. I saw the change in her. Grief had left its mark on her.

I did not mention the recent death of her baby son, but she knew I was thinking of it.

There was so much to talk of. I wanted news of my father.

"He never ceases to talk of you," Mary Beatrice told me. "He wishes you were back with us and reproaches himself for letting you go."

"It was no fault of his. He would have kept me in England if he could."

She nodded. "He could do nothing," she said. "But he still blames himself. This appears to be a pleasant country. The people are very agreeable."

"Orange," said Anne. "It's a strange name for a country."

"I call you Lemon . . . my dear little Lemon," said Mary Beatrice. "Orange and Lemon, you see. Do I not, Anne?"

"Yes," said Anne. "She says, 'I wonder how little Lemon is today among all the Oranges.' "

We were all laughing. There was so much to know. How were all my friends—the Duke of Monmouth, for instance. All missing me, I was told.

I said, "It is wonderful that you have come."

"Your father was so uneasy about you. He would have liked to come himself but he could hardly have done that. It would have made it too official. But when we heard what was happening here . . ."

"What did you hear?"

Mary Beatrice looked at Anne who said, "People wrote home . . . some of the ladies, you know. They wrote that the Prince does not treat you well. Does he not?"

I hesitated—and that was enough.

"Lady Selbourne wrote home and said that you were neglected by the Prince who treated you without respect."

"The Prince is very busy," I said quickly. "He is much occupied with affairs of state."

"He will always be Caliban to me," said Anne. "That was Sarah's name for him."

I said, "Pray, do not let anyone hear you say that."

"Well," laughed Anne. "He is rather alarming. My poor Mary, I am sorry for you. I can't help being glad he is not *my* husband."

I looked at her placid face and wondered who would be found for her. Of one thing I was certain: it would not be long before she had a husband. The thought apparently did not occur to her, or if it had, it had not alarmed her. Very

little did alarm Anne. She had an unswerving faith in her
ability to sail serenely through life.

"I will tell you a secret," she said, dismissing the unpleasant subject of my marriage. "It is very much a secret
at the moment. Only our stepmother knows, is that not so?
But I must tell my dear sister, if she promises to say nothing of it to anyone."

I promised readily.

"It is Sarah," she said. "What do you think? She has
married John Churchill."

"Well, I knew he was courting her. Why should it be a
secret?"

"The Churchills have fine ideas of themselves ever since
Arabella started to advance their fortunes." Anne paused for
a moment, faintly embarrassed. Our stepmother knew, of
course, of Arabella's relationship with her husband and
how, because of it, her family had received many favours.

"The Churchills think themselves far above the Jen-
ningses and that Sarah is not a good enough match."

"Sarah will soon teach them different from that!"

"Of course. Sarah is good enough for anyone. But if he
had to go away with his regiment and Sarah went with him,
what should I do without her?"

"You will have to arrange that she stays behind or let her
go," I said.

Anne smiled complacently, certain of her power to keep
Sarah with her.

"It is a secret until the family has been brought round to
see good sense. Our stepmother thinks that can be done."

"I did hear a whisper that John Churchill was a wayward
young man," I said.

"You must mean the Lady Castlemaine scandal. There
was something. But so many people have been involved
with that woman."

"I have heard it said that the King sent him to Tangiers
to separate them."

"That was long ago. John is now reformed. He thinks of

no one but Sarah. I dare say he will do exactly as Sarah wants."

"Knowing Sarah, I am sure that is very likely."

I wondered how long this deep friendship with Sarah could last. Anne herself must marry one day and that was most certainly to be in the near future.

She said, "How did you get on with Dr. Hooper?"

Dr. Hooper was the almoner who had replaced Dr. Lloyd. I frowned. William did not approve of him. Dr. Lloyd had not minded if I attended the Dutch services, but Dr. Hooper had advised me not to. In fact, he was almost as fierce against it as he was against Catholicism. This had given rise to some unpleasantness, for Dr. Hooper was not a man to keep silent about his opinions. There had been one or two far from felicitous encounters between William and Dr. Hooper.

"He is a man of strong opinion," I said.

"And the Prince did not approve of him?"

"Well, not exactly."

Mary Beatrice smiled grimly and I said quickly, "You know he is returning to England. He is going to marry."

"I had heard that."

"He has promised he will come back again, bringing his wife with him."

"Does that please you?"

"I like him."

My stepmother did not answer, but I knew she was thinking that my husband had probably made life very difficult during Dr. Hooper's stay at The Hague.

He would no doubt make his views of the Dutch court known when he returned to England. He would be quite fearless about that, and with the letters which found their way to England, it would be known that my life in Holland was not as serene as it might have been.

The visit was very brief and I was very sad to say goodbye to them. It had been a mixture of joy and sadness to be with them, for, while it was wonderful to be in their company, memories flooded back of the idyllic life I had led before my marriage. I was beset by such nostalgic longing for the old days that I was not sure whether the visit had been good for me or not.

They had promised to come again.

"The journey is not so far," Anne had said on parting. "Of course, there is that hateful crossing, but I would face that a thousand times to be with my dear sister."

And my stepmother agreed with her.

So I was hopeful that there would be another visit before very long.

The Exile

Soon after their departure, William paid me one of his rare visits. As I was pregnant, it was not for the usual purpose.

He said, "I have a letter from your father."

He handed it to me and I read:

We came hither on Wednesday from Newmarket and the same night the Duchess, my wife, arrived home so satisfied with her journey and with you as never I saw anyone; and I must give you a thousand thanks from her and from myself for her kind usage by you. I should say more on the subject, but I am ill at compliments and I know you do not care for them.

There was more of the letter. He did not give me time to read it, however, but snatched it away as I prepared to do so.

"Well," he said, his lips in a straight line, his eyes cold, "the spies gave a good account of us."

"They were not spies," I said with a touch of indignation.

"Were they not? You surprise me. Their grateful thanks are couched in the language of diplomacy. They are adept in that art at your uncle's court, I believe. Your father is an uneasy man at this time." He waved the letter at me, and I stretched out to take it, but he held it back. He was not going to share it with me. All he wanted me to see was the good report which had been given of the visit.

"There is trouble in England," he went on.

"Trouble?" I said quickly. "What trouble?"

"Your father, I fear, is not a wise man. His obsession with a religion which does not please the people will be his undoing."

"Is anything wrong with my father?"

"Only what he inflicts on himself."

"Please tell me if you have any news." I was losing my fear of him in my anxiety for my father, and I felt bold suddenly. If my father was in trouble I must know.

"Is he in danger?" I asked.

William did not speak immediately. A slow smile crossed his face but he seemed as cold as ever.

He tapped the letter.

"There is a plot being talked of in England. A man named Titus Oates has claimed to have discovered it. This is a papist plot to take command of England and bring back that faith."

"And my father?"

"They will seek to involve him, of course. There is a great excitement in England because of it. All Catholics will be suspect. Your father, your stepmother, the Queen herself. The English will never again have a Catholic on the throne. That is why I say your father is unwise."

"He is an honest man," I said. "He does not pretend. He will not lie to the people."

"Honest . . . and so unwise!"

I wanted to read that letter. I wanted to know exactly what had been written. William knew it, but he would not show me.

I understood later, but I could not then.

His hopes were high. The popish plot raised them. Charles, my uncle, could not live for ever, and then it would be my father's turn. And would the people have him? If not, the next in line was myself. I would be the one and William was my consort. Consort? When he had a claim himself . . . not as strong as mine, it was true, but a claim. He wanted me to know that, however high my rank, he was my husband and I owed obedience to him.

That letter pleased him indeed. Not because my sister and stepmother had not mentioned his harsh treatment of me, but because of the news about a papist plot.

I continued to worry about my father. News came from England. We heard of little else but Titus Oates and the popish plot. Everyone was talking about it. I knew that William was in communication with some of the ministers at my uncle's court. There were several of them who were determined not to tolerate a Catholic king and they turned to William.

I realized that William was aware of the close relationship between myself and my father and he did not want me to be influenced by him.

Although he had a certain contempt for me, and I was sure believed he could subdue me if the need arose, he had to remember that, if my father was removed, he could only secure the throne through me; and I believed on one or two occasions he had seen in me a certain rebellion—a determination to stand up for what I believed to be right, even if it were against his wishes.

He was already conspiring with men in England and must have been anxious to keep me in ignorance of this, for fear I should betray the fact to my father.

Soon after the departure of the visitors I was taken ill again with the disease which had attacked me before. I was suffering alternate fits of shivering and fever and they diagnosed the ague.

I became very ill and during the illness I lost the child I was carrying. It had happened exactly as before.

I was completely desolate, more so than ever. It was a significant repetition. I knew what it meant. The curse of the queens was upon me. I began to believe that I should never have a child who would live.

I knew William was deeply upset. Our efforts were in vain. A child was conceived and that was the end.

He blamed me. Of course. What had I done? I had been careless, stupid. I had let another chance go by.

I was too ill for some time to care much. I thought I was dying and so did some of those about me. I knew this because Anne Trelawny told me afterwards.

There was a great deal of gossip among the women about William's callous behavior. There were occasions when he did come to see me. I supposed diplomacy demanded it. I pretended to be too ill to speak to him.

He stood by my bed, looking at me with obvious exasperation—the wife who could not do what every little serving-maid could with ease—produce a child; and yet I held the promise of a crown in my hands.

He was anxious about me for one reason. I must get well. I must not die, for if I died, I should take William's hopes with me, for Anne would be next. Idly I wondered how she would have acted if she had been the one chosen for William. I thought of her indifference, her lassitude. She would have ignored him and turned to Sarah Churchill for comfort.

Often now I thought of Frances Apsley. One of my greatest compensations was the letters I wrote and received; and I often thought how pleasant it might have been if we could have lived together.

People noticed the change in me. I was a little aloof with my attendants. I had discovered that I had only to look mildly displeased by their conduct and they became subdued.

Dr. Hooper had come back with his wife. She was a charming woman and I wanted her to know how pleased I was to have her join our circle.

The maids of honour had their own dining quarters. I joined them on occasions. I had expected, of course, to dine with my husband, but he still dined at The Hague Palace and the excuse was that he was busy with his ministers. I knew this was commented on and was one of those facts which gave the impression that I was not treated with the respect due to me.

Dr. Hooper had had his meals with the maids of honour in the past but had declined the invitation for his wife to join them when she arrived. He said that, in view of the "great economy" the Prince of Orange practised and his dislike of the English, he thought it better for Mrs. Hooper to dine at their lodgings, and, naturally, he would take his meals with her, thus saving the Prince more expenditure.

This was also noted and I had no doubt that the information would reach England.

So William had a reputation for meanness. It was true he paid the chaplains who came over from England very little. Dr. Hooper, being a man of means, supported himself and his wife all the time he was in Holland. The Dutch were so shocked by his extravagant way of life, for their clergy were so poorly paid, that they called him "The Rich Papa."

This state of affairs had the effect of making Dr. Hooper very independent and he spoke his mind freely in William's presence and, I think, must have given him some uncomfortable moments. Not that William was the man to allow such trivialities to affect him, but he was concerned that Dr. Hooper might influence me in my religion, for it was a fact that, since his arrival, I had adhered to the rites of the English Church instead of adopting those of the Dutch.

William was heard to say on one occasion that if ever he had a say in the matter (which meant that if ever he were King of England), Dr. Hooper should remain Dr. Hooper throughout his life. He would certainly not get promotion from William.

Dr. Hooper was indifferent to such comments and went on expressing his opinion with the utmost freedom.

He did not stay with us for long, however, and his successor, Dr. Ken, proved to be even more outspoken.

I discovered that something of importance was happening in the quarters of the maids of honour, presided over by Elizabeth Villiers. There was a great deal of entertainment there. This was strange for, as Dr. Hooper had pointed out, William disliked any form of extravagance, and the supper parties, which had become a familiar feature of the evenings, must have entailed certain expense.

Then it suddenly dawned on me that there was some purpose in these parties. Some of the maids of honour were attractive and most of them were young; and the most important men at court could at times be seen there.

Among them was William Zulestein, who was a great friend of William's and was in fact related to him, for Zulestein's father was the illegitimate son of Henry Frederick, Prince of Orange, my husband's grandfather, by the daughter of a burgomaster of Emmerich. He had been a faithful friend of William's father and now there was a close friendship between him and William.

William Bentinck was also a frequent visitor to the suppers, as were others of William's circle. William himself had been known to be present. Many of the English visitors to The Hague were invited—among them Algernon Sidney and Lords Sunderland and Russell.

On the rare occasions when I was present I noticed that the English visitors were made much of, and the girls were very agreeable to them.

Elizabeth Villiers acted as hostess. When I was there she paid me all the homage due to my rank, but I was constantly aware of her sly smile and watchful eyes; and I could not help feeling that there was something subversive about those supper parties—some purpose behind them.

I watched Elizabeth Villiers in earnest conversation with Algernon Sidney and I wondered what subject they found so enthralling. I did not believe it was lovers' talk; more than ever, I felt there was indeed something rather sinister behind these gatherings, and that they should be carried on with William's approval amazed me.

There was born in me then a deep feeling of apprehension. I felt we were moving towards a climax of which others were aware and I was ignorant. I felt a little frustrated and helpless, which was due to the fact that I had a faint glimmer of understanding.

Constantly I thought of my father. I gathered that this plot of which they were all talking was directed not only against the Queen but against him also. He was in danger and I wanted to be with him.

These anxieties had their effect on me. I had another fit of the ague and this time I could not rid myself of it. I had to take to my bed and I was very ill this time. People in my bedchamber whispered together and I believe they thought I had not long to live.

William came to see me. He looked really alarmed. Poor William, I thought with newly acquired cynicism, if I died, what hope would you have of the crown? After my father, Anne; and Anne would marry and very likely have sons. Then the prophecy of the three crowns would not be fulfilled. And when I thought of the way in which he had behaved when I had lost my babies, I wanted him to suffer.

I heard him demanding, "Where is the physician? Why is he not attending the Princess?"

And I thought: he is indeed alarmed.

Anne Trelawny said, "The Prince is sending Dr. Drelincourt to attend to you. The Prince has more faith in him than in any doctor in the country."

I said, "He is worried—not for me, but for the crown."

Anne said nothing, but I knew that she agreed with me.

I was young and did not want to die, even to spite William, and under Dr. Drelincourt I began to improve a little.

He had diagnosed that my listlessness was not helping me and that I must revive my interest in the life around me. He said my ladies should be with me: they should chat and gossip of what was going on at court.

Anne Trelawny was constantly with me, Lady Betty Selbourne too, and Anne Villiers. I was beginning to like her more; she had softened and seemed more interesting. She mentioned William Bentinck frequently. I had noticed that she was with him often at the supper parties and seemed to have a great admiration for him. She told me what a wonderful friendship he had with the Prince. She repeated the story of how he had saved William's life when he had had smallpox and how the disease had attacked Bentinck himself. He bore the scars of that episode. She said they were like medals for bravery.

One day William came to me.

"You are recovering," he said.

"I am told so."

"It is clear that you are. When you are a little better, you shall go to Dieren. The climate is good there and Dr. Drelincourt shall go with you. I wish to see you fully recovered."

"I know how important that is to you," I said pointedly.

"But of course," he replied.

"My sister Anne is fully recovered now," I went on, marvelling at my audacity, but enjoying it. "She is in perfect health."

"I gathered so. But she will not be allowed to travel with your father."

He was looking at me with a certain triumph as though to say, do not try your barbs on me. They are so feeble that they glance off almost unnoticed.

I was very anxious to know what he meant about Anne's travelling with my father.

He said, "Your father wished to take her with him when he left England, but that was prevented at the last moment. The people would not allow it. They suspected, and with reason, that he would attempt to make a Catholic of her."

"I do not understand. Where is my father going? Why is he to leave England?"

He smiled almost benignly. "No, of course you do not," he said, implying that I could not be expected to grasp matters of state. "Your father has left England."

"Why?"

A look of pleasure briefly fluttered across William's face.

"Not at his desire. He was asked to leave. You might call it exile."

I was frightened now and he knew it. More than anything I wanted to see my father and hear from him what had happened. I was getting agitated and, fearing the effect it might have on my health, he said quickly, "Your father is now in Brussels. He has heard of your illness and is coming to visit you."

I could not help showing my pleasure and relief and he looked at me with that impatience I knew so well.

I closed my eyes. I did not want to ask any more questions. My father was coming to me. I would prefer to hear what had happened from him.

What a joy it was to see him! We embraced and clung together; we could not bear to let each other go.

"I have been so concerned about you," said my father; and Mary Beatrice stood by, watching with tears in her eyes.

I noticed how they had changed, both of them. My father looked strained and tired. Mary Beatrice had lost the first glow of youth; she was only a few years older than I was, but she looked at least ten.

She had lost her children, as I had, but mine had not been born and hers had lived, if only for a short while; she had come to a new country, as I had, but the people had not welcomed her as the Dutch people had welcomed me. But my father had been a loving husband, although an unfaithful one.

Our positions were not dissimilar and because of this we could understand each other.

My father was bitter and sad.

I said, "I cannot be kept in ignorance any longer. I must know what has happened."

"Do you learn nothing then?" answered my father. "There are many here who are no friends of mine. Surely they would spread the news."

"I learn very little and I must know."

"We have been asked to leave. Even my brother said it was necessary."

Mary Beatrice went on, "He appeared to be very grieved when we left. Yet it was he who ordered it. I told him so. I could not stop myself. It was all so false. I said to him, 'What, sir, are you grieved? But it is you who is sending us into exile. Of course we must go. You are the King and have ordained it.'"

I thought she would burst into tears and my father put his hand over hers.

"It was no fault of my brother, my dear," he said. "He had to do it. It was what the people wanted. It is due to that scoundrel Oates."

"I know," she said. "I am sorry I spoke thus. He is ever kind. He understands. He showed me by his looks that he did."

"Exile?" I said. "How can you be exiled?"

"You do not know what has happened in England. This man, Titus Oates ... he is at the root of it all. He has stirred up such trouble that it has brought us to this."

"I have heard that man's name mentioned," I said.

"I should have thought the Prince of Orange would be deeply interested in what is taking place."

"He does not talk much to me of state affairs."

My father looked grim. His feelings towards William had not changed and he had hated the match from the beginning. I knew that, whatever they showed on the surface, there was deep animosity between them.

"This man Oates is a scoundrel. That much is obvious, but the people cannot see it—or won't."

"They believe because they want to believe," said Mary Beatrice.

"He has accomplices. William Bedloe and Israel Tonge and others. Oates claims to have been a clergyman—a Catholic at one time. He professes to have joined the Jesuits and it is because of this that he claims to have knowledge of this plot."

"What is the plot exactly?" I asked.

"To kill the King, set up a Catholic ministry, and massacre the English Protestants."

"And you?" I said.

"The government thought it wise that I should leave the country for a while, and my brother was obliged to agree with them."

"It will pass," I said.

"I do not know," replied my father seriously. "This is no

ordinary plot to be proved false—as it undoubtedly is—and forgotten. He is rousing the whole country."

I began to grasp the situation. The anti-Catholic feeling was great throughout England and, fomented by this outrageous Titus Oates, it was not safe for my father to remain there. I was very anxious.

I learned that this visit to The Hague was, as he had said of that earlier one made by Mary Beatrice and Anne, "very incognito." The situation was too delicate for it to be a state visit. William was, in a way, involved in English affairs; no one could be unaware of what the refusal of the English to accept a Catholic monarch would mean to him. If my father had a son now he would be taken from him and given a Protestant upbringing, but child rulers usually caused trouble, and at The Hague was one of the most staunch Protestants, married to the present heir to the throne—if my father should be rejected.

When I was alone with Mary Beatrice I realized how troubled she was.

She told me that she had been happier in her first years in England than ever before and now it had all changed.

"I often think," she said, "that, had your father been a Protestant, we should still be enjoying that happy life. The people were fond of him once, as they are of the King. They both have what is called the Stuart charm in good measure. The King is clever and determined to keep his crown; but the fact is that your father is too honest to deny his faith and for that we must suffer."

She told me of how they had had to leave.

"We wanted to bring your sister with us, of course, and she was delighted at the prospect of seeing you, but when it was known that she was coming there was an outcry. The people thought your father might seek to make a Catholic of her, and so she was not allowed to go with us."

"How I should have loved to see her!"

"She said she must come soon. Perhaps it can be arranged."

"What troubles there are in life!"

"You too?" she asked.

"I miss my home—you, my father, my sister, my uncle . . . the ones I loved."

"You have your husband." She looked at me intently, questioningly and I did not answer.

She went on, "The Prince received us well when we arrived in Holland. He had a guard of honour waiting to greet us. Your father was gratified, but he did explain immediately that this was not a state visit and it would be better for him to remain incognito. We went to Brussels and shall return there when we leave here, for, dear Lemon, we must not stay long—we shall have the house which your uncle had during his exile. I think so much of the early years when we were all together, getting to know each other. How happy it was! Who would have dreamed then that all this would happen?"

Poor Mary Beatrice! My poor father! How different everything might have been!

I asked about Isabella and her face lit up with pleasure. Then it was sad again.

"I wanted to bring her with us. She is such a beautiful child. But it was not permitted. Your father is going to write to the King imploring him to allow Isabella to come to us. Perhaps we can persuade him to allow Anne to accompany her."

"I thought the people did not want them to go with you."

"I know, but the King would be happy for them to. He understands. But it will, I suppose, depend on the people. The King will never do anything to offend them."

"He is wise," I said.

"Wise and determined never to go wandering again."

"Yet my father will do what he thinks right, no matter what the consequences."

"Everything is wrong," she went on. "Wherever we look, there is trouble . . . Monmouth . . ."

"What of Jemmy?" I cried.

"He has grown ambitious. This horrible plot delights

him. He mingles with the people. Monmouth, the Protestant. One would think he were heir to the throne. I do believe he sees himself as such. He is the King's son and he wants everyone to remember it and, above all, he is a Protestant."

"Jemmy cannot think . . ."

"I tell you, he is an ambitious young man. He wants the people on his side. I believe he thinks that one day the crown could be his."

"That is impossible."

I thought of my bright and amusing cousin, whose visits Anne and I had looked forward to—and now he had become my father's enemy! What a lot of trouble could have been avoided if my father had not flaunted his religion. It was not the first time that I had felt a touch of impatience with him. The King kept his counsel and all went well with him. If only my father could have been as wise.

I felt ashamed of these critical thoughts. It was disloyal. I brushed them aside and talked about Isabella.

Their stay was brief. They had come to see me, my father told me. They had been so alarmed to hear of my illness, but because of the circumstances they could not prolong their stay.

The encounter had been beneficial to me and my health visibly improved. And then they returned to Brussels.

My father was continually in my thoughts and I greatly pitied not only him and Mary Beatrice but Queen Catherine as well. It appeared that she was in acute danger, for these villainous men were accusing her of being involved in the plot to murder the King, and therefore of treason, for which the punishment was death. This was sheer nonsense, and I was sure my uncle would protect her from her malicious enemies. But what must the poor woman be suffering now?

The King should never have married a Catholic. My grandfather, Charles the Martyr, had married one, too; the stormy Henrietta Maria had been fiercely religious and was blamed for the troubles of that reign which had ended in such tragedy.

Catholics brought trouble wherever they were and that was at the very heart of the popish plot.

I would always maintain my father's honesty, but he really was acting in a reckless, foolish manner, and was causing misery to a great many people.

There was a great deal of activity going on at the supper parties. Elizabeth Villiers was still hostess at these affairs and I was astonished that she should be in such prominence even when William was there. But he did not seem to notice her presumption. I had even seen him talking to her when she joined him and some of the English visitors.

As for myself, I was gaining confidence. I had proved to myself that I could stand up to William and I felt better for it.

I had a feeling at those parties which I attended, that they were all very much aware of my presence and that it put a curb upon them. Perhaps that was just a fancy, for how could I know what they were like in my absence? Perhaps I imagined that there was a watchfulness.

On one occasion, soon after my father and Mary Beatrice had left, I noticed a man who stood out among the others because he was so different. He did not look like a man accustomed to court ways. I guessed him to be English and he was deep in conversation with Sidney. Sunderland joined them and they all talked together very earnestly.

I called Betty Selbourne to my side. She seemed to know everyone and was noted for her discretion.

I said to her, "Who is that man talking to Lord Sunderland?"

She paused for a moment and then replied, "I could not remember for the moment, but I do now. I believe him to be a Mr. William Bedloe."

"Who is he?"

"I do not know, Your Highness. I have not met him. I think he came over with a message for Lord Russell."

"Bedloe," I murmured. I thought the name seemed faintly familiar.

"Would Your Highness like him to be presented to you?"

I looked at the man's mean face and awkward bearing.

"No, Betty," I said. "I think not."

It was later, when I lay in bed, sleepless, thinking of my father and poor Queen Catherine, when I remembered where I had heard the name before. "Titus Oates and his friends—Tonge and Bedloe."

My suspicions were beginning to be formed. William Bedloe was a confederate of Titus Oates.

What were these men who were plotting to ruin the Queen and my father doing here at The Hague? The answer was clear: my father was going to be robbed of his inheritance and William, through me, was going to take the crown of England.

I felt sick with horror. I wanted no part in it. I wanted to break away from it all.

How could my father have plunged us all into this morass of intrigue and misery?

And William? How much was he involved in it?

I had been horribly shocked that a man concerned in the popish plot with Titus Oates should be received at the court of The Hague, and even more so by a discovery I made soon afterwards.

I was really fortunate in having in my service that rather feckless pair Betty Selbourne and Jane Wroth, for I learned a great deal from little details which they thoughtlessly let slip from time to time in their everyday tittle-tattle. Anne Trelawny was discreet and always concerned not to alarm me, and I believe she kept from me any news which she thought might do so.

Some reference was made to my father's visit, and Jane said, "It was the day before his illness."

"His illness?" I asked. "What was that?"

Betty was there too and she and Jane exchanged glances.

Betty said, "Oh, it was nothing much. It quickly passed. It was a day or so before he left."

"Why did I know nothing of this? What sort of illness?"

"It was of no importance," said Betty. "I suppose he did not want to worry Your Highness."

"If it were of no importance, how could it worry me?"

They were both silent and I went on, "How did you know of it?"

"People were talking about it," said Jane. "Your Highness knows how people will talk. The Duchess was so anxious."

I knew there was something mysterious about his illness and, instead of gently urging them to talk and eventually prizing the news from them, I said imperiously, "I want to know the truth. Please tell me immediately."

I could see the expressions on their faces. There was no help for it. They must tell me.

"Well," said Betty. "It was just before the Duke and Duchess left. The Duke was troubled in the night with sickness and gripping pains—so they said."

"Why did I not know of this?"

"We were told not to speak of it. We should not have mentioned it."

"But I insist on knowing," I reminded her. "Go on."

"The Duchess was very worried. Their servants were there. They thought he was . . ."

I found I was clenching my fists. It was hard to control my dismay and alarm.

"What caused it?" I demanded.

Again that exchange of a glance between the two young women.

"It must have been something he had eaten at supper," said Jane.

"But he was much better in the morning," added Betty. "And then, of course, he left for Brussels."

"Why was this kept from me?"

"Your Highness was recovering from your own illness.

The Prince had given orders that you were not to be worried. It was just that your father was briefly indisposed."

"And my father left almost immediately and instructions were given not to tell me."

"No one was supposed to mention it, for it would seem as though the cooks did not know their business."

"And you ladies were told not to mention it? By whom?"

"It was Elizabeth. She is the one who says what we must do or not do now."

I was very disturbed. Had they tried to kill my father? Those men who assembled for the supper parties were his enemies. They wanted to see him removed to make way for William.

And William? I could not believe that such a religious man would contemplate ... murder.

I was ashamed of myself for entertaining for a moment such a thought of my husband. William was stern, unbending, overwhelmingly ambitious, but he would never be a party to murder—and the murder of his father-in-law.

I felt I wanted to make up for such an unworthy thought.

My attitude towards my father had changed a little. There were those who called him a fool and my uncle was one of them. I had heard that the King had said of him: "The people will never get rid of me, because if they did they would have to have James. That is something they would not want. I doubt he would last four years on the throne."

My poor misguided father. Such a good man, he was, apart from that lechery which he shared with his brother; but he could be foolish in the extreme.

It surprised me that I could think this of one whom I had idolized for so long. I began to wonder if I were seeing him through William's eyes.

I was very eager for news of what was happening in Brussels, and I was overjoyed when I heard that my half-sister, the little Isabella, and my sister Anne were going to Brussels to stay with my father for a while.

This appeared to be a great concession, for previously Anne had not been allowed to go with him for fear he should attempt to make a Catholic of her; and I wondered if the feeling in England was less fanatical than it had been, though I still heard that people were being accused by Titus Oates, arrested, tried for treason, and executed. Moreover, my father was still in exile; but the fact that Anne was allowed to visit him in Brussels did seem a good omen.

When they arrived they wanted to come and see me. I was very eager that they should do so, and it was arranged. Once again, it would not be a state visit, for, in view of my father's position as an exile, that would be undiplomatic. I think William was loath to receive him, wondering what effect this would have when the news reached England that the exiled Duke had been received at The Hague.

My husband was in a delicate position. He was certain now that I would be Queen and he, as my consort, would share the throne. No, not consort. If I were Queen, he would insist on being King. After all, he had a claim in his own right. But he had to remember the importance of my position. He had certainly changed towards me since I had begun to show a little spirit.

So I wanted to see my family and he could not deny me that. Nor did he wish to make his ambitions too plain. He had a difficult path to tread.

So they came and he greeted them with a certain amount of warmth. As for myself, I was overcome with joy. We embraced and clung together, mingling our tears. We Stuarts have a streak of sentiment in our natures.

There was one irritation. Anne had brought Sarah Churchill in her suite and as Sarah had refused to be parted from her husband, Colonel Churchill was of the party.

Anne was growing up. She was nearly as old now as I had been at the time of my marriage. So far there had been no one selected for her and she was blithely unconcerned, and she doted on Sarah; she seemed completely subservient to her. It was still "Sarah says this . . ." "Sarah does it this way. . . ." I was tired of Sarah. Anne seemed unable to make a decision without her. But then she had always been too lazy to make decisions.

Sarah was quick to see my irritation with her and she was too autocratic to accept it. I wondered what John Churchill thought of his wife, for I was sure she attempted to control him as she did Anne. I was amazed when I saw them together, for he seemed almost slavishly devoted.

Anne said, "Oh, Sarah is so clever. I am not surprised that he is her devoted slave."

"Does she seek to make you one?" I asked.

Anne blinked at me with her short-sighted eyes. "How could she? She is my attendant."

My dear, simple Anne; she had not changed. She was as ready to accept Sarah's domination as ever and, of course, I noticed, Sarah always couched her orders to Anne in diplomatic terms, for indeed Sarah was at heart a diplomat. But she did not please me.

One day Anne said to me, "Sarah thinks the Prince does not treat you as he should."

"Sarah does?"

"Yes. She says she would not endure if it she were you."

"That is very bold of her."

Anne giggled. "Sarah is always bold. Well, she is Sarah. No one would get the better of Sarah. And she says you are really more important than he is, or would be if . . ."

I said, "Our uncle, the King, will live for a long time yet, and so will our father. My husband is the Stadholder and Prince of Orange, and it is only if our father has no sons that you or I could ever sit on the throne of England."

"Sarah thinks the people will not have our father, nor perhaps a son of his."

"If Sarah were as wise as you think she is, she would look to her own business and leave that of her peers to them."

"Mary," cried Anne incredulously, "do you not *like* Sarah?"

"I think Sarah Churchill takes too much on herself. She should remember her place as the wife of a man who has yet to make his way in the King's army."

I guessed she would tell Sarah what I had said and Sarah would not like it. I was glad of that.

On another occasion, Anne said, "Sarah thinks Elizabeth Villiers gives herself airs."

I agreed with her but said nothing, and Anne went on, "Sarah thinks she has a reason for it."

"What happens in my apartments is no concern of Sarah's," I said. "I think it would be a good idea, sister, if you made that clear to her, and if I discovered her making any trouble in the household it might be necessary to send her away."

Anne looked at me in amazement.

"Send Sarah away! You couldn't do that!"

"Very easily," I replied. "This is *my* household. I do what I will here."

"Sarah thinks you cannot do anything that the Prince wouldn't want."

"Sarah is mistaken. I am the Princess of Orange and our father's elder daughter. I can do as I will."

I was proud of myself. I remembered my power and I was going to exert it. I was my father's eldest daughter and that put me in a very special position. I was going to make sure that people remembered it.

I knew that Anne would have reported this conversation to Sarah Churchill, for I heard of no more comments; but Sarah Churchill and I never liked each other after that.

The visit, like the other, had to be a short one. My poor father could not forget that he was an exile. He was a very sad man. I could understand that. I had hated to leave my country, but at least I had done so in an honoured fashion. I had not been forced out.

It was a sad occasion when I said goodbye to my father, my stepmother, my sister Anne, and little Isabella. There were tears as we assured each other that we should soon be together again.

* * *

There was tension throughout the court at The Hague. Messages were coming from England. King Charles had suffered from a series of fits—one after another. He was no longer young and, in view of the life he had led, it seemed unlikely he would go on much longer.

There were accounts of the people's grief, not only in London but throughout the country. None of the blatant peccadilloes could change their affection for him. His many mistresses, his scandalous liaisons, made no difference. They loved the Merry Monarch. There had never been a king so loved since King Edward IV, tall and handsome, had roamed the streets of London, casting a roving eye on the handsome women.

There were more gatherings at the supper parties in the apartments of the maids of honour, and William was often present in the company of those discontents from England; and now none of them could suppress their excitement.

I wondered what my father was feeling, shut off from it all in Brussels. Then news came from that city that he had left in haste for some secret destination, leaving his family behind.

I was filled with anxiety when he arrived in England, for I knew it was because of popular feeling that he had been sent away.

Meanwhile, we were all tense, waiting for developments.

Anticlimax came. The King had recovered. The ague had disappeared and he was his old self. I could imagine his amusement at all the excitement and his sly comments that he had cheated them out of the fun.

He received my father with affection. Charles was truly fond of his family in his light-hearted way: and it was only because of his determination "never to go wandering again" that he had given way to popular demand for his brother's exile.

Even those who loved my father must agree that it was his own fault. If he had only set aside his scruples, worshipped as he wanted to in secret, none of this would have arisen.

That was a thought which occurred to me again and again. And I must confess it produced a certain impatience with him when I thought of the havoc he was causing.

Well, he was back in England. But would he be allowed to stay?

Everyone at The Hague was watchful and alert. Every messenger who arrived at the palace was immediately taken to William. Everyone was waiting for the outcome.

At length it came. My father was returning to Brussels.

He was going to take his family back to England and would call at The Hague on his way.

In the meantime we heard the news. The people of England would not allow my father to stay there. I wondered what his plans would be and it was with mingled joy and apprehension that I greeted him when he arrived; and as soon as I was alone with him, I demanded to know what had happened.

He told me with great emotion of his reunion with his brother.

"This is no fault of Charles," he said. "In spite of his ministers . . . in spite of the people . . . he would not have me go away."

"Then . . . you will stay?"

"He cannot have that either. There is too much pressure. Only those who have been in London can understand the trouble that has come out of this infamous plot. Only they can realize what harm has been done. The people have been roused to fury. They are shouting 'no popery' in the streets. They are accepting Titus Oates as though his word is gospel. He has inflamed hatred of Catholics."

"And you have let them know that you are one of them," I said with a hint of reproach.

"I am what I am."

"Tell me what will happen now?"

"I am being sent to Scotland."

"To Scotland! Exiled to Scotland!"

"No. Not exiled this time. This time I go in honour. I am to be High Commissioner there. So I shall have work to do."

I could not help feeling relieved.

"Charles thinks the family should stay in London. He says he will care for them. Anne would, of course, be expected to, but Mary Beatrice will insist on accompanying me."

"Well," I said. "It is better than exile here."

He smiled ruefully. "This will be exile in a way . . . diplomatic exile. How I wish we could go back to happier days!"

I felt another flicker of impatience. So might we have done, but for your open declaration of your faith, I thought.

Again there was the sadness of departure and I wondered when I would see them again.

I was to remember that parting all through the years to come.

A Hasty Marriage

Dr. Ken, who had taken Dr. Hooper's place, although slender and of small stature, was a man of great presence and strong character. He made no concession to fashion, wore no wig, and his thin hair grew long, falling down on either side of his face. He was somewhat quick of temper, but good-natured, and, like his predecessor, Dr. Hooper, quite fearless, and would state any view that his conscience told him was the right one.

I felt an immediate liking for him, and I think he did for me; so I was pleased that he had come.

He and William did not take to each other. In fact, William disliked him even more than he had Dr. Hooper. I soon saw that he would like to be rid of these priests who came from England and were put in the place of the Dutch clergy of his choosing. I understood why it rankled.

Dr. Ken was quick to see that William was not as respectful towards me as he should have been. He wrote to my uncle, expressing himself "horribly unsatisfied with the Prince's behaviour towards his wife." He added, "I shall talk to him of this, even at the risk of being kicked out of doors."

He did. William was annoyed, but he must have realized there was little he could do. The position in England was very delicate and he had to consider the effect of his actions there. He had continually to remember that his claim to the throne came through me and that I should be the one who was welcomed, if that longed-for day came. It might seem a small matter to ask Dr. Ken to leave, but who could say what repercussions it would have?

William could accept the pinpricks of a little man like Dr. Ken for the sake of expediency.

Then something happened which demanded a great deal of courage on my part, and I think perhaps it was a turning point in my relationship with my husband. It could never have happened if William had been at court, but he was often absent and in another part of the country on state business, and this was one of those occasions.

I had noticed for some weeks that something was wrong with Jane Wroth. She was naturally a lively girl, given to frivolity. That was why the change was noticeable.

I sent for her. She came to me, quiet, subdued, and then I noticed the change in her figure.

"Jane," I said, "you had better tell me what is wrong." She cast down her eyes and was silent.

I said, "It is rather noticeable. Is it not time that you were married?"

Poor Jane. She lifted her woebegone eyes to my face.

"I am afraid, Your Highness, it is not possible."

"Why not? Is he married already?"

She shook her head.

"Then why not?"

"Because, Madam, of who he is."

"Tell me," I said.

She was silent and I said in my commanding tones, "Jane, I am asking you to tell me."

"It is William Zulestein, Your Highness."

Zulestein! This was William's kinsman, of whom he thought so highly. And who was Jane Wroth? Of no great family, she had been extremely lucky to get a place at court.

"How could this have happened?" A stupid question. How did such things happen? They happened all the time and often in most unexpected quarters. William would want Zulestein to make a good marriage, one which would be important to the House of Orange, for, illegitimate as he was, he was recognized as being a member of it. Oh, what a fool Jane had been!

"How could you have allowed it?" I cried. "So you were seduced by him. He could not have promised you marriage!"

"Yes," she insisted, "he did."

"So he promised. And now?"

"He says the Prince would never allow it. He would . . . but for that."

"Are you sure he promised?"

"Yes, Madam, I am."

"You should know better than to listen to promises. So . . . what will you do now?"

Jane looked at me piteously. She would have no choice. She would be sent home and her family would be filled with anger against her. She had spoilt her chances: with great difficulty a place had been found for her and she had behaved like a fool, allowing herself to be seduced, and was about to bring an unwanted infant into the world to ruin her prospects of a good marriage. Poor Jane! To go home, despised, taunted all her life for this misguided action of her youth.

I liked Jane and I felt very sorry for her.

"Jane," I said, "I do not know what we can do."

She began to weep silently. "I shall go away," she sobbed. "I shall no longer serve Your Highness. I can't bear it."

"Have you talked to Zulestein?"

She nodded.

"And he is prepared to desert you. Is that so?"

"He dare not do aught else. He says the Prince has made plans for him."

"He did not tell you that before?"

"He said he loved me. We would have married . . . in spite of everything."

"Jane," I said. "Go to your room. I will think what must be done."

She left me then. I was filled with pity for her and anger

against this man who had thoughtlessly taken his pleasure and lied and cheated to get it.

Dr. Ken found me in a reflective mood. He asked if aught ailed me. I could see he was thinking that, as the Prince was absent, it could not be due to an unkind action on his part.

I said, "Dr. Ken, I am deeply disturbed. This is due to one of the maids of honour, Jane Wroth. She is with child and in great distress."

"The man responsible is at court?"

"Yes."

"Then he must marry her."

"There is a little difficulty there. It is William Zulestein."

"The Prince's kinsman. That has nothing to do with the matter. He has got the girl with child and he must marry her."

"The Prince will not allow it."

"This is a matter of right and wrong and this man's duty is clear. He has seduced this girl; she is with child and he must marry her."

"I believe the Prince will not agree to that."

Dr. Ken's smooth face was set in firm lines. "Then," he said, "the Prince must disagree."

"He will not allow it."

"He is not here, so he cannot stop it; and when they are married there is nothing the Prince can do about it."

"Do you mean you would . . . ?"

"Marry them? Indeed. Give me your blessing and I will do so."

"But the Prince . . ."

"Your Highness, you are the Princess of Orange. The woman is in your service. It is a matter for you. It could happen that you will be Queen of England. The Prince would in that case only share with you as far as you would allow. You are inclined to permit this man to dominate you. At the moment you are merely the Princess of Orange and he is the Prince. But you are also heir to England. Do not allow yourself to be set aside. You should be strong. If this man is allowed to leave his promises unfulfilled, if that young woman is to go through life in shame because the man who sinned with her is allowed to shirk his duty, and if we do not do everything within our power to prevent this, we are neglecting our Christian duty. Pray for guidance and I will come to you tomorrow morning and we will make it clear to these erring young people what must be done."

"But the Prince . . ." I began.

"This is not a matter for him. He is away. It is our duty to act without him."

"I dare not."

He smiled at me sadly. "Because he forgets your position; you must not."

I said I would think of it.

And I did. All through the night I thought of his anger when he knew what we had done, being fully aware that it would have been against his will. Then I considered Jane, sent home in disgrace. It occurred to me that Zulestein might refuse to marry her even if Dr. Ken insisted that he should.

I am ashamed to say that I felt a glimmer of hope at this. It would be a way out of the dilemma. I realized then that I was a coward. I was afraid of William's wrath. I grappled with myself. I must remember my position. I thought of how his treatment of me had aroused the indignation of Dr. Ken . . . and others.

No, I would stand against him. If any other man had seduced a girl, after promising marriage, he would be made to keep his promise. So why not Zulestein?

I believed the man should marry Jane; and so did Dr. Ken.

I had made up my mind.

Dr. Ken was delighted when he knew my decision.

"You are doing what is right," he told me. "God has guided you in this."

I summoned Zulestein and when he arrived I were waiting for him.

He was not a young man, being some five year than William, but he was very good-looking, with an imposing personality and an air of nobility, which perhaps he stressed somewhat because of his illegitimacy.

I could see that I should need all my newly acquired courage to deal with this man. But beside me stood Dr. Ken, one of the most formidable and eloquent preachers I had ever heard.

I began by telling him that I had seen Jane Wroth and knew of her condition and his part in bringing it about.

He was taken aback and at a loss for words.

Dr. Ken said, "The plain fact is that this young woman is about to bear your child. You promised her marriage and now that promise has been retracted. In view of what has happened, it is necessary for you to marry Jane Wroth without delay."

Zulestein said, "I would do so if it were possible."

"You are already married?" asked Dr. Ken.

"No."

"Then there can be no reason why it is impossible for you to marry Jane Wroth."

"You know of my connection with the House of Orange."

"I know that your father was the bastard son of Henry Frederick, Prince of Orange," said Dr. Ken.

"Then you will understand."

"I fear I do not. If a man makes a promise of marriage, he must honour it, or in the eyes of God he is a cheat and a liar and there is no place for such in Heaven."

Zulestein was beginning to realize the difficulty of his position. He turned to me.

"Your Highness will understand. The Prince wishes me to make a state marriage. It is already being discussed."

I was fortified by the presence of Dr. Ken.

"It would have been before the result of your association with my maid of honour was known," I said firmly. "This,

. course, changed the situation. There is only one action open to you now. I am of the same opinion of Dr. Ken. There must be no further delay."

"Madame ... Your Highness, the Prince will be most displeased."

"If the Prince is a man of honour, he should be more displeased by your failure in your duty," said Dr. Ken.

"This concerns a lady in my household," I put in, "and therefore it is a matter for me to decide. I cannot believe that a member of the House of Orange could fail in honour. I bid you give serious thought to this matter. Come to me tomorrow and give me your answer, and I pray that it will be the right and honourable one."

Dr. Ken said, "I will come with you, my son, and we will pray together and ask God to guide your conscience."

I have said that Dr. Ken was one of the most eloquent preachers I have ever heard, but I do not know exactly what he said to Zulestein. It may be that he convinced him that he would suffer eternal damnation if he did not marry Jane; perhaps Zulestein really loved her. In any case, he agreed to marry Jane and, without losing any time, Dr. Ken made hasty preparations.

It was in my private little chapel that Dr. Ken performed the ceremony and Jane Wroth became the wife of Zulestein.

When William returned and discovered what had happened he was astounded and his anger was great. I wondered what he said to Zulestein, who must have given him an account of what happened. When William came to me I saw that he had difficulty in controlling his rage. Inwardly I trembled, but I forced myself not to show my fear.

"Zulestein married to that girl!" cried William. "Who is she? Nothing ... nobody! And he my kinsman! And you gave your consent to the match! Nay, encouraged it. Insisted on it."

I heard myself say in a defiant voice, "It was a marriage which should have taken place months before."

"Have you forgotten that he is a member of *my* family?"

"All the more reason why he should honour his ——ments."

I felt my courage waning and feared that at any moment I might break down and confess I was in the wrong. But something told me that I must be strong. If I allowed myself to be cowed, his contempt for me would be aroused. I had to be strong now. He dared not harm me. I was too important to his schemes.

I lifted my head and said, "I did what Dr. Ken and I believed to be right."

"That man is at the heart of this. That meddler . . ."

"Dr. Ken is a good man," I said. "He made Zulestein see where his duty lay."

"You had the temerity . . ." He paused. I could see the disbelief in his face. He was thinking that I should never have acted so without Dr. Ken to persuade me.

I said coolly, "Jane Wroth is a member of my household. She is therefore my concern. I believe it was my duty to see right done to her."

This change in my attitude disconcerted him, and he became wary. I knew that, apart from the moral issue, I had done right to stand out against him in this.

Dr. Ken, who must have been listening in the next room, chose that moment to knock on the door and ask leave to enter.

"Yes, come in," cried William. "I hear you have taken upon yourself to arrange a marriage for my kinsman."

"A belated but necessary ceremony," said Dr. Ken.

"You are impudent," retorted William, and I believed he was venting the rage he felt towards me on Dr. Ken.

"You come here instructing the Princess to disobey my wishes."

"It was my own decision," I said, feeling strong with Dr. Ken beside me.

"I have no doubt he advised you."

"The Princess is capable, and has the right, by reason of her rank, to make her own decisions."

He was reminding William that he must be careful in his treatment of me, and I saw William's eyes glint in anger.

"You are an interfering priest," he said. "Pray in the future leave matters which are beyond your understanding to those whom they concern and keep your notions of what is right and wrong for those who wish to hear them. And remember this: I will not have you meddling in the affairs of this country."

"I have come here to practise my calling," replied Dr. Ken. "And nothing will prevent my doing that."

"*I* shall prevent your arrogant interference in my affairs," said William.

"Your Highness, I cannot be obstructed in my duties and shall make preparations to return to England without delay. I believe there are some there who will be interested to hear of the harsh treatment which is accorded to the Princess."

William said, "Leave as soon as you wish. It cannot be too soon in my opinion."

With that he left us.

I looked at Dr. Ken in dismay.

"You cannot go," I said.

"I have no alternative."

I had drawn courage from this man. I needed him to be with me.

"I shall feel so alone without you," I said.

"There is no reason to. The Prince is an ambitious man. He dare not go too far in his treatment of you. Already I have spoken of it. He knows that and he does not like it. Your Highness must never forget your position. He is aware of it constantly and does not like it. He wants to be in control. Do not forget, my dear Princess, that he can only go so far. You have weapons to fight back. Now, I must go and make my preparations."

"Please, Dr. Ken. I have need of you. Do reconsider your decision. I know you are right in what you say. You have given me great strength. Pray do not go. I beg of you—stay. Stay a little longer."

He looked at me tenderly.

"You have heard what was said. You realize my position. I cannot stay unwelcome. I must return to England."

"If you will only stay a little while . . ."

"It will take me a day or so to prepare."

"Please, Dr. Ken, you have given me courage. I need you here. Please do not go just yet."

He said, "I will wait a day or so."

It seemed to me very important that he should stay.

It was later that day when William came again to me. He was calm and cold, his old self.

He said, "Have you seen Dr. Ken?"

"I have asked him to stay," I replied, with a note of defiance in my voice.

I was surprised to see that he looked pleased at this.

"What says he?"

"He says he cannot stay." I held my head high. "I do not wish him to go."

To my astonishment, William said, "It is better for him to stay the appointed time. We shall only have another such in his place."

"But you have made it difficult for him to stay. You have as good as told him to go."

"Only when he announced his intention of doing so. You should persuade him to stay."

I smiled a little wryly. Of course, he did not want Dr. Ken to go home and tell them how badly the Prince treated me. The people would be angry. Their emotions were quickly aroused. He would give them a picture of the poor Princess—their English Princess—who was treated as of no importance by a Dutchman. And when the time came—if it did come—when he rode through the streets of London with me, they would remember the Dutchman who had been harsh to their Princess.

I saw how his mind was working. He had been so enraged by the Zulestein marriage that he had temporarily—and rarely—lost his calm judgement. He had said that which would have been better unsaid; and now he was anx-

ious to keep Dr. Ken under supervision that he might not
go back to England and preach against William of Orange.

I could not help smiling slightly as I turned to him.

"I have tried to persuade him. I think if you want him to
stay, you should ask him yourself."

William seemed taken aback at the prospect.

"You can persuade him," he said.

"I have tried, but I think you have offended him too
strongly and that he will need to be told that his presence
is not distasteful to you."

This was a strange turn of events. *I* was advising William.

He said, "I might see the man."

Yes, he was indeed afraid of Dr. Ken's returning to England and speaking disparagingly of the Prince of Orange.

I saw Dr. Ken a few hours later. He was smiling.

"The Prince has been to see me," he said. "Yes, he came
to me and did not summon me to his presence. A rare con-
descension. He has been emphatic in his desire that I
should stay. He was shocked by the sudden marriage of his
kinsman, he explained, for he had had plans for him. But
he saw the point and realized that I did only what a priest
must do in the circumstances. He said that the Princess had
been comforted by my instruction and was extremely upset
at the prospect of my departure, and for that reason he
hoped I would reconsider my decision."

"And you have?"

Dr. Ken smiled.

"I have said I will stay for another year, but I did imply that I was not satisfied with his treatment of Your
Highness. It may amaze you that he showed no resentment. I thought that he might repeat his desire to be rid
of me, but he did not. Instead he said that, if I would stay
on a little to please the Princess, I should be very welcome at The Hague."

So Dr. Ken stayed with us.

I had certainly changed. I had lost some of my meekness. I had confirmed the importance of the English crown and that William must constantly be reminded that the easiest way to it was through me.

Revelry at The Hague

I was so glad that Dr. Ken stayed with us. He was a comfort to me and at that time I needed comfort.

Frances Apsley had married Sir Benjamin Bathhurst. I
knew that she would marry sooner or later as she was ad-
vancing into her twenties. Her letters had changed. She was
very happy, she wrote to me, and soon after that she was
pregnant. She was still my dearest friend, as she had said
she always would be, but I could see there were more important things in her life now—her marriage, and the child
she was expecting. I envied her and yet I was glad of her
happiness. But it made her remote and I knew that it would
not be the same henceforth. Perhaps it never had been what
I had imagined, but there had been great happiness in the
belief and that had been essential to my comfort.

I longed for a happy marriage, a child of my own. But
I was married to William. Could I ever make him love me
as Sir Benjamin obviously loved Frances? Was it possible?
Should I try?

I have always been fanciful and I began to build up a
picture of domestic happiness which was a complete contrast to reality: William discovering how much he loved
me—a completely different William from the dour, ambitious man I knew. His true feelings had been hidden beneath that stern façade he showed to the world. I had
awakened him to love. My hopes of the crown were of no
importance. Oddly enough, I began to believe that it might
be true.

Then, even in my realistic moments, I began to feel that

there might be just a grain of truth in my dreams, for William and I discovered a shared interest. He was fascinated by buildings and so was I—particularly gardens.

He was in the process of building a palace at Loo and I was surprised when he showed me the plans for it. Perhaps this was due to the criticisms Dr. Ken was still making about his neglect of me—but I did not want to look for that sort of reason.

I was excited. It was to be a wonderful palace.

"The garden will be large," he said. "You might like to choose some of the flowers and say how you would like them to be laid. You will have your own suite there, of course, and you could make some suggestions about that."

I threw myself wholeheartedly into the project. We arranged that under the windows there should be a fountain and, as I showed a preference for statues, they should be placed in the garden at spots of my choosing. It was all very interesting and I watched the erection of the palace with great delight. And what made it so pleasant was William's changed attitude. He was more gracious; he suggested rather than ordered.

Frances wrote of her happiness with Sir Benjamin and the interests they shared, and I wrote back glowing of my life with William.

I loved the palace at Loo, I suppose because I had had a hand in its construction. I set up a poultry garden where I hoped to breed various specimens of fowl. It was a great pleasure to go among them, feed them, and have them fluttering all around me. So I spent a great deal of time at Loo.

Unfortunately, once the palace had been built, I saw less of William. I could not expect him to be at Loo when state affairs demanded his attention at The Hague.

There was news from England. My sister Anne was at the heart of a scandal.

She was sixteen years old now. I had been married before I reached that age. It was different now. The unpopularity of my father had increased since I left. Titus Oates had seen to that. The King was older, and his age and my father's inability to get a son made it seem more possible that I—and William with me—would one day have the throne. And, of course, Anne would follow me, if I had no children, which seemed likely.

It was hard to contemplate Anne bestirring herself sufficiently to become involved in a scandal. I supposed it just happened round her. She was pretty in her way, in spite of being too fat; her complexion, when I had last seen her, had been very fresh and healthy-looking; and her rather vague look—due to her short-sightedness—could be very appealing to some.

In any case, it seemed that John Sheffield, Earl of Mulgrave, had fallen in love with her. Their romance had been discovered and poor Mulgrave was in disgrace.

He was some years older than she was—about sixteen or seventeen, I heard—but a very handsome man with a great gift for words. I think she must have been charmed by his poetry.

However, when it was discovered that Mulgrave had plans to marry her—and had her agreement to this—there was trouble.

I could imagine Anne's demeanour. She would smile her ineffectual smile and it would be realized that it was no use remonstrating with her.

It was different with poor Mulgrave. He was reprimanded and sent off to Tangiers. I heard afterwards that the ship on which he had sailed leaked, and it was hinted that it was hoped to be rid of him at sea; but I did not believe that. My uncle would never be party to such a plan, but there will always be insinuations against people in high places; and when I discovered that the Earl of Plymouth was among those on board, I knew it was false, for the Earl of Plymouth was an illegitimate son of the King. My uncle loved all his children dearly and would never have allowed any of them to go to sea in a faulty vessel.

Mulgrave himself never brought such an accusation and declared that the unseaworthiness of the ship had not been discovered until they were halfway to Tangiers and that if it had been faulty when it set out it would have been quickly revealed.

Anne's little flutter with Mulgrave had brought home the desirability of finding a husband for her before she was involved in further indiscretions.

Prince George of Hanover arrived in Holland. He was on his way to England and we guessed the reason for this visit. It was to give him an opportunity of meeting Anne.

William was always affected by what was happening at the English court. Sometimes I thought it would have been happier for him if Mrs. Tanner had not seen that vision of the three crowns at his birth. Then perhaps he might not have been so obsessed by the need to get them. But perhaps, being the ambitious man he was, he would have wanted the crowns just the same.

George had a claim to the throne. His father Ernest Augustus had married Sophia, the daughter of Elizabeth, Queen of Bohemia, who was the granddaughter of James I of England. His connection with the Stuarts did not please William. I think William would have been happy if Anne had made her clandestine match with Mulgrave.

I had come out of seclusion at Loo for the visit of George of Hanover. I found him singularly unattractive; he was handsome in a way, but he had no charm or manner; he was simple in his dress and it was obvious that he was going to make no concessions to anyone. He had clearly inherited none of the charm of the Stuart clan. I wondered what Anne would think of him.

He did not stay long with us and after he had gone I waited eagerly for news of what had taken place on his meeting with my sister.

There were various versions, but the main one was that it had been far from successful. Elizabeth Villiers, I imagined, was the chief source of information, for she was in constant communication with her sisters who were at the court of England, and that meant she received the latest news from them. It was usually accurate.

It seemed George and Anne had not taken kindly to each other. Poor Anne! I expect she compared him with Lord Mulgrave, and the contrast must have been great.

How I wished I could have been with her, to have known her true feelings. Anne was not a letter writer; she had always avoided taking up her pen. She was quite different from me in that respect and any communication I had from her was brief. I did hope she was not too unhappy at this time.

I heard that George had been averse to the match after meeting Anne and Anne felt the same about him. So there could have been no regrets when the young man was recalled to Hanover and was almost immediately betrothed to Sophia Dorothea of Celle.

So George's future was fixed, and I was sure someone would soon be found for Anne.

There was sad news from home. Little Isabella had died. I was desolate. I had grown to love my little half-sister when she had been with us and I guessed the anguish Mary Beatrice would be suffering. It was so cruel that this child—the only one who had managed to survive for a few years—should be taken from her.

My father wrote very sadly to me. I knew that he would be going through a very difficult time. The King was not in the best of health and there was uneasiness everywhere. He hoped that I was happy. Dr. Ken had reported that he was not pleased with the manner in which I was treated at my husband's court.

I wrote to him and said that I was very well and by no means unhappy. Dr. Ken may have exaggerated. He did not really like being away from his own country and he had had some differences about religion with the Prince.

My father also said that he believed there were rumours circulating about himself, and he hoped nothing would be done to poison my mind against him. He wanted my assurances that the feelings we had had for each other were as they always had been.

I assured him that this was so, although I wondered afterwards if this was entirely true. In the days of my childhood I had thought him godlike, perfect in every way; but recently I had felt a little impatient with him. I hated the conflict and it was becoming more and more clear to me that if my father had not flaunted his religion in such a way, many of our troubles need never have occurred.

When Dr. Ken went back to England he was replaced by Dr. Covell. Dr. Covell had travelled a great deal and was very different from Dr. Ken. He was more gentle, more inclined to keep his opinions to himself, but I quickly realized that he had no great fondness for William, and I was not surprised, for he was shocked, as Dr. Ken had been, by the lack of respect accorded me.

There was more news from England regarding Anne. This time her suitor was another George—the Prince of Denmark. By all accounts, he appeared to be a rather pleasant person, unassuming in the extreme, and because he was only the second son of King Frederick of Denmark, he could take up his residence in England and Anne would not be expected to leave her home. I could well imagine that this would make the young man very agreeable to her—and when I heard that Colonel Churchill was a friend of the Prince, who in turn thought highly of the Colonel, I was sure that Sarah would approve of him and that would count very highly with Anne. So I was not surprised when I heard she was satisfied with the match, and I rejoiced in this, for I did not want my sister to suffer as I had.

I was living a very quiet life at this time. Anne Trelawny was a great comfort and I also had my old nurse, Mrs. Langford with me. Her husband was a clergyman and one of my chaplains. There were the Villiers and Betty Selbourne with Jane Wroth—now Jane Zulestein—and a rather pretty Dutch girl named Trudaine.

Another of the Villiers sisters had arrived in Holland. This was Katharine. She had married a Monsieur Puisars, a Frenchman who had a post at The Hague.

My father was writing frequently to me now and I knew that William was very uneasy about this. He kept a close watch on my actions, and did not care that I should appear often in public. On the rare occasions when I did, I was regarded with great interest by the people and I fancied that they liked me. Their smiles indicated this and, although they are not a people to give vent to emotions, they implied that they approved of me. William noticed this and it seemed to puzzle him and did not, I think, altogether please him. He himself was always greeted with the utmost respect but hardly affection. With me it was the reverse, and this made him rather thoughtful and may have been the reason why he did not want me to appear too often.

He had arranged that, in addition to the maids of honour, who were my friends, there should be several Dutch attendants. They were given orders to attend my needs and make sure I was given the utmost care. When they first appeared, I resented them, for they seemed like jailors, but I soon found that they were pleasant girls and grew quite fond of them.

Now that I had so much leisure, I realized that I had not worked as hard as I might have done at my lessons and my ignorance disturbed me. I discovered a special interest in literature, and as there was little to do but walk in the gardens, do needlework, or, if I were at Loo, amuse myself with the poultry, I became involved with my books. I even painted a little, remembering the instructions of my dwarf, Richard Gibson.

With these occupations the days passed pleasantly. More and more people, though, were asking themselves why I allowed my husband to govern me. It was said, "The Princess of Orange lives like a recluse and this seems to be at the wish of her husband."

But I was enjoying my books and painting. I suppose I have a peace-loving nature. I had never wanted to stress my rank. I think, more than anything, I wanted to live on happy terms with those about me. I have always thought that displays of anger rarely benefit the people who make them. I think, too, that I had become somewhat fascinated by William. I knew he was not handsome, not quite straight in frame, cold, aloof, without tenderness. Set out like that, it would seem he had all the least likeable traits a man could have. But there was something very strong about William. Ambition, I had seen in men, but not that power which I believe is reckoned to hold a certain attraction for some women. It may be that I am one of them.

So I lived my docile life at the House in the Woods, or at Dieren, which I visited from time to time because it was said to be good for me—and of course at the Palace of Loo. And those about me—some of them English visitors to The Hague, Dr. Covell, Betty Selbourne, Mrs. Langford, and Anne Trelawny, continued to complain that the Prince of Orange behaved very badly towards his wife.

The news from England was awaited eagerly. It seemed clear that a crisis was looming. The Exclusion Bill, which was to prevent my father taking the throne in the event of his brother's death, had failed to go through once more, simply because the King had prevented it by dissolving Parliament.

The Duke of Monmouth was very much in evidence— Protestant son of the King, though, unfortunately for him— and for England, some implied—born on the wrong side of the blanket. If only he had been the legitimate son, all this unrest could have been avoided.

But it was not impossible to put this matter right.

I could imagine how the King would watch his son's antics with that amusement he bestowed on all matters, whether of great importance or none at all, as though to say, it is for you to settle when I am no longer here.

My father had returned from Scotland and the King had received him with great joy. Those ministers who had brought about his exile had been overruled by those who wished for his return; but the fact that the heir to the throne had been sent into exile had created a very uneasy situation.

My father had assumed his old duties. He still had his enemies but they appeared to be less powerful and, although he was not popular, it was said that many preferred to have him brought out of exile and at home, where he could be watched.

Everyone did not agree with that. Perhaps that was why the Rye House Plot occurred.

That there should be a plot to kill the King seemed incredible. He was as popular as ever, and all hoped that he would live for a very long time, for while he was on the throne all was well. But he had prevented the Exclusion Bill becoming law, and now his brother was back in the country, heir to the throne. To some it must seem that the King's affection for his brother had overcome his good sense; and there were those who were determined that at all costs the Duke of York should not come to the throne. So they planned to kill him, and with him the King. Hence the Rye House Plot.

Fortunately it was ill-conceived and one of the conspirators took fright and confessed that the assassinations were being planned. The King and his brother were to be murdered on their way back from Newmarket, at a house in Hertfordshire which belonged to a maltster and was called Rye House. I was greatly relieved to hear that my father and the King were safe.

This was particularly interesting to many of the people at The Hague because some of the conspirators were well known there. Lord Russell was one; Algernon Sidney another.

By this time I had guessed, of course, that these men had been at The Hague conspiring with William to be ready for the time when my uncle died.

William was aggrieved, if not for Sidney and Russell— who were executed after the trial, which had shown how deeply involved they were—for the failure of the plot which, had it succeeded, would have removed those who stood between me and the crown.

Anne was married to George of Denmark. How I wished I could have been present in the Chapel Royal at St. James's on that day. By all accounts she had quickly forgotten

Mulgrave and was perfectly contented with the bridegroom they had given her. How rarely that happened, and how blessed were those to whom it did!

Anne would sail through life as she always had done, apart from that minor upset over Mulgrave which she should have known was doomed from the start.

Sarah Churchill was with her and would remain so. Anne would arrange that and Sarah would agree, because of the advantages her position brought her.

Meanwhile, I must pursue my quiet life, reading, painting, walking, seeing few people but those in my immediate circle.

It was with great sorrow that I heard that the Duke of Monmouth was suspected of having been concerned in the Rye House Plot.

I believed he was genuinely fond of his father; he had always shown a great affection for him. I knew that he and my father were not good friends. I was sure Jemmy thought my father a fool to parade his Catholicism as he did; and, of course, my father was not pleased to see Jemmy appearing in public with the airs and grace of a Prince of Wales, as though the role were his by right.

Now Jemmy was in trouble. He had been in trouble before but the King had always been lenient and again and again he had been forgiven. Jemmy possessed the Stuart charm in great measure and was like his father in many ways—alas, though, he lacked his wisdom.

He could scarcely be forgiven this time. Sidney and Russell had been executed for their part in the plot, so how could Jemmy go free? The King did what he always did in such a situation. He prevaricated. There was no imprisonment for Jemmy, but he was sent into exile. Brussels seemed the natural haven and to that city he came.

William made sure that he was given a welcome when he eventually arrived in Holland, and this was noted and commented on.

I was told that when the King heard of it, he was highly amused and in his dry way commented that he was surprised that the Duke of Monmouth and the Prince of Orange could be such friends when they were both pursuing the same mistress—by which he meant the English crown.

There was uneasiness everywhere. Everyone waited for what would happen next. I wondered how my uncle felt, knowing they were all thinking of his death. I could imagine the regrets he would feel that he would not be there to see the results of their actions.

Algernon Sidney had been replaced as English Envoy by Thomas Chudleigh who was not accepted very graciously by William. Chudleigh had been sent to be watchful, for William's preference for Sidney and Russell was well known.

Chudleigh joined the set who were complaining about the Prince's treatment of me, and who were still writing to England about it.

However, the weeks sped by and in fact I was enjoying the occupations which filled my quiet life. I did not want to be drawn into political conflicts, particularly now when there was a growing hostility between my husband and father.

I thought very tenderly of my father every now and then, remembering incidents from my childhood, but my impatience with him for creating this trouble was increasing.

I was reading a great deal about the doctrines of the Church and I was becoming more and more convinced that the break with Rome was a blessing for England, and that a religion which could tolerate an Inquisition with its accompanying cruelties must be avoided at all cost. It was true that there had been persecution by the Protestants, but there had never been such cruelty in England as there was under the reign of Bloody Mary, and it was right that all steps should be taken to make sure that it never happened again. William would prevent it. My father would bring it back.

William came to me one day and said, "The Duke of Monmouth will be coming to The Hague."

"To The Hague!" I cried in astonishment. Jemmy had

been in Holland and William had shown his friendship to him, but to invite him to The Hague—and if he came it must be as an honoured guest—was an insult not only to my father but to my uncle, the King. Jemmy was the latter's son, of course, but he was in exile.

"But . . ." I began.

William waved a hand impatiently. He did not enter into explanations. Suffice it to say that Jemmy was coming at his invitation.

"We must give him a good welcome," he said.

"I?"

He looked at me coldly, annoyed that I should remind him that I was not usually included on such occasions.

"Naturally, you will help to entertain him," he said. "So you will be ready to do so."

He did not linger. He did not want to answer questions. So our brief interview was over.

I was puzzled. The thought entered my mind. Should I allow myself to be treated in this way? To be shut away, almost as though I were under house arrest, and then suddenly to be called out of seclusion at a moment's notice. I knew why—of course. I was my father's daughter. And my father and Monmouth were enemies.

I was never forceful enough, but there were times when I wanted to protest. I did not understand my feelings for William. He was usually cool to me, never tender, never loving; and yet I behaved in this submissive way. I was always aware of that power in him, that quality which made me forget he was undersized, not physically strong when compared with most men; but somehow he managed to tower over them mentally. I knew enough of him to be aware that he railed against his weakness, that he was often in pain from his aching joints. He would never admit this, of course, and Nature had endowed him with towering mental powers with which to achieve his great ambitions.

There was another reason why I was eager to comply with his request. I was very fond of Jemmy. Both Anne and I had looked forward to his visits. He used to dance with us and tell us wild exciting stories of his exploits, of his daring and unmatched courage. They were all fabrications, and we knew it—but we loved hearing them all the same.

So to see him again, if only for a brief time, would be exciting. I would try to forget my uneasiness concerning the part he may have played in the Rye House Plot. I would just look forward to being with Cousin Jemmy.

It was some time since I had appeared at court. There had been one occasion when I had done so most reluctantly. It was one I could not easily forget.

Always at St. James's we had remembered the anniversary of my grandfather's death, and made it a day of mourning. Anne and I used to stay quietly in our apartments, and there had been special prayers for our grandfather's soul. I had always kept up the practice, even since I had come to Holland, and the day had always passed off quietly until the one at the beginning of this year.

I had fasted during that day, wearing a black gown, and was at prayer in my chamber when William came in.

He looked very impatient at the sight of me.

He said, "Enough of this. You are to dine with me tonight."

I replied, "But I am fasting on this day, which is the anniversary of the murder of my grandfather."

"Take off that gown," he said, "and put on the brightest one you have."

I stared at him incredulously. "I could not do that," I said.

"Get one of your women to help. You cannot wear that dress of mourning. I wish you to wear your most splendid gown."

"In England," I began, "we always . . ."

"You are not in England now."

"Here, too," I said.

"I wish you to appear with me. There must be no hint of mourning. You understand?"

"But . . ." I began; and at that moment Betty Selbourne

came in with Anne Trelawny. I realized he must have sent for them.

He said to them, "The Princess must be ready in an hour. Bring out the most splendid of her gowns."

Then he left us.

"But it is the anniversary," began Betty.

Anne was looking at me questioningly. "What does Your Highness want?" she asked.

I hesitated. Then I said, "Bring out the gown and help me to dress."

I could see that Anne was angry and Betty was already thinking of what she would write home. People there would soon know that I had been commanded to ignore the day of mourning for my grandfather.

I felt numb as they helped me dress, but I was ready when the Prince arrived to take me to The Hague.

I remember so well sitting there while the dishes were placed before me. I could eat nothing. I was choked with misery . . . for my grandfather who had been brutally murdered, and for the fact that I could be so treated. It was, as Dr. Ken had said, as though I were a slave.

At that time I despised myself and I hated William. I saw what was in his mind, of course. He wanted the people to know he would have no looking back, no mourning for an ancestor who, through his folly, had lost a kingdom. William looked forward.

It was a long time before I could forgive him for this.

Perhaps I should have been grateful for the secluded life I was leading. I was becoming educated, seeing beyond the obvious, trying to understand my position. There were little, carefree enjoyments in my life which I had not known since I left England.

It was my custom to retire at a fairly early hour, for I liked to have plenty of time to say my prayers and perhaps read a little from some religious books which Dr. Covell had given me. He was anxious, as Dr. Ken was, that I should not turn to the more puritanical Dutch form, which they were sure William was trying to force on me.

One night when I was reading, Anne Trelawny came into my closet and told me that a messenger had arrived and was asking to see me without delay.

He was brought in.

He said, "The Duke of Monmouth has arrived, Your Highness, and is at the Palace of The Hague. The Prince requests you go there without delay."

I said, "I will see him in the morning. I am just about to retire."

"Your Highness, the Prince said that I was not to return without Your Highness. He wishes you to put on suitable garments without delay and come to him at the Palace."

My thoughts went back to that other occasion when I had had to change from my mourning gown at his command.

Suppose I refused? I could not. I dared not. I wondered what he would do if I did? Would he bring Jemmy here? Would he come himself? I very much wanted to see Jemmy.

Only briefly did I hesitate. Then I told the messenger he should wait below and I should be with him very shortly and we would go to the Prince's apartments.

There I found Jemmy with William. It was wonderful to see my cousin again. I forgot all ceremony and so did he.

We embraced and he hugged me tightly.

"Little cousin," he said. "What a joy to see you."

"Jemmy," I murmured, "dear Jemmy."

"Let me look at you. Why, you have grown into a beauty. William, you must be proud of her."

William did not answer and I did not look his way.

"Oh, Jemmy," I began.

He squeezed my hand. "We'll have opportunities to talk, I know."

We dined together. William was very affable. I had rarely seen him in such a mood and I wondered at it, since they both had pretensions to the throne. Jemmy was so good-looking, so charming, he would have a way of beguiling the people and there would be many on his side. He was the Protestant hope—or at least one of them. Could he ever manage to escape his illegitimacy? William and he were rivals.

There must be some devious motive behind William's affability, but I did not want to think of it at this time. Suffice it that Jemmy was here.

William was determined that he should have lodgings worthy of the Duke of Monmouth during his visit to the court of The Hague and he suggested the Prince Maurice Palace.

Jemmy's eyes shone. I knew from the past that there was little he enjoyed more than to be treated with the deference due to rank.

"You must let me know what servants you require," William said, "and I shall see that they are provided."

This was special treatment. William listened with courteous attention to everything Jemmy said and encouraged him to talk—which was scarcely needed.

The thought came into my mind that Jemmy would need to be very alert if he intended to pit his wits against William's.

That was a pleasant evening—perhaps I might say the most pleasant I had had since my arrival in Holland. William treated even me with a show of gracious concern. I felt light-hearted. But there was a tinge of sadness. Jemmy's coming reminded me too poignantly of home.

The next days were some of the most exciting of my life.

I must be seen everywhere with William and Monmouth. I was treated with courtesy; the people cheered me—in fact, I believe they did so more warmly for me than for William. He would notice this, of course, but he showed no sign of resentment. I thought perhaps the people may have heard whispers of his treatment of me and wanted to tell me that they were sorry for me. I could not help being flattered and pleased.

Jemmy was delighted. He was acclaimed by the people. That was of the utmost importance to him. Poor Jemmy, all through his life he had sought to escape the stigma of illegitimacy.

He quickly became popular, of course, and at every opportunity showed his strong allegiance to Protestantism.

I was glad they liked him. As for myself, I looked forward with great delight to his company. He was always so tender and considerate towards me, and so loving that I could almost fancy he was falling in love with me.

It was a ridiculous thought, but I was starved of affection. I was, after all, young, unworldly, sentimental.

I knew that Jemmy shared with the King and my father the particular Stuart failing. One of their main objects in life was to enjoy the society of attractive women.

Lady Henrietta Wentworth had arrived at The Hague and to everyone's amazement had been received as though she were the Duchess of Monmouth, even by William. Lady Henrietta was, of course, known to be Jemmy's mistress of some years' standing. I guessed that the real Duchess, his wife, had stayed in England. It was not a happy marriage. It had been a great match for him but I supposed that once he was in possession of her titles and fortune he forgot whence they came, as so many do.

It was absurd for me to have fancies about Jemmy, but one can be absurd at times, especially when one has lived the life of a recluse for several years, and then is thrust into a world of fun and gaiety.

Lady Henrietta did not, however, intrude, which meant that Jemmy's attention was all for me. It was amazing that William, who had ever before been watchful of all those who were allowed to visit me, now seemed to give Jemmy and me absolute freedom.

Jemmy liked to dance and so did I. In fact, in my apartments now and then I danced with my women.

Jemmy said there were several new dances now fashionable at Whitehall and he would teach me some of them. William raised no objection and this gave Jemmy and me a chance of some private conversation.

I learned the dances quickly and we sat and talked.

"We have heard reports of what is happening to you here," he told me. "Tell me first, are you happy?"

I could talk to Jemmy frankly. I said, "I am getting accustomed to it."

He grimaced. "My poor little cousin. It was hard in the beginning, I know. You were so frightened. My heart bled for you."

"Thank you, Jemmy. But it happens to many people. That was what they told me. I hated leaving everyone I loved."

"And your husband?"

"I did not understand him at first."

"And you do now?"

"He is a man whom it is not easy to understand."

"I'd agree with that," said Jemmy grimly.

"But I am not really unhappy now. I am alone often but I can read ... and think. I can fill my time."

"It is a strange way to treat a Princess of Orange."

I was silent for a while and then I said, "And you, Jemmy? It must be sad for you."

"To be sent away from my country? Yes it is."

"It is not the first time."

He laughed. "I am in a delicate position, you might say. Mary, you do not believe I was involved in a plot to kill your father and mine?"

"If you tell me you were not, I will believe you."

"I would never harm my father. You know I love him well."

"As we all do."

"It is difficult. The English ... you know ... they will never have a Catholic king on the throne."

"If the rightful heir is a Catholic, they must."

"One does not say 'must' to the people, and particularly the people of England."

"Then what?"

He shrugged his shoulders and was silent.

"And Jemmy," I said, "what of you?"

He said, "I am the King's son. None can doubt. The King himself never has."

"But your mother was not married to the King."

"There are some who say there was a marriage."

"That cannot be true, can it, Jemmy? The King has always denied it."

Jemmy's face hardened. "If there were proof," he said.

"How could there be?"

His hand closed over mine. "In life, dear Mary, one should never shut one's eyes to any possibility."

"Jemmy, if it were so . . ."

"Ah," said Jemmy, "if it were! Now I am going to show you another dance. This was very popular in Whitehall before I left."

"Oh, Jemmy, how I wish all this trouble would be over. I hope the King goes on and on. Then it can stay as it is."

"Yes," said Jemmy. "Long life to him! But it has to come, you know."

He stood up and held out his hands to me. I rose and he led me onto the floor, instructing me in the new dance from Whitehall.

There was trouble with Chudleigh, the English Envoy, with whom William had not been on very good terms since his arrival.

Because of William's past friendship with Sidney and Russell, who had both been proved to be traitors, it was inevitable that Chudleigh should be highly suspicious of William, and as he was not the most tactful of men, he had made this clear.

He was shocked—and I supposed many people were amazed by this—that William should at this time pay such attention to the Duke of Monmouth. The King had been surprised and made his wry comments, but the extraordinary thing was that the Duke should have been made such an honoured guest. Moreover, the Princess of Orange, who had previously spent much of her time in seclusion and was the daughter of one of the intended victims of the Rye House Plot, was giving him the most flattering attention.

I could understand how strange this must appear. I should have liked to have explained that it was my husband who had decreed, or more or less commanded, that I should help to entertain Monmouth and I was merely obeying him. I did not believe Monmouth had seriously meant to kill my father or uncle. He was reckless and could be caught up in people's plots without having any real part in them. I was just excited to be with someone who made me feel merry and able to enjoy life.

There was much that would be difficult for people to understand; and I did not entirely understand it myself.

Eager to perform his new duties with efficiency, horrified that William should be honouring an exile from England, Chudleigh took action.

He gave instructions to the English soldiers under Dutch command that they were not to salute the Duke of Monmouth.

When William heard of this he was furious. He sent for Chudleigh. Several people heard what took place and it was talked of freely, so I was able to hear about it.

William demanded of Chudleigh how he could have the temerity to give orders to the Dutch army.

Sure of himself, Chudleigh retorted, "The Duke of Monmouth, Your Highness, is an exile from England on account of his complicity in a plot to take the lives of the King and the Duke of York. It is a matter of great astonishment to His Majesty's Government, which I serve, that he should be so honoured. I consider it my duty to prevent the Duke's receiving the homage which appears to be given to him, for he is a traitor to my country, which is also his."

William replied, "I would have you know that while you are in this country, you must obey its laws."

"I must remind Your Highness," retorted Chudleigh, "that I am not one of your subjects. I am here to serve *my* country and that is something I shall always do."

William was carrying a cane, which he often did. I believed it was because he sometimes felt a weakness and a need to lean on something. He lifted his cane. It came within a few inches of Chudleigh's face and it was clear that it was his intention to strike him. I imagined the awestruck silence and what the effect would have been if William had carried out such an action.

William apparently restrained himself in time, remembering the courtesy due to the envoy of a friendly country.

Chudleigh said coolly, "If I have Your Highness's permission to retire, I will do so."

And the scene was over.

William must have been fuming with rage.

Chudleigh would certainly report what had happened and I knew that there would be surprise that I could be on such friendly terms with a man who had been sent into exile because he was suspected of being involved in a plot to murder my father.

There was a letter from my father. He was hurt and angered by the treatment of the Duke of Monmouth at the court of The Hague, and by the fact that I had not only partaken in it but with such enthusiasm. He was surprised that I could do so. The Duke of Monmouth was in exile, being suspected of planning to murder the King and himself. It seemed that the Prince of Orange, a kinsman of theirs, was acting as enemy rather than friend.

He went on to say that he knew I did not meddle in these affairs, but I should talk to the Prince and tell him what an effect this was having.

I smiled at this, imagining myself explaining to William. My father clearly did not understand the state of affairs here.

He went on, "Let the Prince flatter himself as he pleases, the Duke of Monmouth will do his best to have a push with him for the crown, if he, the Duke of Monmouth, outlives the King and me."

I put down the letter. Did he really think that Monmouth

or William would wait for his death? My poor, ineffectual
father! How could he so deceive himself?

How little he knew of what was going on around me!

The merry life continued. There was a ball in honour of
Monmouth. This was extraordinary, for William hated balls.
To him they were foolish frivolity and a waste of time. But
he appeared at this one—though he did not stay for long.
He actually danced with me once—something I would have
found hard to believe could ever happen.

I think he was anxious to show himself closely allied to
the Protestant cause, and since Monmouth was an avowed
one, he wanted everyone to know that he was anxious to
see a Protestant ruler on the throne of England, and even if
the people chose the bastard Monmouth, he would accept
him because of his religion.

So, there was William dancing—a little inelegantly it
was true—but still dancing!

As for myself, I wanted to dance all the time. It reminded me of home and what evenings used to be like
there. It was no wonder that Monmouth's stay in Holland
was like a dream to me for ever after.

Of course, it was Jemmy who made it so. He was so full
of energy and fun. We used to walk in the gardens together.
William was aware of this and made no protest, although
previously I had never been able to see people without his
approval. It was such a change and I was like a bird which
has been caged too long and has just regained its freedom.

We laughed a great deal. There was always laughter
where Jemmy was. We talked of the past. We promised that
there should be more such visits. We must repeat these
happy days.

The weather grew very cold. We were, after all, in the
midst of winter. There was ice on the ponds.

"We must skate," said Monmouth.

I had never skated before, I told him.

"Then I shall have to teach you how to skate. It is too
good an opportunity to miss. It is so cold that the ice will

be really hard and you need have no fear, for my arms will be ready to catch you. You will be perfectly safe with me."

What fun it was as we slid along, with the skates buckled to my shoes and my petticoats caught up at the knees.

"One foot, then the other," chanted Jemmy. And we laughed and laughed. I lost my balance and was caught in Jemmy's arms.

We were watched by the people who joined in our mirth. I think they were all pleased to see me enjoying life. It was long since I had been so carefree and happy; and I did not have to feel guilty, for I had William's consent to abandon myself to the fun of the moment.

There was one unpleasant incident, however.

It was carnival time, I heard. I did not know there were such festivities in Holland. I supposed that it would have taken place and I heard nothing about it but for Jemmy's presence.

I believe that on every lake and pond in Holland people in fancy dress and masks took their sledges onto the ice.

William had said that he and I must ride together. Jemmy was, of course, very much in evidence with us.

It was so unusual to see William taking part in such frivolity, but he drove the sledge and with me beside him we skirted over the ice.

The pond was fairly crowded and as we swept along, right in our path, a sledge was coming towards us. In this, masked but obviously himself, was the Envoy Chudleigh. He came along directly before us and, as he must have been aware of our identity, we expected him to draw to one side to allow us to pass. Chudleigh, however, did no such thing, and we were obliged to draw to one side to let him go by.

I saw William's lips tighten, and I heard him whisper under his breath, "I shall endure no more of this insolence. I shall have him recalled."

His anger had not abated when we returned and he immediately sent a letter to England and asked that Chudleigh should return to England.

Chudleigh was not a man meekly to take blame for what he considered to have been correct behaviour. He wrote to England. I heard afterwards that he had explained how he had acted as only a man of breeding could act on such an occasion. He had had the right of way and, presuming the Prince and Princess of Orange did not wish to be recognized, as they were masked, he had not done so. He added that, at the court of The Hague, special privileges were given to those English who were ready to work against their own country and continual complaints were made against those who were loyal to it.

In spite of his protests, Chudleigh was recalled to London and soon after that Bevil Skelton came out as an envoy. I think that, in due course, William certainly wished the change had not taken place and it would have been more convenient for him had he retained Chudleigh.

I shall never forget that February day when the news came to The Hague. Jemmy and I, enjoying the days, had no idea that it was all going to end so soon and in such a way.

I had so enjoyed this pleasant interlude and had refused to remind myself that it could not go on for ever; but I had not expected there would be such an abrupt ending.

There came a message from William. I was to go to him at once for he had news which he wished to impart. In accordance with my usual custom, I obeyed immediately, and as soon as I stood before him I knew by the pulse I saw beating in his forehead and his suppressed excitement that the news for which he had been waiting had come at last.

He said, "King Charles is dead. He died a few days ago. It has taken some time for the news to reach us. He suffered a seizure on the first of the month and it was thought that he might recover, but this is indeed the end."

I felt stunned. We had been waiting for it, but when it came it was a tremendous shock. I should never see again that kind uncle who had always had a smile for me, and I was overcome with sorrow, for with my grief came the realization that now the real trouble must start. My father,

William, Jemmy; this meant so much to them all and they were all seeking the same goal.

I wanted nothing so much then as to be alone.

William sounded grim. He said, "Well, there is a new king of England now. They have accepted your father as James II."

I could see his lips were twitching. He had never believed it could be so. They had forgotten James was a Catholic, and because he was next in line they had taken him as their king. It had been a simple passing of the crown from one king to another.

But all I could think of was that kind uncle who was dead and gone for ever.

I sat alone in my bedchamber. I had not prepared for bed. I knew I should not sleep. My thoughts were at Whitehall, and how I wished I were there.

What would happen now? I asked myself. My father was King. I felt we were on the edge of great events and I was filled with fear.

There was a light tap on my door and Anne Trelawny came in.

She said, "The Duke of Monmouth is here. He says he must speak with you."

"So late . . ." I said in alarm.

"He says it will not wait."

I went through into an antechamber and there was Jemmy, dressed for a journey, looking distraught and very sad.

He took my hands and, drawing me to him, kissed me.

"Mary, my dear, dear Mary, I am leaving."

"Not tonight?"

He nodded. "I have been with William for the last hour or so. He says I must go. I cannot stay here. It was different when my father was there. He loved me, Mary, and I cannot tell you how much I loved him. And now he is gone . . . and there is no one . . ."

"What are you going to do, Jemmy? Where are you going?"

"Away from here. William has given me money. He says he cannot offend the new King by harbouring me here."

"It is all so sad," I said.

"Your father is the King now, Mary. I know that he loves you well. If you could plead with him to let me return . . . write to him . . . tell him I am innocent . . ."

"I will see what I can do. It is not quite the same between us as it used to be. There are differences in religion. That seems to sow so much discord. Jemmy, what is going to happen to you?"

"I do not know. I cannot say. If my father had only lived. While he was there I always knew I had a friend."

"*I* am your friend, Jemmy."

"I know it. I know it well. That is why I ask you this. When the time comes . . . you will plead for me?"

I nodded.

"Not yet. It is too soon. He will have other matters with which to concern himself. But you will do this for me?"

"I will," I said. "I will. But Jemmy, you cannot go tonight."

"I must. William has said I must. But I had to say goodbye to you. I shall let you know what is happening to me, and you will do that for me . . . plead with your father to allow me to come home."

"I will do that, Jemmy."

"Dear Mary, dear little cousin."

"God bless you, Jemmy. I shall pray for you."

We embraced and he was gone.

There were letters from my father—one was for me, telling me of his accession and the last hours of the late King. He had been with him at the end. My father then went on to express his undying affection for me. It was a most tender and moving letter. William received a formal announcement of the accession.

William read the letter which my father had written to

me and kept it. I was amazed when he read it to the Assembly, as though it had been addressed to him.

He was evidently accepting the accession of my father, now that it had happened, without opposition and intended it to be thought that it had never occurred to him that it would be otherwise.

Strangely enough, he showed me the letter he wrote in return. He must have realized that during those weeks when I emerged from solitude and mingled with the members of the court and Jemmy, I had learned something of his hopes and schemes.

It seemed now as if he wished me to believe that he rejoiced in my father's accession.

He assured my father that Monmouth had come to the court as a suppliant and because he was the son of the late King Charles and he knew of the King's affection for the young man, he had offered him common hospitality and had now sent him away. He went on to say that nothing could change his affection for my father and he would be the most unhappy man in the world if the King could not be persuaded of it. He would be, to his last breath, King James's friend with zeal and fidelity.

I was amazed that he could write in such language, which was most unusual to a man of his nature, particularly when I knew his true sentiments towards my father. But William was a man who, when he saw a goal ahead, would let nothing stand in his way of attaining it. I wondered what my father's reaction would be to such a letter. Perhaps I should know one day.

In the meantime I was overcome by a great melancholy. I could not stop thinking of my uncle and how different it would now be at Whitehall. I was anxious, too, about my father. He had been accepted as King, but what was to come?

Then I was wondering what was happening to Jemmy— and missing him very much.

* * *

There was a feeling of anticlimax at The Hague. William was certainly bewildered by what had happened, for he had obviously believed my father would never have been accepted. But there he was, secure—so it seemed—and there was no one to raise a voice against him. He was crowned on St. George's Day by the primate; there were a few ministerial changes but nothing to betray the King's preference for Catholics.

However, on Easter Sunday, he did attend the Catholic service, and I could not help feeling that the calm would not last.

Jemmy was constantly in my thoughts. I knew that he was wandering around the Continent, unable to return home, an exile. William would no longer receive him at The Hague as, since my father had been accepted by the people, his great aim was to assure him of his loyalty to him. So poor Jemmy could hope for little hospitality in Holland. How different he must be finding life from the way it was during those happy days we spent together.

I wrote to my father, as I had promised Jemmy I would, asking him to consider removing the ban of exile. I said I was sure that Monmouth had played no part in the Rye House Plot and he was very unhappy and longed for permission to return home. I reminded my father that he himself knew what it meant to be an outcast from his own country.

My father replied that it would not be fitting for Monmouth to return to England at this time. Later he would consider it.

I could see that he did not trust Jemmy, and however much I pleaded for him, he was not going to give that permission which the poor young man craved.

After leaving The Hague, Jemmy had gone to the Spanish-governed Netherlands in search of sanctuary, but not for long. It was soon made clear to him that he was not welcome.

I could imagine how he would feel, how he would make

plans to get home. I hoped he would not do anything rash. Knowing him so well, I feared he was capable of it.

And how right I was proved to be!

When I heard that he was plotting to make war on my father and to claim the throne, I was desperately unhappy. If only I could have talked to him, I might have succeeded in turning him from this reckless folly, I told myself. But he would never have listened to me. He had his dreams of grandeur and he made himself believe in their glorious fruition. I pictured the excitement in his beautiful eyes as he made his plans.

It is well known what happened to those wild dreams. They had little hope of becoming realities. I pictured his exerting that Stuart charm to beguile men to his side. For he did. He made them forget that his was a hopeless cause.

When I heard that he had landed in the West Country, I trembled for him. My father would know him for the thoughtless boy he was. He must not judge him too harshly, but he would, for Jemmy wanted to take my father's crown from his head and put it on his own. He was declaring that he was the heir to the throne; he was his father's son and a staunch Protestant; the marriage of his father to Lucy Walter would be proved. Did the English want their country to be the pawn of Catholics?

It was frustrating waiting for news. Messengers were coming back and forth and William was tense, waiting. The outcome of Monmouth's rebellion could be of the utmost importance to him. There did at one point seem to be a chance of its succeeding. Monmouth's great asset was his religion.

Anne Trelawny came to me. She was always quick to pick up the news.

She said, "The Duke of Monmouth has been proclaimed King in Taunton marketplace."

"Can he really succeed against my father?" I asked.

She shook her head dubiously. "I should have said no, but this . . ."

Later I heard that Jemmy had put a price on my father's head.

"James is a traitor," he had declared, "and the Parliament is a traitorous convention."

This was too much. I knew in my heart that he could not succeed. And if he did, what of my father? But he could not. The army was against him, and what were a few thousand country yokels against trained soldiers?

I could imagine the euphoria. In the West Country, they were calling him King Monmouth. But when he marched on Bath, no doubt expecting the same acclaim he had received in Taunton, Bath stood against him, and it must have been at that stage when he began to lose heart.

As far as I could, I followed his progress. I knew when he began to fear defeat and then recognized it as a certainty. I suffered with him. I knew him so well.

Poor, poor Jemmy, with his grandiose dreams which had no roots in reality.

And then had come the battle of Sedgemoor and the defeat of his followers, when Jemmy escaped disguising himself as a farm worker. I could smile wryly at such a disguise. He would never play the part; his constant awareness of his own royal birth would always shine through.

Inevitably there followed his capture and his journey to the Tower.

There was only one end for him. He knew it and his courage deserted him. He was very frightened.

I wrote to my father and begged him to be lenient with Jemmy. He was reckless, I agreed, but he was our kinsman. His father had loved him dearly. He had forgiven him again and again. This was just a reckless gesture doomed to failure; Jemmy would have learned his lesson.

My father's reply was that Monmouth was a fool. He would never learn his lessons; he was not to be trusted; and fools could be dangerous. He was a coward; he had pleaded for his life; he, who had stressed his loyalty to the Protestant cause when he was recruiting men from the West Country—and many of them had followed him because of this—now he was vowing he would become a Catholic if his life was spared.

There was no hope. They led him out to the scaffold.

The stories I heard of his end were harrowing. Jemmy's courage had returned when he faced the inevitable. He made a declaration that he was a member of the Church of England, but refused to condemn his rebellion. He held his head high as he mounted the block.

Jack Ketch, the executioner, struck five blows with his axe and still the head was not severed, and he had to cut it off with his knife.

And so died the Duke of Monmouth.

He haunted my dreams. I had loved Jemmy. I kept going over in my mind the wonderful days which we had spent together. I kept imagining him on the scaffold, desperation in his eyes. How different from that young man who had taught me to dance and skate on ice! I pictured Jack Ketch as he wielded the axe and Jemmy's head bowed and bloody on the block. And I felt a sorrow which was replaced by a burning anger. He was too young to die, too handsome, too charming. And I could not bear that I should never see him again.

He had been reckless, foolish; he had believed that he could succeed. He had longed for that crown which could not by right be his. He had yearned for it as a child does for some bauble; and for a brief spell he had thought he held it in his grasp. King Monmouth! The King of those good simple people who had laid down their scythes and pitchforks to follow him to disaster and death.

Now he was dead and my father had allowed this terrible thing to happen. He had refused mercy. Jemmy, that poor frightened boy, had pleaded with him, and he had turned away; and so Jemmy, my dear cousin, Jemmy whom I loved, had suffered cruel death on the scaffold.

In those moments of grief the thought came to me that I could never forget . . . and perhaps never forgive . . . my father for the death of Jemmy.

I kept telling myself that he had acted, as most would say,

wisely. But if he had never openly practised his religion, if he had taken the same action as his brother, the King, this would never have happened, for my uncle Charles had been a Catholic, and some said that Catholic rites had been practised at his death. But Charles had been wise, my father foolish. I had loved Jemmy and my father had killed him. I would never forget and I could not find it in my heart to forgive him.

The Mistress

Bevil Skelton, the new English Envoy to Holland, was not on very good terms with William. They had distrusted each other from the day of Skelton's arrival and the reports Skelton sent home were very critical of William's behaviour.

I did not know at this time that my father, who had been against my marriage with William from the moment it had been proposed, was making plans to dissolve it and to arrange a new marriage for me.

William's treatment of me had caused a good deal of anger in England. And it would not be difficult to find a reason for dissolving the marriage.

This would be the last thing William wanted. I had great value in his eyes, though that would seem hard to believe to anyone who did not know the reason and witnessed his treatment of me.

I had, it was true, written to my father telling him that I was not unhappy. I had found much to interest me in life—above all I had had time to study books on religion.

My father knew what books they would be and that did not please him. I dare say he still saw me as a little girl whom he had cherished all those years ago, and he would believe that, if I could be removed from William, my views could be changed.

I learned later that my father had a plan which was to involve Skelton and my chaplain Dr. Covell. Anne Trelawny and my old nurse Mrs. Langford were to be included because I would listen more to them than to anyone else. I

186

was to be weaned from any allegiance I might feel for William.

When a husband is unfaithful to his wife, it is true that usually others are aware of this before that wife, although she is the one most concerned.

William was so serious, so lacking in frivolity of any sort, that I should never have thought he could be involved in an intrigue with any woman.

When Anne and Mrs. Langford were with me one day, I saw them exchange glances, as though there was some secret between them. It was as though they were waiting for a cue to begin something.

Then Mrs. Langford said, "Your Highness, this is difficult to say and I hope you will not be angry, but . . ."

She hesitated and looked helplessly at Anne, who said, "Her Highness should know. There are many who do. It is not fair that she should be kept in the dark."

"Please tell me what you are trying to say," I said.

Still they hesitated. Mrs. Langford nodded to Anne who said, "The Prince has a mistress. It has been going on for some time."

I stared at her unbelievingly.

"It is so," she said. "It has been kept from you, but Dr. Covell and Mr. Skelton . . . they all believe that you should remain in ignorance no longer."

"This is nonsense . . ." I began.

Anne shook her head and went on, "It has been going on for a long time. It is not right that you should not know. Have you not noticed how insolent the woman is?"

"You mean . . ."

"Elizabeth Villiers, yes."

"But she . . . she squints!"

Anne smiled wryly and shrugged her shoulders. "She is clever . . . full of tricks. It started almost as soon as you came here."

"I do not believe it."

They exchanged helpless glances.

"He visits her almost every night," said Mrs. Langford.

"No!"

"Well," said Anne. "We have done our duty. If Your Highness will not believe us . . ."

"Not of William . . . no."

"It happens to most men."

"He is different."

Anne shook her head. "We thought you should know. We have done our part. If Your Highness will not believe us there is nothing else to be said."

"Well," added Mrs. Langford, "it should not be so difficult to prove it."

"What do you mean?" I asked.

"If you hid yourself on the stairs to her apartments you might see him going to her bedchamber."

Anne added, "If you missed him one night, you would see him the next. He is a frequent visitor."

"You mean . . . spy on him?"

Anne shrugged her shoulders. "It depends on how important you think this is."

"You never liked William," I accused her.

"I am not alone in that. There are many of us who do not like the manner in which he treats you."

I said, "Leave me. I should like to be alone."

They immediately obeyed.

I was bewildered. I could not believe this, and yet there was a certain inevitability about it.

Elizabeth Villiers! She was not the most beautiful of women—even setting aside that squint. She had a strong personality; she was not a woman who would be passed by in a crowd. She had dignity. I was trying to think what he could find attractive in her.

But he had no time for women. He did his "duty" with me now and then but that was for a purpose.

Then suddenly I felt an overwhelming jealousy. He did not want me, yet I was reckoned to be beautiful. I know all princesses are said to be, but I was. True, I was inclined to plumpness, but that was not unattractive. Yet he clearly had little time for me and was going to Elizabeth Villiers. I could not believe it.

Then I remembered the tales I had heard of his youth when, under the influence of drink, he had broken the windows of the maids of honour's apartments in an attempt to reach them. He must have masculine needs, the same as any man, but they could not be satisfied by me so he turned to Elizabeth Villiers.

No! no! no! I said. But a voice within me was jeering at me. Why not? I thought of the position she had made for herself at court. She had become a sort of governess to the maids of honour. People took orders from her. When her sister Anne had married William Bentinck, William had made no protest. I remembered the trouble over Jane Wroth and Zulestein. Of course, the Villiers were a noble family, but Bentinck . . . well, he was William's great friend and the marriage had strengthened the tie between Elizabeth and William.

Desperately I was trying to disbelieve, but as the minutes went by the story seemed more plausible.

Anne came to me again.

She said, "Forgive me. I should not have told you."

"If it is true, I should know."

"But it has wounded you deeply. It is the last thing I should wish."

"I know that, Anne," I said. "You have always been my dear friend. I trust you always will be and it is better for me to know the truth."

She took my hand and kissed it.

"He is with her most nights," she said. "If you watched, you could see him and prove it. Yes, it is better to know the truth, however painful. I have pondered for a long time. But Dr. Covell thinks you should be aware of what is known throughout the court."

"Dr. Covell!"

"He is very angry with the manner in which you have been treated. He has written to your father."

"My father knows . . . about this?"

She was silent.

"Anne," I said, "does my father know about William and Elizabeth Villiers?"

"Yes," she replied.

"I can't believe it. It is lies which have been said about the Prince to harm him in my father's eyes."

"You could see for yourself . . ."

I was decided now. I knew I was going to spy on my husband.

We were in our hiding place. It was a large cupboard on the stairs leading to the chamber which had been assigned to Elizabeth Villiers. It was separate from the quarters of the other ladies. The reason for that was now obvious.

Anne was not sure what time he would come, but she was certain that he would—if not this night, the following one, for he was a very frequent visitor.

I hated what I was doing. It seemed a mean and underhanded act. But I had to know and the only alternative was to ask him. I could not bring myself to do that.

Suddenly Anne caught my hand and I listened. There was the unmistakable sound of footsteps on the stairs—quiet and stealthy. They were close now and when they passed Anne opened the door quietly and very slightly. I saw the back of William as he mounted the stairs, I saw him reach the door of Elizabeth Villiers' bedchamber. He went in.

Anne turned to me in triumph.

"You have proof now," she said.

I did not speak until I had reached my bedchamber. Then I said, "So it is true."

"I am so sorry," said Anne. She put her arm round me. "It is better not to be in ignorance," she added soothingly.

"And people know," I said. "Dr. Covell, Mr. Skelton . . . and my father."

"And many more," said Anne.

"What shall I do?"

"Your father will advise you."

"No. I could not speak of this to him. Perhaps when the Prince knows that I have discovered it . . . he will cease to see her."

Anne looked at me disbelievingly.

"I must think about it," I said.

"Do not brood on it. It happened. Few men are faithful."

"Leave me now, Anne," I said. "I will send for you when I need you."

When she had gone, disbelief descended on me once again. It was not true. Other men were unfaithful. Not William. It was not that I thought he would have any scruples in the matter, but that he would not attach any importance to love, to the charm of women, to physical experiences. And certainly not if it meant creeping up back stairs by night. I knew of the exploits of the late King and my father and most of the courtiers of Whitehall, but I had thought William was apart from all that. And now I had discovered that he was, after all, like the rest. I had formed my opinion of him because *I* did not attract him—and therefore I had imagined that no one else could.

I spent a sleepless night. I thought of them all, discussing my affairs, pitying me, courting Elizabeth Villiers, which I now realized they had done.

How had she attracted him with her lack of feminine grace, with her squinting eyes?

I remembered those supper parties in the maids of honour's apartments. I believed she was his spy as well as his mistress. She would be working for him, extracting opinions from the discontented English at The Hague, passing on information. Those parties had been arranged for that purpose.

I felt sick with the horror of it all.

It was not until the afternoon of the next day that I saw William. He came along to my apartments and when I saw him I was so overcome with anger and emotion that I could not consider my words with care and they came rushing forth unchecked.

I said, "I know now that you have a mistress. I am shocked and amazed. You . . . who have pretended to be so virtuous . . . when all the time you are creeping up the back stairs to Elizabeth Villiers' apartments. Pray do not attempt to deny it. I have watched you. I have seen you."

He held up a hand to stop my outburst, but his expression had changed, his lips had tightened, and an unusual colour had risen to his face.

"What are you saying?" he demanded.

"I should have thought it was clear. You have a mistress. She is Elizabeth Villiers. It is not recent. It has been going on for a long time. That is the reason why she gives herself airs. Anyone would think she were my mistress as well as yours."

"You are hysterical," he said.

"And you are unfaithful. You have posed as a man of great virtue . . . and delicacy . . . without human weaknesses . . ."

"I have posed as no one that I am not," he said. "If you have built up an image of me, that is your doing in your lack of reasoning and your inexperience of the world."

"Do you deny this?" I asked angrily.

"No," he replied.

"So you admit that she is your mistress?"

"These matters are not important to people in our position."

"They are important to me."

"Pray be reasonable."

"And say that I do not care if you creep up to the bedchamber of my women at night?"

"Who told you of this?"

"Does that matter? I know."

"Skelton is behind this. I shall find out. I will not have spies in my court."

"My friends know of this and they do not like the way I am treated."

"You are my wife," he said.

"And you are in love with Elizabeth Villiers."

He made an impatient gesture. "I am surprised," he said, "that, brought up in what is reckoned to be the most licentious court in Europe, you should make an issue of such a matter."

"This concerned myself . . . my husband . . ." I began, and felt the tears in my eyes.

He saw them and came to me and laid a hand on my shoulder.

He smiled. "Mary," he said, "you are a child in many ways. When I saw you I determined to marry you."

"Because of what I could bring you. I know that."

"Listen to me. How do I know what you will bring me?"

"The vision of the three crowns. They will come through me."

"I would not marry a wife I did not like and when I saw you, I said, this is the wife for me. Come, understand. I am not like the men you knew at your uncle's court."

"It would seem you are more like them than I realized."

"This is nothing. These things happen now and then— and far less at The Hague than in most courts. The matter is of no importance. Just an everyday happening . . . nothing more."

"Then you will not see her again? You will send her back to England?"

He frowned. Then he laughed lightly. "Oh, you will see it is not important. One must not make an issue of these things. People get wrong impressions. We must think of our position."

Desperately I wanted to be soothed. He was more gentle than he had ever been. I was filled with a desire to oust Elizabeth Villiers from his affections, and I was already beginning to let myself believe that this affair was nothing. It had been exaggerated. It was a passing fancy. Men did have such things. I must try to be more worldly. I was enjoying his efforts to placate me.

I said, "My father knows . . ."

I saw his face change. "Who told you that?"

I hesitated, not wanting to implicate Anne Trelawny.

I said, "I heard it. He is not pleased about it."

William was thoughtful. Then he put his arm about me.

"I am sorry that I have seen so little of you of late," he said.

"You have been seeing Elizabeth Villiers, of course."

"I have seen very little of anyone save my ministers. But we might go to Dieren for a few days."

I thought: he cares enough to try to make excuses, and I felt a certain satisfaction.

He kissed me gently. "Don't forget," he said. "It was you whom I married. It is you I love."

This was startling. I had not heard him speak of love before. He was trying to take my mind from Elizabeth Villiers, I knew. Hence his expression of something near tenderness. I understood it was due to expediency, but I felt a little mollified.

I continued to be disturbed. William's show of affection had had an effect on me. I found myself going over what he actually said to me. That he had been very uneasy about my discovery, I knew. But the fact that he took the trouble to reassure me lifted my spirits. There had been times when I thought I hated him, but I was not sure. My hatred had been fierce but it was due to the fact that he ignored me. I wanted him to notice me. I wanted to be important to him for myself, not just for the crown I might bring him.

It suddenly occurred to me two days later that, since they had told me of William's infidelity, I had not seen either Anne Trelawny or Mrs. Langford. I sent for Anne. She did not come. It was Anne Villiers—Anne Bentinck now—who came in her place.

"Mistress Trelawny is not here, Your Highness," she said.

"Where is she?" I asked.

"She . . . has left."

"Left? Left for where?"

"For England. Mrs. Langford was with her. Dr. Covell has also gone."

"I do not understand," I said. "How could they have left for England without my knowing?"

"They were sent, Your Highness."

Anne Bentinck looked upset. She had never been so hard as her sister and had softened since her marriage.

"Sent? I do not understand."

"Your Highness, the Prince gave orders that they were to leave without delay. They left last night."

"You mean ... they were sent away?"

"Yes, Your Highness. They were ordered to leave."

"Without telling me? They are my attendants!"

"It was on the Prince's orders."

"Why? Why?"

I knew, of course. It was Anne and Mrs. Langford who had told me that it was Elizabeth Villiers who was the Prince's mistress. And Dr. Covell had been receiving letters from England about the matter. So they had been dismissed. William had done this.

Anne tried to comfort me.

I said piteously, "Anne Trelawny is my greatest friend. She has been with me since we were children."

"I know. But she has offended the Prince. He would say that if they were working against him they were working against his country."

I said, "He knew it was Anne who told me ... what he did not wish me to know."

She nodded. News spread quickly at court. I could imagine the talk. The Princess has discovered that the Prince spends his nights with Elizabeth Villiers.

I wished they had never told me. It would have been better for me to remain in ignorance than lose those I loved best.

I was amazed. Now that I had discovered that William had a mistress and he knew that I was aware of it, I had expected him to give her up. He had said that he loved me; from the moment he had seen me he had determined to marry me, that he would not have done so, even for a crown, if he had not liked me. Naturally I had thought he was asking me to forgive him and forget this infidelity with Elizabeth Villiers, that he had been momentarily tempted and the affair had become more or less a habit which he would now discard.

It was nothing of the sort. He continued to see her; and the position had not changed at all. All that had come out of this was that I had lost my friends—even my dearest Anne who had been with me for so long that she was a part of my life.

I was hurt and bewildered and a sudden wild plan came to me. I acted on the spur of the moment. I am sure if I had given the matter more thought I should never have had the courage to act as I did.

I had seen little of William for the past few days. He had said he was engaged on state matters, but I happened to know he was seeing Elizabeth Villiers. I felt bitterly humiliated.

I had been a fool to be so easily placated and to believe all he told me. I was very angry and when I did not see him my courage always rose. It was when he was present that I was overawed.

He was going to be absent for a few days, away from The Hague, and while he was away he was going to do a little hunting.

When I ascertained that Elizabeth would not be with him, the idea occurred to me.

I did not think it out very clearly. There was no one I could trust now to help me carry it through. If Anne or Mrs. Langford had been with me, it would have been different; I could rely on no one else as I could those two.

William had sent my friends away. There had been no opportunity for me to question his decision. It was done before I was aware that it had happened. Well, I was going to do the same to him. I had been robbed of my greatest friend and I was going to rob him of his.

I sent for Elizabeth Villiers. She had to obey, of course.

She was my maid of honour, even if she was also my husband's mistress.

I was not alone when I called her to me. I was not going to give her a chance to talk insolently of her relationship with William which I felt she might have done if there were no witnesses.

When she arrived, I said, "I have an important duty for you, Elizabeth, and I know you will carry it out with your usual efficiency. That is why I have chosen you to do it. There is a letter which my father must have in his hands with all speed, and I want you to deliver it for me."

She looked at me in astonishment.

I felt strong and brave, my father's daughter, heiress to the throne of England. If ever I attained that crown, I should be very important—more so than William. The Villiers family had always been aware of whom they must please and surely I was one.

I expected William had told Elizabeth that I now knew of their relationship; she might think therefore that this was some sort of revenge on my part. However, she could not disobey me and she could not reach William to get him to release her from this task I was giving her.

She smiled at me but I knew she did not feel in the least like smiling.

I knew her devious mind was trying to find some way of evading what I was suggesting, but I was not going to let her do that.

I said, "I shall send an escort with you to put you onto a packet boat and conduct you to Whitehall. There you will deliver the letter into my father's hands. You must go direct to him. Be prepared to leave tomorrow morning."

I doubt whether she had ever seen me so regal as I could be when I reminded myself of my position; it was only William who overawed me and the thought of him out of reach gave me the courage I needed.

She said tersely, "I shall be ready to leave tomorrow morning."

I was amazed how easy it was and I blamed myself for

being so docile in the past. I only had to remind them by my manner who I was and they showed their deference.

I laughed triumphantly, though I did have a tremour or two when I thought of William's return and his finding that I had dismissed his lover. But for the moment I was safe.

Before the night was out I wrote a letter to my father in which I told him I was sending William's mistress to him with a letter. There was nothing of importance in the letter. I should seal it so that it could not be tampered with. When she arrived I wanted him to keep her there. I told him that William knew I was aware of his liaison with her and I had decided to stop it as he refused to give her up.

I sent off the letter by a messenger I could trust, impressing on him its urgency and that there must be no delay in delivering it to my father's hands and his alone.

The next morning Elizabeth left.

It was only then that I realized the enormity of what I had done, and I waited in trepidation for William's return.

He was away for a few days only. I saw him the day after and, to my amazement, there was no difference in his attitude towards me.

I waited. He would soon discover what had happened, for there would be several who knew that I had sent Elizabeth on an errand to England. I was very nervous, wondering how I could ever have acted so daringly.

A week passed without there being any mention of her. Could it be that he had not yet discovered her absence? In that case, the relationship between them could not have been so strong. Perhaps I had been over-rash, jumped to conclusions.

Another week had gone by and still nothing was said of her departure. None of my ladies mentioned it. Of course, they knew I had sent Elizabeth out of the country. They would understand and they usually knew as much about my affairs as I did myself.

One day Jane Zulestein came to me in a state of some excitement.

She said, "Your Highness, I saw Elizabeth Villiers to-day."

"You saw her?" I cried. "Where?"

"In the palace. She was walking quickly. She had a scarf about her head so that it was not easy to see her face, and she was walking with her head down and hurriedly. She was going into the Bentincks' apartments."

"You must have been mistaken," I said.

"No, Your Highness, I was certain of it."

I was shaken. Bentinck's apartments, I thought. They were next to William's and, of course, Elizabeth's sister Anne was Bentinck's wife. If it were possible that Elizabeth was in Holland, that was one place where she might go.

My father would surely have taken heed of my letter. He was angry about William's treatment of me and, in any case, he would do everything to help me.

For a few days I assured myself that Jane had been mistaken. She must have seen someone who looked like Elizabeth going into the Bentinck apartments.

When a letter from my father arrived, I understood what had happened.

He had been awaiting the arrival of Elizabeth. I could rest assured that, had she come, she would not have been allowed to return. The truth was that she had not come. He had had inquiries made and it transpired that, when she reached Harwich, and as she was stepping off the packet boat with her escort, she stopped and said she had left something behind and must go back to get it. The escort offered to go and retrieve the object but she assured him she must do this herself. She left him and that was the last he saw of her.

Further inquiries had been made and it was discovered that she must have slipped ashore unseen and caught another packet boat back to Holland.

It explained so much. I had been foolish to think I could outwit such a woman.

One of the Villiers sisters had recently married a Monsieur Puisars, son of the Marquis de Thouars, and they were living at The Hague. Elizabeth had stayed with them and from time to time she made visits to the palace to see William.

How clever they were! How devious! And how they must be laughing at my feeble attempts to frustrate them.

What was so strange about the matter was that William never mentioned it to me; and his attitude towards me had changed not at all.

William and Mary

About this time there came to Holland a man who was to have a great influence on me. I had reached a point in my life when I was very uncertain. I longed for a perfect marriage. I admired William in many ways but I had been bitterly hurt by his ill-treatment of me. I did not altogether understand my feelings for him; they were mixed and muddled. For so long in my life I had made an idol of my father. And now that image was crumbling. I was blaming him for the friction between my native and my adopted countries. I was lost in a wilderness. I needed guidance and Gilbert Burnet came along to give it.

Burnet was a brilliant man—a master of Greek and Latin, and a student of civil and feudal law. His father had determined he should have a career in the Church and he went through a course of divinity.

He had had an adventurous life before he came to us and his wide experiences had taught him tolerance.

He was a most unusual man, particularly considering his calling. He was tall, his eyes were brown, his brows thick and almost black; and he was a merry man in spite of his serious dedication.

He was even welcomed by William, because he did not approve of the way life was moving in England, and he regarded William and me as the next monarchs.

My father, he believed, was walking straight into a disaster of his own making; and he thought William and I should be ready when the time came for us to take over. He thought this could not be far off. This man helped to draw

William and me together, and he made me understand William more than I ever had before. And I think he had the same effect on William in regard to me.

Gilbert Burnet had the gift of speaking of serious matters in a jocular way, yet in a manner not lessening their importance.

To my amazement, through my conversations with him, I discovered that I had quite an understanding of theology, for during my time of seclusion, I had read a great deal. Now I could discourse with knowledge and perception on these matters, and this impressed Gilbert. He imparted this to William and I detected a new respect towards me from my husband—almost imperceptible but still there.

My father, of course, was not very pleased that Gilbert Burnet should be at The Hague, and there ensued a long correspondence between us about this.

My father was more eager than ever that I should become a member of the Catholic Church. It seemed almost certain now that I should inherit the throne and he could not bear to think of his successor undoing all that he had done to promote Catholicism in England.

His folly alarmed and exasperated me. I loved him as I ever had and always would, but he seemed to me, in the light of all I was learning from Gilbert Burnet, to be acting like a wayward child.

My letters to him began to surprise me. I had for so long thought of myself as a poor scholar. I had seemed less so when compared with my sister Anne, of course, but even so I had never been erudite. Now I was amazed by the ease with which I could express my feelings in those long letters to my father who, although he did not agree with my views, complimented me on my erudition.

I talked a great deal to Gilbert Burnet. During this time I was missing Anne Trelawny very much. I had been accustomed to talk over my feelings with her, and there was no one else in whom I could confide as I had in Anne. With Gilbert Burnet it was different. Of course, we did not talk gossip as Anne and I had frequently done and it is surprising what can be learned from gossip; but I did find my discussions with Gilbert illuminating and a solace.

He made me understand that the break with Rome which had been the great event of the last century had come about through a king's carnal desires, but it had brought great good to the nation. England must never return to the domination of Rome; and it was clear that it was along that path that my father was trying to lead the country.

Reading between the lines of my father's letters, I could see how wild his dreams were. He did not work towards his goal as William did—quietly, deviously, keeping his secrets; he did not plan with his mind but with his heart. He was fervently religious. I thought of my great grandfather, King Henri IV of France, the Huguenot, who changed his religion for the sake of peace. He must have been rather like my Uncle Charles in more ways than one. "Paris is worth a mass," he said, and for that the people accepted him and his great reign began.

My father was a good man, an honest man; and why should I criticize him for that? I had loved him so dearly, but I could not help deploring what he was doing to his country. Then I would see Jemmy's head . . . that beautiful head which I had loved—bowed and bloody on the block; I could see my cousin as he pleaded with my father who had turned aside and left him to his fate.

My emotions were in turmoil.

It need not have been so, I kept saying to myself. What is a principle compared with the lives of people? I had read of the Spanish Inquisition and the torture and cruelty inflicted in the name of religion. Should we have that in England? No, never!

Gilbert advocated tolerance. He was right.

Meanwhile my father planned for me to be divorced from William that I might marry a Catholic husband. Then he planned that I should come to England and with my Catholic husband reign in that Catholic land which he had created. That should never be.

One day Gilbert came to me in some alarm.

"There is a plot to kidnap the Prince and take him to France," he said. "Let us ask him to come to your apartments without delay. It will be quieter there. I want none to overhear this."

William came. He greeted me with that mild show of affection which he had displayed since the coming of Gilbert, for whom he had a friendly word.

"Gilbert has disturbing news," I told him.

William raised his eyebrows and turned to Gilbert.

"Your Highness," said Gilbert, "is in the habit of riding on the sands at Scheveling for a little exercise in the evening."

"That is so," agreed William.

"You must not do it tomorrow."

"I have arranged to do so. It is a favourite exercise."

"Tomorrow your enemies plan to surround you. They will have a boat waiting to take you to France."

William shrugged his shoulders. "I shall not allow them to do that."

"You will be ill protected and they will be in force. Once they have you out of the country, they will not allow you to come back."

"This is ridiculous," said William. "Of course I shall not allow them to take me. I have work to do."

"And Your Highness must be on hand to do it."

I put my hand on William's arm. "I want you to take the guards with you tomorrow," I said.

He gave me a wry look. He could see the real concern in my face and I think he may have been touched, though he did not show that he was. Was he wondering why I should care what became of him after the way in which he had treated me? Many people would. I saw the corners of his lips turn up slightly.

"I think it is unnecessary," he said.

"You must take the guards with you," I entreated. "Please do."

The expression on his face did not change as he turned to Gilbert and said, "Since my wife wishes it . . ."

Gilbert Burnet smiled and the outcome was that when William went riding on the Scheveling sands he took a bodyguard with him. It was fortunate that he did, for an ambush was lying in wait for him and made off with all speed when it was realized that the plan must have been discovered since he was accompanied by his guards.

Burnet's warning had been timely and so had my request that William should take the guard.

This incident was an indication of my changing relationship with my husband. It also showed how far my father was prepared to go in order to get rid of William and replace him with a husband for me of his choosing.

The plan in itself made me angry. I did not wish to be buffeted from one marriage to another, to suit my father's obsession. I was turning away from him and I could not explain how I felt about William, for I was not sure.

I learned more about what was happening in England and I could see that day by day my father was plunging deeper into disaster. He was determined to make England Catholic and the people were equally determined that he should not. Why could he not see what was happening? It appeared that he was adopting his father's belief in the Divine Right of Kings. Had he forgotten that that had led to his father's death?

Sir Jonathan Trelawny—a kinsman of Anne's—was in conflict with him over the Declaration of Indulgence and was sent to the Tower. Seven bishops were on trial for seditious libel. In the Duchy of Cornwall they were singing:

And shall they scorn Tre Pol and Pen
And shall Trelawny die
Then twenty thousand Cornishmen
Will know the reason why.

These were pointers showing what was to come. Why could my father not see it? I believed he could and refused to. He was meant to be a martyr.

I was beginning to know him from this distance as I never had when I was near him. It was like looking at a painting. One must stand back to see the details clearly. Now, in place of that god-like creature, was a weak man who must fall and take others with him because he would cling to a principle which had no roots in possibility.

He continued to write long letters to me, extolling the virtues of the Catholic faith. He was fanatically eager to carry me along with him.

He knew there was a Jesuit priest at The Hague—a certain Father Morgan—and he thought it would be edifying for me to meet him. He would be able to explain a great deal to me, said my father.

I saw immediately how dangerous this could be. If I were to invite the Jesuit to come to me, it would be commented on. I knew how such news travelled. It would be assumed that I was leaning towards my father's faith.

Did he know this? Perhaps. He would do anything to make a Catholic of me and free me from my marriage so that I might make an alliance with a man of his choosing—an ardent Catholic, of course.

I felt angry with him. I had been forced into marriage in the first place, though I could not blame my father for that. I would make my own decision about my religion. I did not want to be freed from my marriage, though a few years earlier I might have welcomed it. But not now.

My father must know that if I were to see Father Morgan, it would be tantamount to a declaration that I was seriously considering the Catholic faith.

"I certainly would not see him," I wrote.

I had an opportunity of speaking to William about it.

I saw the approval in his face and I felt a certain pleasure because I had won it.

"You are right," he said. "You must not see this man."

"Assuredly I will not," I told him. "I hope there will be no rumours of a possible meeting. I thought I might write to someone of authority in England in case there have been rumours that this meeting might take place. Perhaps a bishop or archbishop to state my adherence to the Church of England."

"Pray do that," said William. "It is right that you should."

Excited by his approbation, I wrote a letter to William Sancroft, the Archbishop of Canterbury, in which I set down my feelings, saying that although I had not had the advantage of meeting him, I wished to make it known to him that I took more interest in what concerned the Church of England than myself, and that it was one of the greatest satisfactions I could have to hear that all the clergy showed themselves to be firm in their religion which made me confident that God would preserve the Church since He had provided it with such able men.

In view of the conflict which had existed between my father and the Church of England, this was clearly saying on whose side I stood: and in view of my position as heir to the throne, it was of great significance.

When I showed the letter to William his smile was so warm that I fancied he looked at me with love. All it meant, of course, was that he no longer feared my defection to my father. I had now placed myself firmly beside William.

One day when Gilbert Burnet was talking to me, he said suddenly, "It is not natural in a man to be subservient to his wife."

I agreed. "It is clear from the scriptures that a woman should obey her husband," I said.

"That is so," went on Gilbert. Then he paused for a while before he went on, "It would seem from events in England that the day of reckoning is not far off."

"What do you think is going to happen?" I asked.

"I think they will not have King James much longer."

"They must not harm him," I said. "Perhaps he will go into a monastery." I paused, thinking of his mistresses. How could he live in a monastery? Where would he go? Exile in France? Wandering from place to place, as he had done in his youth, to the end of his days? As long as they did not harm him ... I thought. To lose his kingdom will be grief enough.

I was melancholy thinking of his fate. Then Gilbert roused me from my gloom.

"There is much dissatisfaction," he said. "It has to be. He must be aware of that. Everywhere it is felt that he cannot go on."

I shivered. Gilbert looked at me intently.

"I trust Your Highness is prepared."

"There has been so much said of it," I replied. "So many implications, I could not be unaware of the possibility of its happening."

"If the King were deposed, Your Highness would be Queen of England—the Prince your consort."

Now I saw where he was leading and I said, "The Prince would be beside me. We should stand together."

"Not equally, Your Highness, unless you made it so."

I was silent and he went on, "I wonder whether the Prince could take such a minor position. He is a man of action—a ruler."

"He has a claim to the throne," I said.

"There are others before him."

"Anne," I said. "Her children."

"It would be in Your Highness's hands. If you were to declare the Prince King ... it would have to come from you ... your consent could elevate him from consort to King. As King he would rule beside you. And as you say, he has some right, but you would be the undoubted Queen by reason of inheritance. You would have to give your word that the Prince should be King and you the Queen, to rule together. Would you be prepared to do this?"

I felt a glow of pleasure. I said, "I would not want to rule without him. I should need him. He is my husband. I should be Queen but of a certainty William should be King."

I could see how pleased Gilbert was and it occurred to

me that he had wanted to say this for some time and was relieved that he had achieved the result he wanted. I guessed, too, that William had prompted him to discover my feelings in the matter.

I guessed that Burnet went straight to William and gave him my answer, for William changed towards me from then.

He was more affable; he talked to me of state matters and even showed some affection.

I was delighted and happier than I had been since the days of Jemmy's visit. I understand now that what had been between us was my greater claim to the throne. Now we were equal and, because he was a man, he believed he had the ascendancy over me.

Strangely enough, I did not resent this; I was so happy because of the change in our relationship.

I heard frequently from my sister at this time. She seemed to be quite contented in her marriage and completely recovered from the loss of Lord Mulgrave. George of Denmark appeared to be a very amiable person; and she had Sarah Churchill, whom she had refused to relinquish, still with her.

Unfortunately Anne had taken a great dislike to our stepmother, which surprised me. The Mary Beatrice I had known had been such a pleasant person, very eager to be on good terms with the family she had inherited. Before I left England I had seen how fond she had grown of our father. She had realized she must accept his infidelities—and did we not all come to that state in time—and she took him for the good-hearted man he was.

What came between Mary Beatrice and Anne I could only guess was this matter of religion—as I feared had been the case with myself and my father.

Mary Beatrice was pregnant. This could be very significant, for if the baby were a boy he would be heir to the throne. I should be displaced, and it seemed certain that an attempt would be made to bring the boy up as a Catholic. It all came back to this perpetual factor.

But Anne was quite fierce in her denunciation. She had always loved gossip and to surround herself in her rather lethargic way with intrigue.

She wrote that "Mrs. Mansell" had gone to Bath and come back looking considerably larger. Mrs. Mansell was the name she had given to the Queen and our father was Mr. Mansell. She had a passion for giving people names. I imagined she felt it gave an anonymity to the information she was about to impart.

I knew and I supposed others did, that she had given names to herself and Sarah Churchill: Mrs. Morely was herself; Mrs. Freeman, Sarah Churchill; and although these two saw each other very frequently indeed, Anne still wrote notes to her dear Mrs. Freeman at every opportunity.

However, I was now told that "Mrs. Mansell" was making a great show of her pregnancy and that she looked very well indeed, although, in the past during such periods, she had looked decidedly wan.

Anne was implying, of course, that our stepmother was not really pregnant, but pretending to be so in order that in due course a baby might appear who was not in fact "a little Mansell" after all.

I think she was enjoying this and I was amazed when I remembered how my father had doted on her—almost as much as he had on me—and he had always tried to make us happy, as best he could, for I must not forget that our marriages were quite out of his hands.

We were, of course, all waiting for the birth of this all-important child, and Anne was not the only one who was suspicious.

Meanwhile Mary Beatrice grew larger.

"She is very big," wrote Anne. "She looks well and I do think the *grossesse* of 'Mansell's wife' is a little suspicious."

She wrote that they had quarrelled recently and "Mansell's wife," in a fit of temper, had thrown a glove into Anne's face. Anne implied that the poor creature must be very anxious and she was wondering how they were going to produce this suppositious child. Anne would make sure that she was present at the birth, to see for herself.

I was sorry for Mary Beatrice. I could imagine how unhappy she must be. She would be worried about my father. Perhaps she could see more clearly where he was going than he could himself.

Again and again I tried to make excuses for him, but I could not get out of my mind those images of Jemmy pleading with him, of Jemmy on the block while they hacked so cruelly at his handsome head. But I still loved my father.

Then the day came and the news was out. The child was a boy. This could change everything. There was an heir to the throne. I had lost my place as successor. What of William? Was he regretting his marriage now?

The child's birth was indeed significant. It was the climax. It was that factor which made the people decide that my father must go.

The rumours were rife. Anne had not been at the birth after all. In spite of Mary Beatrice's *grossesse*, the baby had arrived a month before he was due.

Anne was at Bath taking the waters. Our father had persuaded her to go at that time, although the doctors had not advised it. It seemed that every action of my father and stepmother aroused suspicion. Anne implied that my father had urged her to go because he did not want her to be present at the birth.

Anne wrote; " 'Mrs. Mansell' was brought to bed and in a short time a very pleasant-looking child was brought out of the bed and shown to the people."

There was an absurd story in circulation about a baby's being brought into the bed in a warming-pan to replace the one which my stepmother had born—or it might be that she had had no child at all, and had feigned pregnancy and waited for the healthy baby to be brought in by way of the warming-pan. It was a wildly unlikely story and the fact was that the people did not want to believe that the child was the King's.

They had made up their minds that my father must go.

Anne's letters continued to arrive. They chiefly concerned the baby.

"My dear sister cannot imagine the concern and vexation I have been in that I should have been so unfortunate as to be out of town when the Queen was brought to bed, for I shall never have the satisfaction of knowing whether the child be true or false. It may be our brother, but God knows . . ."

I reread the letter. Could she really believe our father would be guilty of such fraud? I could not, yet I wanted to. I was ashamed, but I wanted it to be right for William—and myself—to have the crown William looked upon as his and had done so all his life because of the midwife's vision. As for myself, I wanted it for him, for if he did not get it his marriage to me would be a perpetual disappointment to him. There was another reason: I was now fully convinced that Catholicism must never come to England. There was only one way to prevent it and that was to take the crown from my father.

Anne had turned against him, for the same reason I imagined. Why did she dislike our stepmother so? I wanted to believe this story of the warming-pan although I knew it must be false.

Anne could never have written so many letters before. I wondered if Sarah Churchill encouraged her to write. I believe that Sarah's husband—who was becoming a power in the army—was William's friend. And Anne continued to write of her doubts about the baby.

"After all, it is possible that it may be her child," she wrote, "but where one believes it, a thousand do not. For my part, I shall ever be one of the unbelievers."

And later she wrote with a certain triumph: "The Prince of Wales has been ill these three or four days and has been so bad that many people say it will not be long before he is an angel in heaven."

I could not stop thinking of my father and stepmother and wondering how much they were aware of what was going on.

More and more people were coming from England to the court of The Hague. They were the miscontents who were waiting for the day when William would sail across the sea to take the crown.

The little Prince did not die. He recovered and there was a great deal of activity; more arrivals, secret discussions and throughout Holland men were busy in the camps and dockyards. It was obvious that great events were about to take place.

I heard then from my father. I think he found it hard to believe that I could ever be with those who worked against him.

He wrote: "All the discourse here is about the preparations which are being made in Holland and what the fleet which is coming out from there plans to do. Time will show. I cannot believe that you are acquainted with the resolution the Prince of Orange has taken and which alarms people here very much. I heard that you have been in Dieren and that the Prince has sent for you to tell you, no doubt, of his coming invasion of this country. I hope it will have been a surprise to you, being sure it is not in your nature to approve of such an unjust undertaking."

I could scarcely bear to read that letter. I kept seeing us together all those years ago. A little child of three or four years, waiting for his coming, being picked up in his arms and set on his shoulder, while he talked to his captains, rather naively asking for compliments to be paid to his wonderful daughter. That was the father I had loved so much. And now here he was . . . surrounded by his enemies.

There were more visitors from England, eager to take part in William's expedition. They brought messages urging him to act. William was believing that, instead of a defending army, he would find a welcome.

The fleet was being made ready. Just off the coast were fifty men-of-war and several hundred transports. The climax was coming nearer and nearer and I could see there was no escape from it. I had hoped that there would be some compromise. Perhaps my father would give up his faith. No, that would never happen. Perhaps he would abdicate. That would be the wise thing to do.

I could not bear to contemplate his being at war with William.

He wrote to me, reproaching me for not writing to him.

"I can only believe you must be embarrassed to write to me now that the unjust design of the Prince of Orange's invading me is so public. Although I know you are a good wife, and ought to be so, for the same reason I must believe that you will be still as good a daughter to a father who has always loved you tenderly, and who has never done the least thing to make you doubt it. I shall say no more and believe you very uneasy for the concern you must have for a husband and father."

I wept over the letter. I have always kept it. I was to read it often in the years to come.

And now the time was near. William was with me the night before he was due to sail. Ever since I had told Gilbert Burnet that if I were Queen of England William should be King and there would be no question of his remaining a mere consort, his manner had changed towards me. He talked with me more seriously; he even discussed plans with me on one occasion. I did not ask about Elizabeth Villiers. I was afraid to do so because I knew he was still her lover. She no longer lived in her sister's house but had returned to court and no reference was ever made to the undelivered letter and the manner in which she had returned to Holland, but I had caught her watching me on one or two occasions, a little superciliously, as though to say: do not try your childish tricks on me again, Madam. Rest assured that I shall find a way to outwit you.

In my heart I knew she would, and I was glad the matter was ignored; but I was deeply jealous of her. If she had been beautiful, I could have understood it, but she was a mystery to me—as William was.

It did occur to me that I might have said, give up Elizabeth Villiers and I will make you King of England. Continue with her and remain my consort.

I wondered what his response would have been. I could imagine his cold eyes assessing me, but I could not bargain in such a way.

I had to give freely and for that he was undoubtedly grateful. It had brought him closer to me than any bargaining would have done.

He was really affectionate that night before he embarked for England. We supped together and retired early. He was to leave next day for the Palace of Hounslaerdyke and then go on to Brill where he would embark.

He spoke to me very gravely and with more feeling than he had ever shown before.

He said, "I hope that there will be little opposition when I land. I have been sent invitations to come from all sides. It is clear that the people of England have decided they will not continue with the King. He has shown his intentions too clearly. But, of course, there will be some who stand beside him."

"You mean there will be fighting."

"It is possible. It may be God's will. How can one be sure? And if I should not return, it will be imperative that you marry again."

"You *will* succeed," I said hastily. "I am sure of it. Have you forgotten Mrs. Tanner's vision?"

"I firmly believe that what she saw was heaven-sent. All through my life I have believed that. It has been long in coming, but now it is at hand. I shall come through. I shall be triumphant. But this is in the hands of God and his ways are mysterious. I said if I should not return it is your duty to marry without delay. You know full well that your father will do all in his power to marry you to a papist. That would be disastrous. You must marry a Protestant."

I turned away. It distressed me that he could discuss my marriage to someone else so dispassionately.

He went on talking of what my duties would be in that calm way of his until I could endure no more.

I said, "You must succeed. I will not think otherwise. I do not want to marry anyone else. You are my husband. It is destined that you and I shall rule together."

To my surprise he softened. I think he was a little surprised that I could be so genuinely devoted to him. Indeed, I was myself surprised, but when I contemplated the danger which he was about to face, and the possibility of his never coming back, and the insistence that there would be on my marrying again, I realized the extent to which I was bound to him.

I knew that I wanted to be with him, that my place was beside him.

While William was gratified by my devotion, he could not have forgotten my moments of rebellion. He would remember the grief of the child bride who had begged to be released from her marriage, the woman who had dared to send Elizabeth Villiers to England with a letter for the King. Then he would also remember that unconditionally I had agreed that he should be King of England and not merely my consort. This would indeed seem a triumph—almost as great as victory over the King.

Indeed, he was grateful and never before had he been so like a lover as he was that night.

The next day we left together, for I insisted on accompanying him to watch him embark.

I had bidden him farewell and watched him as he went aboard. I felt a terrible sense of foreboding and could not stop thinking of my father. I tried to convince myself that William would return. I was determined to believe Mrs. Tanner's prophecy. The three crowns must be William's. But what of my father, my poor ineffectual father? I remembered hearing that my uncle Charles had once said to him: "James will not last more than three years after I have gone. The people will never get rid of me, for if they did, it would mean having James—and so I am safe."

Another prophecy!

"Oh, God," I prayed, "spare him. Let him go away quietly. Let him live in peace with his faith."

William and my father. The triumph of one would be the humiliation and defeat of the other. And I must watch this happen to the two men who had been the most important in my life.

William embarked at Brill on the twenty-ninth day of October—not the best time of the year to cross the treacherous Channel. It was the season of gales and it was not surprising that as the fleet moved away from the coast it was caught up in one.

The wind increased. I was panic-stricken. I kept thinking of William's words. Had he a premonition? Then I heard that several of the ships had been damaged and the remains of the fleet was returning to port.

We heard news from England. The Dutch fleet had been destroyed. And where was William?

It transpired that these reports had been grossly exaggerated and I was overjoyed to receive a letter from William. He had been forced to return to Holland and had landed at Helvoetsluys. He said that he would leave again as soon as possible. The damage to the ships had not been as great as had at first been feared and they could be speedily repaired. He would see me before he sailed again.

Meanwhile my anxiety had affected me deeply and I had become quite ill. I could not sleep and was feverish. I hastily summoned a doctor who bled me.

They thought the relief of knowing that William was safe, and that I should see him soon, would help my recovery and I determined to be well enough to make the journey to Brill.

I arrived there on the tenth of November. The weather was dark and gloomy. William was ready to leave Helvoetsluys where he was to embark.

I heard that the road was bad and the weather uncertain, so I waited at Brill, fearing he might not be able to reach me.

With what joy I beheld him! He said his stay would be brief, but he had promised me that he would come to me before he sailed and he had been determined to do so.

I embraced him, weeping, and for once he did not seem impatient. He talked of the coming invasion.

"I do not know what my reception will be," he said. "They have now had time to prepare themselves. They will rejoice over our disaster in the storm. They have circulated rumours that our fleet has been destroyed. But by God's will we shall soon have a different tale to tell."

How quickly those two hours we spent together passed. Afterwards I tried to remember every word we had said, every look which had passed between us.

It was natural that William's mind should be on the great project which lay ahead and I was grateful that he had kept his promise to come back and see me.

Later that day I set out for The Hague, and in spite of the weather the people came out to cheer me as I rode along.

There I spent the next days waiting for news. When it came I could scarcely believe it to be true.

William had arrived safely and landed at Torbay. It was the fifth of November, an important anniversary—that of our wedding. I wondered if William remembered, but I expected his mind would be too engrossed in other matters. There was another anniversary to be remembered on that day. At home we had always celebrated the discovery of the Gunpowder Plot. Significant dates, and this would be another.

There were none to prevent William's landing. He was welcomed by the Courtneys, one of the most important families in Devon, and given lodgings at their mansion.

Nothing happened for a few days and I was afraid that we might have been lulled into a sense of security and that the English army might suddenly appear.

It was never quite clear to me what happened at that time. Everything was so uncertain. There were many who deserted my father. He had been a great commander when he was young. He might have been so again. But I could imagine how disheartened he must have been, how saddened by the defection of those whom he thought were his friends.

I believe what would have hurt him most was Anne's siding with his enemies. It hurt me, though I had done the same. But I was married to William. Need Anne have been so cruel?

Churchill deserted and came to join William, and Anne left London with Sarah Churchill.

So his two daughters, whom he had loved dearly, had deserted him when he most needed their support.

How much more disturbing it is to be away from the scene of action, desperately wondering what is happening, than to be in the midst of it. The imaginary disasters are often more alarming than the actuality. Reports were coming from England. The Dutch fleet had been wrecked, the Dutch army defeated, the Prince of Orange was a prisoner in the Tower. The Dutch had been victorious. The Prince had slain the King. Which was true? I asked myself. How could I know?

The strain was almost unbearable.

Constantly I thought of my father. What was he doing? How was he feeling? And William? What if those two came face-to-face?

When I prayed for William's success, I could see my father's reproachful eyes.

"Please God," I prayed, "watch over him. Let him get quietly away where he can be safe and devote himself to his faith."

At this time Anne Bentinck became very ill. She had been ailing for some time but now her malady had taken a turn for the worse.

Much as I distrusted the Villiers family, I had formed a friendship with Anne. I knew that she was her sister's confidante and that, since she had married Bentinck, she had enjoyed a closer relationship with William. That was inevitable, for William had used Bentinck's apartments as though they were his own and Bentinck was more often with William than with his own family. I liked Anne and although I could not altogether trust a Villiers I did respect her, and was very sorry to see her so ill.

When I went to see her I was horrified by the change in her.

The doctors had visited her, she told me.

"They will soon make you well," I said.

Anne shook her head slowly. "No, Your Highness, I think this is the end."

I was astounded. Anne was young. She had her life before her. The Bentinck marriage had been a happy one. It shocked me to hear her talk of dying.

"You are feeling sad. This is a sad time for all of us."

"It is indeed. I wonder what is happening. I wish we could have some news."

"You shall hear it as soon as it comes," I promised her, and she thanked me.

I stayed with her for a while. To be with people gave me a respite from my continual imaginings of what was happening. I said I would call on her again and I added prayers for her recovery to those I said every day.

There was still no news. I heard that Anne's condition had worsened and went again to see her.

She looked pleased and grateful for my coming.

"It will not be long now," she said, and I had to put my ear close to her lips to hear her.

"My lady . . . we . . . we have not always been to you as we should. You have been a good mistress to us. My sister and I . . ."

"Do not fret," I said. "The doctors will be here soon. They will do something."

She shook her head. "No . . . Forgive . . ."

"There is nothing for which I have to forgive you," I said.

"Yes," she answered. "My husband is with the Prince . . . always with the Prince . . ."

"It was a great friendship between them. Your husband

would have given his life for him. The Prince never forgets that."

She smiled. "The Prince must be served."

"There is great friendship between them."

"The Prince demands much from those who love him. My husband . . . he is like a slave to his master. He has little time for aught else. He is only allowed his freedom when the Prince is otherwise engaged. He is always expected to be there . . . on the spot. It is the way of the Prince."

This long speech seemed to have exhausted her and she was silent for a while.

Then she went on: "My lady . . . my children . . . when I am gone . . . you will look to them?"

I said I would.

"They are young yet. If you could . . ."

"I will see that all is well," I assured her. "You should not worry. Your husband will care for them. He is a good man. Anne, you were lucky . . ."

She nodded, smiling.

"Your promise," she said. "Your forgiveness . . ."

"I give my promise," I told her, "and forgive whatever there is to forgive."

She smiled and her lips moved, but I could hear nothing.

I stayed with her, thinking of the day I had left England, a poor frightened child, in the company of the Villiers whom I did not much like.

There was not much time left for Anne. I was at her bedside with Lady Inchiquin and Madame Puisars and Elizabeth Villiers when she passed away.

We sat on either side of the bed, my husband's mistress and I. Elizabeth was deeply affected by Anne's death. They had been closer than any of the others and I was sure that they had shared confidences about Elizabeth's relationship with William.

Was that what Anne had meant when she had asked for forgiveness? Death is a very solemn state. I could not feel the same anger in the presence of my rival on this occasion as I should on any other. She was suffering the loss of her beloved sister and I could only feel sorrow for her.

It was still difficult to get news. So far I understood that there had been no fighting and I was thankful for that; but I could not understand why this should be, grateful as I was for it.

My father's first thoughts had been for his family. Mary Beatrice and the baby had been sent away to safety. I heard they were in France. Anne was still in hiding with Sarah Churchill.

Thoughts of my father filled my mind but all the time I reminded myself that he had brought this on himself and but for him it need never have happened.

If my uncle Charles could see what was happening he would smile that sardonic smile of his and say "I was right. It happened as I said it would. Poor foolish sentimental James. This is no way to rule a country, brother."

It was heart-breaking. Sometimes I thought it was more than I could bear.

Before December was out I heard that my father was in France. Deserted by his friends, his army depleted, there had been no alternative. But for one thing I was thankful. There had been little loss of life and scarcely any bloodshed.

And then . . . William was at St. James's. It seemed that the enterprise, so long talked of, planned with such care, undertaken with such trepidation, was over and more successful than we had hoped in our most optimistic dreams.

Despatches came from William. They were not brought to me and I was bitterly hurt. There was no word to me personally from William. No tender display of affection. After our last meeting, I had told myself, there was a change in our relationship.

I understood later that he could not suppress his resentment of me. Although he had changed since Gilbert Burnet had told him that I would not stand in the way of his becoming king, now that he was in England, he heard the views of some of the ministers there and the question was raised again. I was the heiress to the throne, they pointed out, and because he was my husband, he was not king in his own right. So, the old resentment was back. William could not endure taking second place to a woman. That which he craved beyond all things, he was told, belonged to his wife and his power depended on her goodwill. So he sent official documents to Holland and no communication to me.

To understand is to forgive, they say. If one has tender feelings towards another, one makes excuses. I wished I had understood then. I need not have felt so wounded, but I told myself that what I had thought of as William's tenderness for me was transient. He had been carried along by the poignancy of the occasion and the possibility that that meeting might be our last on earth.

I heard how William had made his entry into London and thousands had come out to see him. I could visualize their disappointment. I remembered when he had come to London on a previous occasion and how sombre he had seemed beside the King and his friends. William would have no smiles for the people. He did not look like a king. The people were silent. There were no cheers for the dour-looking Dutchman. What had he to recommend him, except that he was a Protestant and the husband of their new Queen Mary? Where was Queen Mary? She should be the one who was riding the streets.

Bentinck, mourning the death of his wife, but first of all slave to William, tried, so I heard, to remonstrate with William, to which William had replied that it had been hinted to him that he was but the consort of Queen Mary and he was not the sort of man to play gentleman usher to his wife.

These little scraps of information came to me gradually and I knew that this was what had affected William's conduct towards me more than anything else.

William Herbert, Duke of Powis, held a meeting of ministers in his bedroom because he was suffering from the gout and unable to leave his bed. Bentinck had been allowed to join them on behalf of his master, and reported what had happened.

Bentinck put forward the view which he had been sent there to state, that the best plan would be for the Prince to be crowned King and myself take the rank, not of Queen Regent, but Queen Consort.

At that, Herbert, infuriated by the suggestion, forgetting his gout, leaped out of bed, seized his sword which he kept close by and, brandishing it, cried that if the Prince of Orange treated his wife so, he would never draw a sword for him again. After that display, he sank back on his bed in acute pain.

Bentinck said that when the Prince heard this he was overcome with melancholy.

He had turned to Bentinck and said, "You see how the people think? I am tired of these English. I shall go back to Holland and leave their crown to whoever can catch it."

After that William scarcely emerged from St. James's Palace. Ministers called on him constantly: he listened to what they said but rarely made any comment.

It was not surprising that they wondered what kind of a man they had brought to England.

And as he had intended, when he considered the time was ripe, and they were growing uneasy, he asked the Marquis of Halifax and the Earls of Shrewsbury and Danby, whom he believed to be his friends, to come to him, and he explained the reasons for his serious deliberations.

"The English plan to set Queen Mary on the throne and wish me to reign by her courtesy. I must make it clear to you that no man could esteem a woman more than I esteem my wife, but I am so made that I could not hold power by apron strings."

The three men looked at him in consternation. Then Danby said he understood his dilemma but, in view of the fact that Queen Mary was the rightful Queen, they could see nothing else that was acceptable.

William then told them that Dr. Burnet had discussed the

matter with me and would be prepared to tell them what had taken place at that interview.

As a result of this, Dr. Burnet was sent for and he gave an account of our talk together when I had most emphatically said that I believed a wife should be obedient to her husband and would be ready to resign sovereignty to William.

Lord Danby's reply was that it would be necessary to have my confirmation of this and no steps could be taken until this was in the hands of Parliament.

As a result I received a communication from Lord Danby stating the case with a request that I should let him know my decision with as little delay as possible.

I immediately wrote back that, as the Prince's wife, I was never meant to be other than in subjection to him and I should feel no gratitude to anyone who would seek to set up an interest dividing me from my husband.

That satisfied them.

The Lords and Commons were assembled and it was agreed that the Prince of Orange should be offered the three crowns of England, Ireland, and France. Scotland, of course, was a separate kingdom and the title of France was a relic from the past. However, the three crowns were William's now. I was to be offered a joint sovereignty and royal acts would be signed in both our names, but the executive power was William's. Any children we should have would be heirs to the throne and if we failed to have them the succession would go to the Princess Anne and her children.

William had achieved what he had always wanted.

While this was happening Christmas had come and passed and we were nearly at the end of January. Then news came from William. I was to leave Holland and come back to England. We were to be crowned King and Queen and the reign of William and Mary was about to begin.

The Queen of England

Coronation

The wind was behind us as we left Brill and our journey was swift. I was feeling very emotional and my thoughts were of my father, but I warned myself that I must stand whole-heartedly behind my husband, and that, but for my father's folly, he might not now be in exile with his sorrowing queen.

I must smile, be merry, pretend to rejoice. William was safe, his mission accomplished, his dream come true. The three crowns were his and I was to share them.

I watched the approach of my native island and thought of that terrified and tearful child who had left it in such misery. I was still young—not yet twenty-seven. I had survived those first years of marriage and had learned to accept what cannot be changed, which I suppose is one of the most important lessons of life.

I was Queen of England, but it was an honour which I wished had not come to me in this way.

Among the women surrounding me was Elizabeth Villiers. I had never felt at ease in her company and now she filled me with apprehension. I was jealous of her. She was an enigma to me, as William himself was. They were two strange people. Perhaps that was why they were attracted to each other. I could believe she had witch-like qualities. Unprepossessing as she was, wherein lay her power to enslave him as she did? He had been her lover for years. Wherein lay this strange fascination?

She was without doubt extremely clever. She understood state affairs; she spied for him, carried information to him

... and William was capable of devotion, as I had seen with Bentinck. These two were the ones he loved. Bentinck had saved his life and I could understand that. But there were many beautiful women at court. Why had he chosen Elizabeth?

My efforts to be rid of her had failed: she had outwitted me, as I fancied she always would. And here she was, on her way to England because William would never give her up.

There was a crowd of distinguished people waiting for us at Gravesend. I had dressed with care for the occasion because I knew all eyes would be on me, and I must stand up and face the scrutiny. I must show them that I stood beside my husband in all things, and I was happy because he was here to rule over them with wisdom and strength. I must not let them see how sad I was because, to do my duty towards them, my husband must destroy my father.

I was wearing an orange-coloured velvet skirt and my page stood by holding my coat of the same coloured velvet. My pearl-decorated bodice was low cut and there were pearls and orange ribbons in my hair.

I walked to the richly caparisoned horse which was waiting for me and mounted the purple velvet saddle.

The people cheered me as I rode with my entourage to Greenwich Palace.

There I was greeted by my sister Anne, and I could not restrain my joy on seeing her. We discarded all ceremony and clung together in rapturous joy.

"I have missed you, sister," I said.

"I am so happy that you have come home," replied Anne.

She was eager to present her husband to me. I could see at once that she was happy in her marriage and that she and George of Denmark were suited to each other. He had an open face and the reports I had heard of him appeared to be true. He was good-looking, good-natured, and easygoing. My father had said he was no conversationalist and was given to repeating certain phrases at intervals, which could be rather irritating. *"Est-il possible?"* was a favourite one. In fact, my father had named him *"Est-il possible."*

It was clear that George of Denmark had made little impression on the court. I was prepared to like him, for he had obviously won Anne's affection, and she his; and it was good to see how happy they were together.

I talked a great deal to Anne while she listened. I had forgotten how fat she was. I, myself, had put on a certain amount of flesh. We were like our mother in that respect. But beside Anne I looked almost slender. Moreover, she was pregnant.

We were all going to Whitehall together and the royal barge was waiting to take us.

As I stepped into it I experienced another pang of conscience. This was now my barge . . . the royal barge, but a short time ago it had been my father's. I braced myself. I must stop these foolish thoughts. The old refrain kept hammering in my mind. It need never have happened. It was his fault.

He could not really have wanted to rule. If he had, he would never have thrown his crown away. He would go to some quiet retreat where he could practise his religion in peace. That was what he wanted.

I must rejoice. William had succeeded and I had come home.

The people cheered as we sailed along the river to Whitehall.

I ascended Whitehall Stairs and walked into the palace. How familiar it was! How memories flooded back! I was smiling brightly. I must show no emotion but pleasure, for I was being closely watched. So I exclaimed with delight as I walked through those familiar rooms. Anne was beside me, smiling.

"You are home now, sister," she said.

"And happy to be here."

I was aware then of Sarah Churchill. She had never been one to hide her feelings, and there was a look of cold criticism in her eyes.

How dare she! I thought. She was thinking how heartless I was. She knew how much my father had cared for me, and here I was, exulting in taking his possessions which were now mine because my husband, with me at his side, had turned my father from his throne.

It was she who had persuaded my sister to desert him! Her husband had led the army to revolt against him! And Sarah Churchill could stand by with that look of condemnation in her eyes!

I hated Sarah Churchill. She might have domination over my sister, but she would have to remember that I was Queen of England.

So I took possession of the royal apartments. I remembered going to see Mary Beatrice there. I recalled her kindness to the poor frightened child who was to be married and sent away from home. Poor Mary Beatrice, how was she faring now? I thought of her with her little baby—the Warming-pan Baby, as malicious people called him—and her futile husband. What was she thinking now? She had loved and trusted her "dear Lemon" who was now flaunting orange petticoats and had come in to take possession of her apartments.

Now that I was installed at Whitehall, William came to see me. It was the first time we had met since we had said goodbye in Holland. He looked tired and strained, and stooped more than I remembered. But it was always like that when I saw him after an absence. I think in my imagination I changed my image of him—making him taller, straighter, more amiable.

After our last parting I expected more tenderness from him, but he seemed to have reverted to the man he had been. I was hurt and disappointed.

It occurred to me, in one of those flashes of disloyalty which I had known in the past, that he wanted me to come to Whitehall before he did because, unsure of the people's reaction, I should be the one to take possession of it.

Nonsense, I told myself. This was the natural way; and yet I had hoped that he would be at Gravesend to meet me.

I wanted to tell him how pleased I was to see him and for him to say the same to me. He did nothing of the sort. He merely kissed me coolly.

I said, "William, you are well? Your cough?"

It was tactless. He hated references to his weaknesses. He said, "I am well."

"You do not ask how I am?" I said a trifle archly.

"I can see that you are in good health," he replied.

"It has been such an anxious time."

"It was what we expected."

"And now you have succeeded, all is well."

"We cannot yet say that all is well."

"But the people want us, William. They know that you will rule them well."

"They were not so eager. They wanted to make you the Queen and me . . ." He shrugged his shoulders in disgust.

"I know. But I made my wishes clear, did I not?"

He nodded. "The sooner we have their Bill of Rights and are proclaimed King and Queen the better. I want to get out of this city. It oppresses me. I believe there is a fine palace at Hampton."

"Hampton Court. Yes, I remember it well."

"As soon as this matter is settled, I shall leave for Hampton, and if it is all I heard—and the situation, I know, is away from the city—we shall take up residence there."

The ceremony took place on the next day. It was Ash Wednesday—not perhaps the best day for such an occasion, but William was anxious that there should be no delay— and with him I went to the Banqueting Hall in the Palace of Whitehall where we were proclaimed King William and Queen Mary.

There was rejoicing in the streets. People put lighted candles in their windows and bonfires were lighted before the doors of the houses. Some of the bonfires were very big and I was told that that was a good sign, for the size of the fire was an indication of the owners' loyalty to the crown.

I had a feeling that night that the people wanted us. Wil-

liam might be austere, as unlike King Charles as a man
could be, but he had a reputation for wisdom: he was a
Protestant—the most important reason of all—and I was his
loyal wife, even if I had betrayed my father to support him.

The new reign had begun; the country was at peace, and
we should go on from there.

William was eager to get on with ruling the country and es-
tablishing the Protestant faith throughout the land. He was
impatient of all the pomp and ceremonies that were thrust
upon him. I was beginning to understand that this was because he had not the physical stamina to endure them. He
grew very tired standing. I knew that his bones ached and
his body was too frail to endure that which affected those
around him not at all. William's mind was active, shrewd,
brilliant, but his body was frail.

I made excuses for his behaviour. His terseness bordered
on rudeness, but it was due to pain and discomfort. I
wished that I could explain to these people but, of course,
that would be the last thing he wished.

Now that I had grown buxom, and I was in fact slightly
taller than he was, his meagre stature was emphasized when
he stood beside me; and my healthy looks accentuated his
pallor and fragility.

He was often morose and rather graceless, which did not
endear him to the people, and wherever we went together
there were cries of "Long live Queen Mary" while King
William scarcely received a mention.

He was deeply aware of this. He complained bitterly of
the London air. It had improved considerably since the
Plague and the Great Fire and the coming of the wide new
streets and new buildings of Sir Christopher Wren, but William found it stifling, malodorous, and not good for his
health.

He had liked Hampton Court from the moment he saw it.
The river and the open country reminded him of Holland
and one of his great interests—as with my uncle Charles—
was architecture.

Bentinck was anxious; he must have wondered what effect William's demeanour would have on his new subjects. They had been accustomed to a colourful court. I remember how they used to see King Charles sauntering in the park with one of his mistresses on his arm, surrounded by witty courtiers, and how the King's remarks were commented on and passed round for all to enjoy. And this new king, whom they had invited to their shores to restore the Protestant faith, was small, without charm, without grace. It was a great price to pay for ridding the country of the Catholics.

However, it was said that he was a clever man and it was early yet; and William did make Bentinck realize that his health would not permit him too public a life. For that reason, Hampton seemed just what was needed, for it was not too far from London and ministers could easily travel there. The air suited William, and he could make the place his headquarters, for a time at least.

He was very critical of the old Tudor palace and soon decided he was going to demolish the main apartments and rebuild them.

The gardens were unattractive and he made plans for these which he allowed me to share.

We spent some time—when he could spare it from state duties—looking at plans, and I was delighted to be able to join in this and even offer suggestions which, on some occasions, were considered. I found a great interest in the gardens, on which work was started immediately, and they were laid out in the Dutch style.

But of course our main occupation must be with the coming coronation, for William said that a king and queen were not accepted by the people as such until they had been crowned.

Therefore it was important that there should be no delay in performing that ceremony.

The coronation was fixed for early April—the eleventh in fact—but it was not going to run as smoothly as we had hoped. In the first place, Archbishop Sancroft, whom we should have expected to officiate, declined to do so.

He declared that he had taken an oath of allegiance to King James II and in no way could he break that oath. Four of those bishops who had been sent to the Tower by James took the same view as Sancroft, even though my father had been no friend to them, and their imprisonment, as much as the birth of the young Prince, had been the final blow which had unseated the King.

William was more silent than ever. He did not like the English and their ways. He had longed for the crown; he had been invited to take it; and now they were making him as uncomfortable as they could.

In due course Compton, Bishop of London, agreed to perform the ceremony in place of the Archbishop of Canterbury; but I think incidents such as this made us feel very uneasy from the beginning.

We were dressed and ready to set out for Westminster Hall when the messenger arrived.

William came unceremoniously into my chamber. He looked paler than usual and very agitated. He was waving a paper he held in his hand.

"What has happened?" I cried in alarm.

William looked at me blankly for a moment. Then he said, "James has landed in Ireland."

My first words were, "Is he safe?"

William looked impatient. He went on, "He has taken possession of the island and has been welcomed by the Irish. Only Londonderry and one or two other smaller towns are holding out against him."

I stared aghast. "What does this mean?" I asked.

"That he will rally forces against us. This is not the end."

I felt sick. Such news, to come at such a time! It seemed significant that this should happen now, when I stood there in my coronation robes, preparing to receive the crown which was his.

"What must we do?" I murmured.

William said tersely, "We must get those crowns on our heads without delay and then we will consider."

He left me and no sooner had he gone than a messenger arrived with a letter for me. I felt faint as I saw that the writing was my father's.

I took the letter, sat down, and began to read. The words danced before my eyes. I wanted to tear off those robes, throw myself on my bed, and weep.

He wrote that hitherto he had made all fatherly excuses for what I had done, and had wholly attributed my part in the revolution to obedience to my husband, but the act of being crowned was in my power, and if I were crowned while he and the Prince of Wales were living, the curse of an outraged father would light upon me as well as that of God, who had commanded duty to parents.

I reread the words and then put my hands over my eyes to shut them out.

I could not move. I could only picture my father's face when he wrote those words.

How could I do this? He was right. It was betrayal. If I were crowned Queen I should be thinking all the time of my father who had loved me so dearly and whom I was betraying by this ceremony.

I sat there with the paper in my hand. William must have heard something had happened, for he came to my chamber. He saw me sitting there and took the letter from my hand. His face grew pale when he read it.

"To send this at such a time!" he murmured. Then, briskly, "Come. The time is passing."

"You have read what he says?"

William lifted his shoulders wearily. "Of a certainty he does not want the coronation to proceed."

"It is right . . . what he says to me."

"The people do not want him," said William firmly. "He does not please them. They have chosen us."

"I cannot . . ."

"You will," he said, looking at me coolly.

"I shall never forgive myself . . . never forget."

I put my hands over my face. He must have thought I
was about to weep, for he said sharply, "Control yourself.
They are waiting for us. You cannot refuse now. You have
given me your word. The people are expecting you."

"My father . . ."

"Your father is a defeated old man. He has gone to Ireland and at this time that is . . . inconvenient. But this day
you are going to be crowned."

"You, William, but . . ."

I saw the contemptuous smile curve his lips.

"What folly," he said, and there were angry lights in his
eyes. I understood my presence was necessary. The people
would not accept him without me.

I was bitterly hurt, deeply wounded and I felt angry with
myself . . . with my father and with William.

I lost my fear of my husband at that moment.

I cried, "You should not have let him go as you did. The
fault is yours. If he regains his authority, you will be to
blame."

I was aghast that I could have spoken so to William, but
surprisingly he was not angry. He looked rather pleased.

He nodded, as though agreeing with me.

"Yes," he said, "he should never have been allowed to
get away." He put an arm round me. "Never fear. We shall
know how to act. It is very important that we should be accepted as King and Queen without delay. Come, we are late
already."

Dressed in my robes lined with ermine, I was carried in my
chair across Palace Yard to Westminster Hall, and there the
people assembled were asked whether they would accept
William and me as their King and Queen. I fancied there
was a pause, but that may have been due to my state of uncertainty.

The acclamation came as was expected and there was
none to say the crown should not be ours.

The ceremony proceeded and I noticed that there were
fewer people there than had been expected. It would prob-

ably be due to the news from Ireland, and there might be some who did not want to show themselves joining in our coronation in case our reign should be a short one, and in that event it would be wise not to be associated with it.

The news of my father's arrival in Ireland would have spread and people would be saying there was something significant about its arriving on the day of the coronation. I sensed the uneasiness in the air.

We were nervous throughout the proceedings, and when the moment came at the altar to make our offering of gold pieces, neither William nor I had the money with us to do so. There was a long pause when the gold basin into which the coins should be put was handed to us. I was aware of the dismay in those about us. We had known what would be expected but I suppose we had been so unnerved by the news as to forget such a detail.

Lord Danby, who was close by, hastily produced twenty gold guineas and the little matter was over, but on such occasions people look for omens.

Gilbert Burnet, now made Bishop of Salisbury as a reward for his services, proceeded with the sermon. His voice rang out through the hall. William was gratified. He could trust Gilbert Burnet to stress the faults of my father while he extolled the virtues of the new monarchs who, with God's approbation, had been set up in his place.

He took his text from the passage in Samuel: "He that rulest over men must be just, ruling in the fear of God."

It was a day of mishaps and I think it all stemmed from the news we had had that morning. It had affected us all deeply. There had been delay in starting the proceedings, the absence of the faint-hearted who feared there might soon be a change of monarchs and did not want to show allegiance to the wrong ones, and we were late in arriving at the banquet.

Then came the traditional challenge when Sir Charles Dymoke rode into the hall and flung down his glove to challenge any who would deny the right of William and Mary to the crown. This was all part of the coronation ritual, and I believed there had never been a time when the challenge had been taken up.

Dusk had fallen by this time and from where I was sitting I could not see the actual fall of the gauntlet. To the amazement of everyone, no sooner had the glove been thrown down than an old woman hobbled over to it, picked it up, and was gone. It seemed incredible that she could have been crippled because her movements after picking up the glove had been quick, and she was gone before anyone could stop her; and in place of Charles Dymoke's gauntlet was a lady's glove.

The challenge had been accepted.

This could only be a supporter of my father.

It was a most extraordinary and upsetting affair. But nothing came of it. Dymoke did not consider it was a true challenge and ignored it. But there were some to say that the next morning a man was seen in that spot in Hyde Park where duels were fought, a man equipped with a sword, waiting for the arrival of Sir Charles Dymoke.

Whether this was true or not, I cannot say. There were so many rumours. I was exhausted when the day was over. I think it was the most unhappy day of my life.

A Gift for Elizabeth

The ceremonies which followed the coronation were a great trial to William. He was very impatient with the ancient customs which had to be observed; what he wanted was to get on with the business of ruling. Trivialities bored him and he was not the man to disguise his boredom.

It was easier for me. My nature was different. I liked to have smiling people about me and I could not bear long silences. I liked to hear opinions and, yes, I will confess it, gossip.

The day after the coronation we had to receive all the members of the House of Commons who came in a body to congratulate us. I knew William would think it a waste of time. The crown was firmly on his head. That was the important matter. He could dispense with the rest.

More attention was given to me on these occasions. It may have been because I was considered the rightful heir to the throne, or simply that they found me easier to talk to. William was aware of this and it made him feel angry towards them and, I feared, with me. I wondered why, as he was so clever, he could not hide his irritation and cultivate a more genial manner which would be more pleasing to the people.

He was glad when he could escape to Hampton Court. Rebuilding there was soon going on apace and a new elegance was replacing the old palace. I was glad that some of the old Tudor part was left so that we could see the contrast.

241

I think Hampton Court would always be one of William's favourite places. It was one of mine too.

I was often in Anne's company. The delight which I had enjoyed on my arrival had faded a little. I was conscious of a certain irritation in her company. She was lethargic. That was understandable as she was in an advanced stage of pregnancy, and indeed was about to give birth at any day.

She would sit in silence, smiling that rather vacuous smile of hers, saying very little. I would do all the talking, telling her about the people I was meeting, whether I liked them or not, about my life in Holland and the differences between the Dutch and the English. She would sit, nodding affably; and I wondered if she really heard what I was saying.

I thought: she will be different when the child is born.

There were times when I was quite alarmed. She was so enormous. She had always been inclined to be fat, of course. I remembered how she used to sit with our mother, nibbling at the sweetmeats which always seemed to be at her side. She was still the same.

When I remonstrated with her, she shrugged her shoulders.

"It is the baby," she said. "This one is going to be a giant."

Anne was very affectionate towards her husband, and he to her. How different from William and me! Of course, George was ineffectual, but how kind and pleasant to everyone. He lacked William's wisdom; he could never have been a great ruler, but what a charming man he was! And how contented Anne was with her marriage and her babies, who appeared regularly, even though none of them survived.

Yet, at times I believed that Sarah Churchill was more important to her than George. She always liked to have her close. Perhaps she felt with Sarah around she need not bestir herself to talk, for Sarah talked incessantly. She was giving herself special airs, too.

The custom was to distribute honours at a coronation,

and this had been done. For instance, Gilbert Burnet had become Bishop of Salisbury and William Bentinck was now the Duke of Portland and John Churchill was the Earl of Marlborough. Sarah was very pleased to be Lady Marlborough and Anne was, of course, delighted by Sarah's triumph.

It was indeed a close relationship—dominating on Sarah's side, submissive on Anne's. I think Sarah ruled Marlborough himself in the same way as she did Anne.

When Anne had chosen the names of Mrs. Morley and Mrs. Freeman for herself and Sarah, she had asked Sarah to choose which she would have and, with a touch of humour I always thought, Sarah chose Mrs. Freeman. Nothing could have been more apt.

Between myself and Sarah there was a certain animosity. There was something in our natures which grated on each other. Sarah, of course, must show a certain respect for the Queen, and naturally she could not offend me openly: but I did wonder whether, in private, she tried to turn Anne's mind against me.

I traced her dislike back to that incident of the two pages, which had happened while I was in Holland. It was when Anne had taken up her residence in the Cockpit, those apartments which were more or less attached to the Palace of Whitehall and where Lady Castlemaine had once had her lodgings.

There had been a rearrangement of staff and Anne had needed two more pages in her household.

People in special places, as Sarah was, had the privilege of selling positions in those households where it could be advantageous to be installed, and Sarah had succeeded in selling these places for the sum of £1,200, which was very profitable for her; but since these were posts in the household of the Princess Anne, who could inherit the throne one day, the price seemed reasonable enough to the families concerned.

She must have been congratulating herself on the sale, when it was discovered that the two pages were Roman

Catholics. This was something which we could not accept, for it was at the time when there was a great deal of feeling working up against King James; and Anne, of course, was said to be a staunch Protestant.

I wrote to Anne and told her that the two pages must be dismissed without delay. This created a difficult situation, for Anne would know of Sarah's profitable deal and the Churchills were always in need of money and sought to find it wherever they could. But, in view of the gathering storm, there was nothing to be done but dismiss the pages.

Sarah was very reluctant to give up the money, which by right she should refund to the families who had paid it for the posts which were not now theirs. There was a certain amount of bargaining and in the end it was agreed that Sarah should keep £400 and refund the rest.

This had been done and Sarah was very disgruntled. She blamed William and me—first for discovering the religion of the pages, and then for insisting on their removal.

I knew the money was of great importance to Sarah and the loss of £800 would never be forgiven.

I was always conscious of her enmity and I did not trust her.

Anne's child was nearly due. The hot weather had come and she was more lethargic than ever. I began to worry about her. She had taken childbearing as she did everything else, and it did not greatly disturb her; and now, in the heat of summer, she just lay about, placidly waiting. I was far more anxious than she was.

She had taken up residence at Hampton Court. She was as fond of the place as I was and I was glad that she appreciated the improvements which William had brought about.

William was often at the palace. He was keeping a watchful eye on events in Ireland and was not very pleased about the support my father was getting there. He talked of it to me a little and said that we must be ready to face James if the need arose.

We often walked in the gardens together. I was very proud of them, having helped to create them. He used to take my arm, instead of my taking his, and I knew it was because he sometimes needed support. He tired easily but would not admit that this was the reason.

I saw looks of amusement on the faces of some of the English, who had not taken to William any more than he had to them. I was taller than William and getting plump. I might seem almost sylph-like when compared with Anne; but it was different when I walked side by side with William.

Sarah said with a smirk, "I saw you and the King walking together . . . he taking your arm. Such a good example to married people!"

She knew why he took my arm and she wanted to remind me of his relationship with Elizabeth Villiers. Sarah was no friend of mine.

One hot July day, Anne's baby was born. I had insisted on being with her and I was so relieved when I heard the cry of a child. It was a boy. How pleased everyone would be!

Anne herself was in a state of ecstasy, and I was overjoyed to see her raised out of her indifference. I had not seen Anne, the mother, before, and the state certainly became her.

She looked almost beautiful, peering at the child with her myopic eyes, demanding, "Is he well . . . every limb of him?"

She was assured that the child was in perfect health and the strength of his voice was like sweet music to us all. A boy! An heir to the throne!

People crowded into the chamber. William was there. George, the father, was highly emotional, proud, delighted, gazing down on his wife and son with adoration in his eyes.

It was a touching and moving scene.

Anne said, "We shall call him William, after the King."

William looked gratified. I knew he was thinking that the

boy had come at the right moment. The people would be
pleased. The child would be brought up as a Protestant and
he would be heir to the throne. At last there was a Protestant male heir and the menace of King James, now trying
to raise an army in Ireland, had receded a little.

This was a very important little boy.

I took it upon myself to share in the nursing of my little
nephew. Anne was rather weak after her ordeal, and was
quite happy to sink back into a state of lethargy. It was a
great delight to hold the baby in my arms. He seemed a
bright little fellow. William had already created him Duke
of Gloucester, and I am sure no child ever had a warmer reception into the world.

However, it was not long before there began to be fears
for his health. He grew thin and fretful. Was it going to
happen all over again? The familiar pattern, the birth, the
hopes that this one would survive, and then the weaknesses
which began to show?

It was unbearable to watch little William grow weaker
every day. He put on no weight whatsoever and we could
not understand what ailed him. Poor Anne was despondent.
The others had been stillborn or lived their brief spells. Not
little William, too.

We were filled with gloom. The child could not live
much longer. Each morning, when I rose, I would say to
my women, "How fares the Duke of Gloucester?" and they
would have the answer ready, knowing that the question
would be asked.

"He is poorly, Your Majesty, but he lives."

Then one day, when the baby was a month old and not
expected to live through until September, I was told that a
woman was without and wished to see me most urgently.

"A woman," I said. "What woman?"

"She is carrying a young child, Your Majesty. A rather
big, strong woman."

"I will see her," I said.

She was brought to me. She was plainly dressed in a

garb I discovered to be that of a Quaker; she had fresh skin, clear eyes and was obviously healthy. She was carrying a plump baby of about the same age as William, but how different this child was from the little Duke. He had smooth round cheeks, and what struck me most was his look of sleek contentment.

She did not bow to me, nor show me the respect due to me, nor did she express any surprise that I had deigned to see her.

In fact, she treated me as a woman like herself.

I said, "Who are you?"

"I am Mrs. Pack," she told me. "I have come here on an errand of mercy because I believe the young Duke is dying."

She spoke bluntly and to the point, in a straightforward, honest way which immediately won my respect. She was very different from the sycophantic people who surrounded me and she went on without preamble, "I believe I can save the boy's life."

"How?" I demanded. "He is already surrounded by those who seek to do that."

"It may be that they do not know what is wrong."

"And you, who have not seen him, do?"

"I would take him to my breast. I would give him of that milk which the good Lord has given me in good plenty that I may save the Duke. A voice came to me in the night telling me what I must do."

I wondered if she were a little mad, but she did have an air of simple piety about her which impressed me. Moreover, my anxiety about the baby was so great that I could not turn away from the flimsiest hope of saving him.

I said to Mrs. Pack, "Come with me."

I took her into the room where the baby lay whimpering in his cradle, and to the astonishment of the nurses, I said, "Take up the child, Mrs. Pack, and show me what you can do."

Mrs. Pack, with simple dignity, laid her own child in the cradle beside little William. She then took him in her arms and, seating herself, undid the buttons of her bodice and gave her breast to him.

There was quietness in the room. I saw the child, his lips at her breast, and I heard him; he was sucking eagerly.

Mrs. Pack sat there, smiling benignly. There was a look of saintliness about her in her simple grey gown and the manner in which she held herself, as though there was nothing unusual about her being in the royal apartments suckling the Duke of Gloucester.

What delighted me was to see the child satisfied, and after he had had his fill, he fell into a deep sleep.

I went along to Anne and told her what had happened. She wanted to see Mrs. Pack without delay, and I took her with me to the nursery where little William was. He looked frail but it was wonderful to see him sleeping quietly.

Anne questioned Mrs. Pack, who responded with that dignity which had already surprised me, and she talked with a lack of self-consciousness, showing that she was not in the least overawed.

Mrs. Pack said that the baby was not getting the milk he needed and that was the reason for his weakness. Her milk was good and wholesome and she had enough for two. She had come on the Lord's business and she believed she could transform the Duke into a healthy child.

Anne immediately asked Mrs. Pack if she could stay and feed the Duke with her own baby, a proposition which was accepted.

It was extraordinary, but from that day William began to grow stronger. It was a fact that the lower classes seemed to rear their children more easily than royalty. It must be something in the milk. Mrs. Pack's child was as healthy as any child could be and the Lord or nature had endowed her with enough milk to feed two. It seemed a miracle.

So Mrs. Pack became a member of the household—not always an easy one. I heard she was no respecter of persons. I am sure she had many a tussle with Sarah Churchill, but even that lady's imperious ways could have little effect on the Quaker, who saw all men and women as equal, and was allowed to act as she pleased since she had saved little William's life and continued to keep him healthy.

I was as grateful to her as Anne was, and we would allow no one to upset her. I loved my little nephew and greatly regretted that he was not my son. He was growing into a very bright child. Anne adored him and she and George gloated over him together. I was continually sending toys. I was glad he was at Hampton Court because that gave me many opportunities of seeing him. Mrs. Pack continued her reign in the nursery with her child and under her care young William grew stronger every day.

Unfortunately, my relationship with my sister was deteriorating. Anne irritated me more and more. I liked lively conversation and I wanted to be with people who could share in it. In Holland, I had lived in such seclusion that I had been starved of it, but I was not going to allow that to happen here. I was the Queen and I would not be shut away as I had been when I was Princess of Orange. Occasionally I reminded myself that it was I who had allowed William to become the King and not merely my consort as many people thought he should be. I wanted Anne to remember who I was—not too formally, of course, but on occasions, and I thought she should make some effort when I was present.

It was not only her slothfulness. I fancied she sometimes annoyed me deliberately. I suspected that Sarah Churchill encouraged her in this. Sarah was my enemy but I was not going to allow her to poison my sister's mind against me. I tried to find out what Sarah said to her in secrecy about people, including myself. But Anne, careless as she was about most things, could be sly and secretive if anything was said about Sarah.

I was sure the matter of Richmond Palace had been suggested by Sarah.

Richmond Palace was enshrined in our memories as the home of our childhood—a time when we were ignorant of the misfortunes of life and had believed we were to go on living blissfully for ever.

Anne needed a place to live, for she could not stay indefinitely at Hampton. As a princess in line to the throne, and moreover mother of an heir, she needed a home of her own, and Sarah had persuaded her to set her heart on Richmond.

It would be wonderful to go back there, she insisted.

"So healthy for dear little William," and she was sure her dear sister would put no obstacles in the way of her having it.

As soon as I looked into the matter I knew why Sarah had chosen Richmond.

Sarah had always disliked William. It was she who had given him the name of Caliban all those years ago, and her feelings towards him had not softened. William had commented on Marlborough with typical candor. "A good soldier—one of the best—which is why he holds his position in the army; but a vile man, not to be trusted, not entirely honest. But, for his military skill, he shall retain his position." And, presumably, be given an earldom, I thought.

I could imagine Sarah's comments to Anne. William might not have a good opinion of John Churchill, and what sort of opinion did Sarah have of William? Morose, graceless, without courtesy, an oaf . . . Caliban. True, Churchill had deserted James to support William. That would have been because he saw James's cause as hopeless. John Churchill was no fool—nor was Sarah. They knew whose side they had to be on—and that was the winning one. But that did not prevent them from criticizing those who did not appreciate the Churchills as they should be.

I soon realized that Sarah had persuaded Anne that Richmond would be an ideal home, because she knew that by asking for it she would be creating an awkward situation.

Madame Puisars, Elizabeth Villiers' sister, already owned a lease on the palace which had belonged to her mother, Lady Frances Villiers, who had been our governess. When Lady Frances died, she left the lease to her family. Therefore, to allow Anne to take possession would mean evicting Madame Puisars.

I could see that Sarah wanted to call attention to the favours shown to the Villiers family, and so discountenance William, and, though his liaison with Elizabeth was not exactly a secret, to bring it into prominence.

I was sure William had other matters with which to concern himself at this time. The news from Ireland was becoming more disquieting. My father was rallying men to his side and there were skirmishes between his supporters and those soldiers whom William had stationed there. And now Anne must come along with this trivial matter of Richmond Palace when there were plenty of other places which she could have taken.

"No," said William, irritated that he should have to give a moment's thought to such a matter. "The Princess Anne cannot have Richmond Palace. Madame Puisars already has the lease and there is nothing to be done about it."

Anne was sulky. Nobody cared for her, she said. She was thrust aside . . . of no importance. Other people . . . the Villiers family . . . came before her.

"I wonder *you* allow this," she said to me.

There was a faint smile about her lips. What did Sarah Churchill say to her during their cosy chats? They would talk of the meek Queen who submitted to her husband's tyranny and even accepted his infidelity without complaint. They knew full well how many other queens had done this. Anne had the example of our own father and uncle. I could imagine Sarah saying, that was different. Their husbands had at least treated them with courtesy. They did not behave like Dutch boors; and those queens were not queens regnant married to a king who was so only because of his wife's good graces towards him.

And so the rift between myself and my sister widened, and there was a new cause for it. This time it was money.

When we had arrived in England, Anne had been receiving an annuity of £30,000 a year as a marriage settlement; and when the Duke of Gloucester had been born Anne had asked for this sum to be raised to £70,000. Nothing had come of that.

Now, to our amazement, the question had been raised in

Parliament. This could only have happened if Anne and her friends—whom I suspected were the Marlboroughs—had instigated this.

When I saw Anne, I could not help showing my disapproval.

"How could you do such a thing?" I demanded. "To go behind our backs and have this matter raised in Parliament. Do you know what demands are made on state funds? Do you know that there is a war threatening in Ireland? And you can behave in this underhanded way ... bringing the matter to Parliament!"

Anne blinked at me, looking helpless and maltreated.

"I am in debt," she said. "I must be able to live. If I cannot have some money I shall have to retire into private life. I cannot go on."

"Anne," I cried. "You are being foolish. You have been persuaded to this and I know by whom. It is Sarah Churchill, is it not? Trust that woman to make mischief!"

"It is my own need which forces me. I am treated with unkindness, as though I am of no importance."

"Tell me when the King or I have ever been unkind to you."

She muttered that she could think of one occasion. It was just before the birth of little William and she had had a great fancy for green peas. It was early in the season and there was only a small dish on the table. Oh, how she had wanted those green peas! It was due to her pregnancy, of course. Women had such fancies at these times. And what had William done? He had taken the dish of peas to himself and eaten them all under her eyes!

I could have shaken her. She was so foolish at times. All the same, there was a certain cupidity in her eyes and when she remembered that she was the Princess and in line to the throne, she could play the autocrat.

Now she repeated that she could not afford to live in her present state if she did not have more money.

I looked at her steadily. I had more than once been reminded of that obstinate streak in her nature. I shall never forget an incident in our youth when we were walking together in Richmond Park and she saw an object in the distance and said, "There is a man over there."

She was short-sighted, as we all knew, and sometimes mistook one object for another. I said to her, "No, sister, that is not a man. It is a tree."

In her stubborn way she insisted that it was a man and when we were so close that even she could see clearly that it was a tree, she insisted, "It is a man. I still say it is a man."

I thought of that now as I saw the same obstinacy in her face.

She said, "My friends are determined to make me a settlement."

Anger rose in me. "Pray tell me, what friends you have but the King and me."

I was so annoyed with her that I walked out of the room and left her.

It was the biggest rift that there had been between us and I knew we should never be the same to each other again.

The outcome was a compromise about the money. She was to have £50,000 a year, and William would pay her debts.

I was very unhappy at this time. My father was constantly in my thoughts. I was upset by the rift with Anne; William was very occupied and I saw little of him. Nothing seemed as we had hoped.

We had come to England at the invitation of the people—or some of them who wanted to be rid of my father—and although they welcomed me with affection, they did not like William. It was impossible to stop certain Dutch customs creeping in and the English did not like them. There was also resentment against the Dutch in high places. William was never affable in company, although it was said that he could be talkative with his Dutch friends, with whom he sat sometimes in the evenings drinking their native schnapps.

On one occasion William said to me, "I do not understand these people. I would as lief be back in Holland. Perhaps I should return and leave you to govern."

I was horrified at the thought and would have been more so had I believed that he meant it. He would never leave. Now he was disillusioned and weary. Possession of the three crowns was not what he had thought it would be. But what in life ever is?

I was very unsettled during that time. Constant anxiety about my father, eagerness to please William, being aware of his restlessness and dissatisfaction, made me reckless for a while.

The years of seclusion in Holland had had a deep effect on me. I wanted to be with people all the time. I needed lively conversation; I wanted to share in everything that was going on. I was like a person who had been abstemious too long and suddenly becomes intoxicated.

I needed gaiety as I never had before; I had publicly turned from my father while, inwardly, I yearned to be as we had been before; I wanted to be back in those days when the court had been merry and the King sauntered in the park with his friends about him and people watched him and laughed and felt that life was good.

They watched us now. They saw ladies in the Dutch costume, prim enough to make the onlookers smirk. They called the avenue at Hampton Court the Frow Walk. How the passing of a king could change the ways of a nation!

Perhaps I acted foolishly. I wanted life around me. I went to the theatre. The King and Queen cannot go to the theatre and no one know. I chose to see Dryden's *Spanish Friar*. It had been a favourite of my uncle Charles, but too late I remembered that my father had banned it because it was not complimentary to the Church of Rome. It was a most unfortunate choice, for it was easy to compare what was happening in the play with our own story.

Everyone knew I was anxious about events in Ireland, that some of our soldiers were there and being harried by my father's supporters. There was a tense silence when the Queen of Aragon, who had unsurped the throne, was on her way to church to ask God's blessing for the army which was marching against the King.

All eyes were turned on me and I was very uncomfortable, being watched throughout the performance.

Before I went to the theatre again, I would read the play which was to be performed.

It hurt me that some people thought I rejoiced in my father's downfall. How I wished I could explain how I really felt!

In my search for excitement, I visited the Indian Houses which were fashionable shops and which had recently come into being. They were full of unusual and amusing merchandise and the ladies of the court often visited them. I did not know at this time that they were also used for arranging assignations—a practice which had grown up during my uncle's reign.

The women who managed them were worldly wise and the best known among them was a Mrs. Graden, who, in addition to her other business, sold some fine ribands and all sorts of fascinating items for a lady's wardrobe.

I went with some of my ladies and had a most amusing time. Mrs. Graden was so overcome by the honour of a visit from the Queen that she insisted on giving us refreshment.

Others in the same profession were a little piqued by the attention given to Mrs. Graden and perforce I must visit the other shops and buy goods from them. I remembered how Mary Beatrice had been attracted by the Indian shops and had visited them several times.

When the news of these visits reached William's ears, he was horrified and wanted me to know it. We were at dinner together, and, in his usual way, he did not wait to speak to me privately, but asked me there if I thought such behaviour wise. This was in the company of several people and was said in a voice which indicated severe criticism.

"I hear that you make a custom of visiting bawdy houses," were his words.

I was astounded, and then suddenly I realized what he meant.

I said, "Do you mean the Indian Houses?"

"I mean what I say. Perhaps next time you decide to go I should come with you."

I was amazed. "Many people visit these shops," I said. "My father's wife often did."

"Do you intend to make her an example you should follow?"

I did not want to enter into a discussion with him in public, so I murmured something about making some interesting purchases at the shops.

He said no more about it and I thought perhaps I had been rather indiscreet to visit the places, and when I discovered what went on there, I did see what William meant.

I should not visit them again, but I could not resist calling Mrs. Wise.

Mrs. Wise was well known throughout the court for living up to her name. She had special "powers" and had been known more than once to see into the future.

I had heard about her predictions from the Countess of Derby who, since I had been in England, had been my Mistress of Robes. I had brought one or two Dutch ladies with me, and the only other English women I had were Mrs. Forster and Mrs. Maudaunt.

They had all been whispering together and when I asked what had excited them, the Countess was loath to tell me.

At length I insisted, and she said, "It is nothing but tattle, Your Majesty. These things will be."

Still she was reluctant, but finally I prevailed on her to tell me.

"Mrs. Wise says that King James will come back to England and that heads will fall."

"I see," I replied. "Do people believe her?"

"There is always talk when such things are said, Your Majesty."

"And this Mrs. Wise, has she a good reputation for foreseeing the future accurately?"

"Like most of these people, she has had her successes," said the Countess. "They say something, which by good luck comes true. But they are often wrong."

"I should like to see this Mrs. Wise," I said.

"Oh, Madam," gasped the Countess. "Do you think . . . ?"

"I should like to see her for myself," I said firmly.

"If people knew . . . they would speak of it. They would feel you must think highly of her to visit her."

"I want to see her. I want to ask her questions."

"Your Majesty . . . should you go . . . openly . . . as you did to the Indian Houses?"

I could see William's cold eyes reprimanding me, and the wondering looks from those about me. Why does the Queen allow this man to talk to her so? they were asking themselves. He is the King by her courtesy. But she is his wife, I thought, and to him she owed obedience. I had learned this from Gilbert Burnet.

William would not, of course, approve of my visiting Mrs. Wise, but I was going to do it all the same.

My women enjoyed the secrecy we must employ. It gave a spice to the adventure, and I went to Mrs. Wise.

She was a woman who did not win my confidence from the first. I could see she was a little shaken by my visit. She had made a pronouncement which she knew would not have pleased me and she was a little uneasy about my visit. I soon discovered that she was an ardent Catholic and I guessed that was why she had made the prophecy.

She was sycophantic, overwhelmed by the honour, she said, and she feared her humble talents were not worthy to serve me.

This, she insisted, prevented her from looking into my future, and she had nothing to tell me. All she could see was that I had been in Holland and had gone there at an early age. She could see nothing beyond that.

She tried to give the impression that the powers were so overwhelmed by my majesty that they felt it would be improper to prophesy my future.

I could not help laughing to myself at this foolish

woman, and I came away with the certainty that she made her prophecies to fit the occasion.

I was relieved that William did not discover that I had visited Mrs. Wise.

That year was coming to an end. It had begun in triumph and was ending in melancholy. I was glad when it was over. But the new year seemed almost more alarming, for it was becoming clear that the situation in Ireland could not be allowed to continue as it was.

William must send an army to face that which was gathering about my father. This would be a battle between Catholics and Protestants. Ever since the conflict had started, I had dreaded the thought of my husband and father coming face-to-face in battle.

It seemed now that it was inevitable, and during the first month of that new year of 1690 I began to wish that I was no longer on earth, so that I need not know the outcome.

It was no use trying to tell myself that my father was in the wrong. He was—but he was my father and I could not forget my happy childhood and the love there had been between us. How cruel life had been to give me William as a husband, the one man who must be my father's enemy. And here was I . . . caught between them.

Yes, it was true, at times I did wish that I could die before that battle took place. I was so torn between them. My duty was to both of them, but what could I do? I was married to William and the scriptures say that a woman must cleave to her husband, forsaking all others.

Dr. Burnet had assured me my duty was to my husband. I must remember that. But I was dreading that confrontation, with such intensity that I would rather die than face the result.

And through those unhappy months preparations for war continued.

I really believed that William sometimes wished he had never come to England. The people continued to show their dislike of him. It had been different in Holland. The Dutch did not expect the same of their rulers as the English did. Moreover, the glorious euphoria of the Restoration was close enough for people to remember. They wanted to laugh and be merry; they wanted excuses for celebrations; dancing in the streets, being delightedly shocked by the King's amorous adventurings. And what had they in his place? War threatening and a monarch who never smiled and who hardly ever appeared in public.

But they did like me. William said, "I am beginning to think it would be better if I went back and you reigned in my place." He gave one of his mirthless smiles. "They would not have that. They would rather have me than a woman ruling over them."

One of those rare streaks of rebellion rose in me and I said, "One of the most successful monarchs this country has ever had was a woman. I refer to Queen Elizabeth."

"Hm. She was surrounded by good ministers."

"Whom she had chosen," I reminded him.

He did not answer, but he gave me a strange look; and in that moment a determination was born to me. If I had to rule—which I might well do if he went to Ireland—I would do everything within my power to succeed.

The thought was gone almost as soon as it came. I dreaded the idea, not only because of his going into combat against my father but also because I should be alone.

Dr. Burnet came to see us one day. We were together when we received him. We looked upon him as one of our closest friends, for he had supported us from the beginning.

He had had a plan put to him and he thought we should consider it.

"I know Your Majesties' feelings in this matter," he said. "The Queen is uneasy to be in conflict with her father and it would seem Your Majesties might see a hope of avoiding confrontation."

I was all eagerness to hear.

"The plan is that a ship manned by trusty men should

call at Dublin, letting it be known that they had come with the intention of joining King James, who should be invited to come aboard. When he does so, the ship should immediately sail for some port—say in Italy or Spain. When the port is reached, the King should be given a sum of money and left there. Without the King, the forces in Ireland will soon be disbanded and conflict averted."

William considered. I imagined it was something which might have appealed to him if it had been practical. But would my father be so careless as to go aboard? And alone? It did not seem likely. But recklessness had been the theme of his life. It had brought him to the position he was in at this moment.

There was another thought which occurred to me. Suppose they took him to Holland? How would the Dutch feel towards an admiral who had beaten them so often in battles?

"I will have no part of it," I said, though I knew that the alternative was conflict with William and his army.

William, I was relieved to see, was in agreement with me. I liked to think that the same possibility had occurred to him, but I suspected he saw the scheme as impractical and, even if it succeeded, likely to prove only a postponement of the battle. My father would still be there to fight another day.

So we declined to consider it, though I fancy Gilbert Burnet was disappointed.

We were now moving towards the time for departure and William must very soon be on his way to Ireland, and I was to rule in his absence.

I felt a certain strength which I had not known I possessed, and the task did not seem so formidable as it had when William was there. It may be that, in order to turn my mind from fears for William's safety and anxiety about my father, I endeavoured to give my entire attention to the immense task before me.

I was surrounded by ministers to help me, the chief of

which was Lord Caermarthen, who had been Lord Danby, Lord Devonshire, Lord Nottingham, Admiral Russell, and Lord Monmouth. Lord Monmouth was not related to Jemmy. The title came through his mother, who was descended from the Earl of Monmouth, and William had given the title to him, in order to impress on Jemmy's son that it should never be his.

I did not greatly care for any of these men. Most of them were ambitious, self-seeking; as for Lord Monmouth, I had always thought he was a trifle mad, though good-natured enough, and perhaps more honest than some, though not, alas, reliable.

I could see I should have a hard task before me, and yet I welcomed it.

I was discovering that I was not the feeble woman William seemed to think I was, and which he had made me feel was true. Neither my sister Anne nor I had been well educated, but whereas Anne had taken advantage of the lack of supervision and hardly ever exerted herself, I had always wanted to learn. I saw now how good for me that period of seclusion in Holland had been, for I had spent a great deal of time in reading, when I was not having discourse with people like Gilbert Burnet and Dr. Hooper; and, although our discussions had been mainly of theology, politics had often been one of our subjects. So it was with a thrill of excitement that I had discovered that I was not as ill-equipped for the task as I had feared I might be.

I went to the Palace of Whitehall when William left. George, Anne, and little William came there, too. I think we might have forgotten our grievances and been as we used to be, but for Sarah Churchill.

Little William was a great joy to me. Mrs. Pack still dominated the nursery. She had installed herself as the boy's chief nurse and he was devoted to her and would have no other. Sarah could not endure anyone to dominate a part of Anne's household except herself and would have liked to be rid of Mrs. Pack; but Anne's stubbornness came out when any matter concerning her son was in question;

and clever Sarah decided that it would be unwise to attempt
to change her mind on this.

I was amused to see Mrs. Pack and Sarah together, for
Mrs. Pack could be as forceful in her way as Sarah was in
hers.

The constant waiting for news was having its effect on
me. My face became swollen. I wanted to shut myself away
to hide it. I had to send for the doctors who applied leeches
to my ears.

In the circumstances, of course, it was impossible for
me to live in seclusion and often I had to receive people
while I was in my bed.

Then came startling news.

The French fleet had appeared just off Plymouth.

This could only mean an attack was imminent. There
were more than seventy French men-of-war coming to attack and rumour said that there were more on the way.

I rose from my bed, my swollen face forgotten. A
number of our ships were still in Ireland, others were in the
Mediterranean. There were Dutch squadrons in the Channel, but with them, and those of ours which were available,
there would only amount to some fifty men-of-war.

The Earl of Torrington, as Admiral of the Fleet, had been
a supporter of William and me from the beginning. That
was why he held the post. He was an adequate sailor but
not such a good one as my father had been, and he was at
this time a little disgruntled because he had not been included among those selected for the governing body when
William left for Ireland.

He had acquired the nickname of Tarry-in-Town which,
although it was on account of his name, did suggest that he
might not be the most energetic of men.

These were dreadful days. The French, of course, were
seizing the advantage of our weak position. There was murmuring against William. Why should he be in Ireland when
England was in need of protection? The French were and
always had been our greatest enemy and we should always
be on guard against them. I thought there might have been

an insurrection. William should never have gone, I thought. This would not have happened if he had been here.

But the fact that the French were close to our shores had its effect on the nation. At such moments the English could be relied on to stand together.

There was consternation among the governing body. Was Torrington the man to lead the fleet in this time of danger? Hot-headed Monmouth offered to go out and take over from Torrington if the need arose. I refused to allow that, for I was sure interference from Monmouth would be disastrous. Caermarthen thought that we should send Admiral Russell to take Torrington's place.

I pondered this for a while but I came to the conclusion that, as Torrington was Admiral of the Fleet, it would be unwise at such a time to make a change.

"Torrington holds the post," I said. "I am sure he will do his duty. He is an honest man."

Meanwhile Torrington reminded us that he had frequently warned us of the growing strength of the French Navy. He was unhappy about the situation for which he was unprepared.

I cannot bear to think even now of the disgrace of that battle. It was a disaster from the beginning. Torrington abandoned the Isle of Wight to the French and retreated up the Channel. When he saw the French hoving into sight, he gave the order to attack. The Dutch fleet were in the van. There were less than sixty ships against eighty French. Only a Francis Drake could have succeeded in such circumstances and Torrington did not have that kind of genius. The Dutch fleet fought bravely, without much assistance from Torrington and his ships. Torrington took refuge up the Thames and the Dutch fleet was shattered.

The only relief which came out of that action was that the French did not take advantage of their victory and contented themselves with merely burning the town of Teignmouth.

But what a disgrace it was! People were saying that there had been no luck in England since the new King came.

They blamed William more than they did me. He had left the country in a time of peril; ships which should have been defending England were in Ireland. People were saying that if King James returned he would find it as easy to defeat the Orangemen as the French had.

I knew it was no use to mourn over defeat. I must take action. The ships which had been damaged must be immediately repaired. Who knew when we might need them again? I ordered twelve new ships to be built without delay.

I was ashamed that Torrington had allowed the Dutch to bear the full brunt of the battle, and I sent an envoy to The Hague with my regrets and I gave orders that the wounded Dutch were to be given the best attention and compensated for their losses.

Any dissatisfaction which might have followed was forgotten in the fear that the French would show their strength at sea by attempting an invasion.

Then suddenly our fortunes changed.

There was news from Ireland. William was victorious. He had defeated my father at the Battle of the Boyne.

My relief was tempered with anxiety. William had been wounded. There were reports in France that he had been killed. The French went wild with joy at the news. I heard that there were celebrations in the streets of Paris with caricatures of my husband, irreverent and cruel. It was an indication of how important they held him to be. By that time I had heard that William's wound was slight. He had grazed his shoulder blade. My father had escaped to Dublin, which was another great relief to me.

Considering the importance of that battle, the losses were not great. Five hundred of our men lost their lives and one thousand five hundred of our opponents died. But how significant was that battle! My father was in flight. What would he do? Return to France? Wait for another chance? He was getting old and would be losing hope, so perhaps this would be the end of the conflict.

How I hoped so, and how I rejoiced that he had escaped.

What I had dreaded most had been avoided. It was good to hear the rejoicing in the streets. William was almost a hero. They would never forgive his solemn ways but at least he had won a great victory and was given credit for that.

The Catholics were lying low; there were expressions of loyalty from several sources. The defeat of Beachy Head was forgotten in the all-important Battle of the Boyne.

My face had ceased to swell; William was coming home; and my father was safe. I was happier than I had thought possible only a short time before.

I was sorry though that Torrington was court-martialled, but that was later—not until the end of the year. I always thought it was unfair to blame him. William did; but he had never liked him, and that was mutual. Torrington defended himself with dignity and said that he had not had the strength to engage the French. The English fleet was not in home waters. If he had imitated the recklessness of the Dutch, the result would have been not only a lost battle at sea but a disaster for England.

I was relieved when he was acquitted. He did not, however, take another command, but went to live in the country.

Meanwhile William was home. Ready to welcome him as the victor of the Boyne, the people expected a triumphant procession through the streets of London. They assembled to cheer and there he was, riding in his carriage instead of on horseback. I dare say he was fatigued. He was indeed recovering from his wound. He wanted only the peace of Hampton Court. He did not raise his arm or give an acknowledgement of the cheers. How I wished he would understand the needs and wishes of the people!

There was another matter which spoilt his homecoming. I heard about it from Caermarthen just before William's arrival. I fancied Caermarthen's smile was a little sly as he told me.

"Your Majesty must know," he said, "that considerable Irish lands have fallen to the King. There are some 90,000 acres of King James's estates which are now in King William's hands."

"That should represent a great deal of money."

"It does indeed, but King James had given many of the rents away to various ladies." Caermarthen coughed. "There is but £5,000 in rents left out of some £26,000."

"Still considerable," I said.

"Indeed, Your Majesty. The King has already disposed of the 90,000 acres."

"To whom, may I ask?"

Again that little cough. "To . . . er . . . the Lady Elizabeth Villiers."

I felt the blood rush to my face as I turned my head away and said, "I see. It would be well for us to turn some of the acquired estates to the good of the Irish poor."

"Doubtless there will be other means of doing this, Your Majesty. It is a great victory."

"A very great victory," I said.

When he left me I sat down and stared ahead of me.

How could he do this! He must realize that I should discover it. Yet he did it, blatantly uncaring. Ninety thousand acres for Elizabeth Villiers!

I knew I should not be able to speak to him of it, so I took up my pen and wrote.

I have been desired to beg you not to be too quick in parting with confiscated estates, but consider whether you will not keep some for schools to instruct the poor Irish. For my part, I must needs say that I think you should do very well if you would consider what care can be taken of the poor souls there. The wonderful success you have had should oblige you to think of doing what you can for the advancement of true religion and promoting the gospel.

Would he understand the reproof? I was sure he would. I had rarely come so near to criticizing his actions.

I was so angry that he should do this. After all this time

he still cared for her. I was his wife, his Queen. I had given him my obedience and what he had wanted most—a crown. All this I had given him—and he had bestowed the Irish estates on Elizabeth Villiers!

Traitors

In spite of my diplomatic reproach, William did not mention the matter of the Irish estates and they went to Elizabeth Villiers as arranged. This was tantamount to a public declaration of their relationship and it was hard for me to bear.

I tried not to allow myself to feel humiliated. I had to remember that I was the Queen and for a time had taken over the reins of government—not unsuccessfully, I flattered myself, for I could not be blamed for the defeat at Beachy Head.

I avoided being in the company of Elizabeth Villiers. She was very confident. She was a clever woman, making up for what she lacked in physical beauty in mental ability. She was on good terms with Bentinck. Moreover, she could keep a sharp eye on what was going on at court; she would be able to sort out the important from the trivial and discuss it with William. I was sure he regarded her as an acute statesman and, because her interests were his, he trusted her absolutely—as much as he could trust anyone except Bentinck.

Soon after he returned home, William acquired a mansion in Kensington which he bought from the Earl of Nottingham. It was a fine house in about six acres of park.

William became a different man when he could plan the restoration of a house; and I could share in this enthusiasm. Thus we set about recreating Kensington Palace.

Hampton Court had been completed and was much admired. Now we could turn our attention entirely to Kensington Palace.

We discussed plans; we engaged architects and the work was soon in progress. Grinling Gibbons was called in and did some beautiful wood carvings. I was going to work on William's closet and, with my ladies, began on the tapestry which would line the walls and cover the seats of chairs.

Anne, cheated of Richmond Palace, as she said, had moved to the Cockpit. I was still very sad about the decline in our friendship and I often thought of the old days when she had always wanted to do what I did, when I was the elder sister, to be admired and imitated.

Little William was growing up into a bright, amusing, and intelligent child, though his health still gave concern: but Mrs. Pack remained with him and his devotion to her increased. Anne resisted Sarah's urgings that the woman should be sent away. Anne was devoted to her son and his welfare, his happiness, could bring out all the stubbornness in her nature and she would fight even Sarah for his sake.

Mrs. Pack and Sarah had naturally become the most bitter of enemies. I was amused to see them together and delighted that Sarah could not get her way this time.

I often took presents to the child. He was very interested in me. I realized it was because he had heard I was the Queen.

He would call me imperiously to his side if he wanted to show me some picture or a castle of bricks.

"Queen," he would cry, "Here, Queen. Look."

Anne talked of his cleverness—quite volubly for her. Sarah might grow impatient but it was no use. Anne would go on talking.

The boy had a small carriage made for him. There were miniature horses—the smallest that could be found—and they were attached to his little carriage and led by George's coachman.

People used to come to the park to watch the little boy in his carriage. They would cheer him as he passed along. He would regard them solemnly and then raise his hand

and wave. When he did this they laughed and cheered the more, which clearly excited him for he bounced up and down in his seat with glee.

The little Duke was always popular, and so was Anne. She had somehow conveyed her devotion to him and that touched the hearts of the people. Whenever she appeared, the people made it obvious that she was a favourite. They were kind to me, too. It was only William who was received in silence.

Marlborough had gone to Ireland where there was trouble in the south. He did very well there and when he came home, I heard that Sarah thought he should receive an honour.

Anne spoke to me about it. "Sarah thinks that Marlborough's services should be recognized. He should have the Garter or a dukedom."

"He has already been made an earl."

"Think what he has done since that."

"He has done his duty as a soldier, yes."

"Sarah thinks good service should be rewarded."

I said tersely, "Sarah does not make the laws in this country, though doubtless she would like to."

Anne dropped into one of her silent sullen moods, so I began to speak of young William—a subject she could never resist.

I mentioned to William what she had said. "Marlborough thinks he should be rewarded," I said. "He thinks, as the Garter will soon be available, he should have it."

"The Garter! Marlborough!" cried William. "That is quite out of the question."

"I thought you would say that. It is his wife's idea, I dare say."

"That woman interferes too much."

That was something with which I could whole-heartedly agree.

He told me then that he would soon be leaving for Holland and it would be for me to take over the government again.

This did not alarm me as it had in the past. I was realizing that I could be stimulated by the prospect of stepping into first place and taking decisions. I was learning that, in spite of the accompanying anxieties, it is exciting to be in command.

"I must attend the Congress of the Powers," he said. "The French are more to be feared than James, and now he is in France, we can be watchful of him. He is weak, but the French are strong, and those nations who are against the French must stand together. We shall make plans to do this during the Congress."

It was only a few days before he was due to leave when the plot was discovered. It was reckless in the extreme. The plotters were making a proposition to my father. If he would make a solemn promise to rule England as a Protestant country, they would bring him back. He was to gather together a French force which would bring him to England where a secret landing place would be arranged. The French force would then be dismissed and sent back to France. His friends would then rally round him and set him on the throne.

They were rather naive if they thought my father would keep such a promise, even if he made it in the first place.

Three of the conspirators, Lord Preston, Major Elliot, and a Mr. Ashton, were selected to take the proposals to France. Suspicions had already been aroused and before their small boat was able to leave the Thames, it was boarded and the papers which were intended for my father were seized.

As a result the three men were now in the Tower.

William said he was pleased that this matter had been settled before he left England.

Now there was another problem. Prince George wanted to go to sea.

"Could he not do so?" I asked William.

My husband looked at me scornfully. "We cannot afford to encumber the service with those who will be no good in it."

"Surely some position could be found for him?"

"It would have to be a position of some importance because of his rank. That is the trouble. Think of Torrington."

"Torrington was a good man. He was just short of ships."

"A good man accepts difficulties and overcomes them."

"He has to have good luck to do that. Torrington did not."

William clearly did not want to discuss Torrington. He was concerned with George. He despised George, who was all that he was not; and he was determined that George should not go to sea. How could he prevent him? It must be done.

"For," he added, "he shall not join the fleet. On that I am determined. But it would be better if he were persuaded not to, instead of forbidden."

"Forbidden?" I cried.

William's face hardened. "If necessary, yes. He shall not join the fleet which must be manned by only the best. We cannot afford more incompetence."

"Who will persuade him?"

"Anne, I suppose."

"She never would."

"Well, you must persuade her to it. Get the Churchill woman on your side. I am told that you know how to deal with people."

"This would not be easy."

"Dealing with foolish people never is."

He dismissed the matter and the next day he left for Holland.

I was anxious about him for the weather was not good, but he would not delay his departure. It was necessary for him to be in a country where people behaved reasonably, where they understood him and he them.

Poor William! I wondered, as I had before, whether he would have been happier if he had never realized his dream and inherited the crown.

It was a relief to hear that he had arrived safely and emerged with nothing more than a cold. The Dutch had welcomed him warmly—in that undemonstrative way, I supposed, which was so much to his taste.

Before me lay the difficult task of "persuading" George that the sea was not for him.

I made several attempts with Anne but that stubborn look came into her face when I mentioned what George proposed to do and questioned the wisdom of it.

"So," she cried, "he is to be given no post! He is expected to spend his days sleeping, drinking, and sitting around. The King treats him like an usher ... of no importance at all."

I could make no headway with Anne. The only way would be, as William had suggested, to get Sarah to try to persuade Anne.

With some misgivings I sought out Sarah.

I said, "Lady Marlborough, I know you have great influence with my sister, and it is for this reason that I wish to talk to you."

"The Princess honours me with a rather special friendship, I believe, Your Majesty," she replied complacently.

"Well, I know that she always listens with attention to what you have to say. This is rather a delicate matter. Prince George has conceived an idea that he should take command of the fleet."

"I believe that to be in his mind, Your Majesty."

"It is really not possible, and I want you to persuade the Princess that it would not be good for him."

"Oh?" said Sarah, her eyes widening in innocence.

I tried flattery, to which I suspected Sarah was not entirely immune.

"If anyone can make the Princess see the wisdom of this, it is you. And when the Princess realizes it, she can persuade the Prince. That is all I ask of you, Lady Marlborough."

She hesitated for a moment and I saw speculation come into her eyes.

"Madame, Your Majesty, I ask your forgiveness for my forwardness, but I am in the employ of the Princess Anne and therefore owe my allegiance to her, and I hold it as a matter of honour. I will tell her that it is your opinion that it would be unwise of the Prince to join the fleet and you have asked me to persuade her to this. I would tell her that this is your command, for I should be obliged to tell her whence it came. I trust Your Majesty understands my meaning."

"I understand you well, Lady Marlborough," I said rising. She immediately stood, as she could not remain seated when I was not. "I pray you, say nothing of this matter to the Princess, for I see little good could come of it."

With that I left the insolent woman. I could see that more harm than good had been done. Now it would be necessary to give an outright refusal to Prince George. It would have been better to have refused him in the first place.

One of my most unpleasant duties at that time was signing the death warrant. I hated the thought that someone had died because I had penned my name to a paper and ordered it to be done.

I must obey the law, of course, and there were the three prisoners who had been caught in an act of treason. It was harder because that act of treason was one of loyalty towards my father. Ashton, with Lord Preston and Major Elliot, had been caught with treasonable documents in his possession. So there was no help for it. They would have to die.

This weighed heavily on my mind. I wished that William had been there. He would have signed those documents without a qualm. He would be contemptuous of me for my soft feelings.

I had read a great deal about my predecessor, Queen Elizabeth, for whom I had a great admiration. She had been a strong woman and had ruled despotically in her own right. She had talked of her proud stomach, and she would never have allowed a man to unsurp the smallest part of her power.

And there was I—Queen of this Realm—beside a husband to whom I gave the right to come before me. Elizabeth would have despised me, and perhaps she would have been right.

I did remember that she had suffered pangs of conscience when she had signed the death warrant of Mary, Queen of Scots. These men were not close to me. I did not know them, but I deplored what I had to do, and would have given a great deal to have had that burden taken from me.

The people understood my feelings, I believed. They may have thought me weak, but they liked me as they never could like William.

While I was suffering from these pangs of conscience, I had an experience which made me even more sad. It happened in Kensington Palace, which was now beginning to look very fine. In the great hall, when William and I had bought the place, there hung a big picture of my father looking splendid in all his regalia. It was still there.

One day when I came down the stairs I saw a young girl sitting on the lower step, staring fixedly at my father's portrait.

I said, "What are you doing here, child? And why do you look so intently at that picture?"

She stood up and curtsied.

"Your Majesty," she said. "That is your father." She fixed melancholy eyes on me and went on, "My father is in the Tower. He is Lord Preston. They are going to kill him. It is sad that my father is going to be put to death for loving your father too much."

I was stunned. The child curtsied again and ran off. I wanted to call after her, to bring her back, to say her father should not be killed. Instead, I went to my apartments and prayed, as I always did in moments of intense unhappiness; but I found little comfort.

I wished, as I had so many times, that I was that child's age and happy in the love of my father.

When I thought about the matter afterwards, I guessed that someone had primed that child to be at that spot where I would pass and told her to say what she did. They knew

I was not hard like William. How I wished I could give those men their freedom, but I could not remake the laws.

I was relieved when Lord Preston revealed the names of his fellow conspirators—which was not a noble thing to do, but it saved his life and eased my conscience to a certain extent.

There was bad news from Holland. The French seemed to be triumphant everywhere. At home the people were growing more and more dissatisfied. They wanted to hear of victory, not defeat; and when the news was not good they immediately asked themselves why they had exchanged one unsatisfactory ruler for another who was equally so.

The good old days under Charles were remembered. How had he managed it? I often wondered. I thought of the manner in which he had averted trouble. He was not always sincere, but he always pleased the people, and the art of governing was to do that.

I was rather proud of the manner in which I handled the sailors' wives of Wapping.

Funds had been low for some time. The wars were responsible for that. Payments which should have been made had been temporarily suspended, and because of this the sailors' wives had decided to bring a petition to Parliament to air their grievances.

This state of affairs must not be allowed to go on, I decided. These debts must be settled even if it were from the Privy Purse. The poor must not be made to suffer. It was important that those who had only a little money should be the first to receive it.

There was consternation when, in the midst of a Cabinet meeting, the angry wives of Wapping arrived.

This was the kind of situation which could quickly result in a riot; and when one started others could spring up. The matter had to be settled at once.

I said, "I shall speak to them."

"Your Majesty . . ." several of the ministers cried in horror.

But I was determined.

"Down there is a mob of angry women," I said. "Go down and tell them to select four who will speak for them and bring them to me."

They tried to dissuade me. There was I, wearing the state robes which I wore for Cabinet meetings, and I was preparing to see those women, dressed so!

I waved aside their protests and insisted that the women be sent to me.

They came in a truculent mood, angrily determined to demand their rights. I must say they looked taken aback at the sight of me in my splendid robes, and, being somewhat rotund, I must have made quite a regal sight. I could not believe that they would be pacified by the contrast they made in their poor patched garments.

But I have a very soft and gentle voice, I am told, and when I spoke and told them how sorry I was that their husbands had not been paid and they had been right to come to me, I saw the expression on their faces change.

"Tell me all about it," I went on.

They were taken aback. They had not expected soft words.

One of the women, bolder than the rest, stepped forward. She told me of the poverty they had endured, how hard it was to make ends meet, and when there was no pay coming for good service, they could endure no more. So they had come to demand it.

I agreed that what had happened must immediately be put right. Everything due to them must be paid. I would see that this was done.

They hesitated. They had been promised payment for work done in the first place. They wanted action, not promises that might not be kept.

"I want you to believe me," I said. "I shall make sure that the money is paid to you without delay."

I realized suddenly that I had won the confidence of these women. They did believe me. I was moved and gratified when the leader went down on her knees and said, "I believe you. You are a good woman."

Then the others knelt with her.

"God bless Your Majesty," they said.

I went back to the Cabinet meeting. They all looked shocked. They had been ready to hurry to my aid should I have been attacked and were astonished when I said calmly, "The amount owing to the sailors' wives must be paid immediately. I have promised this and my promise must be honoured."

My orders were promptly carried out and I believe the action I had taken averted danger.

My popularity increased after that. Alas, it did not help William.

The people of London liked to express themselves in verse; and when someone wrote a couplet—usually anonymous and unflattering—it was often set to a tune and sung in the streets.

The people saw William as the ruler and I, though the true heiress, was the retiring woman who had hitherto been kept in the background, occupied with her needle. This was not so now. I had been brought forward in William's absence and I had won the hearts of the sailors' wives.

The couplet they were singing now was:

> Alas, we erred in choice of our commanders
> He should have knotted, she gone to Flanders.

I was glad William was not in England to hear that and hoped that they would be singing a different verse when he returned.

Since William's refusal to allow Prince George to go to sea had not been arranged discreetly, he had to be told officially by Lord Nottingham that the King would not sanction it.

I could imagine Anne's fury, and George . . . well, he would have been mildly disappointed. I could imagine his raising his eyes and murmuring, *"Est-il possible?"* William was the one they blamed, and Sarah, of course, would do all in her power to add to the resentment.

Anne and Sarah would discuss the matter. Caliban was the loathesome creature who had refused to recognize the good services of Marlborough, and now behaved as though George was a nobody—and he was the father of the male heir to the throne.

William returned to England. The continental war had been his chief concern now that James had been driven back to France. The people of England had been taxed to pay for the war and there were no successes to report.

It was clear that they were not pleased with their King. I guessed there was a certain amount of gratification in the Cockpit because of this.

My sadness at the discord between my sister and myself was compensated a little by my young nephew. I liked to visit him and have him brought to Kensington. He enjoyed those visits. He liked to watch the soldiers in the park.

He would point to them in glee and shout, "Soldiers, Queen, look!"

I gave him toy soldiers, which pleased him, but of course they were not real soldiers who marched and saluted.

There would never be harmony between Anne and me while Sarah dominated that household. She had two enemies, however, and because of circumstances it was not easy for her to dislodge them.

The first was, of course, Mrs. Pack. There was that special bond which is often there between a nurse and the child she has suckled, and this was certainly the case with William and Mrs. Pack; and because of his devotion to her, Mrs. Pack must remain.

The other, and perhaps more to be feared, was Lady Fitzharding, who was one of the Villiers sisters. The closeness of that family was legendary; the advantages acquired by one were shared by all. They stood together, as they always had.

I had no doubt that Lady Fitzharding kept her sister well

informed of what occurred at the Cockpit, and of course
Elizabeth would pass this information on to William.

Lady Fitzharding's position as governess to little William
could not be more convenient for Elizabeth and my husband.

She would have to tread very warily, no doubt, for Sarah
was too shrewd not to realize the inevitability of the outcome. It occurred to me that Sarah would be desperately
seeking an excuse to be rid of her, but she could not expect
an easy victory against the Villiers family, as she—and
Anne—had discovered over the controversy of Richmond
Palace.

William did not pass on to me the information he received from Elizabeth by way of Lady Fitzharding, but I
had my own source which gave me a good idea of what
went on there.

It was obvious that Sarah remained incensed by what she
called the lack of appreciation of her husband's genius, and
through Mrs. Pack I heard of the constant railing against
"Caliban's ingratitude" and the treatment of Prince George.
According to Mrs. Pack, it was Sarah's view that Caliban
was jealous of Anne and of Marlborough.

This was no news to me. I could have told Mrs. Pack
that was exactly what they would say. I had heard something like it from Anne herself.

Mrs. Pack was grateful to me. In my turn I was grateful
to her, for I was convinced that she had saved little William's life. I agreed with her methods. Although William
was a delicate child, she never coddled him. She would insist on his going out in all weathers, although she always
made sure that he was well wrapped up.

I had arranged for her husband to have a job with the
Customs Office; and although she was actually in Anne's
service, she believed that her loyalty should be to me. A
sensible, down-to-earth woman, she would have little pa-
tience with Anne. She found the relationship between Anne
and Sarah Churchill quite incomprehensible and, of course,
there was the antipathy between herself and Sarah. She

knew that Sarah would have done everything in her power
to have her removed, and that Anne would have been easily
persuaded but for little William.

She came to see me at Kensington Palace because she
had news which she thought was important and I should
know.

When I was alone with her, she said, "The Princess
Anne and the Churchills are writing to King James."

"The Churchills! That can't be true!!"

"I have heard them talking. The Earl of Marlborough is
concerned in this. I heard Lady Marlborough telling the
Princess what she should say to him. The Princess is writing to tell him that she is filled with remorse. She made a
bitter mistake and craves his forgiveness. They want him to
come back."

"My sister . . . I understand her remorse. I know how she
feels. But Marlborough . . ."

"They have been angry, Your Majesty. They say Lord
Marlborough is not appreciated, that the Dutch get all the
best posts. They do not want to be ruled by Dutchmen.
They say they want to bring King James back."

I was astounded. I could not believe this. She had not
heard correctly. How could she know this merely by listening at doors? If it were so, Lady Fitzharding would have
discovered it. Then William would know.

"It seems," said Mrs. Pack, "that their plan is to bring
back King James, although they would not let him reign.
They would set the Princess Anne on the throne—and then,
as you can guess, the Marlboroughs would rule through
her."

This amazed me, but I could see the reasoning behind it.
It would be typical of the Marlboroughs.

But when Mrs. Pack had gone, I wondered again if it
were plausible. Had she heard aright? I could not be sure.

But the Marlboroughs were disgruntled, and Anne was in
leading strings. Marlborough might have decided that there
was no hope for him under William. Here was one of the
most ambitious men alive. He was not one to be set aside

by anyone, even a monarch he had helped to the throne. My father had trusted him and it was in a large measure due to Marlborough that he had fallen, for when Marlborough had defected, he had taken a large part of the army with him. Surely he would never trust Marlborough again?

No, they would not want my father back. But Anne, that was a different matter. Sarah had Anne in thrall. Yes, it was reasonable. They would rule England through Anne because there was no hope of doing so through James.

Before I could speak to William of Mrs. Pack's discovery, he came to me. He looked very grave.

He said, "I want that Churchill woman out of the Cockpit."

"You have heard?" I asked.

He nodded. "And I want her out of the Princess Anne's service without delay."

"You have heard then of Marlborough's plans?"

He looked startled, and I could not help saying that I was sure Lady Fitzharding would have passed on the news to her sister.

William looked faintly embarrassed. It was rarely that I spoke up so frankly. The approval of the people and their expression of it had made me bold.

I went on quickly, "The nurse, Mrs. Pack, does not like Lady Marlborough. She has told me what she believes to have overheard."

He nodded again, not wishing, I was sure, to reveal the source of his information.

"You must talk with your sister," he said. "Tell her that Lady Marlborough must leave her service."

"And Marlborough?"

"I will deal with Marlborough."

"Do you believe it is true that they are in communication with my father?"

"Yes."

"He surely would not trust Marlborough."

"He would be a fool if he did, but then he has done

some foolish things. I think, though, he would see through this. The plan is to set Anne on the throne."

I said, "The people like her and they love young William."

"I believe they do not dislike you."

I wished that I could say the same of him, but I could not. I was silent for a while, and then I said, "I cannot believe she will listen to me."

"You are the Queen," he said.

"She will never give up Sarah Churchill."

"Then she will be forced to. But explain to her. Talk to her. You are her sister."

"It will be useless."

"Try," he said.

It was like a command.

It was some time since I had been to the Cockpit. When I did go, it was usually to see little William.

Anne received me with some surprise.

"This is an honour, Your Majesty," she said with mock respect. "I wonder to what I owe it?"

"I trust you are well," I said.

"As I see you are, sister," replied Anne.

She was lying back in her chair, and every time I saw her I thought she had added to her weight. I suppose I had done so too, but always beside Anne I felt almost slender.

"I have come to see you on a very important matter," I went on.

"I guessed that was so. You rarely see me now."

"And dear little William?"

Anne's face softened. "He is adorable. He was in the park this morning, watching the soldiers. He saluted when they passed and they saluted him in return. He crowed with joy and you should have heard the people cheering."

"He is very bright," I said, and wished I could have gone on talking about the charm of our darling.

I said, "I have come to talk to you about Lady Marlborough."

Anne looked a little startled—not exactly alert, but wary and less placid.

"I think it would be an advantage if she left your service."

"Left my service! Sarah! Sarah has always been with me, right from the beginning. You remember those days when we were in Richmond ... when we were little."

"Yes, I remember, but it seems that it would be better now if you dispensed with her services."

"Why?"

I could not tell her what had been discovered. I must wait until William had dealt with Marlborough. Then Anne would understand. Perhaps I should have waited for that.

"I am of the opinion," Anne was saying coolly, "that I am the best person to judge who shall and who shall not be in my household."

"You allow her to guide you. She is the mistress here ... not you."

"She never forgets that I am the Princess."

"Mrs. Morley, Mrs. Freeman," I reminded her.

"We always liked names. What about you and Frances Apsley?"

"We were young. This is different. Think of your position."

"My position tells me that I should choose my own household."

"It is obvious that that woman rules you. She gives herself airs such as I never saw before. She behaves as though she is the mistress."

"Oh dear," said Anne. "You are upsetting me. In my condition ..."

She trailed off and watched me warily. Of course, she was *enceinte*. When was she not?

"The doctors said I should not excite myself," she said plaintively. "They say I should rest more."

"Rest more? How could you possibly do that? You are always resting. There would have to be more hours in the day for you to rest more."

She took up her fan and feebly fanned herself.

"Oh dear," she murmured.

I believed she was play-acting, but I could not be sure, and as she had often attempted childbirth and the only result was little William, I dared not provoke her in any way.

I said to her, "Think about it."

"I do not have to think about it," she said. "Sarah is my greatest friend. I could not lose my greatest friend."

"You have good friends. William and I have always been good friends to you."

"Sarah has always been my greatest friend."

"You are ungrateful."

She looked at me coldly. "We could both be accused of that, could we not . . . by some?"

She had put on a pious look, and I was sure now that she had written to our father. I wondered if she knew of the grand plan to put her on the throne.

If so, it did not disturb her; she would remain in her chair resting, while she nibbled her sweetmeats and handed over the power to the Marlboroughs.

She must have seen the hopelessness in my face, for she said, "I will never give up Sarah."

There was nothing more I could do.

I took my leave and went back to Kensington.

The next morning, when Marlborough presented himself at the palace to perform his duties as one of the Lords of the Bedchamber, Lord Nottingham drew him aside and informed him that his services at court would no longer be required.

There was consternation throughout the capital. The great Marlborough, dismissed from court, stripped of his appointments! What could this mean?

The main theory was that he had been guilty of fraud. There had been occasional rumours that he had not been entirely scrupulous, and his love of money—as well as power—were well known.

I wondered what the reaction would have been if they

had known he was suspected of conspiring against us and was in touch with my father.

It was all so distressing. I was filled with anxiety, and had been so ever since I became Queen.

I was anxious about William. If only he could win the people's affections. My uncle had had that quality in abundance; my father had had it to some degree. If only *he* had not become a Catholic . . . I was back to the old theme.

They were still talking about Glencoe and blaming William for it. William had doubtless acted carelessly, being at the time concerned with weightier matters. The fact was that he had signed that order hastily, without realizing what effect it would have. And the people were only too ready to lay the blame on him.

The Civil War in Scotland had continued even after the death of John Graham of Claverhouse, Viscount Dundee, known to his admirers as Bonnie Dundee. Some few months ago a proclamation had been issued to pardon all those who, by the end of the year, signed an oath to live peacefully under the government. MacIan of Glencoe, head of the MacDonald clan, went to Fort William to give the pledge, but finding there was no magistrate there, went on to give it at Inverary. It was a long journey; the roads were snowbound, and he did not get there until the sixth of January; and before he could sign the oath, the Campbells, the sworn enemies of the MacDonalds, taking advantage of the fact that the oath had not been signed, sent word to William that it would be right and proper, in the vindication of public justice, to extirpate that "set of thieves" who refused to obey the law. Knowing nothing of the reason for the delay in signing, William agreed and so gave his permission for the massacre of Glencoe, which was carried out in the most barbarous manner.

When this came to light through those who had escaped to tell the tale, William received as much of the blame as the bloodthirsty Campbells who had been responsible for the outrage. But, of course, the people seized on anything they could bring against a king they so much disliked.

The Marlborough scandal, though, was the topic which held everyone's attention, and there were unscrupulous people who sought to turn it to advantage. I remembered how Queen Catherine had suffered through Titus Oates and his popish plot, and Titus Oates had made a fortune out of it. He had lost it in the end, it was true, but people who make such plans believe that they will be wiser and will profit from the experience of those who have gone before.

People were now talking about a man named Robert Young. He had uncovered a conspiracy. He said there was a plot to kill the King and Queen and bring James back and leading men in the country were involved in this. He had news of a certain document which they had all signed and which was hidden in the house of one of the conspirators—Thomas Sprat, Bishop of Rochester.

If they would search his house, they would find the incriminating paper hidden in a flowerpot—the Bishop's hobby being gardening, this might not be as strange as it sounded.

It all seemed wildly incredible, but such accusations must be investigated and a search was made.

To the astonishment of all, the document Young described was found rolled up and hidden in a flowerpot. As Young said, it set out an intention to murder William and me and bring back my father. It was signed by a number of well-known men—among them Sprat himself, the Archbishop of Canterbury, Lord Salisbury, Lord Cornbury—and Marlborough.

I do not believe much credence would have been given to the authenticity of the plot, had William not been waiting for an opportunity to put Marlborough under arrest, and he seized on this.

Marlborough was in the Tower.

I could imagine the fury at the Cockpit. Sarah would be frantic and Anne would share her grief and anguish.

William declared that Anne could no longer shelter Lady Marlborough and she must leave the Cockpit at once.

I wrote to Anne. I told her she must let Sarah go. It was

not fitting that the wife of a man who was now a prisoner in the Tower should be in her service.

Anne replied: "Your Majesty must be sensible enough of the kindness I have for Lady Marlborough to know that a command from you to part with her is the greatest mortification in the world to me, and indeed of such nature as I might well have hoped your kindness to me would have always prevented. There is no misery which would be greater than that of parting with Lady Marlborough."

I was exasperated when I read this letter, and, as William had said that if Lady Marlborough did not leave the Cockpit then Anne herself could not stay there, the task fell to me to tell her to depart.

Anne prepared then to leave and fortunately the Duchess of Somerset offered to lend her Sion House.

Little William was staying at Kensington at the time, which gave me great pleasure, but Anne ordered that her son leave Kensington at once and accompany her to Sion House. I was desolate and William was really angry. He sent a command to Sion House demanding that Lady Marlborough leave without delay.

Anne's obstinacy came into play. She would *not* give up Sarah. William was in a quandary. What could he do? Send guards to Sion House? Remove Sarah by force? How would Anne react to that? We all knew her stubborn nature, and with Sarah beside her, what mad act would she be capable of?

The people liked Anne. They loved the little Duke of Gloucester. Poor Anne, they would say. She cannot have whom she likes to attend her. The Dutchman must even decide on her servants. It could be a dangerous situation.

So it was allowed to pass, and Sarah stayed with Anne at Sion House.

The Prophecy

The mystery of what was called the Flowerpot Plot was solved without much difficulty. It proved to be preposterous and even more farcical than Titus Oates' Popish Plot.

The perpetrator, Robert Young, had modelled himself on the famous Oates. He was, when it started, in Newgate Jail on a charge of bigamy. He called himself a priest and had documents to prove it, but Robert Young had no difficulty in providing documents to prove anything, because he was an expert forger.

Therefore, to produce the incriminating evidence against some of the most important people in the country, all of whom could be suspected of antagonism towards William, presented no difficulty to him at all. It was fairly easy for him to see signatures of these men, and all he had to do was study them for a while and produce replicas.

He wrote the document, but it had to be found before it could be of any use.

Stephen Blackhead was a fellow prisoner with a grievance against the State. He had been set in the pillory and badly treated, for he had lost one of his ears. He wanted revenge—no matter on whom—on someone rich and famous, someone who had everything while he, poor Blackhead, had nothing.

He was a simpleton, Young knew, but he was all he could get. Blackhead had served his time and was at liberty. Therefore he could work for Robert Young, who could promise him rewards for his labour such as the poor man had never had before.

It was quite simple. All Blackhead had to do was to take a letter to the house of the Bishop of Rochester in Bromley. He had had instructions, he would say, to deliver it into the hands of the Bishop and no other. Young would also give him another paper which he must hide on his person and show to no one. If he did, there would be no money for him—only trouble. Everything depended on his doing exactly what Robert Young told him.

He would be put into a waiting-room when he arrived and would certainly not be taken to the Bishop immediately. He must look round. The Bishop was noted for his interest in plants and there would be a great many of them in pots around his house.

While he was in the Bishop's residence, Blackhead must find some means of slipping the document into a flowerpot, making sure that it was well hidden. Then he would hand the letter to the Bishop and depart.

Blackhead was not very bright, but he did need the money badly, and Robert Young had hinted that this action of theirs would bring disgrace to some very highly placed people—and that appealed to him.

Strangely enough, up to a point the plot succeeded. The letter to the Bishop—written of course in Young's expert hand—was reputed to be from some nonexistent deacon of a far-away parish, and served its purpose, for the Bishop must have received many such letters—most of them left unanswered; and being left in a room which contained numerous flowerpots, Blackhead had no difficulty in disposing of the document.

When Young received word that it was safely in the Bishop's house, it was time to act.

He disclosed the fact that he had heard that there was a plot to assassinate the King and Queen and set James on the throne. He announced that the Bishop of Rochester was involved and that in his house they would find the incriminating document, signed by all the conspirators.

The search was made and nothing found, but Robert Young said he was certain the paper was there and he was given permission to join the searchers. He knew exactly, of course, into which flowerpot Blackhead had placed it.

He had to act with care, but he prided himself on being a very subtle man. He called attention to the displacement of the earth on one of the pots. He did not wish to discover the paper himself—only to lead someone else to do so.

And indeed there it was.

Thus, as a result, those who signed the document—including Marlborough—were taken to the Tower.

It did not seem possible that Anne could keep Sarah with her now. If Marlborough were found guilty of treason, it would be impossible for her to remain.

I received a letter from Anne.

I had heard the sad news of her confinement and had contemplated going to see her. She had given birth to a little daughter who, like so many of her predecessors, had died a few hours after she was born.

I was sorry for Anne and felt very miserable. How sad it all was! I had been happier in Holland.

William said we should have no communication with Anne until she dismissed Lady Marlborough, but I had to see her at such a time.

She lay in her bed and was clearly pleased that I had come.

"I am sorry," I said.

She smiled wanly. "I feared it would be so," she answered. "It seems ever so."

"You have dear little William."

"My treasure! But I fear for him. I watch him constantly."

"He will stay well. There are many to care for him. There is good Mrs. Pack."

Anne looked a little sullen and I guessed Sarah was bothering her about dismissing the woman.

"I have made the first step in coming to see you," I reminded her. "I like not this trouble between us. It should not be. Nor would it but for Lady Marlborough. She must go now."

"The charges against Lord Marlborough are false."

"Who told you so? Lady Marlborough?"

She did not answer.

"You must take the next step," I insisted. "You must send Lady Marlborough away."

"I have never in my life disobeyed you except in one particular, and I believe in time that will seem as reasonable to Your Majesty as it does to me."

"You mean to say that, in spite of everything, you will not let Lady Marlborough go?"

"I mean that," said Anne, her lips set in the well-known stubborn line.

I went away very sorrowfully.

William was angry because I had been to see her and more so because I had been unable to persuade her.

Shortly afterwards Anne's guards were sent away and she moved from Sion House to Berkeley House; and Sarah continued to stay with her.

Then, when Robert Young's documents were examined by experts, the signatures were proved to be forgeries; and Marlborough and his fellow prisoners were released from the Tower.

But William still suspected him of treachery.

Mrs. Pack had left Anne's service by her own desire. Lady Derby, one of my trusted ladies, told me what had happened.

"It seems, Your Majesty," she said, "that Lady Marlborough caught her actually reading the Princess's letters. She did not deny it. She said it was her duty to make sure there was no treachery against the Queen."

"She had always been a faithful servant to me," I said with gratification. "What happened then?"

"Lady Marlborough went straight to the Princess."

"In triumph, of course."

Lady Derby smiled in agreement.

"The Princess was very upset. She was thinking of the little Duke, of course. He dotes on Mrs. Pack and all know that it is for his sake that Lady Marlborough has had to endure her all this time. The Princess was most unhappy, for the woman's reading her correspondence was a very grave matter indeed. Mrs. Pack herself then asked for an audience and, before the Princess could speak—Your Majesty knows Mrs. Pack's way—she said she could no longer remain in the Princess's service."

"The Princess must have been very relieved," I said. "I suppose Mrs. Pack realized she could not stay after what she did had been discovered."

"It may have been that she thought her usefulness was at an end. But, of course, there was the little Duke to be considered. Mrs. Pack said her health was not good. I think this may be the truth, because she would never tell a lie. However, she insisted on going. Lady Marlborough is delighted and the Princess, of course, is happy to please her friend."

"And what of little William?"

"He has been strangely quiet about the matter and did not protest as he was expected to."

"He is a strange child—so unusual. I have never known another child like him. There are times when I think he is wise beyond his years."

There was something strange about the child. There were occasions when he spoke like a young man and then a few seconds later would become a child again.

The unusual qualities of the boy were brought home to me afresh by an astonishing story.

He was grave after the departure of Mrs. Pack, but he had not cried, and seemed to accept the story that she had to go away to Deptford for her health.

"She is not well," he was reputed to have said. "I would not have her ill."

In his grown-up way, he sent over to Deptford every day to inquire about her health.

He went about his daily life, giving a great deal of attention to his favourite game of soldiers. He had now several boys a year or so older than himself whom he called his "men." His mother was so anxious to please him in every way and the boys were fitted out as soldiers in miniature uniforms and William took them to the park and exercised them. People used to come and watch. It was one of the most popular sights.

There he would command them—this little boy of four years or so—just like a general shouting orders as they marched to his direction.

I always felt there was something strange about him.

His head was long and there was a mature look in his eyes. Anne told me proudly that his hat was the same size as a man's. His face was oval, his hair, doubtless inherited from his father, very fair, and his complexion was a glowing pink and white. His body was well-made and seemed to be strong, but he had difficulty with some movements; he always needed a rail when he went up stairs, and help to get up if he had been sitting on a low stool. In addition to this, he had an air of extreme gravity which accompanied certain remarks so that they seemed more like those of an adult than a child.

So when I heard the story I was a little shaken, yet not altogether surprised.

Lady Derby said the whole court was talking about it.

"It is very strange, Your Majesty. But . . . how could he have known?"

I waited for an explanation and Lady Scarborough, who was also in attendance, said, "Your Majesty knows how fond he always was of Mrs. Pack."

"Indeed I know."

"They were all amazed at how calmly he took her departure. The Princess had expected him to refuse to allow her to go, and in that case, she would have had to remain."

Lady Derby put in, "But he always sent every day to see how she was."

"Yes, I heard that."

"This is the strange part of it, Your Majesty. Two days

ago, when the messenger, in accordance with the practice, was about to take the message to her, the Duke said he would not send that morning. Mrs. Wanner—Your Majesty may remember her, she was in his household—asked him why he did not send. He just looked past her, as though he were staring at nothing, and said, "There is no need. She will be dead before the messenger arrives there."

"What a strange thing for a child to say!"

"Stranger still, Your Majesty, he was right. It transpired that Mrs. Pack had died."

"He must have heard it."

"No, Your Majesty. It seemed she died just at the moment he was speaking."

"How could he have known?"

There was silence.

I was thinking of the little boy and Mrs. Pack. There had been a very special bond between them. I believed that without her he would never have survived.

He was indeed a very strange little boy.

I was unwell and had been for some months. I think it was due to the strain of perpetual war, William's comings and goings, the burden of greater responsibilities taken up and then taken away. This was all having an effect on me. Sometimes I felt old and tired. I was only thirty years old and never free of remorse on account of my father.

I was beset by continual anxiety. Every time a messenger came I would tremble and wonder what ill news he brought. If only there had not been this coldness between my sister and myself. My great consolation was little William. He seemed to be the only one who could lift my spirits. He did visit me often, and I could always be brought out of my melancholy to smile at his drolleries.

I looked back over the last months and thought of the torments I had suffered over the Grandval plot.

Grandval was a French officer who had been hired to assassinate William. Fortunately, his design had been discovered in time and he was arrested by the English.

At his trial it was revealed that, before he left Paris, he had had a meeting with my father and stepmother and that my father had told him that if he carried out his plan successfully, he, personally, would see that Grandval never wanted for anything as long as he lived.

So ... while I could rejoice in William's escape, I was overcome with sadness because my father had given his blessing to this murderous plot.

It made me very weary of life.

I suffered from the ague, from heavy colds, from a weakness of the eyes, and a swelling in the face. I longed for the war in Europe to be over; I wanted William to come home. Sometimes I felt myself drifting into fancy and believing that our troubles were over. William would come back a hero, the people would be cheering in the streets, my father would come home and announce that he realized he could never reign as a Catholic and it was right for William to take his place, William loved *me*, Elizabeth Villiers had married and gone far away and we all lived happily together. What a fantasy! What a dream! But dreams were useful at times when reality was hard to bear.

There was no end to disaster.

It was June when one of the greatest of them occurred. This was the expedition to Brest. It had been essential that this should be a surprise attack, but the plan had been foiled and the French had had warning and strengthened their defences so that when the English landed they found the enemy waiting for them. General Tollemache was mortally wounded and four hundred soldiers were lost.

It was a major disaster. But the most shocking feature of the affair was that the French had been warned, and there was a strong suspicion by whom. Lady Tryconnel, Sarah Churchill's sister, was with my father and stepmother in France, and Sarah, it appeared, had written to her telling her of the activity in London concerning the coming attack in Brest.

It was an act of treachery and left no doubt in my mind as to what the defeat was due to.

When William questioned Marlborough on the matter, he swore that he had had no part in the betrayal. His wife? Well, women will gossip. She may have mentioned, casually, to her sister, that there was much activity in progress. These things happened.

I knew William would like to have sent Marlborough back to the Tower for trial. But Marlborough had many friends and there was a lack of evidence against him.

What a melancholy state of affairs! So many deaths, so many disasters, suspected treachery all round us, and worst of all, my family in conflict. I was tired. I suppose it was because my health was deteriorating, and there was no end to the aggravation.

When I think of my idyllic youth, I see that already in the household were those who were to plague me. Strange that they were already there, a part of my childhood. Elizabeth Villiers, who had caused me great grief, and Sarah Churchill, who had done her share.

They were clever, those Marlboroughs. How could they be so blatantly treacherous and escape? They were devious, and Marlborough was undoubtedly powerful, so William must be careful when dealing with him, otherwise he would have been safe in the Tower and found guilty—as he undoubtedly was, and his wife with him.

She was a malicious woman, and I was sure she was responsible for the scandal which arose about Shrewsbury and myself.

It was quite unfounded.

Charles Talbot, Duke of Shrewsbury, was about two years older than I. He was very charming, tall, well-made, and reckoned to be one of the most attractive men at court. He was very handsome, in spite of the fact that there was an imperfection in one of his eyes. This did not however detract from his charm—but rather added to it, and made him more distinguished.

His early life had been overshadowed by the conduct of his parents. His mother, Countess of Shrewsbury at the time, was the mistress of the notorious Duke of Bucking-

ham, who had created such a scandal during the reign of
my uncle Charles. The Countess had lived openly with
Buckingham after he had killed her husband in a duel.

It had been one of the great scandals of a scandalous age.

I liked Shrewsbury because he was a good, honest man,
not afraid to state his opinions. After the disastrous defeat
of Beachy Head, when he was out of office, he came to me
and offered his services; and in March of that year, he had
accepted the post of Secretary of State, which meant that I
saw him frequently in the course of the country's business.

We had a great deal to discuss together; and in addition
to state affairs, he liked to talk about his health and he was
very interested in mine, and at that time, when I was suffering from a great many ailments, I found that comforting.

And so Sarah Churchill circulated rumours that I was in
love with Shrewsbury. She said that when he came into my
presence it had been noted that I turned pale and trembled.
If I did, it must be because I feared what news he might
bring.

It was a trivial matter and I suppose there will always be
unfounded rumours about people in high places; such will
always have their enemies and Sarah Churchill was, without doubt, one of mine.

Of course, it was not all gloom. There were times when
I could feel almost happy. At last I had begun to realize
that I could be successful in my role. The people were
growing more and more fond of me. Indeed, I think they no
longer cared that the King was so often away fighting battles on the Continent. They had Queen Mary. She was a
good Protestant; she was English and their rightful Queen;
they had never wanted a Dutchman to rule over them. If
only he had been different, they might have been reconciled. I knew he suffered pains in his back and arms, but he
looked quite magnificent on horseback when his low stature
was not evident. If he would have taken a little more care
to make a more acceptable image of himself, it could have
been so different; but he would consider such things frivolous and unimportant. I knew he was wrong.

It began to dawn on me that I could have been a good queen. I understood the people. I had had my successes when I had been in charge. That was why the people chanted: "God bless Queen Mary. Long life to her." Silence was usually what greeted William. Perhaps if I had gone my way, doing what I thought was best, with my ministers to help me, of course, the monarchy might not merely have been tolerated, but loved.

After the action at La Hogue, which must have been a crippling blow to my father, I had made sure that the people realized what a great victory it was.

We had had so many defeats, so much depression, that when there was something in which we could rejoice, I was determined this should be done whole-heartedly.

I made it a great day when the ships, bringing the victorious men, arrived at Spithead. I sent £30,000 to be distributed among the common soldiers, and the officers received gold medals. I wanted them to know that their loyalty and bravery were rewarded. I would persuade William that it was money well spent, though I was sure he would not agree with me.

I arranged rejoicing in the streets of London and I myself, attired in all my regalia, rode among the people.

They cheered me delightedly. There were no complaints at that time.

It was during William's absence that the question of new coins arose. These were to have our heads—mine and William's—engraved on them.

There was a very fine artist named Rotier, who had made the engravings when they had last been done during my father's reign, but, when approached, he said that he worked for the King, and as the King was across the water, he could not work for him. He had a son, Norbert, who offered to do the work in his father's place, and as I was aware what trouble might grow out of disloyalty to William and me, I decided to forget the father and employ the son. I was rather horrified when I saw the result, for William's likeness had certainly not been flattering. He was made to look satanic. I was disturbed, not only by the coins, but by the hostility of the people towards William.

I did hear a little later that the Rotiers had fled to France, fearing some kind of retaliation.

William returned from the Continent and I handed over the reins to him. Although I had felt some confidence in my own government, I was not sorry to do this, for I was beginning to feel quite ill and tired.

I had hoped that William might compliment me on my rule, for I knew there were many who were pleased with it, but he did not. He just nodded without comment when I explained certain of my actions to him, and I was expected to slip back into my old place of consort.

There was one happy occasion which gave me great pleasure. Little William had, for some time, had his band of soldiers—youngsters of his own age with whom he played his game of soldiers. Every day he would drill them in the park.

He had persuaded his mother to procure a uniform for him—and of course this request was granted. Mr. Hughes, his tailor, arrived and William was fitted out in a white camlet suit with silver buttons and loops of silver thread.

Young William himself told me about the incident of the stays. Mr. Hughes had said that if he would look like a general he would have to have stiff stays. The uniform demanded it. William was not very happy at the idea, but he was willing to try anything that was necessary for a soldier.

He wore the stays, which not surprisingly he found to be uncomfortable. The tailor was summoned by William. The boys surrounded him and threatened him with dire punishment for having made their commander uncomfortable and insisted that he go down on his knees and promise to make the stays less stiff.

The exploits of the young Duke never failed to amuse everyone and when I heard that he was to have a field day and had said he would be honoured if the King attended in person, I rather timidly put the question to William, hoping that he might comply with the Duke's wishes.

To my delight, and amusement, he agreed. He had quite an attachment to his little namesake and I knew he often wished that this was our son.

And so the day came. I shall always remember those little boys looking so quaint in their uniforms, doing their drill, marching before the King. William did his part well, walking along the line to review them, young William proudly beside him.

The toy cannon was fired and everything went off with military precision. William declared himself content to be assured of the loyalty of the Duke's men. He gave the little drummer two guineas because he played so loudly.

The parade over, young William stood before the King and said, "My dear King, you shall have both my companies to serve with you in Flanders."

The King thanked him and gravely accepted the offer.

I had rarely seen William relaxed and pleasant. Little William had the power to charm us all.

That was a gloomy November. I could not rid myself of a feeling of foreboding. I was feeling listless and more unwell than ever before.

I was in Whitehall Chapel when John Tillotson, the Archbishop of Canterbury, was preaching a sermon. I had always liked Tillotson. He was a courteous and tolerant man. It was not very long ago that he had been appointed Archbishop—some three years, I believe—and during that time he and I had become good friends.

It was a shock, therefore, when, in the middle of his sermon, he suddenly stopped speaking, though it was clear that he was trying to, for his face twisted and his lips were alarmingly distorted. There was a tense silence throughout the chapel, and then suddenly the Archbishop slid to the floor.

He had had an apoplectic seizure and within four days he was dead.

It was necessary to appoint another Archbishop of Canterbury and the choice should have been mine. I immediately thought of Stillingfleet, Bishop of Worcester, one of the most active men of the Church, handsome and vigourous, although not in such good health as he might have been.

William objected to Stillingfleet. He maintained he was not well enough for such responsibility and the arduous duties which would be expected of him. He would prefer Thomas Tenison and, of course, he had his way.

I was disappointed, but felt too tired to protest, but I suppose William would have had the man he wanted in any case.

However, Tenison was a good man; he had always taken a great interest in promoting the gospel. My father had said that he was dull and a man who had a horror of levity in any form. But perhaps that was not a fault in a priest.

Tenison was a popular choice, but I believed Stillingfleet would have been more so. There were many to remember that at the time of Nell Gwynne's death, Tenison had preached a sermon in praise of her which, in view of the life she had lived, seemed not exactly fitting. Then it had transpired that she had left £50 in her will to the priest who would make her the subject of such a sermon when she died.

I dare say the £50 had played its part in Tenison's willingness to preach that sermon, but I said that, in my opinion, he must have known of her repentance or he would not have been persuaded.

It was Christmas of the year 1694 and William was in England. We were to spend the season at Kensington Palace, which I think had become William's favourite of all our residences.

There would be as little ceremony as possible and I was glad of this, for I was feeling quite ill. I had a fit of the ague which I could not throw off. I knew in my heart that it was more than that. I was overcome with such listlessness that I had to force myself to keep aware of what was going on around me.

I was very anxious that none should know how I was feeling, but it was growing more and more difficult to disguise.

I was not old. I had been thirty-two last birthday. I could not forget Tillotson's sudden death. I would dream of him as he had stood in the pulpit and that sudden horror when his mouth twisted and he became incoherent. I remembered the bewilderment which followed.

It was terrible that death could come so suddenly without warning.

It was growing increasingly difficult for me to hide the state of my health. I was confined to my apartments for a few days, and of course rumours immediately began to be circulated.

I was so relieved when I felt well enough to venture out and I was amazed at the tumultuous welcome I received in the streets.

Young William came to see me. I was always delighted to be visited by him. His coming lightened my spirits.

He talked for a little about his soldiers, and then suddenly he said, "The people love you dearly, Queen. My servant Lewis Jenkins has been most unhappy because of your illness."

"The people have always been good to me," I said.

"He saw you riding in the park. He came back and looked so pleased that I asked him what good fortune he had had. He laughed and said, 'Your Grace, I have seen the Queen. She is well again.' I said, 'I am glad of that with all my heart.' Then Lewis took his hat from his head and cried, 'The Queen is well again. Oh, be joyful!' "

He looked at me very strangely then and seemed suddenly unlike a child—more like a wise old seer. His eyes looked beyond me, as though he did not see me. It was a strange moment.

He went on, "I said to Lewis Jenkins, 'Today you say "Oh, be joyful!" Soon you may be saying, "Oh, be doleful." ' "

There was a deep silence in the room, and I thought I

heard a strange rushing of wings. It was as though the Angel of Death was passing overhead.

William had become himself—precocious, it was true, but a child again.

He did not attempt to explain his strange words. Indeed, it was as though he were unaware of having said them.

He went on to talk about his "men" and a new parade he was planning. He hoped the King would come to receive the honours he was intending to pay him.

I sat still.

I knew that death was close.

The Last Request

My return to health was short-lived. Within a few days I was confined to my apartment. There was concern and people were praying for me in the churches.

Archbishop Tenison was often with me. He was a good man and a great comfort to me in those days.

I had known from the moment young William had said those strange words to me that I had not long to live. There was a feeling of unreality all about me.

My father was constantly in my thoughts. I kept going back over those happy days. There were times when I blamed myself. I had had to choose between them. Dr. Ken, Dr. Hooper, all those who had guided me, who had inspired me with the desire to lead a Protestant life, who had instilled in me the virtues of being a good, submissive wife, had led the way. But it is also written "Honour thy father." I had wanted to be a good wife, but a good daughter too . . . a good daughter to the best of fathers.

But life had ordained that my duty towards one was my betrayal of the other.

Was anyone ever put in such a position?

I wished I could go to my father. I wished I could explain how it had happened. I think he understood a little but his letters had shown me the depth of his wounds. And William? What had I been to him? An easy way to a crown. And what had the realization been? He was not a happy man. Poor William, I could feel sorry for him.

And then sudden fierce anger came to me. I had brought him the crown. I, the Queen, beloved of the people, had been submissive to a man who had never been faithful to me through all the years of our marriage.

How soon had his passion for Elizabeth Villiers begun? Before we left for Holland? Almost certainly immediately afterwards.

I had been the one with whom he must do his duty. I was the one to whom he must cling for all those years.

And for this, I had betrayed my father, for the sake of a man who had never loved me, never wanted me except for what I could bring him, a man who had been unfaithful to me throughout our married life.

If he had been such as my uncle Charles or my father it would have been different. Women had been a way of life to them, and they had always been good and kind to their wives, asking only this one concession. But Elizabeth Villiers had been his only mistress. There had been whispers that he had dallied with Anne Bentinck, but I did not believe that. The four of them, Elizabeth, William, and the Bentincks had been close friends because Anne was Bentinck's wife and Bentinck was the closest of William's associates.

It hurt more perhaps because he could be faithful, but not to me. I had been the foolish child whom he must take because of a treaty, the tearful bride who had in the beginning been unable to hide her disgust for him and her dislike of the match. So he turned to Elizabeth Villiers.

They had sold me into marriage. My father had hated it and he had tried to save me, but it had been beyond his power to do so.

Could I blame William altogether? Yes, I did. He had never been kind, never understanding; he had always been brusque, insisting on domination. And I was the Queen, the one the people wanted, the one they loved. "Oh, be joyful." "Oh, be doleful."

I sat down to write to him.

I said I was going to die. I told him that I had suffered a great deal through his liaison with one of my women. There was nothing he could do now to atone for his neglect of me, but for the sake of his mortal soul, I wanted him to repent of his adultery and give up Elizabeth Villiers. I should not be here to know whether he respected my last wish, but for the sake of his own salvation, I hoped he would.

I sealed the letter.

Then I sat there, thinking of Elizabeth Villiers—her air of superiority, her contempt for me, her sly squinting eyes, and all I had suffered through her.

I wished I did not hate her as I did. I should be thinking of my own sins rather than those of others.

If I could go back, how should I act? I could not be sure. But one cannot go back in life and say, "There was the turning point." There is no quick turn in the path along which Fate has chosen one shall go.

Archbishop Tenison came to see me. I could see that he was aware of the deterioration in my health.

"I have been writing a letter to the King," I said.

He looked surprised, no doubt wondering why I should write when he was here and I could speak to him.

"I am entrusting it to you," I went on. "I want you to give it to him when I am dead."

"Your Majesty," he protested with that false note of disbelief which people used to deny they are aware of something which must be obvious.

I lifted my hand. "You will do this for me, Archbishop?"

"I am at Your Majesty's command. Will you join me in prayer?"

We prayed and I asked forgiveness for my sins.

Early this morning I saw the spots which were beginning to appear on my body. The dreaded smallpox has come to Kensington. I am certain now that death is close.

I lay down my pen. There are certain matters I must put in order, for there is little time left to me now.

Bibliography

Aubrey, William Hickman Smith, *National and Domestic History of England*

Bathurst, Benjamin, Lt-Col, the Hon., *Letters of Two Queens*

Bryant, Sir Arthur, *King Charles II*

Burnet, Bishop, *History of His Own Times, with Notes by the Earls of Dartmouth and Hardwick and Speaker Onslow to which are added the Cursory Remarks of Swift*

Chancellor, Frank, *Sarah Churchill*

Chapman, Hester W., *Mary II, Queen of England*

Clark, Sir George, *The Later Stuarts*

Corville, Mrs. Arthur, *Duchess Sarah*

Hopkinson, M.R., *Anne of England*

Hume, David, *The History of England*

Macauley, Lord, Edited by Lady Trevelyan, *History of England from the Accession of James II*

Oman, Carla, *Mary of Modena*

Renier, G.T., *William of Orange*

Sandars, Mary F., *Princess and Queen of England, Mary II*

Stephen, Sir Leslie and Lee, Sir Sidney, *The Dictionary of National Biography*

Strickland, Agnes, *Lives of the Queens of England*

Traill, H.D., *William III*

Trevelyan, G.M., *England Under the Stuarts*

Trevelyan, G.M., *History of England*

Van der Zee, Henri and Barbara, *William and Mary*

Wade, John, *British History*

Look for the new historical novel by

JEAN PLAIDY

also known as VICTORIA HOLT.

The Rose Without a Thorn

——— •◆• ———

Published by Fawcett Books.
Available at bookstores everywhere.